**FROM
"ONE OF THE MOST GIFTED [WRITERS]
IN THE ROMANCE GENRE TODAY."***

Shadowheart

Allegreto is a charismatic, dangerous man who will stop at nothing to regain his rightful place. And the perfect tool has just fallen into his hands, in the lovely form of Lady Elena—the long-lost Monteverde princess. Only she can solidify his claim. But the dark passion that grows between them is more dangerous than any treachery mortal men could devise . . .

Praise for the bestselling novels of
LAURA KINSALE . . .

"Readers should be enchanted." —*Publishers Weekly*

"An absolute gem, virtually flawless . . . I can't find the words to praise it highly enough." —*Rendezvous*

"Poignant and sensitive . . . hard to forget."
—*Heartland Critiques*

"Once in a great while an author creates a story and characters so compelling that the reader is literally placed on an emotional roller coaster . . . Ms. Kinsale once again takes the reader on that roller coaster . . . The story is rich with life, the writing beautiful, and the characters unforgettable. This is a book readers will long remember and turn to again and again." —**Inside Romance*

Shadowheart

LAURA KINSALE

BERKLEY BOOKS, NEW YORK

SHADOWHEART

A Berkley Book / published by arrangement with
Hedgehog, Inc.

PRINTING HISTORY
Berkley edition / April 2004

Copyright © 2004 by Amanda Moor Jay.
Cover design by Lesley Worrell.
Interior text design by Kristin del Rosario.

For information address: The Berkley Publishing Group,
a division of Penguin Group (USA) Inc.,
375 Hudson Street, New York, New York 10014.

ISBN: 0-425-16232-X

BERKLEY®
Berkley Books are published by The Berkley Publishing Group,
a division of Penguin Group (USA) Inc.,
375 Hudson Street, New York, New York 10014.
BERKLEY and the "B" design
are trademarks belonging to Penguin Group (USA) Inc.

PRINTED IN THE UNITED STATES OF AMERICA

10 9 8 7 6 5 4 3 2 1

For Sage and Keeper and Folly,
dogs and muses and a reason to smile

One

~~~~~~~~~~~

*Forest of Savernake,
in the fifth year of the reign
of King Richard II*

ON PLOW MONDAY, all the chickens died.

Elayne knew she shouldn't have tried to substitute a chicken feather for the quill from a magical hoopoe bird. But Savernake Forest did not harbor hoopoe birds. In truth Elayne had no notion what a hoopoe bird looked like—the only place she had ever seen the name of the creature was in the handbook of charms and experiments that contained her formula.

Elayne felt that it was hardly certain her small attempt at a love spell had caused the complete demise of the Savernake poultry. But Cara's suspicion would fall on Elayne. Cara's suspicion always fell on Elayne. It could not be hoped that her older sister would overlook the sudden termination of every fowl in town. In a larger locale, in London by hap, or Paris, the loss of a few dozen chickens might pass unremarked. But not in such a minor place as Savernake.

Elayne pulled her mantle close, striding over the frozen ground away from the village. She could feel the black feather and small waxen figure hidden beneath her chemise, tickling her skin like a finger of guilt. She had ventured to substitute for the magical hoopoe quill because another recipe in the volume called for a feather from the wing of a black chicken. But it was a foolish experiment. The other recipe was meant to cause a man's beard to grow. Perchance that goal did not sympathize well with the ingredients for arousing a man's affections, and the result had a deadly effect upon all the poultry for ten leagues round-about.

She only hoped that Raymond de Clare, in whose image she had formed the wax, would not now suddenly sprout a beard.

As she neared the abandoned mill, a small herd of the king's deer looked up from browsing at a frost-rimed thicket. They bounded away as Raymond stepped out from behind the great mill wheel. He held out his gloved hands to her, but Elayne turned her face away, suddenly shy. She thought him the handsomest man in Christendom, but in her agitation and guilt, she could not quite look at him just then.

"No welcome for me?" he asked, amusement in his voice.

"Yes," Elayne said. The word came out a breathless squeak, barely audible. She forced herself to raise her eyes, assuming worldliness and experience with a lift of her chin, and made a little courtesy. *"Bel-accoil!* Kind greeting, Sir Knight."

"Oh, we are on ceremony, then," he said, grinning. He gave a bow worthy of the king's court—not that Elayne had ever been within a week's ride of the king's court, but she felt certain that Raymond's great sweep, showing the red-and-black slashed sleeves of his doublet under his fine scarlet cloak, must be admirably suited to such rarefied spheres.

She evaded his gaze as he straightened, feeling that if she could not touch his face—only touch his face, or take a loop of his thick chestnut hair about her finger—that she would die of unrequited love before the night was gone. Instead she put her foot onto the frozen millrace. Eluding his offered hand, she jumped over the icy channel and started to walk past him. He turned as she did and walked with her, brushing her shoulder. Elayne made a skip, moving ahead of him, pushing aside a bare branch that overhung the doorway of the old mill.

He laughed and flicked her cheek. "You are avoiding me, little cat."

She looked up aslant, a covert glance at his jaw. He was perfectly clean-shaven—no sign of a beard. With a sense of relief she said cheerfully, "It is a favor to you. In faith, sir, you can't wish to dally with such a rustic as I!"

He caught her shoulder, turning her to face him. For an instant he looked down into her eyes—she felt his hand, his fingers pressing her through the thick gray wool of her cote-hardie. "Nay, how could I not?" he asked softly. "How could I find a sparkling diamond at my feet and fail to pick it up?"

Elayne stared at his mouth as if she were the one bewitched. He leaned his hand against her, gently pushing her against the wall. The stone pressed hard into her shoulder blades. She glanced aside, afraid they might be discovered. The leafless bushes cast a wavering light in the doorway, but the old mill was empty and silent. She put her palms against his chest, as if to hold him off, but inside she was praying that he would kiss her, that at last, after weeks of this dangerous play and ferment between them, she would know what it was like. She was seventeen, and she had never been in love, never even been courted. She had not known that a man who stole her sleep and dashed her prudence, a man like Raymond, could exist.

"I am only another lady, like the rest," she whispered, her heart beating against his hand. "Haps not so meek as some."

"You, my love, are an extraordinary woman." He bent his head close. Elayne drew in a quick breath. His lips touched hers, warm and soft in the crisp winter air, softer than she had expected. He tasted of mead, very strong and wet—not completely to her relish. As his tongue probed between her lips, he breathed heavily into her mouth. In confusion and a sudden distaste, she pushed him away so quickly that he had to put out a hand to the wall to catch himself.

He lifted his eyebrows at her. He stood very straight. "I do not please you, my lady?"

"Nay, you do!" she said quickly, patting his sleeve. She was already ashamed of herself, to be such a coward. "It's only—if someone should see us—oh my . . . Raymond!" She bit her lip. "You make me so abashed!"

His stiff expression eased, for which Elayne was grateful. Raymond de Clare did not bear any affront lightly, even the smallest. But he smiled at her and brushed back her woolen hood, pulling her earlobe lightly. "I shall not let anyone catch us."

"Let us go to the Hall. We can walk together there, and talk."

"Among a throng of people," he said dryly. "And what do you wish to talk of, my lady?"

"You must make a poem to my hair and eyes, of course! I'll help you."

He laughed aloud. "Indeed." He smiled down at her, a strange smile, as if his mind had gone to some distance, but his eyes never left her lips. "Do you suppose I need help?"

"I feel certain that any knight could profit from a lady's fine ear for these things."

"All this reading and writing of yours. Haps you will compose my proposal of marriage also."

"Certainly, if you should require my aid," she said airily. "Mark me the bride of your choice, and I shall study upon her, to discover what will be the most persuasive words to win her hand."

"Ah, but only tell me what words would persuade you, little cat."

"La, I shall never marry!" Elayne declared, but she felt her lips curl upward to betray her. To hide her mirth, she tilted her head so that her hood fell down across her cheek as she gave him a sidelong glance.

He snorted. "What, then—will you wither into an old crone, reading books and stirring over a pot of hopeless spells?"

"Hopeless!" she exclaimed. "Mark me, such incantations are not so vain as you suppose!"

He nodded soberly, in just such a way that she could see that he was making a fond mock of her.

"Wella, then," she said, shrugging. "You may believe me or not. I cannot see why I should cease my learning only because I marry."

He shook his head, smiling. "Come, in serious discourse now—though I know how it pains you to speak soberly."

Elayne straightened. "I do not tease on that point, I assure you, Raymond! Married or maid, I shall pursue my study. Lady Melanthe does the same."

"I hardly think her example is one to be followed—" He broke off as Elayne looked up quickly at him, and added, "Of course your godmother is admirable, may the Lord preserve her, but Lady Melanthe is Countess of Bowland," he said. "Her manners are not those of the wives of simple knights."

"Then I must take care not to marry a simple knight!" Elayne said. "Happen that some foreign king will be looking about him for a queen."

"How sad for him if he lights upon you, my dear heart—since only a moment ago you proclaimed that you would never marry."

"Nay—" She made a wry face at him for catching her out. "I shall become a nun."

"You? A celibate?" He pulled off one of his gloves and leaned an elbow against the doorjamb, tracing the soft leather against her lips. "That I cannot conceive. Not while I live."

His certainty pricked her a little. "Can you not?" she replied, keeping her face solemn. "But I would rather reverence God than be subject to a husband."

"Hmmm . . ." He trailed his finger across her mouth. "I do not think the church will see you casting magical spells any sooner than your husband will," he said.

Elayne was breathing deeply, creating wisps of frost between them. "And how, pray, would this mythical husband prevent me?"

"My foolish darling, do you suppose I'd beat you? Nay, I'll keep you warm and happy, and too busy for reading books."

Under his touch, Elayne felt that she would turn to steam and float away. But the excitement held an edge of terror. Elayne was not afraid of him, oh no—and yet she was frantic.

"Still!" she exclaimed with a flurried laugh. "I shall not marry! I do not propose to be commanded by a mortal man. I will have visions instead, and order the Pope what he ought to do."

"Little cat," he murmured. "Not commanded by your husband? What jest is this?"

"Another of my unholy fancies." She flicked her tongue at him and ducked away, catching his hand. "Come to the Hall, and I shall tell you all about it."

But he did not let her lead him. "Nay. Your sister will be there, looking daggers at me." He drew her close, his hands at her waist, sliding them upward. "I have a better purpose, Elayne."

He began to walk her backward, bearing her into the darkness of the empty mill. She laughed to cover her confusion, allowing him to push her step by step into the abandoned room where old reed baskets and rotten barrel staves lay scattered.

She felt him lifting her skirts. His other glove fell to the ground. She tried to dance away, but he held her confined between his legs as he backed her into a corner. His mouth came down upon hers again. His bare hands searched into her chemise.

This was too jeopardous by far. She had only meant to make him love her and wish to marry her. She gasped a protest, but he seemed deaf to it, his fingers working to unbutton her cote-hardie. He grasped her loosened gown, pulling it up, exposing all the length of her legs to the cold air.

"Raymond," she yelped as he touched her skin.

He spread his palms under her breasts. "I want you," he said huskily into her ear. "You witch, you make me mad with it!"

"Please. Not here." She grabbed his wrists through the fabric of her skirts, pulling his hands away. But he wrenched free with an easy twist.

"Where then? Elayne—you slay me! Great God, you are so warm." His hands explored freely under her smock, from her hips to her back to her breasts again. He squeezed them together. She whimpered, thrilled and horrified at this brazen touch.

He was a courtier; he knew the ways of high-born ladies, while Elayne knew no more than the hall of a country castle at Savernake. She had not had any suitors at all before, much less a worldly knight like Raymond. Until this moment he had been a gentle and gallant admirer; had done no more than kiss her hand and tease her and call her delightful names.

Her chicken's-wing love charm, it seemed, had unleashed another man entirely. He was not gentle now. His mouth on hers drove her head back against the wall. He pushed his knee between her legs. She wrestled, ducking away with an awkward shove. He pulled at her, grabbing her chemise. She felt the thin thread on the charm around her neck give way and fall as she stumbled free, brushing her skirts down frantically.

"Raymond!" she exclaimed between gulps of air.

He stood back, his cheeks red. "You don't desire me, then," he said, breathing hard himself.

"I do!" she cried, holding her arms around her. "But not like this."

"I beg your pardon, my lady." He stood straight. "I did not aim to offend you."

"I'm not offended, but . . ." She blinked in the dimness. Her voice trailed off. She should never have met him here. It bespoke an invitation she had not meant.

"Is it marriage?" A rat scurried into the far corner as he knelt to retrieve his gloves. "A-plight, I intended that. Do you doubt me?"

She had doubted, of course. He came in his fine court clothes, on business of purchasing horses for his lord John of Lancaster, and lingered for weeks at a remote castle like Savernake where there were no entertainments or amusements to be had. But his talk of marriage seemed all in jest. He never spoke of it seriously, and there had been no open negotiations between their families, though Cara had inquired thoroughly into Raymond's circumstances. Her sister was not impressed. He was well-bred and widely connected, even if a landless younger son, but Elayne herself had a good dowry and Lady Melanthe's pledge of a grant of property upon her marriage. Cara felt she could do better. But Elayne cared nothing for that. She had known from the instant he first smiled at her that he was the one.

"I don't doubt you," she said. "I love you."

His grim look eased. "Little cat. You will drive me to distraction!" He smiled at her. "I am sorry. I should not have handled you so brutally. I don't know what caused me to lose my head."

She tried not to look at the black feather and small waxen figure that had fallen to the floor and now dangled unnoticed from the gloves he had retrieved. "Never mind," she said brightly, hoping the charm would drop away unobserved in the dim interior. "You shocked me. I've never before—I should not have—Cara would be wild if she knew that I'd come to meet you here."

"Aye," he said. "It was not wise of you. Another man would not have let you go so lightly."

She dropped a courtesy. "You are kindness itself to spare me, Sir Knight!"

He frowned a little. "Elayne, I speak soberly. You must promise me that you will be more circumspect."

Elayne blushed. "Circumspect?"

"Aye," he said. "If we are to wed, you must leave off your childish ways. It is charming in a girl, by hap, to run about the countryside and trifle with foolish spells and mischief as you do, but I will not tolerate such in my bride."

She lowered her face, thinking of the dead chickens. Verily, she had always been too impulsive. Cara and Sir Guy complained of it often. *Why cannot you delay for a moment to think, Ellie? Why cannot you hold your tongue, young lady? It is not for a woman to say such things. I beg you will be restrained, Ellie, don't laugh so much or ask so many questions.*

"I will do better," she said, staring helplessly at the love charm that still dangled from his hand. At any moment he would look down and see it. "I will try."

"And I want your pledge," he said, "that you will do no more of these small spells and magics. I know you mean no harm, but it is sinful."

She nodded. He meant to marry her. The charm had worked. What other magic did she need to do?

"Your promise," he said firmly. "I wish you to say it aloud, that you swear in the presence of Almighty God, you will not use spells or make magic."

"But, Raymond—"

He frowned.

"Such a heavy oath should be in a church, before a priest, should it not? I will make it in confession, come Candlemas. And urge him assign me a penance as well, something very grave and painful, to help me remember," she added.

"Well—" His mouth twisted. He shook his head. "Mary,

I don't want to cause you pain! Only swear in the church in your mind, when the Host is present, not to do it anymore."

She nodded, lowering her eyes.

"Good." He reached out and raised her face, his fingers under her chin. "Don't look so wretched, little cat. I do love you."

She looked up at him, wetting her lips. He loved her. Without taking her eyes from his, she caught his hand and drew his gloves away, closing the charm within. "May I have them for a keepsake?"

"They are yours, and gladly," he said. "I ride tomorrow to Windsor, to seek out consent of my Lord Lancaster and the Lady Melanthe."

ELAYNE HAD AN angel, a guardian watching over her, Cara always said—usually in disgust when Elayne emerged unscathed from some illicit adventure. But it was true. Not that she would ever say so to Cara, but Elayne saw him now and then—in dreams, or half-waking. She could hardly describe it or even remember it clearly. A vision, not a friendly one, but full of darkness and power. She did not speak of it because someone who did not know her angel might misunderstand, and think him something of the Devil's sending. But he was not from the Devil, that she knew, any more than her natural spells and potions were. He was simply . . . her angel. If he was more dark than light, haps it was because he held many evil things at bay.

She had been under his protection this eve, for certain. No one had seen Raymond kissing her—Elayne's blood pounded at the thought of that kiss, of being caught in dalliance, but eluding the danger only made it all seem more a marvel. A quiver ran through her. She glanced about the empty chamber as if her older sister might suddenly leap out from under a stool or behind the hangings. She put down the book in her lap and checked again to make certain the buttons on her cote-hardie were secure. *An ex-*

traordinary woman, he had called her. *A sparkling diamond.* And then he had kissed her.

Elayne had never dreamed of anything like this. With the deepest reluctance she had joined Cara and Sir Guy in the great hall the first night of Raymond's arrival, expecting yet another lengthy, dull meal with some stout guest— a visiting warden or a lay brother from the nearby abbey grange; yet another opportunity for Cara to scold Elayne's unseemly manners.

The older she grew, it seemed, the more a stranger Elayne felt among the people she had loved for as long as she could well remember. She loved Savernake Forest: the ancient oak groves and the enormous beech trees, the wild fey places and silent haunts of deer and pheasants. She loved to ride the fine horses that Sir Guy bred and husbanded for the Countess Melanthe on her pasturage at the edge of the royal wood. She loved her nieces and nephews and the pack of dogs and children that adventured with her about the countryside, against all of her sister's and the priest's strictures on chaste and virtuous behavior.

She even loved Cara, though they chafed at one another so. It was only that the ordered round of daily life at the castle that was Cara's greatest pride and comfort seemed an intolerably narrow prospect to Elayne, as predictable as the cattle chewing their cuds in the fields.

But Raymond de Clare had transformed it. He was not merely some agister come to collect *pannage* for grazing pigs on the acorns of Savernake. He was one of Lord Lancaster's men—a knight from the court of the great duke himself, elegant and clever, delighting in Elayne's free custom. He had grinned at her, winking when Cara fussed at her unfettered laughter—and Elayne had found herself floating. He contrived with her in merriment and defended her from her sister's chiding. When she was with him it seemed as if she were in a wild trance—it was when she was away that she felt her heart swell with true affection and ardor for his gentleness, his wit, his long swift stride.

Cara said he was merely toying with Elayne; that she

had best have a care with a man who had experience of Lancaster and the King's court both. Even Sir Guy had cautioned Elayne about Raymond. A man might praise an unbroken filly, Sir Guy said, but he would buy a well-gentled mare when it came to laying out his gold.

Elayne huffed softly, recalling that advice. She set aside her book and pen, holding her skirts back at the hearth, and lit a tallow candle from the fire. See what they would say when Raymond returned with her guardian's blessing on the match!

She sat down again on the chest where her books were stored, holding Raymond's gloves to her lips. She drew in a full breath, taking in his scent, and then laid his keepsake in her lap, the charm still entwined inside. She warmed her fingers between her knees for a few moments, and then pulled the writing pedestal near. Elayne had long ago ceased to speak aloud of her deepest questions and thoughts and dreams, holding them to herself like the secret of her dark angel. But she had a place to keep that silent part of herself—the gift of the one person who seemed to understand her. Her splendid, enigmatic godmother, the Lady Melanthe.

Elayne had seen her godmother and guardian only a few times in her life, and yet those times persisted in her mind like waking dreams. Lady Melanthe—black-haired like Elayne, regal as a tigress, and as dangerous. Even thinking of her made Elayne lift her head and stare as if into a deep forest. There was no one to compare with Lady Melanthe, no simple description to encompass her. Cara was plainly frightened of her, though she would never speak of why. Sir Guy was in awe. Both were meticulous in every attention to their liege lady. Yet they never mentioned her without a blessing, without gratitude, even something like affection mingled with the dread. As if the Lady Melanthe were a mythical goddess rather than a mortal woman.

When Lady Melanthe approved of Raymond's proposal, they would have no more to say.

Elayne stirred the inkwell, contemplating. She meant to

write a verse on the day, on the moment Raymond had said he loved her. Cara always dismissed her attempts at poetry as an idle occupation, suggesting that Elayne's needlework stood in far more urgent need of improvement. Elayne gave the unfinished basket of mending a shamefaced glance. It was true enough—compared to Cara's exquisite embroidery, Elayne's hems and laces always looked as if a porpoise-fish had tried to ply a needle with its flippers.

But Lady Melanthe herself had provided for Elayne's instruction in letters, in both the Italian and the French style. She insisted that Elayne be able to comprehend any documents that her godmother sent her. A number of manuscripts, both interesting and tedious, had arrived at Savernake with regularity, fair copies of letters by persons in every sort of station from archbishops to journeymen tailors.

Elayne seized such packets from the messenger's very hands, already untying the twine before his mount was led away, and bore them to her corner of the privy parlor. It did not matter what her godmother gave her the opportunity to read. Even the dullest Latin writ could challenge her to ponder things she had never considered before. Was an oath valid if extracted under threat of a red-hot plate? She followed a judge's reckoning on the point with anxious interest, relieved to find at the end of the legal document that he decreed the wife in question need not undergo the ordeal that her husband demanded to test her honor.

But even better were such implausible volumes as *The Description of the World.* Cara claimed she had heard of that one long ago in Italy, where they called it *Il Milione*— "The Million Lies"—because everyone knew it was only a fable made up by a Venetian rascal. But Elayne devoured every word of Signor Polo's tales of his travels to far China, and wondered if such things as birds the size of elephants and money made of paper could be real. Even if Cara did not always approve of the texts, she never prevented Elayne from studying them. That the Countess Melanthe entrusted

Elayne with such valuable articles as her books and letters was plainly a singular compliment.

Lady Melanthe also sent Elayne gifts each year, and the gift on her twelfth birthday had been a daybook, blank pages bound in beautiful blue-dyed calf hide, locked with a finely made hasp and golden key. No instruction had accompanied the book, but Elayne had taught herself to scribe in it, making careful copies of the most interesting documents before they had to be returned. It had not been long before she was composing text of her own, as unworthy as it might be. Her prayers and weightier thoughts she recorded in Latin, and experimented with the sweet dance of the French tongue in little poems and ballads. But as she grew older, she found her best pleasure in writing down anything she liked, in a language no one else would know.

In an earlier year Lady Melanthe had sent the wisewoman, Mistress Libushe of Bohemia, who was to teach Elayne the lore of herbs, along with such surgery and practice of medicine as a noblewoman should require. That, at least, was what the letter said. But there often seemed to be more to Lady Melanthe's gifts than met the eye, for Elayne learned of much beyond simple ointments and curatives from Libushe. It was the wisewoman's strange native tongue, so unlike the French or Latin or Tuscan or English, that Elayne borrowed to write her uncommon speculations and musings in her daybook.

Cara had taken an instant dislike to the wisewoman. She forgot to order wood for Mistress Libushe's fire, complained that she was teaching Elayne to speak useless, barbaric words, and fussed that the wisewoman's feet, bare in snow and sunshine, were unseemly, when she could well afford to buy shoes on the stipend Lady Melanthe provided for her. But Mistress Libushe said only that her feet did not feel easeful in shoes, for she wished to feel the earth. Cara could do no more than reckon her grievances and indulge in small discourtesies. The Countess Melanthe had sent Libushe, and so Libushe had stayed.

Elayne sighed, tapping her lower lip with the quill. She

did not dare to write her love poem in any other tongue, but her grasp of Libushe's Bohemian language was hardly adequate to convey the chaotic feelings inside her. Elayne longed for Libushe to talk with now, as they had so often while walking through the meadows. Mistress Libushe had a way of making confusion into sense. But the wisewoman had departed Savernake of her own accord when Elayne reached her sixteenth year, leaving an abiding sense of loneliness that had not subsided until the day Raymond sat down to the table in Savernake's great hall.

She took another deep breath against his gloves and bent to her agreeable labor, pondering a beginning to her verse of love and joy, then drawing each letter with slow care. She did not wish to make a mistake and waste any of the fine vellum pages.

"Elayne!" Cara's voice interrupted her work with a shrill note that boded ill. Elayne slammed her daybook closed without even blotting the ink. She leaped up and stuffed the love charm and Raymond's gloves in the chest while her sister was still laboring up the stairs to the solar. Elayne dropped the lid and sat down on it.

"Elayne!" Cara's generous figure appeared under the carved wooden portico at the door. A man followed close behind her, bringing a scent of livestock and sweat in his coarse woolens. Elayne recognized the husband of a village woman who kept a large hen-roost—the same roost that had yielded the black chicken feather in exchange for a thimbleful of ginger powder pilfered from Cara's coffer.

Elayne stood up, bowing her head and giving Cara a deep courtesy. "Fair greeting, sister!" she said warmly.

Cara made a huff of dismissal. "Do not play innocence, Elayne," she said in her accented English, still heavy with the inflection of Italy even after years. "What you done to Willem's fowl?"

"Was no ordinary fowl, lady," Willem said angrily. He glared at Elayne, gripping his cap between grimy fingers. "Was my fighting cock, the best bred cock I was hoarding for Shrovetide! And my wife's chickens, dead to a hen!"

"Nay, I heard of that, but I hoped it wasn't true!" Elayne exclaimed, brazening it out. "Sir Guy said that all in town were taken."

"Aye, there's not a poultry to scratch," he said. "Between last night and morn they all took dead, and we found 'em laying about the yards and streets."

"Dread news," Elayne said. She wanted desperately to sit down, but she remained standing. She knew what they would say next.

"Aye, dread enough. 'Tis the Devil's work," he said harshly, staring at her.

Elayne crossed herself. She assumed her most profound air of concern. "Does the priest say so?"

He instantly looked away, crossing himself, too, as she met his stare, and glanced aside at Cara. "Happen your sister has the Evil Eye, lady, God save us," he muttered.

Cara looked flustered. "What a wicked thing to say!" she snapped. Her ire turned from Elayne to the villager. "I not never allow such words in this abode, I warn you!"

"'Tis the color," he said. "It is no natural blue."

"You show ignorance," Cara said. "Lady Elayne descends of noble blood. Such purple tinge be a mark of wellborn in our people."

"Aye," Willem said forebodingly. "Foreigners."

Cara's mouth pursed. Her eyes and complexion were their own betrayal of distant birth—Cara was olive-skinned, with eyes of deepest brown. She far preferred to speak her elegantly fluent Italian tongue with Elayne. But she always took ill to any suggestion that she was not as thoroughly English as the man she had married. "Bah, I am too busy with you. You take this complaints to Sir Guy," she said with hauteur.

"That I will, lady," Willem said. "I want ten crowns of him to repay my fighting cock, and another twenty shillings for the loss of the hens."

"Ten crowns!" Cara cried. "You not never saw ten crowns in your wretched life. Why Sir Guy should pay for your dead cock that took ill?"

Willem narrowed his eyes. "He's your husband and master over your sister, now aren't he not? Me wife says the girl was there, giving her fine gifts for to be let at the hens, and the next day they all die. . . . 'Tis witches' work, and I know it. You kept that foreign witch woman here, and she taught this girl her heretical ways, and now look you! My cock as was to fight at Shrovetide is lifeless as a stone!"

"Mistress Libushe used no heretical ways," Elayne said firmly. "She was sent by the Countess Melanthe herself, God keep her, to instruct me in herbs and medicines."

"Aye, and ask what else she instructed you in. Creeping about the countryside and meeting with men at the mill, even this very day!"

At the sudden look Cara cast her, Elayne lost her courage. She evaded her sister's eyes. "I did naught to harm your fowl, Will," she said. "Libushe taught me to heal the sick animals, not hurt them!"

"Meeting with men at the mill?" Cara demanded in Italian. "Meeting with men at the mill?"

"I only passed Sir Raymond there on his way to leave town," Elayne replied quickly in their native tongue. "I spoke to him briefly, to tell him farewell."

"Elena, you are the veriest little fool," Cara hissed. "Great God, you will end a whore upon the streets in your recklessness!"

Elayne bowed her head. She had no defense for herself.

"Foreigners," Willem grumbled, watching them with his jaw pushed forward.

Cara turned to him. "This was certainly not Elayne at the mill," she snapped. "All day she do my bidding here at the castle. And you—I do not like you with your Evil Eye and rude claims to defame my sister. Be gone now."

"I will see Sir Guy," Willem said.

"Be gone at once!" Cara demanded. "Or the guard will cast you from the gate."

"Foreigners!" Willem snarled, and turned without even a bow for the ladies of the castle. "Heretics! The priest will hear of this."

Two

ELAYNE SAT ON a bench in Lady Melanthe's solar, her hands locked together in her lap so tightly that her fingers were white. The hard, clear sunlight poured through the tall windows, sparking a ruby in one of her rings, sending rosy rays over her skin. In the background, like a dreary dream, she heard the voice of the elderly Lady Beatrice raised in sharp contention, echoing even through stone walls, but the only thing distinct in Elayne's mind was the declaration of scornful dismissal in Raymond's letter.

After weeks she could remember each burning word that Cara had read aloud over their needlework at Savernake. Elayne remembered it upon waking; it was the last thought to haunt her as she fell asleep.

It did not matter that Sir Guy sent word the ecclesiastical court in Salisbury had dismissed the summons for heresy as unreasonable. It did not matter that the dead chickens were replaced and the villagers reimbursed beyond their wildest hopes. A seven-day past at Westminster, Cara read, unfolding the page of Sir Guy's message and glancing up with significance at Elayne, the banns for Raymond de Clare's marriage had been asked, the bride to be one Katherine Rienne, widow of a Bohemian knight.

"My lady." Elayne flinched as a man's low voice startled her. She looked up to find the chamberlain dressed in red-and-white livery. He bowed. "Her Grace will see you in her bedchamber."

Through the high oriel window, the sky sparkled with ice crystals, blown snow swept from the rooftops of Windsor Castle by the wind that had brought a Lenten blizzard. Elayne realized that the Countess Beatrice of Ludford and her long-haired spaniel were being escorted from Lady Melanthe's presence-room. In spite of the choleric tone of her voice, Countess Beatrice did not appear ill-pleased with the results of her interview with Lady Melanthe. Elayne courtesied as the venerable lady limped past, resplendent in her stiff wimple and heavy brocades, and received a disdainful nod and a growling yap in reply.

Elayne kept her face low. Everyone must know she had been sent up to be interviewed by her godmother in utter disgrace. It should have been an honor to be received in Her Ladyship's privymost room—even Countess Beatrice had only been admitted as far as the presence-chamber—but no doubt it was because Lady Melanthe wished to interview her scandalous goddaughter in strictest privacy concerning her affairs with chickens and gentlemen. Elayne followed the butler through the presence-chamber, past the silk wall hangings and silver candlesticks as tall as she was, the canopied chair of audience. In the bedchamber, Lady Melanthe was just stripping off her ermine-trimmed surcoat, while her maidservant lifted the tall headpiece from her hair—a single peaked cone glittering with emeralds and silver bosses.

She turned, her loosened hair falling down over her bared shoulder in a black twist. With the steady gaze of a cat, her eyes a strange deep violet hue, she watched Elayne curtsy.

"God save and keep you, my beloved lady Godmother," Elayne said, with her face still lowered, holding her skirt spread wide over the carpeted rushes. She kept her courtesy, looking down at an indigo cross woven into the Turkish rug.

There was a moment of silence. "I fear I do not find you well, Ellie," Lady Melanthe said quietly.

Elayne bit her lip very hard against the unexpected rise of tears in her throat. She did not look up, but only shook her head. She had kept her proud countenance in the face of Cara's censure, in front of the servants and the priest and the village. She had allowed nothing to show.

"Your hands are trembling. Mary, take that stool away and set a chair by the fire. Bring two pair of slippers, the fur-lined winter ones. I will wear my green robe. Malvoisie wine for us, well warmed and sweetened. Sit you down, Elena."

As her godmother turned away, Elayne lowered herself into the chair. She felt the tears escape, tumbling down her cheeks as she stared bleakly into the fire. Lady Melanthe removed her golden belt and pulled the green robe about her shoulders. When the maid had left the room, she sat down, brushing a glowing coal back into the hearth with the fire rod.

"When you have composed yourself, tell me why you are unwell," she said, dropping a linen towel into Elayne's lap.

Now that the tears had begun, Elayne could not seem to find a stop to them. She took up the linen and covered her face with her hands. The wind moaned outside, sending a cascade of snow crystals against the stained glass behind her.

"Your hands are thin," Lady Melanthe said.

"It is Lent. Nothing tastes, my lady."

"Are you ill?"

"No. At least—" She lifted her face and put her hand to her throat. "No." She turned her face to the fire, hiding a new rush of tears.

She felt Lady Melanthe watching her. Elayne had not intended to speak of it, or admit her despair. But she could think of no excuse for this absurd behavior before her elegant godmother. She bit her quivering lip and held it down.

"Are you perchance in love?" Lady Melanthe asked gently.

"No!" Elayne gripped her hands together. Then the tears overcame her again, and she buried her face in the linen. "Not anymore. Not anymore."

She leaned down over her lap, rocking. Lady Melanthe said nothing. Elayne felt the sobs that had been locked in her chest for weeks overcome her; she pressed her face into the linen and cried until she had no breath left.

"My maid returns," Lady Melanthe said, in soft warning.

Elayne drew a deep gasp of air and sat up. She turned toward the fire, keeping her face down as the maid set two ornate silver goblets on the stool between Elayne and Lady Melanthe. She placed the furred slippers beside their feet and then withdrew.

"Here." Lady Melanthe held out wine to Elayne. "Drink this up directly, to fortify yourself."

Elayne tilted the goblet and took a deep gulp of the sweet heated wine. She held it between her hands, warming her frigid fingers against the embossing of dragons and knights. "It is all my fault!" she blurted. "I ruined everything. He called me a sparkling diamond, and a extraordinary woman. And then he said I was arrogant and offensive to him. And I am. I *am!*"

"Are you, indeed!" Lady Melanthe sipped at her malmsey, watching Elayne over the rim. "And pray, who is this paragon of courtesy?"

Elayne took a breath, and another gulp of wine as she looked up. "I beg your pardon, my lady Godmama. I thought he would—he did not seek an interview of you?"

The countess lifted her eyebrows. "Nay—none but your sister Cara and Sir Guy have entreated me regarding you of late."

Elayne blushed. She could imagine what Cara had said of her that had resulted in a summons to Lady Melanthe's own bury hall of Merlesden at Windsor. "I am sorry, my lady! I am so sorry to be a mortification to you!"

"I am not so easily mortified, I assure you. I quite enjoyed Cara's history of the blighted poultry. And the Bishop of Salisbury is a reasonable man. With a small token, it was no great matter to persuade him of the absurdity of a charge of heresy over a parcel of chickens."

Elayne took a sobbing breath, trying to keep her voice steady. "Grant mercy, madam, for your trouble to intervene on my behalf."

"But to this paragon again," Lady Melanthe said. "He was to seek me out in audience? I may guess his purpose, as he had pronounced you a sparkling diamond and extraordinary woman."

"His heart changed from that," Elayne said bitterly. "He said I am sinful, and a liar, and to make no presumptions nor claims upon him now." She took a deep swallow of the malmsey. Then her throat tightened with a rush of remorse. "But it *was* my fault! I made a love charm to bind him."

Lady Melanthe shook her head. "How depraved of you," she said lightly. "I suppose that was the source of this awkward matter of the chickens."

Elayne felt her eyes fill up with tears again. "I tried to say that I was sorry! I sent him a letter of repentance. I sent three! I could not eat, I felt so sick after I sent them each, for fear of what he would think when he read them."

Her godmother stroked one bejeweled finger across another. "And what did he reply?"

Elayne stared down into the dark hollow of her wine. "Nothing," she mumbled. "He did not answer. The banns were published for his marriage to another in church last Sunday."

She hung her head, awaiting her godmother's censure, mortified to admit she had drawn such humiliation upon herself.

"*Avoi*—who is this amorous fellow?"

"He is not a great man, my lady, only a knight." She hesitated, feeling a renewed wave of shame that she had chosen a man so inconstant. "More than that, it is not meet for me to say."

Lady Melanthe sat back, resting the goblet on the wide arm of her chair. Even with her hair down and the informal mantle about her shoulders, she seemed to glitter with a dangerous grace. "Yes, I think not." She smiled. "I might not resist the temptation."

Elayne glanced up. "Ma' am?"

Her godmother made a quick riffle with her fingers. "It occurs to me to have him arrested for some petty theft and subjected to the trial by boiling water," her godmother murmured.

"I should not mind to see him boiled," Elayne said darkly.

But Lady Melanthe merely said, "Do not tell me his name, Elena. I am not to be trusted, you know."

Elayne drew a breath, not taking her eyes from the moon-shaped reflection in the surface of her wine. It was true—she had not thought of it before, but one word from Lady Melanthe would ruin Raymond forever. Elayne had revenge at her fingertips, like a tigress on a light leash.

For an instant, she allowed herself to imagine it. He had said she was arrogant and offensive to him, after all. She pictured him and his new wife reduced to penury, proud Raymond the boot-kicked messenger boy of some ill-tempered noblewoman—Lady Beatrice, by hap—skulking in kitchens and longing for the days when Elayne had been a sparkling diamond at his feet. While she herself, recognized as a extraordinary woman by far nobler men than Raymond de Clare, could hardly choose among the proposals of marriage from dukes and princes as far away as France and Italy.

"We might arrange a prince for you," Lady Melanthe said idly, startling Elayne so that she nearly tipped her wine. Her godmother looked at her with amusement, as if she knew she had read Elayne's mind.

In the midst of a small, choked laugh at this absurdity, the tears flowed anew. Elayne covered her face again and shook her head. "I don't want to marry a prince." She took a shuddering breath. "I want *him* to love me again."

"Hmm!" Lady Melanthe said. "I think it is time and past that you ventured beyond Savernake, Elena. The experience of a worldly court will do you much good." She made a dismissive gesture toward the bannered walls visible over the treetops outside, as if Windsor Castle were a cottage. "You will accompany the Countess of Ludford, who has just been beseeching me to write introductions for her pilgrimage to Rome. She goes by way of Bruxelles, and Prague. You will not wish to go to Rome yourself; it is naught but a heap of ruins and rubbish, but you may await Lady Beatrice in Prague, at the imperial court, and then return in six or eight months with a great deal more polish than you have now. There is no place more worthy to refine your education and enlighten you in all ways. It is a brilliant city. Your Latin is yet commendable?"

Elayne blinked, taken aback. She nodded.

"We shall practice a little, between us. The Countess does not journey until Midsummer's Eve—we have the whole of springtime to prepare you. I will see that you have an introduction to Queen Anne. She is just come of Prague, and shows an admirable degree of style and understanding for her age." Lady Melanthe made a little grimace. "Doubtless London must appear a tawdry place to her, but she seems satisfied enough with the King, may God keep him, and he is besotted of her." She paused, tapping her long fingers. "Tomorrow we will look over my wardrobe and find you some apparel fit for court."

Elayne sat silent, stunned. She could only gaze at Lady Melanthe as her godmother arranged her future with such casual dispatch. The sound of the door latch barely reached her, but when it swung open and a tall, simply dressed knight ducked through, clad in black and carrying a dark-haired boy child, she rose hastily from her chair and fell into a deep curtsy. "My lord, I greet you well!"

"Nay, rise, my lady," Lord Ruadrik said, extending a large, weapon-hardened hand to Elayne even as he easily deposited the wriggling four-year-old in Lady Melanthe's lap. He had the north country in his speech, and an open grin. "Take this goblin, lady wife, 'ere it slays me!"

The boy slid immediately from Lady Melanthe's lap and ran to cling to his father's leg. He stared at Elayne. She spread her skirt and made a bow toward the child. "My esteemed lord Richard, greetings. God bless you."

The boy nodded, accepting the salutation, and then hid his face against Lord Ruadrik's black hose.

"This is your kinswoman the Lady Elena, from our hold at Savernake," Lord Ruadrik said to the child. "It would be courteous in you to hail her warmly."

The boy peeked again at Elayne. A warm greeting did not appear to be forthcoming, but with downcast eyes, he said, "You look alike to my mama."

"And you look very like to your lord papa," Elayne said.

The boy smiled shyly. He gripped his father's muscular leg. "You have flower-eyes, like Mama."

"God grant you mercy, kind sir. You look very strong, like to Lord Ruadrik."

"Gra' mercy, lady," he said solemnly, and seemed to feel that this concluded the interview, for he turned, gave a fleet kiss to his mother, and ran from the chamber through the way they had come.

Lady Melanthe moved quickly, half-rising, but Lord Ruadrik shook his head. "Jane hides behind the door—that was the bargain, that he would come and meet his cousin Elayne, did I vow a line of retreat remain open the whiles."

Elayne realized with shame that she had yet even to inquire about Lady Melanthe's daughter and son, she had been so swept up in her own wretchedness. Knowing her face must be ravaged by tears, she stood with her head bowed as she asked after the young Lady Celestine.

"She is learning to dance," Lady Melanthe said. "I doubt me we shall see her again before Lady Day. My lord, what think you of a journey to the imperial court at Prague for Elena?"

Lord Ruadrik looked sharply toward his wife. He frowned slightly. "To what purpose?"

"To enlarge her wisdom and instruct her in the wider ways of the world. Some hedge knights hereabouts seem to believe they are worthy of her attention, but I do not believe the Donna Elena di Monteverde is temperamentally suited to become wife to a rustic."

"Too much like you, I am certain," Lord Ruadrik said, nodding soberly.

"Fie," Lady Melanthe said, flicking her hand. "I adore bumpkins."

He laughed. "To my misfortune! Wella, if it is your desire that Lady Elena be trained to bring poor rustic knights to their knees, after Your Ladyship's heartless manner, then let it be so."

Lady Melanthe smiled. She looked toward Elayne with a little flare of mischief in her languid glance. "What think you, dear one?"

Elayne pressed her lips together. "Oh, madam," she murmured. "Oh, madam!" She could not even imagine herself with the elegance and bearing, the confidence of Lady Melanthe. To inspire awe among rustics like Raymond! It was worth any price, even a journey with Countess Beatrice. She sank to her knees, taking her godmother's hands. "God bless you, madam, you are too kind to me."

"And when you return, we shall look you out a husband who can appreciate your superiority," Lady Melanthe added serenely.

"God save the poor fellow," said Lord Ruadrik.

AFTER A FORTNIGHT Elayne still had not become accustomed to her court headpiece. It was a double piked-horn, only modestly tall, but she felt her neck must bow under the weight of the dense embroidery and plaiting that seemed to tower above her head. Cara's strictures on a proper pose and attitude became practical at last—when Elayne could not remember to hold herself perfectly erect and turn with slow grace as her sister had charged her to do, the head-piece swayed in perilous reminder.

The new queen of England, younger by several years than Elayne herself, seemed to have no such difficulties. As her splendidly dressed ladies pinched and smoothed her royal train into place, she moved with confidence under a looming creation the height and breadth of a tympan-drum, encrusted with jewels and topped by a golden crown. But such fashionable elegance earned Queen Anne no love among the chilly English noblewomen. The royal match was not a popular one.

The English complained that the girl and her retinue were too foreign, and too great a drain on the King's purse. Feeling foreign herself at Windsor, Elayne found it easier to like her young Majesty. She admired the way Anne kept an earnest smile always on her round face, bravely ignoring the poisonous unkindness of her new court as she tried to make acquaintance of the English ladies. She seemed pleased at Elayne's ventures to speak in her native tongue, though it was speedily plain that the parlance Elayne had learned of Libushe was more suited to a peasant than a lady. When the Queen learned that Elayne was bound for Prague, she had proposed that they make a trade of study—courtly Bohemian for English. To her wonder, Elayne found herself rapidly elevated to one of the Queen's favorite companions, with a daily invitation to the royal presence-room.

In spite of Anne's benevolence, Elayne could not be so charitable in her feelings toward all of the girl's retinue. As the Queen stepped up to her throne, aided by two gentle-women, Elayne began to wish that she did not command so much of the Bohemian tongue after all, did she have to listen one more day to the tiny lady who spoke too shrill, her voice often rising above the rest as she talked excitedly of her betrothal to such a handsome English knight. Only the trumpets announcing the King's approach could seem to silence the Lady Katherine Rienne on the matter of her coming wedding.

The fanfare seemed tremendous to herald a mere boy.

Elayne had seen King Richard before; he came often to visit his queen, running in to embrace her with all the fondness of an adolescent youth for his sister, but this day was a formal visitation. Everyone fell to their knees as he entered, a slender figure flanked on one side by his mother and on the other by his uncle, the Duke of Lancaster. He looked too slight and young to bear the burden of the ermine robe that lay across his shoulders. But he met his queen with a happy smile, and the two of them clasped hands like bosom friends, heads bent together in instant concert.

Elayne had not expected to see the Duke of Lancaster arrive with the King. Quick fear seized her, that she might see Raymond among his entourage. She bowed her knee in a deep courtesy like the rest, straining her neck to balance the headpiece. As the courtiers arranged themselves, she rose and walked backward in her turn—a skill that she had never mastered and mismanaged badly, becoming so entangled in her train that a page had to hold her elbow while she freed herself.

In a mortified flurry she found herself pushed out by the others coming after her, pressed bodily into the waiting throng in the anteroom. Just outside the Queen's chamber, attendants from three noble households and Anne's Bohemian retinue were packed together like gaudy sheep. The rumble of voices echoed to the heavy rafter-beams. She glanced over brightly clad heads and shoulders, looking about the crowded chamber with a growing sense of dread.

Lancaster's men wore the red-and-blue of England quartered with France; but so also did the attendants of the King's mother and the King himself. The room was full of like costumes. The English colors merged with the purples, silvers, and blacks of Anne's retinue, creating a flow of bright confusion. Elayne felt hot and flustered with the press of people and alarm at the chance that Raymond might be near.

She did not believe that he was. She thought she would know instantly if he were within a league of her—her heart would know of its own accord. More and more people seemed to be pushing into the room. The air was warm and stifling. Even above the clamor she could hear Lady Katherine's voice in a giggling complaint that she could not see her own feet.

Elayne had never been in such a close and crowded quarter. A rising unease gripped her throat, a powerful sensation that she must get herself free. She began to edge toward the entry to the great hall, holding her hand to her headdress in an attempt to avoid entangling herself with the elaborate peaks and horns of the other ladies.

It was a vain effort. She found herself caught in the netting of an Englishwoman's steeple-crown. With forced smiles, they worked to free themselves of one another and gave stiff, upright courtesies to avoid repeating the predicament.

As she straightened, still trying to free her train from beneath someone's slipper, she saw Raymond staring at her from not half a rod distant.

She lifted her chin, turning quickly away. It was evident from his expression that he was astonished to perceive her there. To her consternation, her passage toward the door had vanished. Her hem was still caught, no matter how she tugged. She could not move a step in the throng.

She tried to slow her breathing, feeling suffocated in the press. The need to flee Raymond and the entrapment of the crowd made her feel light-headed. She closed her eyes and then opened them wide at the touch of a hand upon her shoulder. She glanced back. He stood next to her, impossibly close.

"Elayne!" He bent to her ear. As she pulled back, his fingers closed on her arm. "Elayne, for Christ's pity, why didn't you tell me?"

She yanked her elbow free. "Do not speak to me," she said.

He let go, but a courtier forcing his way through the

mass of people pressed her back against his chest. She arched upright, trying to shun touching him.

"You should have told me," he hissed in her ear. "I would have done all differently."

"God's mercy, Raymond—what could I tell you?" she exclaimed between her teeth.

"Who you are," he said, his voice very low by her ear. She could feel his breath on her skin. "That you are Lancaster's ward!"

She cast a glance back in spite of herself. "Lancaster's ward! Don't be foolish." She struggled to turn clear, her nose at a level with his chin. On all sides people pressed against her, shoving her inexorably against him. The din of talk made a tremendous roar in her ears. She began breathing in short gasps, trying to think beyond the growing sensation of being crushed to death. There was a strange horror welling up inside her; she was shaking, wishing desperately for clear air.

He frowned down at her, his mouth a set line. "Come." He gave the lady standing on her hem a brisk elbow in the ribs. The woman turned with a sharp curse, freeing Elayne's skirt so suddenly that she tumbled hard against him. He began to move, his arm at her waist, using his leverage to breach an opening toward the door. Raymond was the last person she wished to converse with, but it was his strength that maneuvered them toward escape from the throng. She did not think she could endure this congested place one more moment.

They reached the entry to the anteroom. The guards allowed them out, pikes lifted and then lowered quickly to prevent access to any of the hopeful petitioners pressing forward from the great hall. Raymond guided her swiftly among them, sidestepping the King's subjects of every class and description. He pushed her into a low doorway and up around the first curve of a spiral stairwell.

Elayne stopped there, overwhelmed with faintness and relief. She turned around, slumping her shoulder against the wall, feeling the blessed coolness of the stone under her flushed cheek. She drank in fresh air that flowed down from the tower above.

"Grant mercy," she said, taking a deep breath. Raymond's hands were at her waist. She leaned against him, grateful for the support. "Depardeu—I was near to falling in a trance in there."

His hands tightened. She opened her eyes. He looked up at her, his features in a shadow that hid his expression. Suddenly his arms slid around her, and he pressed his face into her breasts. "Elayne," he whispered. "Oh, God forgive me, I have missed you."

She stiffened. The muffling blanket seemed to lift from her mind. She tried to push him away. "Raymond . . . don't."

He released her with a faint sound. He took her hands between his palms, staring down at them. "I have been a very fool," he said hoarsely.

Her heart beat harder. In her wildest dream she had not hoped he would ever say so. But she pulled her hands away. "That is done with now."

He grimaced as if she had struck him. He looked up, his face tormented, and it was all she could command to prevent herself from leaning down and pressing her lips to his.

"Aye," he said painfully. "I did not know, Elayne. You should not have led me on so, to believe it was ever possible."

"Led you on!" she cried softly. "And what of me? Now that you have your banns and your widow for comfort!"

He scowled and looked away. "Don't tease me for that, I beg you. What was I to do?"

"You might have stood by me," she exclaimed, "instead of disavowing me as meanly as you could!"

"Disavow you?" he said. "Nay, I never could. I never would, but my lord commanded me to abandon my suit."

"Commanded you? But your letter—you said me to make no presumptions upon you."

"Oh, that letter," he said. "I was angry. I meant it not, what a scribe wrote for me—you know that!"

"Raymond," she breathed. "Do not make a fool of me."

"Make a fool of you!" he snapped. "I'm the one be-fooled, Elayne! I'm the one fool enough to plunge in love with a country chit, only to be told she's royal blood! I'm the one who couldn't buy her hand with all the gold I could beg or borrow in my sorry lifetime. I'm the one ordered to marry a woman twice my years and shrill as a peahen, and do it before St. George's Day!"

"What are you speaking of?" Elayne whispered. "I believe you have run mad!"

"Mad enough," he growled, "when my liege told me who you were in truth."

"Who I am?" she echoed, baffled.

"Aye, you need not deny it now. I know all. I submitted to him for permission to wed, and gave his clerk your name and dwelling, and thought no more of it but to await his blessing and then go to the Countess Melanthe. I suppose you meant it to be a good jape, to let me find out that way. And shamed I was, Elayne, to stand before my lord Lancaster and be told I was too lowborn to think of you. He was kind enough, God assoil him, but he made it plain. You are his ward, and he has higher designs for you."

"His ward! What nonsense!" she exclaimed. "My ward belongs to the countess!"

"So I thought. But the clerk read it to me himself. Lady Elena Rosafina of Monteverde, that is you, is it not?"

She nodded. "Yea, my font name it is."

"Wella, then you are upon the rolls of widows and orphans in the king's gift, and my lord John is appointed your guardian."

"No," she said. She drew in a breath. "That cannot be so. I know nothing of this."

"It is so."

"But—Lady Melanthe—she is my godmother. I always thought . . ." Her voice trailed away. "Raymond!"

He shrugged. "It makes no difference. You are a princess. I'm beneath you."

"A *princess!* Have you lost your very reason?"

"A princess of Monteverde." His jaw grew taut. "I believe there is some prince of the Italian blood he has in mind for you."

"No," she said faintly, bewildered.

He looked up at her. "You didn't know?" he said, his voice wistful. "Truly?"

"I don't believe it. There is a great mistake."

He smiled weakly. "That is something, at least," he said. "I thought you had done it all to mock me."

She sank down onto the stone step. "I don't believe it."

"Ask your godmother. She must know."

Elayne stared at him dazedly. "I don't believe it." She put her fist to her mouth. "Raymond, this cannot happen. It is a mistake. We must do something."

He looked hard into her eyes. "I have no means to change who I am, nor you."

"Do you have to marry her?" Elayne cried.

"I have no choice!"

"I can't stand it!" she whimpered. "I can't bear it."

He put his hand over hers. "We can pray to God for Providence to aid us. More than that . . . Elayne . . . fare you well." He turned.

"Raymond! Wait!"

She stood up, reaching for him, but he was already descended the curve of the stair and gone.

"I DID NOT conceal her from His Majesty," Lady Melanthe said in a calm voice. Her tone was soft, but she sat very still in a carved armchair as she faced the Duke of Lancaster across a table laid with wine and sweetmeats. "She is not King Richard's subject by blood or birth. Therefore her wardship was never eligible to be counted among the orphans in his gift."

Lord John glanced at Elayne huddled on her stool. "She greatly resembles you, my dear countess," he said, equally languid. "It is quite astonishing."

Lady Melanthe nodded. "So I am told, my lord. Though

we are relations only of the fifth degree, through my mother's descent."

The duke smiled slightly. He was a striking man, graying at the temples, with powerful shoulders and finely molded hands. His scarlet sleeve swept the table-carpet as he gestured toward a folded document that dangled many seals. He looked toward Melanthe. "I still hold your quit-claim to Monteverde, Princess—after all these years."

"It is yours, sir, and welcome," Lady Melanthe said.

"Mine?" He raised his brows. "But I have no income from it, nor sovereignty in your Italian princedom." He gave an amused snort. "Alas, I cannot even get a loan from the celebrated treasury."

"I did what I could to aid you," the countess said. "I regret that it was of no advantage to my lord's grace."

"Ergo," the duke said, "it might be reasoned that you yet owe me."

"For what debt, my lord?" Melanthe asked instantly. She did not move, and yet Elayne thought her godmother grew taut as an unseen bowstring.

"Melanthe . . ." He said her name softly, like a mild reproof.

The countess smiled. "Come, do not deny me, Your Grace," she said lightly. "I'm old and vain enough to wish to hear that you regret me still!"

"Not so very aged, madam." He grinned, a sudden boyishness on his hard features. "I vow you could make a lovesick calf of me again, were we both free."

Elayne realized with amazement that they seemed to be speaking of some past connection between them. She felt a twinge of disapproval on behalf of Lord Ruadrik.

"We might have done much together, my lady," the duke said, his smile fading. "I have regretted it, from time to time."

"Nay, sir. You are made King of Castile and Leon by your Duchess Constanza, may God bless and keep her. What could I have ever brought you to match that?"

"Ha. Now you mock me," he said. "I have no more do-

minion in Spain than in your Monteverde. But you and I—
and our lands united here . . ." He shrugged, then narrowed
his eyes. "You do owe me a certain debt, my lady, for your
love-match with my green knight."

"I do not see it," she said. "You dismissed Lord Ruadrik
from your service into mine. None could foretell that God
willed I would be wedded to him by and by."

He made a sound of discontent. "I dismissed him, aye.
And nothing did go well for us after that cursed tourney at
Bordeaux. By hap I should call him back to our service, and
make some use of him to recover our losses in France."

Lady Melanthe said nothing. The duke looked at her
long.

"Would that please you, my lady—to have your husband
lead some archers into Aquitaine?"

"Lord Ruadrik is at the behest of His Majesty," she said,
her eyes meeting his steadily.

"Do not forget it. You may argue that this girl is not our
loyal subject, but do not fail to remember that you now
are."

"Certainly," she said, unruffled.

He sat back, drumming his fist upon the table. He turned
his look suddenly upon Elayne. "Have you a sweet, child."
He pushed the platter of sugared nuts and tarts in her direction. She glanced toward Melanthe, who nodded. Elayne
took a handful of lozenges and looked dumbly down at
them.

"I don't think they have been poisoned," the duke said
dryly.

She ate several, forcing them down against the anxiety
in her throat.

Lancaster took up a parchment, narrowing his eyes and
holding it out at arm's length to read it. "You aver, then, that
the King has no claim to her guardianship," he said.

"We do," Lady Melanthe said. "I am her guardian, appointed by my late husband the Prince Ligurio of Monteverde, God assoil him."

"Alas, His Majesty does not concur. He asserts that she

has been given succor and safe harbor in England these many years since forsaking Monteverde, and therefore claims her as his rightful subject. By his good judgment, His Majesty has been pleased to affix responsibility for her lands and person upon myself until such time as she may be legally wed."

Elayne bit her lip, but her godmother did not flinch. "His Majesty may be interested to discover that Lady Elena has no lands nor income but what I intend to bestow upon her at my chosen hour," Melanthe said. "Will he persevere in his opinion when he learns of this?"

"He will," Lancaster said. He bowed his head toward Elayne. "He has a great affection and concern for the last princess of Monteverde, now that her location has been revealed to him."

"How much did you pay him?" Melanthe asked frostily.

He folded the parchment and smoothed the seals. "His Majesty would not entrust the young lady's welfare to me for less than three thousand crowns. Of course her merit renders it but a trifling sum. Arrangements for her marriage and return to her rightful throne have been well in hand since Shrovetide." He smiled and nodded at Elayne. "We will do favorably by you, child, I promise."

FROM LADY MELANTHE'S solar, Elayne watched the maidens of Windsor returning with their armloads of sweet blossoms and sheaves of greenery. For every May Day morning that she could recall, Elayne had woken before dawn and roused her little niece Maria. They had put on their new kirtles of linen and their summer gowns, and joined Sir Guy and Cara and the whole of the castle folk at Savernake, all decked in their fairest garments, to go into the meadows and green woods at sunrise to gather flowers.

This May Day, like all the others, she heard the birds singing. The scent of fresh-cut garlands wafted into the open window. The sky was misty with low clouds that al-

ready began to disperse, promising a sunny day for the celebrations of the May.

She had never felt so bitter.

"I cannot keep it in my head," she said, releasing the
edges of the scroll. The family tree of the House of Monteverde rolled closed with a crackling rustle.

Her godmother looked up from her writing. "You must,"
she said simply.

They would be standing before the church door this
morning, Raymond de Clare and Katherine Rienne. Before
the bells rang midday, before the May pole was raised, before the crowning of the mock-king and the bonfires in the
streets, they would be married.

Elayne stood up. She gazed out the window.

"Do you wish to join the May?" Lady Melanthe asked.
"Take a few hours, then, and make merry."

"Thank you, my lady," she said. "I don't wish to make
merry."

She felt her godmother's observant gaze upon her. She
had not told Lady Melanthe that today was the day. She had
not once mentioned Raymond's name, though she thought
perchance her godmother had guessed it.

"It is true that you would do better to put your mind to
what you must learn. The time grows short," Melanthe said.

"I will learn it," Elayne said. "It is only a lot of Italian
names."

"Elena," Lady Melanthe said softly, "your life there will
depend upon what you know and understand."

Elayne did not like the squeeze of alarm in her breast.
She lifted her chin. "I'm not afraid of those people. Cara is
the one afraid. I'm not."

Her sister—her half sister, it was now revealed—had
traveled up to Windsor and begged; gone down on her
knees and wept before Lady Melanthe, pleading that
Elayne be saved from a return to Monteverde.

Monteverde . . . Elayne had a faint memory of red-tiled
roofs, of narrow alleys, of tall towers and mountains and
misted water. Though she recalled so little of it, in the very

silence that had surrounded her birthplace and Cara's, she had understood something of the peril. She had never been so timid about life, so apprehensive of every shadow as her sister who had lived far longer there, but she was not utterly blithe. She did not want to go to Monteverde.

But Lady Melanthe had given her sister a look of the coldest ice and said there was nothing she could do. And Cara had cried and whimpered and sworn to kill herself before she would let Elayne go, but in the end she only sobbed and embraced her tightly. Then abruptly turned away, as if Elayne were dead already.

"Fear will not serve you," Lady Melanthe said. "Sharp wit and knowledge will serve you. God in his judgment provided that no child of Ligurio's and mine would survive. Your own father would have been the successor to Monteverde if he had lived. Remember that you have worth in yourself—in your blood. You are their only heir."

Elayne turned sharply from the window. "Why did Cara never tell me of my father?" she demanded. "I thought we had the same father."

Lady Melanthe sighed. She put down her pen. "In truth we had hoped that you could grow up here in quiet and safety, and be spared a return to Italy. Though in hap that was wrong, to keep you from your birthright. We had our reasons. Both of us. The Riata . . . Elena, you should know that they searched for you. For some years they searched. We set about the rumor that you had died of a fever, and finally they ceased looking."

Cara had never told Elayne that she was born of their mother's second husband, or who he was, or that she had even had a second husband. No one had made mention of what Lancaster's clerks had discovered in their customary investigation into Elayne's lineage on behalf of Raymond's suit. She was directly descended from the ruling house of Monteverde. From the Lombard kings. She was the granddaughter of Prince Ligurio himself, by his wife before Lady Melanthe. If Elayne had been a boy, she would have been his certain heir. She was the last unmarried princess of the Monteverde blood.

Her head throbbed with the tangled history that her godmother tried to impart. Her own father had been murdered before she was born, a brutal loss of Monteverde's only male successor. There was the family called Riata, usurpers who had grasped their chance at Prince Ligurio's death to defeat their mortal rivals in the house of Navona and seize power in Monteverde. There was a quitclaim to the princedom that Lady Melanthe had long ago given up, and somehow it was devolved to the Duke of Lancaster. He had a claim, Elayne had a claim, the Riata had only the volatile sway of their own raw power—and the treasury of Monteverde was unthinkably rich, overflowing with silver from underground mines, with levies from trade with eastern potentates and oriental kings.

"Why were they looking for me?" she asked bleakly. "If the Riata rule now—why look for me?"

"Because a Monteverde should rule," Lady Melanthe said. "You should rule, and the people know it."

"I don't want to."

"That is little matter." She made a small grimace. "We are pawns of our own heritage, Elena. The Riata hold their place because there was no one remaining of the true blood. Because they were ruthless enough to make certain of it."

"But now I am to marry one of them. This Franco Pietro." Elayne felt she was ensnared in a trance, illusory and menacing, with no means to wake and escape it. Her dark angel, having carried her through the little dangers and trials of Savernake, seemed to have deserted her now when she most needed him. "I don't understand how the Duke could arrange for it. Why? If they want no one of Monteverde blood to remain alive!"

"Nay, they prefer you alive, my beloved. Alive and safely wed into the Riata. Navona is finished. You and the quitclaim that Lancaster holds are the only things that threaten them now. Once you are the bride of Franco Pietro, you give them—and their descendants—the final right to the throne they took by force."

"But why does the Duke of Lancaster care?" she cried. "What is it to him?"

Lady Melanthe smiled and shook her head. "It is gold to him, Elena. Gold and advantage. I have read the betrothal contracts—he has succeeded in trading his quitclaim and your dower for a right to tax the mines of Monteverde. Upon your marriage, he is in alliance with one of the richest states in the whole of Italy; he gains influence in Aragon and Portugal that he hopes will aid him to conquer Castile—as long as you favor him. And that is what I want you to remember—you have value. You can be more than a pawn. You do not have to dance to any tune they play for you."

"How? I don't know how."

"Learn. You have a fine intellect, that I know—do not shrink from it now. Listen to what I tell you. Watch for those who claim to wield power, and discover who wields it in truth."

She pressed her lips together. "I suppose I will try."

Lady Melanthe rose. The rings on her fingers glittered. "You must do more than try. Let nothing escape your notice. You must beware of poison; you must distinguish between mere flattery and enemies who smile and compliment you as they plan your ruin. There are a hundred dangers!" She closed her eyes. "God forgive us, I see now that to keep you sheltered here was a grave mistake. There is no time to teach you all that you must know, Elena. Things will not always happen as you expect. Be ready for anything—be clever, be bold if you must, and act on the edge of a moment. Opportunities will come. Use your wits, and your nerve."

"Oh!" Elayne turned away, frightened. "Do everything that Cara has told me all my life I must not do!"

Her godmother's cold laughter echoed in the chamber. "In very deed, Cara is not a fair teacher for you now. She was a fawn among wolves in Monteverde. But you—I have some hope."

"Yea, I am different, am I not?" she said resentfully. "An extraordinary woman! I only wish I were extraordinary enough to run away."

She thought Lady Melanthe would chide her for saying such a thing. Instead her godmother only said, "I did not want this for you, Elena. But it has come."

Elayne stared out the window. She listened as the church bells began to toll for midday, then broke into a clanging peal of celebration. She bit her lip and looked up at the carved stone at the top of the window, blinking hard.

"Be warned." Lady Melanthe spoke quietly, standing at her shoulder. "Never say the truth of what is in your heart. Trust no one, Elena. Trust no one."

Three

THE KNIGHTS-HOSPITALLERS OF Rhodes sweated in
their black robes sewn with white crosses of Saint John,
dark skull caps drawn tight under their chins, their tasseled
rosaries clashing lightly against their swords with each roll
of the waves. A militant order they might be, but they were
no match for Countess Beatrice. The only things that
seemed a match for Lady Beatrice's piercing voice were the
spaniel's barking and Elayne's memory of Raymond,
which felt as if it grew stronger and more tormenting instead of dimmer as the distance between them grew.

The glare of the sun already heated the deck, reflecting
a brilliant shimmer off the heaving surface of the Middle
Sea. Elayne had departed England on Midsummer's Eve,
with great fanfare, aboard her own ship commanded by the
sober Hospitallers, sailing with a convoy of thirty vessels
bound for the cities of the south. Her bridal wardrobe filled
the hold, along with gifts and strongboxes marked with the
Duke of Lancaster's seal and the King of England's white
hart. At the stern flew the red cross of Saint George and the
white cross of Saint John, and atop the mast a pennant full

twenty feet in length spread the green-and-silver colors of Monteverde across the sky.

None of this pomp moved the elderly Countess Beatrice and her testy spaniel. While Lady Beatrice had readily agreed to alter her mode of transport to Rome and lend her venerable countenance to Elayne's protection—at a considerable increase in speed and comfort and no expense to herself—the Countess of Ludford seemed no more pleased than Elayne at the unexpected reversal in their positions. In spite of being on Christian pilgrimage, Lady Beatrice practiced unkindness as a virtue.

By the time they reached Lisbon, she had chased all of the handmaids to the lower deck, and insisted upon treating Elayne as her servant within the cramped confines of the ship's castle. Elayne did not object to the labor; she was glad enough for some occupation on this dismal voyage, but nothing she did was done well or to the countess's taste. In the night her lantern was too bright. In the day she did nothing to prevent the sun from overheating the cabin. It was Elayne who made the ship roll without mercy. She caused the spaniel to bark angrily at seabirds. Her step was too quick and her voice was too loud. When she tried to be slow and quiet, she was chastised for skulking like a snake.

It appeared that being a princess had no benefit at all that Elayne could fathom, beyond wearing a great deal of velvet and miniver in a climate that grew ever more sweltering, and being addressed by everyone but Lady Beatrice with a number of empty praises and compliments. She could not even write or read in the rough sway of the ship. Her only escape was into prayers of desperate penitence and petition to her guardian angel to turn back the months and let her become simple Elayne of Savernake again—humble appeals that were somewhat adulterated by the simultaneous desire to be turned magically into a falcon, fierce and ascendant, and fly away to some vague place that greatly resembled her own bed at home.

To no one's astonishment the Countess of Ludford and the Knights of Rhodes did not accord. If the Hospitallers recommended a position midway in the convoy for the sake of safety, Countess Beatrice wished to sail at the periphery, to catch a greater breeze. If the knight-brethren suggested a Benedictine monastery as having guest lodgings that were clean and cordial in port, the countess insisted that she could not tolerate the inflated Benedictine order and could only rest easy with poor nuns. But the most painful disagreement arose from the fact that the famous fighting order of Saint John was divided into seven Tongues, its members drawn from all of Europe. The two Hospitallers appointed to command Elayne's escort had the effrontery to be French, and no amount of hectoring or contempt could make them English.

Elayne spent most of her days holding a basin for Lady Beatrice. She saw nothing of the fabled Pillars of Hercules as the ship passed into the Middle Sea. Instead she was rinsing the countess's wimple in tepid seawater and attempting to contrive some way to hang it to dry in the steamy cabin that rolled and creaked with every wave.

By this morning, five days beyond their last view of the Spanish shore, Elayne had long discarded the elegant fur and stiff layers of clothing that swathed the countess. She wore the simplest gray smock that she could uncover from her chests, with just a white scarf thrown over her head and bare shoulders for modesty. She had even put off her rings and dressed her own hair in a loose pair of braids wound up around her head and off the damp nape of her neck.

She gathered the remains of the countess's breakfast and prepared to take it away. Lady Beatrice, in spite of claiming the seasickness held her prostrate, was sufficiently hale to finish the last of the Portugal wine and berate the Hospitallers for their incompetence. The knights stood just inside the stern castle, bearing the countess's tirade with perspiring fortitude and a few scattered apologies, when they could insert one. As well they might, since this dawn had discovered the ship alone on the empty Middle Sea, with no sign of the convoy's sails in sight.

No one seemed quite certain how this misfortune had

occurred. Before Lady Beatrice had awoken, the two knight-brethren in command had hastened to assure Elayne, when she emerged for morning prayers, that a correction had been made in the ship's compass. The convoy would be back in sight before midday, they reckoned.

The crusading Knights of Saint John were celebrated as the greatest fighting sailors on the Middle Sea, so Elayne supposed they knew well of what they spoke. Lady Beatrice was not as sanguine. Or at least not so forgiving, when furnished such an excellent opportunity for scorn.

"We can only pray to God that you are better warriors than seamen, when pirates fall upon us!" she declared. She bore a close resemblance to her snub-nosed spaniel in a temper, pushing up her lower lip while her jowls quivered with disgust. " 'Tis fortunate that the princess has chosen to dress like a miller's wife—she, at least, may escape the notice of a pack of infidels who would relish nothing better than to abduct a Christian noblewoman such as myself!"

The knights murmured and bowed as Elayne moved past them out the door with her bundle of linen and soiled dishes. She thought there was a little shame in the glance that passed between them. Or it might have been amusement at the idea that any pirate could be unwise enough to abduct Lady Beatrice. Elayne gave them a sympathetic nod. She was in no haste to rejoin the convoy. If she could have an answer to her prayers, they would toss the compass overboard and miss her destination entirely.

SHE LINGERED BELOW deck, helping her maids to rinse the plate in a great tub the sailors had hung from a beam and filled with seawater. None of them paid any mind when the first loud cry sounded overhead—it was common enough to hear the hails of the crew as they went about their business. Elayne swished a goblet through the saltwater. She paused as more shouts broke out. The sound of sailors' feet thudded above them.

They all looked up.

The deck tilted. Her maids squealed as the ship lumbered into a sharp turn, wallowing down with a force that threw them all flat to the floorboards. Dishes clattered as the tub swung aside and came back with the force of a huge boulder, pouring water and plate thunderously across the lower deck as the vessel rose and fell.

Elayne lay stunned for a moment. The countess began shrieking orders from the stern castle above. The spaniel yapped shrilly and the maids succumbed to paroxysms of terror. Elayne realized that her foot was trapped in a tangle of hemp rope and pewter-ware. She had to duck, pressing herself flat to the flooded deck as the tub came swinging in her direction, pouring water over her back.

It only wanted this, she thought, but her exasperation dissolved into a flash of panic as the cry of *"Pirate!"* ran through the ship.

Pirates! For an instant, Raymond's name hovered in her throat, as if he could somehow save her, but instead an older guardian came, enfolding her in dark wings. She had no time to think or pray; she only knew that if she did not yield to the frenzy that surged up inside her, she could carefully relax her foot and wriggle herself free, sliding back from the reach of the massive tub.

She rose, drawing a deep breath. She clamped her hand over a maid's mouth, stopping her wailing. "Hush!" she whispered. "Do you want them to discover us?"

The ship was lolling, the sails flapping loosely, but Elayne heard no sounds of fight or boarding yet. By fortune, none of the maids seemed to have been injured by the force of the swinging tub. They lay staring at Elayne in the dim light of the lower deck, their eyes wide.

"Conceal yourselves!" she whispered. "Under the bed-litter!"

While the maids scurried to find hiding places amid the bundles of straw and canvas, Elayne clambered up the ladder, pulling her wet skirts around her.

In the stern castle, the countess still screeched out hoarse directions while her spaniel barked. Elayne held on to the

edge of the deck, craning out of the hatch. The commander-
knights were nowhere to be seen, but the crew and men-at-
arms lined the sides of the ship, crossbows and spears at
ready. The green-and-silver banner of Monteverde hung
limp, its fringed tip nearly reaching the deck. It fluttered
and rose as the ship spun slowly, finding its way to the wind
again. At first she saw no sign of any other vessel—then, as
the ship's sails filled, beyond the high structure at the bow
she saw a bare mast. It too spun, the great spar rotating and
tilting in the sun. The distant sound of men chanting drifted
across the waves, a low hollow sound, terrifying in its reg-
ular deep timbre, as if fiends hooted their displeasure up
from Hell.

Elayne gripped the hatch and bounded onto the deck.
When she reached the mast, she could see a second pirate
galley, the oars flashing, speeding toward them with a white
spew of foam before it—as it rose on a swell, the apex of a
vicious bow-ram split the air and then ripped through the
water again, throwing spray aside like a racing sea monster.

As if in a dream, she stood with the crew and the soldiers
and watched helplessly, the creak of the ship and the sound
of the chants filling her ears. Their own vessel had regained
some faint speed. The pirate galley seemed misaimed with
its wicked prow—it did not pull straight toward the belly of
the ship, but seemed to direct a line that fell away from collision with each passing moment as the sails collected wind
and the ship added speed.

Elayne held her breath as the pirates came at them,
clinging tight to a rope ladder at the mast, staring at the
painted bowsprit above the ram, at the crossbows raised, at
the ferocious bearded faces under infidel turbans—each instant seemed to unfold with a crystalline slowness; each
second increased the chance that their ship would slip a
hairsbreadth ahead of the galley's strike.

At one and the same moment, roars of command issued
from above her on the stern castle and from the deck of the
pirate galley. The near oars on the galley swept upward as
one unit, pointing toward the sky; at the same instant a

flight of arrows hissed from the ship. A great sound rent the
air, as if the heavens cracked open as the galley struck the
ship's huge rudder. Elayne fell to her knees with the impact.
The pirate slid past under the stern amid a hail of screaming shouts, carrying the rudder away.

The ship still sailed, but it was like a wounded bull now
between two wolves. The second galley came on swiftly,
the chants a relentless rising tempo, unmindful of arrows
flying as it swept alongside with men hanging from the
spars and ropes. She saw that they were going to leap
aboard in mass; she saw an arrow take one down; his body
twisted as he fell like a broken bird into the sea.

The other galley was turning toward them again. Amid
the war shouts, a heavy hand pushed her, half-dragged her
toward the stern castle. Elayne stumbled inside just as the
pirates began to leap aboard; the door slammed and she
turned, scrambling for a bolt, a chest, anything to block it
closed.

"Help me!" she screamed to Lady Beatrice. The old lady
for once seemed to pay attention: she sprang with a startling
energy to push one of their chests against the door. Elayne
grabbed the other end as the spaniel scrambled aside. Together they hauled the heavy wood against the entry and
gasped and heaved and flung the other baggage on top.

Elayne sat against it, her back to the muffled sound of the
battle outside. The two of them huddled down behind the
barricade of wood, waiting in the suffocating heat. Even
the spaniel was quiet, panting from its hole under the sleeping berth. She could hear the infidel's urgent shouts, and a
renewed roar of command from directly above them.
Splashes and thumps and incomprehensible cries followed.

Lady Beatrice reached out and took her hand. The
countess's fingers were trembling, but she gave Elayne a
hard squeeze and a nod. In her other hand, she held up a
tiny dagger, one of the pretty jeweled toys that court ladies
wore on their girdles. With a grim look, the old lady made
a thrust in the air, as if plunging the knife into an attacker,

and then pressed it into Elayne's hand. "Don't tell them who you are, girl," she whispered harshly.

For the first time, Elayne felt a tinge of admiration for the countess's fierceness. She accepted the dagger soberly. Crossing herself, she sent a prayer to her enigmatic guardian angel, begging that he not desert her now.

As if in answer, a strange hush fell over the ship. Elayne stared straight ahead at the one tiny porthole in the stern, listening. Through the bulkheads and the door and the sound of her own heart beating, she could make nothing of the faint voices from outside. She stiffened as the chant of the galley oarsmen seemed to draw near again, but then— amazingly—it began to fade away.

Elayne lifted her chin a little, peering over the countess's bowed head. Through the porthole, beyond the chaos of the cabin, she caught just a glimpse of bright blue water and the white sails of another ship.

FOR SOME TIME Elayne waited. After many minutes she began to grow a bit impatient. If they had repelled the attack, then it would be benevolent of their own escort to come and inform them of it. She felt a strong urge to climb over the baggage and present herself with a demand to know what went forward. But the countess caught her arm tightly as she moved, and Elayne lapsed back.

The ship shuddered, a deep thump as another vessel came alongside. Elayne and Lady Beatrice stared at one another. Then, unmistakably, Elayne heard a voice shout, *"Pax!"*

She could not make out the exchange that followed, only that they all sounded quite calm. Even convivial. Elayne began to breathe again.

"Madam?" One of the knights finally addressed them in a loud voice, to the sounds of shoving and pressing upon the door. "Madam, we are out of danger, God be praised."

Lady Beatrice did not answer. But she took care, with Elayne's aid, that she was standing proudly, leaning upon her cane with her chin up and her wimple in good order, as if nothing had disturbed her. The Hospitaller pushed past their barricade without much effort, glancing down at the chests and bags. He looked up. "Ladies, you are unharmed?"

Lady Beatrice thumped her cane against the chests. "See to this disarray."

While Elayne stood back in her wet smock and the countess held herself like royalty on the rolling deck, seamen hastened to set the baggage back to order and clear the passage. The spaniel began to bark again, but hushed when Lady Beatrice struck the deck an inch before its nose.

"Who is this varlet?" she demanded, staring with a stern distaste at the richly dressed stranger waiting behind their escorts. It might have been that he had just saved their lives, but Lady Beatrice gave no compliments for that.

"Captain Juan de Amposta, madam. He brings news." The knight bowed solemnly. "He respectfully wishes to make known to madam that the Moorish pirates in the Middle Sea have become abundant and incorrigible."

The countess stared at the stranger. "I take it that you jest."

The captain moved into the cabin and went to his knee with a lavish greeting. "Forgive my impudence, that I wish to serve a lady of your grace and gentleness!"

She tapped her cane. "I daresay you are of France," she said scornfully.

The captain looked up, grinning without rising to his feet. "Nay, my lady. I am a Portugal, here to offer you armed and Christian escort, if it please you."

"I have armed and Christian escort," the countess said, flicking her hand disdainfully toward the knight. "Such as it may be."

"My lady, it is my galley that I offer, to shepherd these slow-sailing craft. She is swift and well-equipped, to prevent a corsair from boarding you." He hesitated, glancing about at the confusion in the cabin. "I mourn that we did not arrive in time to spare you such a fright. We've been on the hunt for that pack, my lady." He made a sorrowful gesture with his hands. "But they scurry off like mice when they espy us."

"You must be more fearsome than our fine brethren of Saint John, then," she snapped, glaring at the Hospitaller. The knight narrowed his eyes slightly, but made no reply.

"Madam, your men did well," Amposta said courteously. "I saw five bodies afloat, and none of them Christian. Your pardon—it is impossible to defend a round ship such as this from galleys. It is by God's grace that we came upon you when we did, or . . ." He glanced toward Elayne, then shook his head. "I do not like to think of the consequence."

"And what is your proposal, Captain?" Lady Beatrice asked peremptorily.

"I offer protection, my lady. We can rig a steering oar for your rudder, and accompany your ship into safe waters."

"How much?"

Amposta tilted his head, making a negative gesture with his hand, as if the question shamed him. "I am told you are on Christian pilgrimage, my lady. A token, by hap. It is not important. Whatever you feel moved to grant once we have reached a parting."

"Fortune indeed, that you came upon us!" Lady Beatrice said. "After these fellows from Rhodes have made such a ruin of the thing. But they are French, God forgive them."

The captain smiled and glanced at the dour Hospitaller. "God bless them. We are fast friends of the Holy Order of Saint John."

The knight inclined his head, but did not return the tribute. He seemed to have little to say—Elayne feared that the weeks of humiliation by the countess and now disgrace over their navigational blunder had rendered the knight-brethren somewhat disenchanted with their service.

Amposta lowered his voice. "Nay would I propose such an invitation to any common wool monger, madam, but if my lady and her maid should wish to sail aboard my vessel, as a part of the pact, I make you free of her, and with honor.

The accommodation is . . ." He shrugged and smiled. "By hap it would be a degree more to Your Ladyship's taste."

"Countess!" the Hospitaller said sharply. "I cannot advise it."

Elayne might have thought that the Knights of Saint John would have learned something in their dealings with Lady Beatrice by now—the moment he stated a conviction, her decision was a foregone conclusion.

"An admirable proposal, Captain," the countess said, thumping her cane on the deck. "See to the removal of our baggage."

The Hospitaller's mouth twitched once. He bowed deeply and stepped back, giving way to the captain. It was possible, Elayne thought then, that he had learned something of Lady Beatrice after all.

A NUMBER OF uneasy prospects passed through Elayne's mind as they went aboard Captain Amposta's galley. She had heard of seraglios and slaves, and this captain had a dark Saracen look about him, even if he wore a Christian cross at his throat. But his first act upon installing them in the spacious cabin, among carpets and cushions, was to present Lady Beatrice with a silver rosary. The crew was courteous and disciplined, the food wholesome; altogether it was a marvelous increase in comfort and speed. The galley was so swift that it could circle the wounded sailing ship as it lumbered along like a greyhound could range about a plodding ox.

By tacit accord, neither the Hospitallers nor Lady Beatrice mentioned Elayne's rank or destination to these strangers—an omission that suggested the countess might not be entirely convinced of Amposta's good offices. But under the amiable influence of the captain, Lady Beatrice became better-humored; almost jocund. He was generous with gifts, and full of ghastly stories of his own captivity among the Moors, both of which recommended him to the countess, who delighted in tales of torture. His crew, unseen below, was so well-trained, the oars pulled with such steady vigor, that Elayne could even walk about on deck while the galley cut smartly through waves that tossed and rolled the sailing ship.

She was perfectly content to be regarded as a simple handmaid. A breeze lightened the oppressive heat of the Middle Sea. Like Lady Beatrice, she found her mood much improved. Her melancholy began to lift; her longing for Raymond became a gentler thing, a yearning that he might be there with her to see the glorious sunsets and the luminous bow wave under the stars. She was sure he had never seen the like of this transparent sea. The lookout did sight one corsair, red sails on the horizon, but when Captain Amposta's galley turned in swift pursuit, it fled. The captain lamented that he dared not leave the damaged ship to chase it down.

"Is that the coast?" Elayne asked on their third day aboard, pointing to a faint smudge of grayish-white on the blue skyline.

"You have excellent eyesight!" the captain said approvingly. "Nay, not yet. We are still a week out from Italy, rowing against these contrary winds. That is the isle of Il Corvo, the Raven. A beautiful place, and well-protected. By hap you will inform your mistress—if Her Ladyship the countess wishes to rest there for a day, we will put in and refresh our water."

The thought of standing upon dry land, even for only a day, was blessed. Elayne hurried to inform the countess.

THEY GLIDED INTO the shadow of Il Corvo at twilight. Elayne stared up at the towering walls of the tiny harbor, at the white rock glowing pink against the last of light. A bridge crossed a ravine, supported by three dizzying stone arches that dropped sheer to the water, vaulting so far above her that she could see the radiant blue of the sky beneath them. There was no other sign of human habitation, save the huge mooring bolts sunk into the cliff wall. As one of

the sailors dived into the water to secure the mooring cable,
a dolphin surfaced and then vanished again into the clear
green depths.

"Welcome," Captain Amposta said, with a bow and a
brief smile. "Il Corvo awaits."

"GOD'S TOES, WHY should I toil any further up this cliff
to honor some foreign rubbish!" Lady Beatrice exclaimed.
She leaned upon her cane, breathing heavily, and glared
about the empty tower room. They had come to be presented to the lord of Il Corvo, climbing a steep narrow stair,
escorted by Captain Amposta in the lead and an armed
guard behind. "Let him wait upon me. Come, girl!"

The captain reached out and caught her arm as she
turned. "I think not, madam."

"You wretched devil!" Lady Beatrice hissed, jerking
away. "Unhand me! Are you possessed by the Fiend Himself?"

His lively demeanor had changed. "You speak more
truth than you know. You may find that you fancy the Fiend
better than my master."

The countess ignored him, limping with quick conviction toward the tower door. When the guard moved his
pike, barring the stairs, Lady Beatrice shoved her cane into
his belly-plate. "Stand aside!" she declared, her voice ringing off the rough walls.

Elayne stood silently, watching. The understanding
slowly bore in upon her that they were made prisoners.

"Remove the weapon, varlet," Lady Beatrice ordered,
flipping her famous reed cane under the man's helmeted
chin, pushing his head up and back. Elayne well knew that
murderous tone of voice: it had reduced dukes and archbishops to quailing pageboys.

But the guard stood his ground. He merely looked over
his nose at the captain, who laughed and shook his head.

Lady Beatrice's translucent skin flushed with rage. She
whirled about quickly, belying her fragile figure. She was

three hands-breadth smaller than Amposta, and had not a single means to enforce her command as a countess here in this savage place, but her lip curled and her back arched as she spat, "You insolent harlot!" Her cane sliced the air, a supple snap of her wrist. The captain had not the reflexes of Lady Beatrice's servants, or perchance he had not thought she would dare—his hand came up too late and the blow caught him smartly on the ear, a resounding smack that sent him recoiling, his shoulder colliding with the stone wall as he bent over himself.

"I do not suffer fools," Lady Beatrice said calmly.

The captain straightened, sucking air between his teeth. For an instant, Elayne thought that he would leap at Lady Beatrice like a wild animal. The countess had lowered the cane, but she held it lightly, drawing a circle with the tip on the floor.

"My dear lady—has this fellow been disrespectful?"

The quiet voice came unexpectedly, a shock in the small tower room. Elayne saw the captain's face change—beneath the vivid red mark across his cheek, his skin drained stark white.

She turned about. There had been only the four of them present. Now, though the guard beside the door had never moved, there was a fifth.

He stood tall and still, watching them—arriving from nowhere, as if he had created himself out of the ether. Jet-dyed folds of silk fell from his shoulders to the floor: an iridescent cape of black. Beneath it he wore silver, a tunic fitted perfectly to his body. His hair too was black; the color of fathomless night, long and tied back at the nape of his neck. He was like to a statue of pure metal, something—some *thing,* inhuman—elegant and fantastic. Elayne was not even certain for a moment if he were real or a marble figure come to sudden life, but dark as sin, as gorgeous and corrupt as Lucifer himself.

For he was corrupt—and the master of this place—no one need bow to make that evident, although both the captain and the guard fell to their knees with haste. Elayne dipped into a reverence, keeping her head lowered, though she watched him from under her lashes. She could not tear her eyes away. Even Lady Beatrice leaned upon her cane and made a brief courtesy.

He smiled. "My lady, you must not bow to me. I do not require it." Though his words were deferential, though he smiled, it seemed less a courtesy than a mandate. "You have been served ill, I fear, to be asked to climb so far. My regrets, Countess. You may beat the man senseless if you like."

"And who might you be?" Lady Beatrice demanded—with considerable audacity, Elayne thought.

"Alas, I have no noble titles, my lady. They call me only Raven, after the name of this island—Il Corvo."

He might have no title, but he carried himself as if he were a prince. His cloak sighed and stirred like something living, light woven into black.

"Humph," Lady Beatrice said. "A graceless cur, I think, if it be your order that I wait upon you. I am the Countess of Ludford, on Christian pilgrimage, fellow!"

He studied her, and then his glance drifted to Elayne. She wanted very badly to lower her face, but it was as if a viper had her for its mark, his black eyes glittering with that subtle smile. She did not dare to look away.

"By hap you will muster the patience to enjoy my home and table while you are here, my lady Countess," he said, still watching Elayne. "My port-master tells me that your ship is in need of some repair—I hardly think it safe for you to venture forth in a leaking vessel."

"Trumpery!" Lady Beatrice exclaimed. "Do not suppose I am any such fool as sails into your harbor every day! That ship is sound enough. We shall not impose upon your idea of hospitality a day longer."

"I fear that you will," he said softly. He wore no ring or jewelry, but on the shimmering black robe there was a strange emblem embroidered in silver, not a coat of arms, but some entwined letters or symbols, like an astrological sign, or Mistress Libushe's characters, but neither of those nor anything Elayne had ever seen before. "But Your Ladyship will like us better after I have Amposta here tossed onto the rocks below."

The captain made a dreadful sound, as if a protest had been choked to a gurgle in his throat. The man called the Raven looked toward him. Elayne could see Amposta freeze under that faint smile just as she had.

"A poor jest, though," the Raven said. "I see that you do not comprehend my humor."

The captain grinned, baring his teeth, the red mark on his cheek burning.

"Come and dine with me privately, my dear friend," the Raven said amiably. "We'll talk of Moors and pirates. *Mes dames,* the sergeant will guide you to your accommodations. We do not keep great ceremony here, but it is my hope that you will find them comfortable."

"SO WE ARE hostage," Lady Beatrice snarled, pounding her cane on the tiled floor. "Sold like sheep! Those treachers of Saint John sold us!"

Elayne said nothing. The spell of the Raven's presence still seemed to hover about her, strange and familiar at once. Besides, the countess would not like to be reminded that it was she herself who had chosen to go aboard the captain's galley.

"Judas knights!" Lady Beatrice gritted her yellowed teeth. "You may be sure that their Grand Seigneur will hear of this, if I must go to Rhodes myself to complain!"

They did not seem to be going anyplace at present. The chamber allotted to the countess was richly furnished, covered with eastern rugs and silken hangings, lit by enameled oil lamps that burned without smoke. But the arrow-slit windows looked out on a moonlit sea lying so far below that Elayne could not even see the shoreline. The tower wall and cliff beneath were invisible to her, as if the room floated high above the water by sorcery.

A servant had come, a Moorish girl who seemed to

speak no language that Elayne knew, but only brought a
tray of superb fruits in syrup—figs and grapes and oranges.
She placed a vase of flowers, too, poppies, such a dark purple they were black, and then vanished silently. Elayne
served Lady Beatrice, who never ceased railing against the
Knights-Hospitallers as she ate. But the countess grew
weary at length, and willing to lie down on the feather mattress. Elayne drew the bed hangings and heard the countess
snoring before she had even shielded the lamps.

Elayne sat down on a bench at the foot of the bed, toying with the stewed fruits. This Raven was a pirate, of
course. They were his prisoners, had walked open-eyed and
guileless into an elegant snare. She could not seem to quite
apprehend it. She licked at the syrup on a fig and took a
very small bite. Eating was still a burden to her. On Lady
Melanthe's strict injunction, she took enough to keep herself from wasting, but had no enjoyment in it. She lifted a
section of orange, and then ate it. Her fingers grew sticky.
She dipped them in the little bowl of water on the tray.
When she looked up from drying them, she was not alone
in the room.

Elayne started so that she upset the water as she came to
her feet. "Sir!" she murmured, staring at the dark lord of the
place as he stood in shadow not two yards' length from her.

"My lady," he said, bowing.

"I did not hear—" She glanced toward the planked door,
which she herself had barred from within. The heavy rail
was still in place. She blinked nervously. "How came you
here?"

"Talent," he said. "And study." He moved near, standing
over her. Elayne stiffened as he touched her. He took her
chin between his fingers, tilting her face up to him. She suffered his leisurely inspection, having no choice. He lost
none of his inhuman perfection at closer range. His face
was still that graven image of proud Lucifer, fallen from
Heaven to stand over her and examine her with eyes as
deep black and wickedly beautiful as the poppies.

"I know you," he said pensively. "Who are you?"

She lowered her eyes. "Elena," she said simply, using the name of her Italian christening, which had long ago transformed on English tongues to Elayne.

She hoped it would sound common and unremarkable in this part of the world, the name of a girl who had no ransom value to anyone. But his hand fell away as if she had just uttered some dreadful iniquity. Like a priest probing a heretic under inquisition, he leaned closer, searching every inch of her face.

"Who sent you?" he demanded.

Elayne swallowed. She shook her head slightly. She was afraid—and yet she felt remote, as if she were not really in this chamber, but safe somewhere, watching from afar.

He took her chin hard between his fingers. "Who?" He smiled with an affection that seemed warm and terrible at once. She stared at him. Though she had no intention of speaking, she felt the answer hover on her tongue, as if his smile alone could compel her.

"Tell me now," he said gently. "You must tell me."

"Lady Beatrice," she whispered, clamping her lips closed against saying more.

His black eyebrows lifted. "Nay, tell me who sent you. Who put you in her service?"

"The countess," Elayne mumbled. "I serve the countess."

"The Countess of Bowland?" he asked kindly, his voice very quiet. "Melanthe?"

Elayne's eyes widened. But he seemed now not so threatening, more human. He looked at her with a fondness that made regret well up inside her; it was the way she had longed for Raymond to look at her, with love and tenderness. It seemed that if she did not tell him what he wished to know, she would be wrong; unfeeling. "The countess," she murmured. To gaze up at him made her dizzy. "She said . . ." She tried to remember, but all the voices of the past months seemed to clamor together in her head, a tumble of instruction and warning. "She said . . . she told me . . . trust no one."

She felt his hand tighten on her chin. He drew in air with
a soft hiss. "Did she?"

"I don't know," Elayne said in confusion. She put her
hand on the bedpost. "I'm not sure."

He smiled, like the Devil speaking from the shadows.
"Then trust me," he murmured, or Elayne thought he did.
She could not seem to see him clearly. He faded, or the light
faded, or the shadows crept into her eyes. The lamps went
dark, leaving her standing in the blackness, with nothing
certain but the wooden carving beneath her fingers and the
sound of Lady Beatrice's snores.

UNDER THE INFLUENCE of the hot southern atmosphere, the countess succumbed to a sleeping sickness. She
would not rouse to sense except to complain weakly of her
head aching, and to take drink and a little gruel. Elayne
watched over her, worrying. She seemed to have no fever,
even in this stifling heat. Indeed, she seemed cold and mori-
bund, so Elayne tried to ask the Moorish girl for herbs to increase warmth and blood flow. She asked in every tongue
that she knew. The girl only nodded agreeably and went
away, returning with the same wine and white bread to soak
in it. Elayne asked for a physician, and the girl nodded
again. But no doctor came.

Elayne sat in the window embrasure, where she could
catch the breath of a cool breeze in the tower chamber.
Their baggage had been returned, no doubt after being thoroughly searched for anything of value. It seemed nothing
had been alluring enough to steal, for all of Elayne's possessions from her traveling chest were intact, including her
daybook, still locked and undisturbed.

There was no bolt or bar on the door beyond the one she
set herself from the inside. She seemed to be unimpeded in
coming or going from the chamber, but she did not want to
leave the countess. As disagreeable as Lady Beatrice could
be, she was familiar and undaunted and English. Elayne
had no knowledge of what had happened to the Hospitaller

knights or the maids who had remained aboard the sailing ship. But the idea that the countess might succumb to her illness and leave Elayne utterly alone in this place was unnerving.

In the fourteen nights of slow imprisonment that passed, Elayne had far too much time to think, watching Lady Beatrice lie in heavy slumber with her ill-tempered spaniel curled up at her knee. Elayne's earliest impulse—vague thoughts of escape—died a quick death under cold reason. Their chamber was not left unlocked through any carelessness on the part of their guards. It was clear enough that the island of Il Corvo was a prison in itself.

She thought of their captor. A memory teased her, a difficult image, too indistinct to catch. The Countess of Bowland, he had said, as if he knew all about her godmother. She had not told him of Lady Melanthe. But she had some apprehensive notion that indeed she had, only she could not remember when or how.

He was a pirate. He would be striving to obtain the highest ransom for Lady Beatrice. He would want to know if Elayne had any value. Possibly he intended to force her to write a begging letter for her release, full of dread and pleading.

She ought to be full of dread. She was surprised and a bit guilty to find that she was not. She had no notion of what was the best thing to do. But she was not, in truth, in any hurry to resume her journey to Monteverde and her marriage. There was a dreamlike quality to the days that passed in silent waiting, marked only by the rhythm of Lady Beatrice's hoarse breathing and the cries of the seabirds outside. Elayne felt be-spelled: suspended between the earth and the sky in this rich carpeted room that seemed to hover like the gulls in the sapphire haze.

In such a reverie, anything began to seem possible. Lady Beatrice had only spoken of her own self to the pirate; she had not revealed Elayne's destination or her consequence. If he discovered her identity, there was no surer thing than that he would try to ransom her back to Lancaster or her betrothed husband. But as long as he thought her merely a handmaid to Lady Beatrice, she did not see how she could hold much interest for him.

In her most secret heart, Elayne even dared hope that her destiny might change with this turn of events. If the pirate did not discover who she was; if he intended to negotiate a ransom for Lady Beatrice's restoration to her family, Elayne ventured to dream that fortune might favor her. It might fall out in some way that she would be returned to England after all with the countess, still unmarried. It might even fall out . . .

She thought, in spite of herself, of Raymond's last words. He had not wanted his marriage, any more than she wanted her betrothal thrust upon her. She prayed earnestly and repeatedly that his wife was in good health, and carefully did not allow any other sinful hopes or wishes to enter her mind as she recited her Aves each eventide. She prayed that Lady Beatrice would mend, and that they would be freed of this pirate's clutches.

Then she sat in the window and gazed out at the sea, lost in the empty beauty of the blue night, not knowing what else to ask for.

Four

———∞∞∞———

SHE WAS ROUSED from deep sleep by a candle in her eyes
and a sharp hand on her shoulder. Elayne rolled over, her
heart jolting, disoriented by the sudden awakening.

"Il Corvo summons you," a young woman's voice said.
Blinking, Elayne stared at the hooded figure but caught no
glimpse of her face, for she stood back, illuminated only by
the single candle that guttered and shone bright enough to
blind.

"My garments," Elayne said hoarsely, with a wild fear
that she would be brought before the pirate wearing nothing, exhibited and sold as a naked slave.

"Wear this," the girl said. Her voice was unfriendly. She
held up a robe of deep royal blue trimmed in gold. Elayne
pulled it over her smock. She was given hose and slippers,
but offered nothing to cover or bind up her hair. Countess
Beatrice snored on in unheeding slumber.

"A comb—" Elayne said tentatively, trying to tie up the
garters with shaking fingers.

"Hurry. It is no matter. He will prefer it so."

Elayne took a deep breath. All the fear that she had not

felt seemed to come upon her at once. She was shuddering
deep inside, unable to think past the sound of her heart
pounding. She said nothing more to the girl, only followed
her cloaked guide through long passages and up endless
stairs until they came to an arched door standing open on
blackness.

"Go in," her escort said. Elayne stood frozen. "Go in,"
she repeated. "He awaits you."

Elayne stepped through the door. With a soft boom, it
shut behind her, closing her in darkness. Her heartbeat rose
as she put out her hand to grope at what was before her.

She encountered smooth metal, intricately carved. It
moved as she touched it. Elayne jerked her hand back. But
it was only another door, swinging open outward, cool
fresh air rushing into the tiny room where she stood.

She felt that she was looking outside before her eyes
were certain of it. Slowly they lost the bedazzlement of the
candle. She could see that the door opened onto a platform,
a wide terrace surrounded by white columns, unroofed beneath the night sky. The floor was tiled in white, scored by
dark lines that spread out from her feet as if beckoning her
to walk forward.

It was silent. Even the air that moved past her cheeks
made no noise. But above the pounding of her heart she
could just make out the sound of the waves at the base of
the sea cliffs, a resounding echo at the edge of hearing.

She crossed herself. As she stepped out onto the terrace,
the whole sky opened above her, set off by the wheel of
columns, thick with countless stars. She stood transfixed by
the heavens, looking up. Never had she seen so many stars,
as if the sky were not black but a living brilliance, a
sparkling sheet of icy fire. They looked near enough that
she might put out her hand and pluck one, and yet unfath-
omably distant.

The place seemed an incarnation of starlight. She turned
in a slow circle. The stars swung above her, cold and
stately. When she stopped, she distinguished the outline of
a man against the column before her. It did not alarm her—

she was too amazed. She stood still, gazing toward him as the starlight poured down on the pale pavement between them.

He walked forward, his cloak reflecting silvery highlights. Elayne saw that he wore the same shimmering tunic of silver in which she had first seen him.

"What is this place?" she asked, her voice almost lost in the stupendous silence.

"My observatorium," he said. "You are standing upon it." He opened his hand, and she looked down at the intersections of lines scored across the floor, marked at intervals by numbers and symbols.

"You are an astrologer?" she asked.

"I trifle," he said. "I could cast your horoscope with fair accuracy, I daresay."

"Pray do not," Elayne said. She did not want to give him any further power over her than he had already.

His soft laugh echoed from the columns. "As you wish." He tilted his head a little to one side, looking down at her with dark eyes. "Afraid? I had not thought you so orthodox."

"I am faithful in Christ," Elayne said guardedly.

"Come, admit it," he said. "You are a heathen."

"Nay, I am not."

"A pagan. I shall have no qualms about selling you to the Saracens."

"They will not thank you for it," she said, ignoring the chill that touched her.

"You are mistaken there, my lady. A virgin female bred to courtly manners, young and fair of skin, with your extraordinary eyes—worth five thousand French crowns, I venture."

The breath left her chest. She stood very still, trying desperately to calculate. She had no idea what a French crown might be worth, but five thousand of them sounded a ransom for a prince. Or a princess. "If this be a ruse to make me afraid, I only wish it might be successful. I am only maidservant to the Countess of Ludford."

"What choice have I, then? As a sparing merchant, sweating over my reckonings."

She said nothing, her meager defense already exhausted.

"In haps, you would like your fate cast after all?" he asked.

"As it lies in your hands," she said stiffly, "little wonder if you can foretell it."

"Perchance it is not so dreadful as this moment would suggest." He looked up at the stars. "Saturn ascends. All things appear melancholy on such nights. Have you not sometime felt it, when you wake deep in the night, at the wolf hour, and all you loved seems hell and cold, no matter how bright the day before?"

She gazed at his starlit face. His expression was as cool as the stones. "The wolf hour?" she repeated slowly.

"But you are young and innocent," he said. "Haps you do not know it."

Elayne thought of Raymond, of the nights she had woken and stared into the darkness of the bed-hangings. "Aye," she said. "I know it."

A silence grew between them. He seemed to gaze at their faint shadows on the pavement, as if he had gone away to the stars somewhere. Or haps he was merely calculating his profit when he sold her to the Saracens. There was no way to read his expressionless face but as an exquisite work of art, a mystery like the enigmatic angels carved above an altarpiece.

"Come," he said abruptly. "I will show you more."

She followed him as he turned away, all thought of sleep vanished now. She felt as wakeful as she had ever been in her life. Each shape and surface was sharp and perfectly clear to her eyes, each sound distinct. Her own footsteps echoed, but his were as quiet as the rustle of wings. He paused before a pair of columns, then stepped up onto the dais and lifted a slim scepter from its jeweled rest. As he did it, the wall behind the columns seemed to subside into darkness.

Elayne realized she was looking through a door. A faint

illumination rose up from below, carrying with it a strange scent, acrid but not unpleasant, as if flowers or herbs were burning. The bluish glow provided just enough light to see the stairs sinking out of sight. He turned to her, bidding her enter.

She was not at all pleased to be descending this staircase. "Sir, I prefer not to go down."

"You are afraid?" He seemed surprised.

"God's mercy, yea! I like not the look of it."

"It is the way to my library."

She shook her head, taking a step backward.

"What do you fear?"

Elayne looked up at his face. "Tell me what you do there."

"I conjure the Devil as a black goat," he said, with an impatient sweep of his hand. "He arrives in a great cloud of hail and brimstone, and does whatever I bid him. Don't you wish to watch?"

She drew a quick breath and crossed herself. "You are too bold to make such a jest."

"Nay, madam," he said softly. "If I make bold, be certain that I know the Devil too well to summon him. I have lived by his hand and under his rule, and no power he could grant be worth that cost."

She gazed at him, wide-eyed. "You made a pact with—" She could not even summon the nerve to say it.

"I made no pact!" he said abruptly. "That is done with. It was a human devil I spoke of merely. This is what I do in my library, my lady: I read. I study. I am no foolhardy mage, who imagines he can command Hell itself. I have not the disposition of a priest, that I grant. I'm no meek sheep in the holy flock. It is the natural powers in the world I would divine. Come and I'll show you, if you will. If you won't, then go back to your snug bed and your prayers."

He turned sharply, his cloak sweeping wide, and strode across the dais to the top of the stair. He ducked into it and went down two steps, then paused for an instant, looking back at her. The faint blue illuminated his cheek and jaw, the frowning wing of his black eyebrow.

If he had tried to force her; if he had threatened or tempted, she would not have gone. He was a pirate. And a wizard, it now came clear—a real one.

"Do you think I should not be afraid of you?" she asked suddenly. "It seems to me that I would be a fool if I were not."

He stared back at her for a long time. She could not see the expression on his face, only the shadowy planes of it. "Yes," he said. "You would."

"Very well," she said. "I am afraid. But I will come down."

He stood straight and still. The blue light outlined his figure in the stairwell, the black sweep of his shoulders and cloak. The scepter that he held seemed to sparkle like starlight.

"Come, then," he said quietly. "I will go before you, my lady, for your safety on the stairs. Put your hand upon my shoulder."

THE STRANGE SAPPHIRE illumination in his library came from flasks of glass set about the room, some on shelves, some on the floor, gleaming like bog-fire. Elayne had happily hunted beside springs and moats as a child, chasing frogs and salamanders in pure defiance of Cara's disgusted admonitions, but that had been long ago; she drew in a sharp breath as she made out the skins of snakes dangling from a rafter. Still, those were mere snakes.

"For mercy!" she gasped, gripping his shoulder as she halted on the last stair. Against the far wall, a stone furnace glowed red with burning charcoal, lighting the white underbelly of a monstrous lizard, longer than two men, that hung suspended overhead by iron chains. Its tail was thick and scaly, and its huge mouth opened on fangs such as Elayne had imagined only in her nightmares.

"It is a crocodile," he said.

Eleanor stared at the hideous beast. It lay stiffly in its chains, dead and dry, the clawed feet dangling and the great mouth propped open by a stake, but still it was fearsome.

"A small water-dragon, of Egypt," he said. "As you see, it has no wings."

"Did you slay it?"

He chuckled. "Not I. I leave that work to noble knights. I merely paid a large heap of gold to obtain it, my lady."

"Why?" she asked in amazement.

"I find such things useful, from time to time," he said.

Elayne realized she was clinging to his shoulder. She let go, but the glossy feel of his cloak seemed to cling to her hand. She brushed her palms together.

"I have read of them in a book of beasts," she said.

"Is it so?" He turned to her. "I have not met before a maiden who reads of beasts."

"Nor have I met before a gentleman who collects them as serviceable goods!"

"You read much, madam?"

"Yes, I read the Latin, Tuscan and French, and English, too." The moment the words left her mouth, she regretted the pride that had engendered them. It was hardly the education of a simple maid.

He made no comment upon it, though she did not hope that he took no notice. "Sit down," he said, indicating a round table at the center of the room. It stood inside a circle painted upon the floor, a golden star drawn inside it. "You need not mind the pentangle," he said, as she hesitated. "It is the sign of Solomon, and betokens truth spoken within the margins of its power." When she still paused, he said, "By hap truth is not to your liking."

Elayne could think of no clever reply. Unquestionably telling any truth was not to her liking at this moment.

"Also it protects from demons, should I conjure any by mischance," he said. "By whiles I have done it, I will confess, and so it is the safest place to stand."

"You said you did not invoke the Devil!" she cried.

"I do not," he answered calmly. "But—" He shrugged.

"Sometime, a smallish imp has appeared. It is a hazard of my inquiries. So I take care to stand inside Solomon's five points, my lady, as I advise you to do."

She looked about at the vials and flasks and bizarre vessels that lined the room. There were scrolls laid neatly in racks; mortars and pestles of all sizes, the skulls of unknown creatures. His tranquil mention of demons made the hairs stand along her neck, but she felt a curiosity dawning that was the equal of her fear. He was a magician. He had mastered what she had only attempted to learn. "What is in them?" she asked. "The parchments."

"You would like to see?" He nodded, as if she satisfied him. "Then sit down."

Elayne wet her lips and stepped over the golden lines. She sat in the chair he pulled out for her, and watched him bring a box to set upon the table. He made no special sign or bow as he crossed into the circle, which eased her mind a little. She did not think a demon would come, even by mischance, unless particular words and signals invoked it. Still, she was not so certain of it as to stand outside the pentangle at this moment.

The box, beautifully carved and polished, had a scent of myrrh that wafted stronger as he opened it. He lifted out a stock of cards and spread them, all painted with figures, men and women like something from a moral tale, carrying suns and moons and scythes, some showing devils and some monks. Each was named and numbered in Latin: The Beggar, The Artisan, The Emperor; Grammar, Music, Logic, Poetry.

"These are the Triunfi," he said. "The emblems of the Taroc."

She had heard of the Taroc. Libushe had mentioned it, but Elayne had never seen the cards. Before she could discern many of the figures, he turned their blank sides upward and stacked and cut them apart, then stacked them again. The rare odor of myrrh filled her nose. He wore no rings. His hands moved with simple grace, as if he had done it many times, touching the cards lightly, reverently, as a man would touch living things that he loved. His silver sleeve gleamed like light sliding up and down a sword blade as he moved.

He set the deck before Elayne and reached into the box again. This time he opened between them a parchment adorned by the figure of a naked man, the arms and legs spread wide, the body enclosed in a wheel of astrological signs. She was determined to show as little as possible of her emotion, but her cheeks flamed at the immodesty of the drawing.

The Raven glanced up, as if he had sensed her abashment. His dark, beautiful eyes rested upon her. He smiled with one corner of his mouth and reached across for the cards, placing them in the center of the figure as if they were a loincloth. "Haps that pleases you better, my lady," he murmured. "Take off some cards, and keep them with you."

"Why?" she asked. "Is this a spell?"

"We are philosophers. It is purely contemplation and study."

"Study of what?"

"Of you."

She stared at him warily across the table, realizing belatedly that he had lured her into his pentangle of truth. "I do not think you will find that there is a great deal of me to contemplate."

"So it may be. Gentle young ladies often lead dull lives, and have characters to match."

"As you say," she murmured, dipping her head briefly.

He grinned, a dark flash of humor. "Take up the cards, madam," he said.

SHE GREW WEARY of breaking the stack and handing him one card after the other from the top, over and over, while he placed them in a pattern over the points of the human figure. It seemed to go on for hours, although she had no way to keep the time. Her neck and shoulders ached.

Night and lack of sleep were overcoming her resolution to remain vigilant.

If the Raven were fatigued, he gave no sign of it, but seemed to be deep in thoughtful meditation as he examined each card, placed it, and then studied the evolving spread. At some cards he seemed to smile a little, and when she handed him The Pope, he even laughed and shook his head as he laid it across the unclad figure's private members. At another he lifted his black-winged eyebrows, whether in surprise or incredulity, she could not say. Finally she came to the last two cards in the stack before her.

"Take the one from the bottom," he said.

Elayne offered it to him. He turned it up and laid it down facing her, in the center of the figure.

"The Knight," he said. "From the first decade, the stations of humanity. I do not think you are a humble maid-servant, my lady Elena. Your birth is much higher than you tell me. But you need not look so alarmed." He leaned upon his elbow lazily. "The degree of your nobility is not what I wished to discern."

She had grown wide awake in an instant. The elegantly dressed Knight posed before her mockingly.

"Here—" He spread apart two cards that lay at the lowest part of the wheel. "Your establishment interests me more. The Duke and the muse Clio, the giver of fame. But you see . . . here at her feet, this herb. Do you know it?"

Elayne peered at the card in spite of herself. "It seems to be a rose?"

He looked surprised. "No. Perchance it might appear so, though for myself I cannot see it, but the plant is not so noble. It is only the poor gith flower."

"Oh," she said.

"Haps you know it by another name. I have heard it called melanthy, too." He smiled at her, and suddenly Elayne saw her danger.

"Is it?" she asked stupidly.

"Yes. Does it not grow near Bowland Castle?"

She blinked. "I know not. I have never been there."

"But you are in the household of my Lady Melanthe, the Countess of Bowland."

He spoke with simple assurance. Elayne answered nothing. She thought that someone must have told Amposta, but she kept a careful silence. There were any number of minor handmaids in the household of Lady Melanthe.

"You see, a little study of the details reveals much," he said. "Here in the ninth house, we can see more—in your childhood you made a great journey out of danger . . . recovery from a morbid illness?" He tilted his head, turning over another card and considering. "Nay, I think not. The Emperor in the sixth position. Your health has always been superb."

He glanced up at her, as if to confirm this. She could not deny it; she had never been seriously ill. Even the measles had treated her lightly.

"A journey in truth it was," he said. "Over land and water. A vital cusp. Everything in your life changed at that turning. I don't think you would have lived long if you had not traveled so young." He frowned at the cards before him. "From the south to the north. Was it winter? Was there snow? And a fortification—a castle—a woman with child."

Elayne stared at him. He could not know of her childhood journey from Monteverde to England; Lady Beatrice could have told him nothing of that. Elayne recalled it only dimly herself. But in her mind, even as he spoke the words, a memory stood clear, of arriving at Savernake in a snowfall, of Cara's bulky form, nearly to term with little Maria, of being swept up into a joyous welcome.

"You called out," he said. He rested his forefinger on a female figure named Melpomene, a singer holding a double flute. He smiled a little, as if remembering it himself. "A horse foundered in the drifts. You made a ball of snow and threw it."

She sat frozen, stilled by the strange precision with which he described her own memory. She could see the horse struggling, the empty, snowy road that led away from

Savernake Castle. "How know you these things?" she whispered.

"Some I read on the cards," he said. "Some seem to be—given to me. But look now, the last card. That represents your future. Turn it up."

Hesitantly she lifted the card, holding it so that she alone could see its face. It was exquisitely painted like all the rest, but here the artist had traded the bright colors and land-scapes for a darker hue. On a background of midnight blue, the winged figure glowed: an angel arrayed in robes of sable black and silver, resplendent against a sky of infinite stars. Elayne felt her breath fail her.

It was her own dark angel. Beautiful and powerful, radi-ant with mystery, a perfect rendering upon the artist's card. And as she lifted her eyes, she saw the same face alive be-fore her, watching her, in the person of a nameless pirate.

She sprang up, sweeping the card away and knocking over her chair as she escaped from his circle of Truth. "It is a trick! It is some artifice with the cards!" She stood breath-ing quickly, angrily. "He can't be you."

The Raven never took his eyes from her face. He tilted his head a little, as if he too were doubtful. "Do you re-member me, Lady Elena?"

"Nay—remember you? Have we met?" She shook her head helplessly. "I don't understand this! It's not—I don't mean—not in life! Remember you from where?"

He smiled. "It is merely a card, as you say. I only won-der why it disturbs you so."

"It is not merely a card, as you well know!" she cried. "It is you! And he can't be you. I don't know how you have discovered this, or made it come about, but he is not you."

He lifted his eyebrows. "You confuse me greatly, Lady Elena, I do concede. The card is me, and I am not him? Who is 'he'?"

She set her jaw and reached to pick up the card, slapping it face-up on the table. "I am quite sure this is some prank you play with your victims, as it must be known to you that this card is a perfect rendering of your person."

His mouth worked, as if he were subduing a smile. "I confess, you are correct in that point."

She hesitated, taken aback by this easy admission.

"It is a little game. I delight in games. It is a pursuit of mine to observe the human character. Your response has been the most interesting of all so far. Tell me, who is this 'he' that I cannot be?"

"No one," she said, truthfully enough. " 'Tis naught but a resemblance to a . . . a statue I used to gaze on during mass."

"Of a saint?"

"Um, an angel," she said.

"Ah, that would account for it," he said placidly. "I've oft been told I resemble an angel."

Elayne blinked at him. He did not appear like any angel she had ever seen, except her own.

"I expect it is my cherubic expression," he said, and gave her a smile so wicked that her throat shrank.

"You are very frightening," Elayne breathed.

"I mean to be," he said. He riffled through the cards and spread them in a fan upon the table. "And yet . . . you do know me."

"No." She shook her head, twice. "I don't know you."

"I'm in no mood to harm your lovely face, Elena," he said. "None at all." His lip curled slightly. " 'Tis your good fortune that you remind me more of Melanthe than of your sister."

Elayne felt herself frozen. She answered nothing.

"Ah, the house of Monteverde. Do they either of them suppose that I would forget those night-flower eyes? Your half sister's are only brown, but you have that infernal Monteverde tint of blue and purple in yours. Foolish of Melanthe, to be so careless. But better for you in the end, as I don't hold the timid Madame Cara's visage very dear."

If he had only spoken names, or even of faces, she might not have believed he could be speaking true. But when he called her sister timid, Elayne knew that he must have some close and vivid knowledge of her. "You have met my sister?" she asked faintly.

He made a short nod. "Aye," he said, "and hated her as she despised me."

Elayne stared at him. She could not even imagine her fainthearted sister in the same room with this man, far less that they knew one another enough to have hatred between them.

He turned his full gaze on her again. "Either you dissemble well, or your education in your family heritage has been sadly neglected, Princess Elena Rosafina di Monteverde. I am of Navona, and you have no greater enemies on earth."

She stiffened in her chair. "Nay," she whispered. "That is all gone now. Lady Melanthe told me!"

"Oh, did she!" He laughed. "And how did she convince you of this fantasy?"

"She only said—there were once three families, Monteverde, Riata, and Navona—but I need not study deeply on Navona, for they are finished."

"Finished! And that is all? I am stung."

"I'm sorry," Elayne said, ducking her head. "But in truth she made no mention of a pirate."

"Pirate!" he exclaimed languidly. "What a low opinion you have formed of me, my lady, on such small acquaintance!"

"A very princely pirate," Elayne said, giving a shaky wave of her hand about the chamber.

"Grant mercy!" He bowed his head in mockery. He picked up the angel card and glanced at it. "Finished," he said, tossing it down. His beautiful face became a devil's mask as he narrowed his eyes. "Indeed."

"Haps she only meant—that we are not enemies anymore. I have no hate for you myself."

His dark eyebrows lifted. He looked at her as if she must be lying, and he would kill her for it. Elayne tried to hold his gaze.

"How should I?" she asked earnestly. "I don't know who you are."

After a moment he lifted the angel card again between two fingers, turning it to examine the shadowy figure. A faint curve appeared at the corner of his mouth. "Alas, you make me smile too easily. I fear things will go hard for you here."

He did not appear amused. Elayne knew not what to make of him. "You object to smiling?"

"Not at all," he said. "Only I find that I do not do it often—so it may be I will decide to keep you with me longer than you find convenient. Should you object?"

Elayne looked away uneasily. "I do not comprehend you."

"Oh, you will, my lady Elena," he said. He pushed himself to his feet, standing over her. He did not touch her, and yet as he looked down, his eyes seemed to move over her face with the depth of a caress. "I promise that you will."

Somewhere very far away, at the outermost edge of hearing, a trumpet called three notes. It called again, and was gone, dreamlike in the silence.

He laughed suddenly. "Franco Pietro, eh? What a tragedy that would be!" With a gesture, he beckoned her. "Come, Elena. Your future awaits."

Five

"SIT!" HE SAID, waving her to the place beside him on the dais. They stood upon a gallery overlooking the sea, with laden tables lining the row of open arches. Elena was vividly aware of her hair falling loose down her back. Her insides quivered from lack of sleep, making her brain dance with flashes of illusion in the corners of her eyes. Torches burned, but the growing light of dawn made them dim. As he bid her sit down at the head table, child-servants passed back and forth, carrying platters and trenchers, casting long sharp shadows across the tiled floor. The prospect from the gallery was magnificent, the sky ablaze with pink and orange, the sea a soft blue. The Raven himself was a figure cast in silver and black, lit by the golden beams. He made no move to eat or speak to her—he sat still, his hand upon his wine cup, watching the sun rise over the sea.

Elayne sat quietly also. There seemed to be no other diners but themselves. The white linen tablecloth swayed gently in the open air, brushing her hands in her lap. In spite of his stillness, she felt a sharpened vitality in him; a sense that he kept himself motionless by resolve, alert, like a hunter listening for the distant sound of the hounds.

As the sun rose slowly above the sea, Elayne saw his glance flicker aside from his fixed focus on the horizon. At the same instant, she became aware of another drift of linen at the corner of her eye; a cloth moving lightly—a table that had not been there—but as she turned toward it she saw that it was a man. He seemed to appear from the dawn breeze itself, tall and insubstantial, dark-skinned like the Moors, his long wrists as thin as a skeleton's in the full white sleeves of his gown.

He made an elaborate bow, dipping his bronzed, bald head almost to his knees, like a court jester. He wore a white linen robe, cut simple and full, with a peasant's rough cord knotted about his waist. The flourishes of his hands in his sleeves were overwrought, dramatic, his tapered fingers mercurial. They almost seemed to gossip, speaking a silent language of their own.

"Il Corvo!" he exclaimed, lifting his gaunt head on a slender neck and stretching out his arm, addressing the pirate with a bold ease that Elayne had seen no one else use.

The Raven nodded. He smiled dryly, tapping his wine cup with his forefinger. Elayne could not tell if he was annoyed or entertained.

"I bring tidings," the strange man said in thickly accented Latin. "I bring great news."

The quiet figure beside her made no move. But Elayne knew that this was what he had been listening for.

"Tell us," the Raven said.

"I have found it!"

Still the pirate did not move, and yet it was as if a silent quiver ran through him; or through the air itself. He took a sip of his wine and waited.

The stranger was in no hurry to explain what he had found. Instead, he began a discourse on his travels, beginning in Byzantium and progressing—with extravagant gestures to show the length and hardship of his journeys—to Jerusalem, to Damascus, to Athens, and thence to Alexandria in Egypt. He endured storm and wrack, he rode upon camels, he sailed the River Nile in leaking vessels, he walked the hot sands of the desert wilderness. "At length I came to Thebes of the Temples," he declared, "Thebes the Colossal, the Everlasting, the Divine."

He paused, staring into the distance, the tendons in his neck springing clear and taut against thin skin. His dark eyes widened, as if he saw it before him.

"There I went into the temples," he whispered. "The empty sand-filled temples of ruin. I looked upon the columns, the statues—stone icons of men as tall as this fortress." He looked sharply at Elayne, as if he had seen her doubt. "You may believe me, my lady. I am a native of that country. They were the ancient kings, like unto gods themselves, and their statues are immense beyond your cunning to imagine. Their temples are defended by curses that must be disarmed—it is a lifetime study I have made, so that I may enter them safely in my search. I am a magician. Any other man would not emerge alive—or if he be unlucky enough to live, his maddened wits will slay him soon enough."

Elayne glanced aside at the Raven, to see how he accepted this. He looked back at her blandly, giving nothing away.

"It has cost me greatly," the Egyptian magician said, gesturing wide. "In coin, a king's fortune. In strain, it has cost me near my life—as you see by my withered frame."

His frame was indeed spare, although Elayne would not have called him withered. He seemed more as one of those men who might eat all they could consume and still burn it away with the flame of his eager temperament.

"I found nothing in the temples," he announced. "Nothing that would interest the least boy sorcerer in the land. Their bones were picked dry long ago by others."

"I thought no others could dare to go in," the Raven said dryly.

"Oh, I am not the only magician who can turn away a Pharaoh's cursed writ. You yourself could do it with some ease—I dare to say that even your gentle lady here, flying under the Raven's wing, would be as safe as I," he replied, glossing any contradiction with a rolling presentation of his hands, at the same time that he managed to give an air of great compliment to his host. "But—" He paused. "There are other places of power in Thebes." He lowered his voice. "The tombs."

The Raven said nothing, but he listened.

"Even such a master as I was forced to become apprentice again in order to reach them," the magician said. "When I found the man who could make me an adept in the secret art of entry, I had to pay him dearly, with a hundred pounds of marcasite and cinnabar—and then for a further compensation, to make him fulminating gold from aqua regis."

The Raven lifted his eyebrows. "Fulminating gold."

"A jeopardous undertaking, I know," the magician said, nodding deeply. "If it had erupted, I should not be standing before you now."

"Continue," their host commanded. Of all the food that lay before them, he had not taken a bite, nor invited Elayne to eat. She was hungry, but had more sense than to risk tasting anything on the pirate's table.

"In the end, I was successful," the Egyptian said. "When he judged me skilled enough, he took me to the city of Hermoupolis, to the mouth of the tomb of Hermes Trismegistus."

The Raven made a soft sound, like a sleeper's sigh. But he was not asleep.

"You will judge for yourself my tumult. Hermes Trismegistus, Lord of Wisdom, he who instructed Asclepius himself in the divine way. I will spare your lady the tale of my entry into that place. It is not lovely, nor fit for gentle ears. But I returned with treasure beyond compare. Not gold or jewels!" He flourished his sleeve. "Nothing so common. You of all men know what manner of treasure I describe."

"Tell me," the Raven said softly.

"Scrolls." The magician lowered his voice. "Still sealed with the device of his caduceus." He swept his hand wide, and suddenly he held a rolled paper. He strode forward and placed it on the table before them. Dust fell from it onto the linen; Elayne could smell the musty odor. On the clay seal, deeply incised, she saw the badge of an upright wand entwined with two snakes.

The Raven nodded slowly. "How many?"

"Twenty," the magician said. "And . . ." He began to nod also with his zeal. "A single tablet."

"Describe it," the Raven said sharply.

"It would seem to be made of onyx, though nothing I can use makes a scratch upon it. The inscription—" He became suddenly reticent. "But you must judge for yourself. I tell you verily, I cannot read it. It is in no characters that I know."

"The Black Tablet?" the Raven demanded.

"I know not. I would not take it upon myself to say. Those who do not wish you well have made me a bountiful offer, but I tender it for your examination. I brought it to you first."

For a long moment the pirate stared at him, as if he could see into the man's brain. Elayne did not think she could have stood still under such a scrutiny. But the magician looked back, directly into the Raven's eyes.

"How much do you ask?" the pirate said.

"I have brought the treasure first to you. We have dealt well before with one another," the magician repeated. "Ten thousand ducats of Venetian gold."

The Raven glanced toward his young steward, who instantly went about tasting and serving the meal that had been waiting. "Sit down to my table," he said to the magician. "I will examine them in my library later."

"YOU WISH TO accompany me?" The Raven slanted a look toward Elayne, offering her dried fruits and honeyed wafers from his own plate.

The breaking of fast was done, the torches and candles gleaming fitfully along the length of the gallery in the full light of morning. Elayne was giddy from lack of sleep.

"To your library?" she asked, hardly knowing what she said. The question ended on a yawn she could not stifle.

"I thought the Egyptian's wares might interest you." He shrugged. "But it is true that they will be in my library, where I conjure Beelzebub for sport. You need not come, if you do not like it."

Elayne felt as if she were swimming through some fantastic dream. "I will come," she said, hearing her own acceptance as if someone else had said it.

"Good." His demeanor lightened. He rose quickly, offering his hand. His fingers closed about hers a little more eagerly than was courteous. But as soon as she was on her feet, he let go and strode away down the gallery, his cloak sweeping out like the wings of the raven he was named for.

Elayne glanced about her at the silent child-servants. The magician had departed some time before, to prepare his goods for viewing. She was left to follow in the Raven's train, hurrying after with what dignity she could muster.

He did pause and look back for her at the head of the stairs. But as soon as he saw that she was coming, he passed ahead, moving as silently as shadow, as ardently as a boy on his way to some glad game.

She nearly lost him several times as they wended among passages and stairs, through empty rooms, where the only sign of the way he had gone was a slight crack in one of the heavy doors. But he waited for her at the burnished brass door to his observatory, standing and looking back, his dark cloak hanging back over one shoulder.

"You are slow," he said, smiling. "Has no one taught you how to follow properly?"

"I am not usually so pressed," she said, still panting a little from hurrying up the last set of stairs.

"Pressed!" He shook his head. "I'll teach you, sweeting."

"Teach me?" she replied carefully, taken aback by the endearment.

He brushed his hand over her cheek and hair, lightly, without touching it. "I shall teach you all manner of things," he said, his black eyes alight. He seemed to emanate his own dark flame, burning brighter as they drew closer to the Egyptian's cache.

Elayne gazed after him as he pushed open the door and strode out across the etched wheels and curves on the gleaming white floor. A thought of Raymond flitted through her mind—he seemed a simple knight indeed in comparison to this pirate. Elayne did not doubt for a moment that the Raven could teach her all manner of things—the kind of things she had never been allowed to learn under Cara's strictures. Her spirit rose fiercely at the thought, bounding like a hawk from the glove. Lifting her skirt, she hastened after him down the curved stairs into darkness.

The scrolls lay upon the same table where he had read her the cards of the Taroc, within the protective circle. But Elayne was not so unsettled now—she gave the mysterious blue lights merely a glance, and then turned to the center of the room.

The Egyptian magician stood silently by, his white garment dyed blue by the lights. The Raven was already occupied with the dusty treasure, but he looked up as she left the stairs, beckoning her nearer.

"I shall not need you for the moment," he said to the magician.

The Egyptian drew himself up, sweeping his arms behind his back. "I do not think it safe—" He paused. The Raven merely looked at him, one eyebrow lifted. With a negligent flick of his sleeve, the magician said, "For any other, I would not deem it safe. I do not recommend it to you, but if you insist upon my absence, it is upon your own head."

The Raven made a polite bow. "I do."

With a stately tread, the magician passed out of the library. When the sound of his sandals on the stairs had faded, the Raven gave Elayne one of his sudden, devilish grins. "An easy victory. I did not think to be rid of him for hours."

"He fears you would toss him from a cliff if he disobeyed," she said boldly.

"Not he! He supposes he could fly if I did." He tilted his head, observing her. "Do you think I have ever in truth had someone flung down?"

She looked down, her momentary boldness crumbling. "I don't know," she said. In the blue half-light the sculptured planes of his face seemed like a marble statue. Elayne lost her nerve for saying more.

"Do you think I am a murderer?" he asked.

"I don't know what you are," she said impulsively. "I don't know!"

"But you are sure that I am dangerous."

She glanced up at him, and then bent over the scrolls, pretending to examine them, keeping her hands locked behind her back. Her brain felt as unsteady as a ship's deck, tilting and spinning with exhaustion. It seemed madness, that he said such things. Yet it awakened something in her, a will for the wild sky that was nothing like her blissful love for Raymond.

"What do you think of them?" he asked.

Elayne straightened. She rubbed her nose, subduing a sneeze. "They are quite dusty!"

"Dust from the tomb of Hermes Trismegistus!"

"Who?" she asked.

"Perchance a god, perchance a man—let us call him the patron saint of magicians and sages. He lived in ancient times."

"A pagan."

"Without doubt, a pagan."

"Did he write these papers?"

"That, my beloved, is the question before us." He stared at the table without touching anything, then turned and took down one of the blue lights from a shelf. He set the glowing flask upon the table. As he leaned over the Egyptian's musty treasure, the shadows and light drew a glitter from his silver tunic.

Elayne watched him as he unrolled the scrolls one by one. She was learning to see emotion where he seemed to show none—he betrayed nothing in his face, but in the swift lift of his hand, the stillness of each pause as he examined the antique papers, he revealed a fascination as intense as the fiery lamplight. She could not tell what he saw there—only that it held him rapt.

She had thought Raymond handsome. But the Raven was something beyond handsome. Beyond gallant manners and teasing glances. He was like the old, old stories, like the unknown man who waited on a darkened hill, the mist around him, hand outstretched . . .

In the stories, if a woman went to him . . . she did not return.

.But she wanted to go . . .

She wanted . . .

Elayne blinked, her head swaying. A long time had seemed to pass. She sat down in the opposite chair, looking at the items spread across the table. She did not dare let herself drowse again. A pair of brass boxes sat beside the scrolls, unopened. In the center of the table, still wrapped heavily in linen, lay a flat package the size of her open palm.

To keep herself waking, she stood up again and wandered about the library, staring at snakeskins and strange devices, contrivances of metal and glass, furnaces of stone with chimneys protruding from all sides.

"Take care," he said. "Not everything here is benign."

Elayne snatched her hand away from a sealed jar she had been about to tap—it seemed to contain a live toad. The animal stared at her phlegmatically, perchance alive, perchance stuffed; not divulging any secrets.

"So inquisitive!" He shook his head.

She turned back to the table, made heedless by the weary spinning in her brain. "You asked me to accompany you," she said. "What am I to do?"

He lifted his eyebrows. "Sit quietly?"

"I have never excelled at sitting quietly. My sister has often said so."

"Ah, your sister," he said. Nothing more than that, but Elayne felt as if somehow another presence had entered the room.

He gazed at her steadily, with such a dark reserve that she felt blood rise in her cheeks. "Well, I will sit down," she said. She pulled out the chair and sat again, folding her hands in her lap.

"The picture of feminine obedience," he said. "Did you learn that of your sister?"

"Aye," she said, pursing her lips.

"Good. I would not like to think that you had wasted much of your life in that coy pose."

"Alack, you are difficult to please!" she said impatiently.

He startled her once more with his sudden flash of a smile. "Why, I only wish for you to please yourself—you are by far the more interesting that way."

"Hmmm," Elayne said, taking a deep breath to try to clear her brain.

"Hmmm," he replied, and went back to his scrolls.

She sat for a few moments, tapping her fingers against her lap, opening her eyes over and over as they tried to fall shut. She knew she must have some occupation or fall asleep. "May I open one of the boxes, then, to please myself?" she asked.

He looked up at her. "You have not changed an atom, you know," he said.

"What do you mean?" she asked, stiffening.

"You have always been so. A mobile spirit. Curious and inquiring."

"What do you know of me?"

"I read your cards," he said, dismissing her question. "Let me open the box, then, Pandora—to be safe."

If he said any protection spells or performed any rites of propitiation, Elayne did not see it. Instead, he simply drew one of the boxes toward him, took a knife as slender as a reed from his belt, and unpicked the ornate lock with the skill of a seasoned thief. The lid sprang open suddenly, making her jump.

"No demons," he said, glancing over the top at her. "Some pretty things." He pushed the box across the table toward her. "You may have them if you like."

She touched the box gingerly, peering inside. It was filled with a jumble of golden brooches and buckles. No dust dulled their glory—jewels winked and sparkled in the lamplight, tiny rainbows caught in the black depths of the box. "Benedicite!" she breathed, suddenly waking. She drew forth a breast pin shimmering with the red fire of rubies. "You do not mean to give me this!"

"I am sure it will become you," he said, without looking up. "If it will only keep you still for a quarter hour, I shall be delighted."

With his slender knife he flicked a cut across the bindings that held the linen package. He spread open the cloth, revealing a flat stone, badly cracked across the carvings that swirled over the dark, rough surface.

For a moment it seemed only to be a half-finished work, as if the stone carver had left off before smoothing his design. But even as she looked, she could make out incised letters in an unknown language, interrupted by the crack and the broken edges.

"The Black Tablet," he murmured.

She gazed at it curiously, seeing nothing in it to invoke extraordinary interest, but the rich pile of jewels lay ignored as he moved his palm and fingertips lightly over the stone. If the hours of waking wore on the Raven, there was no sign of it in his elegant features. He only paused to reach for a flagon of wine from a sideboard, pouring into a pair of silver goblets.

.While he inspected the tablet intently, she took a deep sip from the offered cup, trying to rouse herself. She toyed with the sparkling breast pin. The twisting, teasing smoke of memory rose and twirled like a spent candle's smolder in her mind, that sense that she had seen something, or said something before, without remembering when or where.

She was losing the battle with sleep. Her eyes drooped. She drank more of the tart wine, in an effort to keep herself vigilant, but toads and soaring falcons drifted and spun in her brain. *Things will not always happen as you expect,* Lady Melanthe said, as outlandish notions and stratagems formed in a reverie, dreams of escape and nightmares of wandering. He had discovered who Elayne was. He was her enemy; he might try to ransom her to Monteverde, to Franco Pietro. But he said he would teach her and called her tender names. It seemed that Lady Beatrice was railing at her for her incompetence. *Use your wits, girl! Use your wits!*

Elayne came upright with a little jerk of her head. "Where is Lady Beatrice?" she mumbled.

"Asleep," the Raven said, and Elayne realized where she was again.

She blinked at him and rubbed her hand across her eyes. He sat back in his chair, stretching out his leg, watching her.

Opportunities will come, Lady Melanthe had said. *Use your nerve.*

"Sir," she said, struggling through her lethargy. "You are a pirate."

He shrugged. "By hap I am, if you insist."

"Hence—people pay you ransom to go free."

His black eyes glittered. "They do. Unless I cast them off a cliff."

She frowned at him. It was impossible to decipher whether he was in jest or in truth. She squeezed her palms together. "My lord, I have a proposal for you."

He waited, steepling his hands and looking at her over the tips of his fingers.

"Sir—could I pay you to keep me here?"

For a long moment he said nothing. Then he tilted back his head and began to laugh.

"It is not so absurd!" she said thickly. "I have nothing of my own, I confess, but you could write to the Duke of Lancaster—he's been appointed my guardian by—by—" Her weary brain could hardly find the name. "King Richard. Of England." She took a deep breath to clear her brain. "And I believe that you would find him eager to pay a goodly sum for my release. You could have all of that, but keep me here instead."

"Now, there is an admirable design!" he said. "I believe you have a pirate's heart. But what if the duke refuses to pay?"

"Then—" She hesitated. "I believe—you seemed to know of Franco Pietro of the Riata. . . ."

"Indeed! I should write to Franco Pietro, and say the duke did not see fit to ransom you, so will he kindly defray a proper sum to obtain his contracted bride?"

"But do not send me to him, after you receive it," she prompted.

"Of course not! Why not write to both of them at once? I could ransom you twofold and still sell you to the Saracens. An excellent plan."

"No, I mean for you to keep me here."

"And what am I going to do with you here?" He tilted his head. "You would be awkwardly in the way when Lancaster and the Riata send their fleets to obliterate me."

"I doubt they would send fleets. Fleets? Not over me."

He nodded. *"Avaunt,* let us take that chance, then. No doubt I'll sink them if they come. But still I don't know what to do with you, if you can't be sold," he said mildly. He filled her drinking cup again. "Do you wish to become my concubine?"

"No!" she said with a furious blush. Heat rose up through her body, awakening her. She avoided his eyes. "I don't mean that at all!"

"There is no choice, then. I would have to toss you from the cliffs."

She set her jaw and took a quick swallow of the wine. "Never mind. I don't speak in jest, though you laugh. You said you might keep me here longer than I like, but in truth, you cannot delay me long enough for my taste."

He traced the incisions on the black stone. "You don't wish to marry the Riata?"

She drew a deep breath and took another generous swallow of the wine. "No. I abhor the idea."

"We are in wondrous accord, then, my lady." He looked up at her as he ran his fingertip over the carvings. "I had no intention of allowing it to happen."

There was nothing visible to betray it, but Elayne felt as if some faint lightning rushed between them, like a storm far off. The Raven stood, his tunic gleaming in the blue light. The water-dragon seemed to sway slowly overhead.

"Navona is not finished," he said in a voice that caressed the words. "Not yet while I breathe." He leaned on the table, his black cloak flowing down over his hands. Nothing he had discovered among his purchased treasures had elicited a look like the one he gave her now. "You may have your desire to linger with me, my lady Elena, but I need no payment from the duke. I demand another ransom, sweeting. I require you for my wife."

Six

LADY MELANTHE HAD warned her of poison. *Beware what you eat,* the countess had said. *Take heed of what you drink.*

Elayne lay very still as the headache gripped her, looking through her eyelashes at the room, trying to remember how she had come there. There was a scent of flowers, a soft breeze that lifted the bright silken bed-hangings of saffron and blue and red ochre. From the coolness of the air, she thought it must be morning. Slowly she realized that she was naked underneath the sheet, her hair spread loose across the pillows.

She held her hand to her temple and closed her eyes. When she opened them, a blurry gleam of gold caught light through her lashes. She lifted her hand, staring at the ring on her third finger.

On the broad band, letters were engraved. *Gardi li mo,* she read.

Guard it well.

She frowned. Through the ache in her head, she found a memory of the pirate, standing over the table in his library.

A young maid started up from somewhere in the room, hurrying to the side of the huge bed. "Good morrow, Your Grace!" she said in English. She made a deep bow down onto her knee, her head disappearing below the level of the bed for an instant. "Your Magnificence slept well, I pray?"

Elayne let her head fall back onto the pillows, trying to still the spinning in her brain. "I don't know how my magnificence slept," she grumbled, her eyes closed, "but my forehead is like to split in two."

"My lord said it might happen so," the maid said kindly. "He sent a remedy for such, in the juice of grapes. Will Your Grace take it now?"

Elayne looked at her suspiciously. The girl was yellow-haired, much younger than Elayne, with pale blue eyes and a round face. A sprinkle of blond freckles gave her a cheerful countenance. She seemed out of place on this island of wizards and pirates.

"I will bring it," she said, as if Elayne had agreed.

In a moment she returned to the bedside with a tray of hammered brass. She held up the ornate ewer and cup, pouring carefully. Light gleamed on the brilliant enamel designs.

"You drink of it first," Elayne said.

The girl nodded, unsurprised, and took a draught. She wrinkled her nose and then smiled with a purple-stained upper lip. "I fear it has a trace of bitterness, ma'am. But my lord says it will cure your head."

Elayne waited a few moments, to be sure the girl stayed waking. "What is your name?"

"Margaret, if it please Your Magnificence." She gave another bow of courtesy.

"Pray do not address me as 'magnificent.'" Elayne put her hands to her aching eyes and saw the ring again. She sat up, drawing the sheets to her chin. Her head pounded. Margaret did not seem to have fallen into a faint, or expired, so Elayne took up the cup of grape juice and drank a large swallow.

She worked at the ring. It would not come off.

"Does it pain you, Your Grace?" Margaret asked anxiously.

"It does not belong to me," Elayne said. She took another swallow of the purple liquid, and then finished the entire cup. A metallic taste lingered on her tongue. "I am not entirely foolish, though I took his drugged wine."

Margaret bit her lip. She took the cup from Elayne and set it carefully on the tray.

Elayne held the sheet close about her shoulders. As luxurious as the chamber allotted to Lady Beatrice had been, this one was richer by far. No king would be ashamed of the artistry in the bright frescoes and carvings that adorned the domed ceiling. At first they seemed like religious tableau, or scenes of gentle parties in beflowered gardens, but a second glance revealed astrological signs woven into the ladies' headdresses. The creatures that lolled at their feet like pets were not lapdogs, but small monsters, or fairies, or something indescribable. The tall bed frame was gilt, swathed in tasseled silk. Scrolls and books lay piled on a velvet table-covering—Elayne counted twelve volumes in three stacks, more books than she had ever seen collected in one place apart from the pirate's library.

"What chamber is this?" she demanded, holding the embroidered coverlet close.

"It is my lord's bedchamber, Your Grace," Margaret said cautiously.

"Why am I here?" Elayne was burningly aware of her nakedness beneath the sheet. "Is he coming here?"

Margaret bobbed her head. "In a little while, he will return with the lady and some others. I am to prepare Your Grace and the chamber for inspection."

"Inspection!"

"The sheets, madam." She gestured toward Elayne's knees in the bed. "I have some flowers, too! I will spread them very pretty beside you in the bed, if it would not make you shamefast."

"I don't know what you mean." Elayne felt panic. "Inspection? Who is coming? Am I to be sold?"

Margaret shook her head vigorously. "Your Grace, of course not! If he would not tolerate the least one of us here to be enslaved, how should he allow such a thing for you?"

"He spoke of it several times. He threatened me with it."

The girl looked disapproving. "My lady, may God forgive me, I cannot believe you. He would not countenance any such thing."

"What is this inspection, then? Who does he bring?"

"I believe he will bring your lady attendant, madam—the elderly lady. She will wish to be assured of the proper consummation of your marriage to my lord."

Elayne gave a gasp. "She will wish to be assured of no such thing!" She sat straighter. "Where is my chemise? I must rise."

"Nay, Your Grace, it would be best to stay—"

"I have not said that I would marry him! My gown!" Elayne said forcefully. "Make haste!" She pushed herself off the bed, dragging the sheets around her. As she pulled them from the mattress, she saw spots of blood-red amid the white folds. "Deus!" she exclaimed. "What—"

She stood still. A wave of mortification and horror rose to her cheeks as understanding came upon her.

"No," she whispered. "Depardeu, no!"

"Do not be abashed, ma'am," Margaret said. "It is an honorable mark upon your wedding bed."

Elayne stared at her. She almost declared the girl a lunatic. She had not consented to any marriage with this pirate. But the ring upon her finger, his bedchamber . . . she remembered nothing of how she had come there.

She turned away, holding the sheets tight about her. "He would not dare!" she exclaimed under her breath. And yet even as she spoke, she knew he could commit any transgression that he willed. Marriage would be a favor compared to other prospects.

Lady Beatrice's sharp voice penetrated the chamber, an ill-tempered forewarning that caused Margaret to hurry toward the door. Just before the maid reached for it, the latch

swung open silently, as if it had no weight. Margaret stood
back, bowing down to the floor.

Elayne conquered a fervent urge to hide herself. She
stood as straight as Cara had ever demanded, holding the
sheets and tangled tresses of her own hair close to her
breast as she glared toward the door.

The countess entered, rapping her cane with each step.
Whatever sleeping illness had possessed her, she seemed
suddenly recovered now. She paused, her thin eyebrows
lifted almost to the tight line of her wimple as she looked
Elayne up and down.

I am a princess, Elayne declaimed in her mind, and returned Lady Beatrice's look with defiance. She would not
bow or even nod. Not now—when one move might cause
her meager coverings to slip.

Behind Lady Beatrice the pirate stood in the doorway,
dressed in pure indigo, his long hair tied behind his neck.
He wore two daggers on the belt at his hip. A silver pendant
dangled from his ear, giving him an even more pagan aspect. Beyond, she could see that there were others waiting,
but he blocked their faces from the door. As he met her
eyes, she lifted her chin angrily.

He seemed amused. He might even have made a wink at
her as he gave a formal bow of courtesy, but she was not
certain, for he lowered his face as he went to his knee. His
reverence was easy and elegant—as polished as any at the
court of Windsor. He rose effortlessly and stepped into the
room, closing the door on the crowd.

"And what have you got yourself into, girl?" the countess demanded. "This poor fellow seems to think you have
some noble blood in you, and so he'll wed you on the spot."

Il Corvo said, "You may spare us any play-act, Lady
Beatrice. I know her bloodlines to a fine degree."

The countess turned her head and shoulders toward him.
She thumped her cane and shrugged. "You seem to have
made sure of your mark on her. If you are so convinced of
who she is, what ransom do you suppose to get now that
she's besmirched?"

The pirate walked to Elayne. She turned her face away. He lifted her hair and traced his fist down her throat. The velvet of his sleeve brushed her bared shoulder. "Do you wish to make a more certain examination? I would not like to send you back to Melanthe with any doubts in your mind."

"Send me back? To England? Aye, and you suppose I will be pleased to carry news that you have ravished the goddaughter of the Countess of Bowland for your whore?"

"Taken her as my beloved and honored wife," he countered calmly. "As I told you, we gave our vows in my own chapel here not a few hours since. I am grieved that you were too ill to be in attendance, but now you may see for yourself that all is sealed."

Lady Beatrice tapped forward and reached for a fold of the sheets around Elayne, bending over to examine one of the bloodstains. She flicked it away and straightened. Elayne felt like one of Sir Guy's horses at the market.

"It will never stand, once Lancaster is informed," the countess said, gripping the cane's head in her bony fingers. "If you know who who she is, fool, you know she's contracted for a portion enough to buy your little island a hundred times over. You'd have done better to hold her for a handsome profit than to defame her virginity."

He gave a cold nod of assent. "You, too, have a pirate's mind, I see, my lady. As it falls out, however, a handsome profit is not my desire."

"What is it you expect, knave?"

"I expect you to return forthwith and convey tidings of the marriage of Princess Elena Rosafina di Monteverde to Allegreto Navona, along with my cordial gratitude to the Lady Melanthe."

"Gratitude! You'll have the armies of England and Monteverde upon you in gratitude! What of her betrothal contract?"

"You may further advise our good lady Melanthe to hold the armies of England in check," he said, "if they wish to be arrayed on the winning side." He looked down at

Elayne. "But Melanthe will understand. She owes me this.
Read closely how she chose the words of that wedding contract." With a half-smile, he slid a lock of Elayne's hair
through his fingers. "She owes me. But by Heaven, I do
thank her for it."

Elayne tweaked her hair away. She was trembling.
"Whatever it is you want of me, whatever enemy I am of
yours—you did not need to do it this way." She glared up
at the pirate, clutching the sheets close. "I had no wish to go
to Monteverde, nor bring armies upon anyone. If you could
prevent me from wedding the Riata in some way—I told
you I abhorred the match. I would have obliged you in
whatever manner I could. But not this!"

"You regret our vows already?" he asked. "You wound
me!"

"You know there were no vows made!"

He touched her cheek like a lover. "Have a care of what
you say in the heat of the moment, *carissima*. You were not
so unwilling in the night."

"Oh! You are full of lies!"

"That I am, my lady." He shrugged. "It is one of my
many mortal sins. But these blemishes upon our sheets are
not a lie. And there are a score and more of my people outside this chamber who witnessed our pledge, and our lying
down together, and come at present to wish us well. To
withdraw now from your given word is a matter to consider
gravely."

She wanted to shout that it was not true—there had been
no pledge or oaths exchanged. But like a cheating opponent
at chess, he had maneuvered her when she was not attending, and she found herself with no escape. She could declare she had made no vow to be his wife—but what would
she be then? Besmirched, as Lady Beatrice said. It might be
that Franco Pietro would still have her, or the Duke of Lancaster would send armies, but at best she would end up
where she had dreaded to go, under a cloud of stark humiliation.

She could feel Lady Beatrice's judging look. She was no

longer chaste. She did not feel different; she had no memory of what had been done to her—but the pirate made her sound as if she had been eager for it.

In haps she had been. When he touched her so lightly, she felt as if there were a flash between them, a sting, an ache that ran from his fingertip across all of her skin.

"Well, girl?" Countess Beatrice demanded.

He moved away, as if to allow her freedom to choose. As he walked behind the countess, silent as a cat on the carpeted floor, he paused. He slipped the dagger from his belt and turned it in his hand, so that the morning sunlight caught the white diamond in the handle and sent a prism of light across his palm. The maid Margaret watched him placidly. He looked up directly into Elayne's eyes.

"What do you say?" The countess leaned upon her cane, her back to him. The stiff wings of her old-fashioned wimple made a screen around her face. "Has he forced you into this, child?"

The Raven did not move, or take his eyes from Elayne's. His face was gentle, perfect, his hand balancing the dagger and his dark brows slightly raised as he waited for her answer.

And she understood him. With a clarity as brilliant as the gemstone on his weapon, she understood that he would kill the countess if Elayne denied him. Lady Beatrice would be a messenger with no doubt in her mind, or she would not be a messenger at all.

"Do not think you are friendless," the countess said gruffly, unknowing of the viper poised to strike. "There is recourse for this kind of villainy, if you've spine enough to demand it."

Elayne swallowed. She shook her head.

"There was no villainy," she said faintly. "We are truly wed."

The countess snorted. "God spare us, you witless chit! Not a moment since, you claimed there were no vows."

"I only pretended to repent of it—for fear of your displeasure, ma'am."

"Play me no May games! You tell me true if you've been plundered and forced to bed, or take your fine chances of life with this whoreson."

Elayne saw his fingers close on the dagger; she saw him make a leisurely move.

"I was not forced!" she cried. "We are wed; I said I took him for my husband before God."

"Willingly?" the countess persisted, leaning forward. "This baseborn outlaw?"

"Willingly!" Elayne flashed her hand outward. "More than willing! I wear his ring! I was eager to bed with him. Now take that message to my lady godmother and leave me. Leave me!"

Lady Beatrice thumped her cane and raised her chin. "Bah! So I shall, then. Harlot."

The pirate sheathed the blade without a sound. He inclined his head to Elayne.

She pulled the sheets close around herself and turned her face to the wall. "Leave!"

FROM THE TILED and arcaded gallery, Elayne watched Lady Beatrice sail away. It had not taken long for the countess to embark once she made up her mind. The Raven had Amposta's ship prepared and waiting, laden with letters and gifts to soften the shock of the news she carried. Before noon the countess was departed.

The craft moved swiftly, manned by two tiers of oars as it made boldly for the horizon. Elayne gazed after it from behind the fronds of a potted palm. She did not want to stand openly beside the parapet where anyone could see her. In a two-month, she supposed, Lady Beatrice would be safely back in England, spreading the word that Elayne was a harlot married to a pirate.

She stood very still, containing shame and wrath and bitterness like a smooth-faced vessel with a whirlwind inside. From somewhere far below, invisible, the smoke and bustle of cooking drifted upward. People laughed. Someone seemed to be rehearsing music on a psaltery, plucking the same faint string of notes over and over.

Elayne passed her hand over the pattern of silver-and-green leaves twining through the silk of her cote-hardie. There were hundreds of pearls embroidered into the low sweep of the neckline. The gown was a gift from Il Corvo, Margaret said, for Elayne to wear at the wedding feast. It lay heavily across her bathed and perfumed shoulders, more luxurious than anything she had ever donned, even at the Queen's court—and like enough stolen from some passing merchant ship.

Behind her, through an open arch in the faceted black stone of the castle, Il Corvo's sumptuous bedchamber and anterooms waited. He had not returned there, only sent a courteously worded notice of Lady Beatrice's imminent departure, describing the array of comforts and the strong guard he was sending with her. Their handmaids were no longer detained, made free to accompany her back to England as her attendants. He did not wish for Elayne to be concerned about the countess's ease and protection.

Elayne was not concerned for the countess or her maids. She felt the approach of evening like a descending hand.

"My lady." Margaret's voice came meekly from behind her. "My lady, the repast does not please you?"

Elayne had refused to take any of the food or drink that Margaret had brought her. It sat disregarded on a table in the open gallery, covered by a diaphanous linen cloth.

"I am not hungry," she said. She had no intention of being asleep when he came this time.

"I will take it away." Margaret made a courtesy. "Pray, madam, if you will give me leave, I must begone for a short while to feed my son before the banquet."

"Your son?" Elayne glanced at her. The maid seemed young to have a child.

"Yea, my lady," Margaret said, keeping her face lowered. "I know it is blameworthy. I was in a bordel-house, to my shame, until my lord gave me sanctuary here." Her hands fluttered. "But I have full repented and done penance! I pray Your Grace will not cast me off."

"Of course I would not cast you off."

"God grant you mercy, madam. You are as kind and good in your heart as my lord. I will make a loyal servant to you, as he bid me." She bowed deeply again. "If you will give me consent, I will not be away long. I brought your privy chest, with your combs and fillets. We will have ample time to dress your hair when I return, I pledge."

"Certainly, go," Elayne said. "Take as long as you wish."

Margaret retreated, giving a courtesy with each step. Elayne turned back to the horizon, staring hard, unable to find the ship any longer.

The weight of the pearl-encrusted cote-hardie was stifling in the midday heat. Elayne turned suddenly, walking from the gallery into the bedchamber. She looked at the bed, the vibrant hues of the silken hangings, the clean sheets and pillows that showed no imprint now of what had been done upon them. The very essence of the pirate lingered here, like a sinful promise, a perfume too faint to perceive. She remembered him touching her bared shoulder; the back of his hand sliding lightly against her skin. A strange shudder overtook her, a weakness beyond understanding. With trembling fingers, she yanked at the false sleeves until the threads gave way. She tore free the buttons of the elegant gown. It fell to the floor, where she left it in a costly heap.

She instantly felt lighter. Amid the exotic furnishings was one small familiar coffer. She lifted the cover, inspecting quickly inside, relieved to find everything in place as she had left it.

Her hair was still loose, but she managed to stuff all but a few disorderly strands into a net. As she hunted through the chest, she moved with more urgency. She found her journal and writing tackle, and thrust them into a leather purse, girding herself with a plain silk cord for a belt. She did not know what she was intending, dressed only in her short-sleeved smock, but she would not remain in this chamber any longer, meekly awaiting her fate.

BLACK STONE WALLS surrounded the castle yard, stone that was like to some gem itself, glittering with tiny surfaces of peacock iridescence within the dark hue. There were no milk cows or friendly cook-fires in the courtyard; only racks of the guards' staves and a water well at the center. Two great white dogs patrolled the court, their rough coats the hue of purest snow. They stood and stared with deep-eyed majesty, aloof and unapproachable.

It seemed lonely for a castle. Deserted, as if it had been built for some high lord whose retinue had departed, though she still heard voices and smelled the kitchen somewhere. A goat stood tied in harness, the cart loaded with baskets of fruits and soft cheese. No one guarded the food. It was as if the human inhabitants were invisible.

The heavy main gates were closed, but there was one small doorway that opened from the courtyard to the outside. Elayne looked through, seeing a path along a corridor cut in the earth. It ended in steps that led upward and vanished around a corner. From inside the wall, she could see a gnarled tree and some sky.

If he expected her to be humbly waiting, dressed and trussed like a prize fowl for his false celebration, he would be disappointed. She stole three plums and a pair of white-meats from the cart, and bolted through the doorway.

Outside, it did not require long to make certain of what she knew already—that no unwilling bride would be making her escape merely by leaving the castle yard. The island was a natural fortress, girt by seacliffs only the screaming gulls could occupy, riven by tiny harbors and gorges spanned by the fabulous stone bridges. But the energy of anger—and something else, some hot misery that she could not name—propelled her feet, though she could find no destination. Below the castle, she could see whitewashed houses and a quay clustered around a diminutive beach.

Fishing boats came and went in a bustle of activity. A pack of war galleys lay serenely off the shore, like wolves resting before their next hunt.

Elayne could observe the village clearly from the cliff heights, but try the countless bridges and paths as she might, she could not find the way down to it. Her head still throbbed with an echo of drugged wine. Sea wind blew strands of her hair from the net as she wandered the maze of trails that seemed to lead nowhere but back to where they began. The frustrating twist and coil of the pathways back upon themselves only made her more furious at the pirate, enraged at the cheating games he played. She could all but feel him watching her from his black towers, laughing at her inability to reach the village that it seemed he must have placed deliberately, so tantalizingly close. She was breathing hard when she emerged finally onto a wind-blasted headland, surprising a goat that gave a kicking leap and vanished among the gnarled bushes.

At the cliff's rim, arising suddenly from the raw rocks, a smooth block of limestone lay uprooted from the ground. She made her way among the wind-racked shrubs to the huge ruined pedestal. Putting her hand upon it to steady herself, she looked down into a vertical chasm at dolphins playing in the jewel-blue water of the narrow inlet below.

She glanced back, upward to the castle itself mounting the highest point of the island. The slender, fantastic spires of black stone seemed to dazzle in the afternoon sunlight like the Raven's cloak. She looked down at the water again and took another careful step up around the pedestal, watching her feet to keep clear of the edge. Not until she felt safe did she look up, and then had to grab a bush and stifle the involuntary urge to jump backward.

Enormous stone eyes stared at her. A colossal head, blind and tipped askew, lay broken on the ground where it had fallen from the pedestal. Elayne stared back at it, gripping the rough bush tightly. She had seen nothing like it in her life; it was the size of three wagons, the nose alone as tall as she. Once it had been painted—traces of red and black clung about the eyes and the strange headdress. Carefully she reached out and touched the barbaric figure, running her palm down the full lips that were as smooth and perfect as a woman's.

She looked about her. She was hidden from the castle's view, blocked by the peculiar, fan-like headdress of stone. With a sense of deliberate insolence, she dropped the bundle of cheese and fruit on the ground and hiked her skirts above her knees. She clambered up onto the statue's neck. From there, balancing on the broad cheek and temple, she walked out and sat down against the headdress. It made an excellent throne and windbreak, blocked from the castle and commanding a view of the crevice and inlet.

She pressed her hands over her hot cheeks. For a long while she sat still, hidden in this strange and magnificent place between the sea cliffs and the sky. Out of sight of the pirate's citadel, she felt her furious breath come easier.

As a girl she had wandered such wild places, sought them out when she was troubled or distressed, drawn there by that unwomanly side of her nature that Cara deplored. Lately that urge had seemed far away, lost in her passion for Raymond, in the bright colors and crowds at the King's court. There was nothing here so gentle as the woods and pastures of Savernake, but she took some melancholy consolation in the emptiness, in the vast prospect that revealed every hue of nature before her.

She put her fingers to her eyes. Green fool that she was, she had thought the Raven fascinating—dangerous—God save her, she had thought him almost alluring. For a deluded hour she had even believed she had found an ally, that she might make of him a friend.

Shame flooded her. Shame for the loss of her honor, shame for the word that Lady Beatrice would carry back to England—shame and anger that for even a moment she had trusted him. Bargain, would she? Bargain with a treacherous outlaw, her sworn enemy; even her sister had despised him, by his own admission, but Elayne had not had wit enough to wonder why.

And she knew why she had not wondered. Because she was frail. Because she was weak. Because he was so beautiful and mysterious that he had blinded her with it. And even now she felt the place he had touched her throat, even now she closed her eyes and ached with a hot, nameless ache when she thought of it.

She leaned down with her skirt about her knees, hiding her face from the world. She rocked back and forth with her eyes squeezed shut, trying to erase from her mind the image of him in the dawn light, the figure of black and silver, the trace of a fleeting smile. Trying not to imagine him lying beside her, over her. Abruptly she took out her journal and ink-horn. In Libushe's language she penned an insulting description of Il Corvo, in unfettered, grisly detail, making him a good degree more hideous and rough than was truthful.

She gazed out at the horizon for a few moments, then dared to leaf back through the pages to the poems she had written to Raymond.

She bit her lip. He would never hear her poems, never laugh with her, never kiss her or call her his foolish darling, his little cat, again. Until this moment, the truth of it had not penetrated her heart. It had seemed that somehow, someway, she would return to him. She stared down into the ravine and wondered if she flung herself off she might turn into a dolphin and swim away, as Libushe had once told her of a girl who transformed into a seal and vanished into the misted sea.

She stood up. For a long, dreadful moment she thought of it.

She thought of the fall, the rocks . . . the water.

She had not the nerve.

Bowing her head, she turned from the edge—and gave a low cry at the sight of a white dog tugging at her forgotten bundle of food. The animal startled and looked up at her, no more than a large puppy, almond-shaped black eyes in a downy white face. But it did not retreat or snap as she jumped down and grabbed the bundle away, only stood and stared up at her hopefully.

"A fine thief!" she said gently, unable to scold such a sweet face. "Where is your family?"

The puppy moved toward her, sniffing at her hem. It leaped up and rested its big paws on her thighs, grinning. Clearly it was no wild animal. She thought it must be from a litter of the great white dogs that guarded the castle, although as it began to play with the folds of her gown, it had none of the majestic dignity of those beasts. It was more a disgraceful tumble of white fluff, wriggling and turning its belly up to invite a pet.

She bent down, stroking its soft fur as it twisted happily under her hand. She had missed her own dogs badly since leaving home. Lady Beatrice's spaniel had been unfriendly, never loving when it could nip instead.

She reached into her bundle and broke off a bite of the white meat. The puppy rolled upright and took it politely, nibbling the tidbit from her fingers. It sat before her with its tail wagging gently, looking into her face. Elayne sat down and let it wriggle onto her lap. She rested back against the statue, stroking the dog's soft fur, distributing the cheese between them and biting into the sweet plums herself.

After they had devoured all there was, she wiped juice from the corner of her mouth and sat with the warm weight of the puppy in her lap. The sun heated her bare arms to a flush of pink. Her head ached. She supposed Il Corvo would be searching for her. Let him search. Let him have his wedding feast without a bride.

It was quiet here, and so empty. There was no one to order her or caution her or arrange her future with an uncaring snap of their fingers. There was only the young dog, a friend with no demand or desire but to nestle close and share a meal.

Its nose bumped her in greeting. The pup licked her chin and settled against her, heaving a sigh. She could feel its quick heartbeat against her skin. She bent her head and rested her cheek on fur softer than any costly pelt, smiling in her misery.

Seven

WHEN SHE OPENED her eyes again, it was to see the pirate sitting on a rock, examining the pages of her journal by the angled pink light of the setting sun. The white puppy was playing with the tip of his boot. She sat up quickly as she realized what he had in his hands. "That is mine!"

He was dressed differently now, plainly, in black hose and a simple white shirt belted with silver and onyx, his sleeves pushed up past his elbows. His hair fell loose about his shoulders, longer and blacker than any Christian man's should be.

"Then it is you who pines so sweetly for this Raymond," he said.

It was as if his dark eyes saw through her body and into her past and future. She evaded the look, unsure if it was mock or menace in his voice. "Raymond?" she mumbled.

"The name is not familiar to you?"

She half-shook her head, denying it by instinct.

"Perchance another wrote his name several times in your book, then."

"He is—a friend."

The corner of the pirate's mouth lifted in a knowing smile.

"Very well!" she exclaimed. "Why ask? If you perceive so much by your magic, then I have no secrets!"

"Mere speculation and deduction, Lady Elena." He smiled again. "But here—" He looked down at a page. "I am grieved that I myself don't appear in such a kindly aspect in your text. Am I truly such an ugly, uncouth fellow?"

"You *can* read it!" she said sullenly. "How can you read it?"

"I make an earnest study of alien texts," the Raven said. He flipped through pages of her journal lightly. "As any philosopher must."

"Philosopher! A mere pirate, who forces himself on unwilling maids."

He tapped the toe of his boot back and forth as the puppy pounced on it happily. "Alas, no wonder you describe me in such unflattering terms, if that is what you believe."

Elayne took a deep breath. She twisted the gold band around her finger. "Then you will not be surprised if I do not attend your celebration feast, since—whatever you may claim—I do not believe that we are truly wed."

"Before you cast off my ring, Lady Elena," he said gently, "let me survey your situation for you. You have two choices. You may accept me as your husband, or you may be sold to some kind Moor who treats his concubines better than his wives, and no one in Christendom will lay eyes upon you again."

Elayne brushed a thick strand of hair back from her cheek. "How should I believe that? The girl Margaret declares that you would never sell anyone as a slave."

"Very well—" He stood up. "If you wish to stake your life upon a maidservant's notion of me."

The puppy bumbled over to Elayne. She busied herself in petting it. The pup put its paws on her knee, licking her fingers. Its fur was the softest thing she had ever touched.

Elayne leaned over the pup while it nosed her face. "Are

you a lost princess?" she whispered. "Did you refuse to do what you are told?"

The puppy bit her nose. She drew back with a yelp. The pup jumped away and then came back to chew at the hem of her robe.

"Ever naïve," he said dryly.

"Avoi," she said, touching her nose and finding blood on her finger. "She is only a baby."

"Do you always trust what appears innocent?"

Elayne daubed at her nose with her sleeve. "I do not ascribe deep devices to puppies, it is true."

He squinted at her face. "I hope it doesn't leave a scar."

"A scar!" She touched the cut carefully, wincing at the sting.

"It would lessen your value when I sell you to the Saracens," he said.

She drew her hem away from the puppy's teeth as she stood. The sun was going down behind a bank of dark clouds, turning everything to brilliant golden light and harsh shadow. His loose white sleeves billowed in the dying breeze.

"May I have my book?" she asked, holding out her hand.

Somewhat to her surprise, he returned the journal without dispute. "How came you to write in that tongue?" he asked.

"Lady Melanthe sent a wisewoman," Elayne said shortly. "She taught me of many things."

"You seem to have made a broad study indeed. Wide learning is not common in a maiden."

"Haps it is not common, but there is nothing wrong with learning."

"Nay, it is excellent," he said, nodding. "I hope you will continue apace. Make yourself free of my books and manuscripts. They are full of dust and interesting ideas."

She was not accustomed to approval of her studies. Nor to men who encouraged her to entertain interesting ideas. "Well," she said, "for such time as I remain here, I shall."

"Good. I doubt me you will find much to read in the

harem." He gave her a dark-eyed look. "But at least you'll have ample hours of leisure to meditate on your vast knowledge, between carnal visits from your master."

Elayne felt the blood rising to her face. She had no memory of what he had done, but Libushė had emphatically explained to her, for her protection, just what a woman could expect from a man. She wished that he would not be so comely in his body and face as he stood with his boot braced against an overturned block of stone. It made her angrier at him still, that he was not abhorrent, but made her feel hot and willing to be touched by him.

As ever, he seemed to see into her mind. "We will endeavor to find you a buyer not so ugly as myself," he said. "But I can make no certain promises."

She turned away, pulling her skirt free of the branch of a windswept bush. "You mock, but it was fiendish of you to do what you did. To put some potion in my drink, and then to—" She pursed her lips and broke off a piece of the branch. "To humiliate me." She twisted the stick between her hands until it cracked and splintered. "And then to announce it before Lady Beatrice and those people, so she will carry the news of it to England, and tell them that I— that I desired it."

The clouds on the horizon were darkening, rising over the sun. A sharp puff of renewed wind blustered across the headland.

"You told me that you did not want the Riata," he said. "You begged me to keep you here. Would you have consented to wed me, if I had asked?"

She whirled around. "No."

"So—I merely spared our recital of that chapter, then." He shook his head. "Lady Elena. Iniquitous I may be, I do not deny it, but you would be wise rather to reconcile yourself and see what you can make of it, than to struggle against me like some doomed moth in a spider's web."

"Reconcile myself to ravishment by an outlaw? What good end could I make of that?"

"Alack, the only subject that your teachers seem to have

neglected is your own history." He leaned his shoulder against the broad, broken pedestal of the stone head and tossed a stick for the puppy to chase. "And how does my lady Cara appear in these latter days? Is she quite beautiful?"

Elayne tucked her chin at his sudden change of direction. "Cara? She appears as any matron in good health and generous flesh, I suppose."

"Become a fine English peasant, has she? And what of that churl she chose to wed?"

"Sir Guy is a knight, not a churl."

The Raven gave a flick of his hand. "Naught but a varlet with the dirt still on him. It is too bad you were obliged to reside in such company as would only grace a sheep sty. No doubt that's why you conceived this debased affection for some common English fellow."

Elayne sucked in a sharp breath. "Debased! How dare you!"

He snorted, tweaking the stick from the puppy's mouth in spite of its quick attempts at evasion. "No? For what purpose did you want him? Not marriage, in the name of God."

"Of course I wanted marriage!" she said. "I love him."

He looked at her as if she were mad. "You're Monteverde."

"What of it? Cara always said I might marry a man I could love, and Lady Melanthe, too."

"Bah, you would never disgrace the name of Monteverde in that manner!" He hurled the stick. The pup bounded away after it, sniffing among the rocks. "I would not have allowed it."

"You!" She stared at him. "What do you care?"

"The devil take your sister and Melanthe! They knew I didn't save your skin and carry you five hundred leagues to marry some common English muck bucket!"

"Save me?" she echoed in bewilderment. "You haven't saved me—"

"Ignorant infant! They've told you naught in truth, have they? You were toddling poison-bait for the Riata in Monteverde. The last of your line still there, in their hands, while they knew Melanthe had lied to them till her tongue turned black. She didn't get you out of there. You're alive by my hand—*I'm* the one who brought you out and conveyed you safe to your sister's godforsaken mud pit in the woods. Little though you seem to know or remember of it." His lip curled. "Though I apprehend that Melanthe and your sniveling sister had their reasons enough to keep you unwitting."

"What raving is this?" Elayne sputtered. "I don't believe you!"

"Did you think you had been wafted there upon some angel's wings? I smuggled you out of the Riata fortress in a laundry basket, and a bold child you were too, at a bare six years. We crossed the mountains with a dog for a guide—one just such as this, the white guardians of the flocks—I lost the way and the rain turned to ice; I carried you until I thought we would both be dead. But that dog came to you, and you held on to it, and it took us. You don't remember." He shook his head. "You don't remember any of it?"

"Nay, I've never—"

But she looked at him as he stood in the last of the evening light, the fading sun on his black hair and flawless face. With a terrible insight, she saw too clearly what she had struggled to deny. Even curved in disgust, his mouth was well-formed; his features lit with real emotion more beautiful than ever—so like her dark angel, so painfully familiar.

"It is not possible," she said. She shook her head furiously. That a pirate in the midst of the vast sea would know her past—know more of it than she did herself . . . She did not want to give credence to what he said, and yet . . .

And yet . . .

"No one ever said aught of anyone such as you!" she exclaimed heatedly.

"Nay, I doubt your sister would have the name of Allegreto Navona on her lips."

"You make no sense. You said me yourself the house of Navona was our enemy."

"Aye," he said. "Your mortal foe."

"Then why would you go to such length for me?" she demanded. "Why?"

"Oh, for love," he said with a sneer. "I supposed myself in love with your sister."

Elayne's mouth dropped open. "With Cara?"

He posed in an ironic bow.

"No," she said. "I don't believe it! She would be terrified of you."

"She was." He looked out at the horizon blazing in gold and pink above the storm bank. "She was," he repeated slowly.

"Cara?" Elayne could not even imagine such a thing. Cara, who seemed so sedate; so plump and wifely and bound to Savernake and her home. A pirate had loved her. This pirate, this angel-demon man with his magic and life of hazard. "I cannot conceive of it," she said faintly.

"No more can I conceive how you want some English peasant in your bed," he said. "But then, so did your sister. By hap it is some taint in your mother's blood."

The manner in which he said it was like a slap across the face. Elayne drew herself straight. "Sir Guy is no peasant, nor Raymond. And who are you, after all?"

"Your husband now, sweeting. You may call me Allegreto—the bastard son of Gian Navona," he said, "since you seem so woefully untutored in your own history."

"Whoever Gian Navona might be."

"A man you may thank the merciful Lord God you could dare to forget. Your sister and Lady Melanthe be in full debt to me for their easeful lives today." He smiled bitterly. "If I had done my father's bidding, your sister would have had me after all, in the stead of her English commoner, and Lord Ruadrik would be long rotting in his grave."

"I don't believe it! I don't! How can all this you say be so?"

"No one told you, so you think it can't be so? Then haps

you don't know that your faithless Melanthe was promised to wed my father after Ligurio died," he said. "But she was so bold as to run away to England, and foolish enough to find a husband there instead. So Gian ordered me to poison her inconvenient Ruadrik, to free her from that bond."

"Poison him!" she gasped.

"Poison him unto death. But Lord Ruadrik lives, does he not? And he ought to go on his knees every night in dread thanks to me." The pirate touched his dagger, his fingers sliding over the jeweled haft. "My father was not pleased. He left me to drown in a stone well after he found I had not done his will with Melanthe's knight."

"Sweet Mary," she breathed.

"I betrayed him." He shrugged and rested back against the statue. He drew the dagger, sending it into a shining spin around his hand and catching it as if it were a plaything. "I was brought up to do exactly as he bid me—to slay in silence, from behind, so that no one knows where or whence it comes." He gazed at the tip of the blade. "It was said I murdered him myself."

She thought of him standing at Lady Beatrice's back, of his casual touch on the knife. She felt the powerful presence of her dark and mysterious angel, and knew now why she had never spoken of those dreams to Cara.

"Did you?" she whispered.

"Nay." His eyes did not meet hers. He turned the dagger in his palm. "In truth, I doubt I could have killed him. I loved him. I was terrified of him." He sheathed the knife. "He was my father."

She wet her lips, taking a deep breath. He lifted his eyes, impassive.

"Ask of your sister how he died," he said. "No doubt the Devil wanted him in Hell." He knelt, snapping his fingers at the white puppy. It rose from where it had been lying in the cleft of some rocks, chewing on the stick, and trotted to him. He sat back on his heels. "If Melanthe sent you to me, it is fair payment," he said.

Elayne watched the young dog lick his hand. "I don't think she sent me to you."

"That may be. Still, it is strange that you traveled with such a paltry escort," he said, "and the brave Knights of Saint John gave you up so easily. But however you came here, I'll take you."

"Why? It makes no sense to me!" she cried. "What great use am I to you?"

He looked up at her. "What use?" He shook his head in disbelief. He stood again and swept his hand across the horizon. "Do you still think I am a trifling pirate in truth?" He took a step toward her and tilted her chin up, holding her face hard between his fingers. "For a decade of years I have worked for this, and it matters not if you were sent by Melanthe or fell into my hands by the grace of God or the Devil's devices. The house of Navona is not finished, though a bastard son be all that remains." He narrowed his eyes. "I'll have what my father meant to take. Monteverde belongs to me. You cleanse the taint of my left-handed blood. You seal my claim. So abandon your love poems and do not imagine that you will be suffered to dally with any mongrel such as this Raymond who pants after you."

Elayne put her hand on his wrist and wrenched free. "If you are not a pirate, then do not handle me as if I am a pirate's trull."

He spread his fingers. The wind blew his hair back from his face as he stepped away. For an instant he had such a look that she did not know if he would reach for his dagger and use it upon her. She held herself rigidly still, like a rabbit beneath a circling hawk.

Slowly he smiled. "You remind me greatly of Melanthe sometime. We will deal favorably together, I think."

"Favorably?" She gave an incredulous laugh. "I did not consent to be your wife."

"You prefer Franco Pietro?"

"I wished to wed a man I could love."

"And I wish I were the Pope," he said. "You remind me as well of your witless sister."

"It may be I am witless, but I don't want Monteverde," she said savagely. "I want nothing to do with it. Or poison and murders and—what you are."

"Of course," he said in a cold voice. He turned away from her and walked to the edge, looking down into the blue depths of the ravine. "I do not ask you to be what I am."

Elayne sat down hard on the ground and let the puppy crawl over her. "That seems to be the only thing you don't demand, pirate."

He tossed a stone into the chasm and watched it fall. "Call me Allegreto, if you please."

" 'Allegreto!' " Elayne gave a scornful sniff. " 'Tis hardly a fitting name."

"Indeed, I'm not the most merry of fellows, am I? I should have been named Destruction instead. But my mother was fond of me when I was an infant, as mothers are wont to be."

"Oh, did you have a mother?" She rubbed the puppy's ears vigorously.

He looked at her aslant, his silver earring dangling down on his cheek. "Nay, I sprang full-grown from Hell, of course."

Elayne hugged the pup to her. "I thought so."

His black hair swept over his shoulder as he turned to face the sunset. In faultless profile, he seemed like a vision suspended between the black storm depths and the lucent sky, something painted for a king's pleasure, too perfect to be real.

"The sailors say a tempest brews," he said coolly. "It is time to return, before dark."

Elayne buried her face in the young dog's fur. She squeezed her eyes shut.

"Why do you weep? Your future is not yet writ," he said. "At six years you were a hellion, not afraid to scale mountains with me."

"And now a pawn to anyone's ambitions," she said, muffled.

"You are not a pawn, madam, but a queen upon this
board." His voice hardened. "Commit yourself to the game,
or you will find yourself a hostage to fortune in truth. I cannot indulge sentiment this time, even if I desired to do it. It
is not within my power now. Melanthe owes me this. Cara
owes me this. Before God, you owe me this! I carried you
to sanctuary once, at infinite cost to myself. I cannot do it
again, and will not."

She remained with her cheek pressed to the warm furry
body, refusing to look at him. When she finally raised her
face again, he was gone, leaving her with the sea breeze
growing colder as the storm clouds rose to swallow the sun.

THE GALE CAME on with the lowering night, turning the
headland to a roaring mass of gloom, of whipping branches
and glistening rocks. The statue provided some shelter, but
not enough to prevent the wind from blowing cascades of
stinging drops against her cheek as she sat hunched in
angry grief, struggling to relinquish the final delusion that
she had been watched over by an angel of shadows; a fearsome angel, dark but good.

He claimed that Elayne had a debt to him; a debt for her
life. As if the sweet safe years in Savernake—so brief they
seemed now, as if all her memory of girlhood crystallized
into one endless, merry day in May—had been a bargain
made without her knowledge. A bargain with this devil, and
now she had to pay.

A brigand, a bastard, a murderer. And Lady Melanthe . . . she knew not what to believe of her godmother.
Things that had seemed forthright before now appeared sinister. Why had no one told her of her past? That she had
been left behind in the hands of her family's enemies? She
had not inquired, but the silence around the subject of how
she and Cara had come to England had felt like a barrier
that forestalled questions before they were asked. Somehow, without thinking of it clearly, she had known that any

query would make Cara angry, and so she had not questioned.

The last outlines of her surroundings disappeared with the light, lost in the tempest and black night. As the darkness thickened, rain began falling in sheets. The statue no longer offered any protection. She rose, keeping her face down, holding the wriggling puppy close as the downpour soaked them both. Wind caught her thin skirt and tangled it about her legs.

She had no idea where the path might be, only a sense that the cliff lay to her left and the castle somewhere ahead. She hardly cared. The cold rain pounded her head and bare arms, pouring down her back. It seemed fitting that any step she took would only bring her to ruin.

But the pup rested its chin on her shoulder, its paws splayed in a heavy, trusting hug about her neck. She took a few steps where she thought the path should be, ran into the thrashing branches of a bush, and edged her way around it. The wind pushed her hard, as if to insist on a direction, then veered capriciously, propelling her another way.

Another few steps, and she knew it would be impossible to find her way. She turned back into the wind, seeking the scant refuge of the fallen statue.

But it was invisible in the black rain-driven obscurity. She edged carefully, blindly, her head lowered against the wind. With each step she slipped on the uneven stones. She had not moved far from the statue. It seemed she should have reached it in a few paces, but when she searched forward with her toe, she met nothing.

She froze, buffeted by the wind, afraid to step forward or back. Below the roar of the storm, she could hear the surf, a deep echoing boom that seemed to come from all around her. The puppy began to struggle again. She held it tight, afraid that if she let it go, it would vanish off the edge in one bound.

She stood petrified, no longer indifferent to her fate. She was certain that the cliff lay one step before her, or perchance beside her, or left or right or she knew not where.

She could see nothing. She dared not take one footstep, but the wind shoved her like a huge hand. Slowly, with her wet skirt battering her legs, she went to her knees. The puppy wriggled madly and began to bark.

It made a frantic leap, tearing free of her hold. Elayne cried out in terror. She could see it for a moment, a vague white shape as it sprang and disappeared. A faint whimper escaped her throat. She stared through the rain pelting her face, panting, certain it had hurtled from the cliff.

Then with a vast relief she heard it barking again, high-pitched notes from the howl of the storm. As she squinted against the rain, she saw a large white form take shape in the gloom. A huge dog—and then a man loomed up over her from the dark.

Elayne grabbed his hands. He pulled her up roughly, his grip slick with coursing water. She stumbled forward, half-dragged as he turned and followed the pale shape of the dog through the lashing gale.

Eight

‒‒‒‒

IN A PASSAGE lit by one of the strange blue globes, the pirate halted. Rain still poured into the rough opening behind them, spilling in a stream down the rugged steps, trickling from the rock walls. He turned, her outlaw-savior, a dark lock of his hair plastered down to one cheekbone. Blue-tinged droplets glistened on his eyelashes and ran down his face.

Elayne stood in a puddle of her own making, shivering like the puppy that hugged her legs. She did not even pull away from his brutal grip on her arm. They had not struggled far to reach this cavern entrance, but she would never have been able to find it herself. The white dog had led them unerring to the shelter.

That instant of terror in the dark, feeling no ground before her, made the blood beat in her ears yet. The big dog shook itself vigorously, sending a hail of water over them all.

"Grant mercy," she said to it, heartfelt. Her teeth chattered as she reached out to stroke the big white head. "God protect you."

The dog sat down and glanced at her with brief disinterest, ignoring the puppy trying to lick its muzzle. Suddenly the animal leaped up with a roaring bark, hurling itself down into the passage with the pup racing behind, a minor echo of its elder's throbbing voice.

The Raven looked after them, watchful. But when the dog ceased barking, leaving only the puppy's excited yap resonating faintly amid the drumming of the rain and wind, he turned back. He released her.

"Listen better to me in the future," he said, "when I tell you it is time to go."

"You have my thanks," she said stiffly, though it tested her to show gratitude to him.

"I did not expect you would endure so long there." He wiped a trickle of water from his temple and flicked it away. "A dire mistaking of your obstinance."

She hugged herself, shivering. "I beg your pardon for causing you to bestir yourself."

"Aye," he said, "I'd hoped to be lounging in bed with my bride on such a night. It is too bad she resembles a drowned rat."

"A pity!" Elayne said, hardly able to pronounce the words as a shudder overtook her.

"But even rats dry," he said. He reached up and took the glowing sphere from a hook, cradling it in his palm. It cast no heat, only the cold light that gave everything an uncanny hue.

He began to descend the passage after the dogs. She hesitated a moment, and then followed. It was that or be left soaking wet in the dark, with the storm still screaming above. The sound of the tempest receded as they went down, replaced by the crunch of their footsteps on loose stone. The tunnel grew narrow and twisting, marked by seeping water on the walls. In some places other routes branched off, passageways that danced with the blue light for a moment and then vanished again. The dogs seemed to have disappeared, gone among the tunnels like foxes would fade into the woods, intent on their own business.

The passage took a sudden turn back on itself. She ducked a low ceiling, following him up a staircase—each step more smoothly carved than the last—until they reached a massive bronze door.

"Watch," he said, holding up the lamp.

Carving marked the door, designs of sheep and a shepherd in one panel, in another a fierce battle between dogs and a bear. The doorway seemed a barrier, with no handle or hinges. Incised deeply down the center were three words. *Gardi li mo,* as on the ring she wore. Guard it well.

He touched the first letter, and then the shepherd's staff. His hand moved in a pattern, from letters to the carved scene and back again. In the utter silence of the underground, Elayne heard a faint click. Gently he drew his palm down the carving of the battle, and the creatures slid apart to reveal a latch.

"Can you do it?" he asked.

She glanced at him. He stood back, closing the panel with a sharp sweep of his fist. The sound of it echoed in the passage.

Elayne stepped to the door. She reached up and felt the wood under the letter G give way beneath her light touch. She tried to copy his pattern, but when she moved her hand down across the carved dogs, nothing happened.

"Like this," he said. He put his open palm over hers, pressing the heel of her hand down. "Softly."

With a smooth motion he slid their hands across the carving. She could feel the wood slide away beneath her hand; she could feel his palm on her skin, warm against the chill of the cave and her wet smock. He stood behind her, close enough that he touched her with each breath. For a moment she thought he would take her in his arms; for a moment she had a vision of his bed and bodies entwined there. The air seemed to leave her throat.

He flipped the latch, and the door swung inward.

"Remember it," he said.

Elayne stepped through. Beyond the door was a small chamber carved in the stone, furnished with a rush cot and some sturdy stools. Chests lined the walls, trunks of all shapes and sizes. The atmosphere was warmer than in the tunnels, the stone walls and floor spread with Turkey carpets.

The door closed silently behind them. "Behold," he said. "My innermost sanctum."

He said it with his derisive tone. And yet there were things of astonishing value scattered about—golden bowls and pieces of bejeweled armor; baskets nearly overflowing with loose pearls, a miniature device of silver wheels with a face like the king's clock tower at Windsor. On the floor beside the cot lay a stack of books surmounted by a blackened candle.

Elayne paused, wishing it were not so small a chamber, or so full of things. She would have liked to strip off her sodden gown, but she saw no hope of being private here.

He moved past her, brushing close, for there was no room to give way. From one of the boxes he drew a multitude of fine linen towels and tossed them on the cot.

He was as drenched as Elayne. With his back to her, he unclasped the belt at his hip, spreading it carefully across the top of a chest. With a practiced glance, he examined the evil gleam of each dagger in turn, sheathing them with their hilts toward him. His shadow fell across the stacked chests and loomed on the walls.

He pulled off his dripping shirt and held his hair back, wringing it between his fists. Blue light glinted on the pendant that dangled from his ear. Water slipped down between his shoulder blades.

He was such a heathen presence in the small space that she felt half-suffocated. She grabbed up a towel and wrapped it around her hair. She pressed another over her smock, trying to soak some of the water out of it.

"You would do better to disrobe," he said.

"I have nothing dry to wear."

He leaned back against a stack of chests. "What do you need, in bed?"

"Don't," she said, her breath coming shorter.

"That is not a word I favor," he said. "It is a shrinking maiden's word."

She pulled the towel over her shoulders. Her skin that had felt so chill was growing warm. "Do not berate me as a maiden, when you put an end to my maidenhood yourself."

"Did I?"

Elayne flashed a look at him. "So you declared to all the world!"

"Such deceits are sometime required. It was necessary to convince Countess Beatrice."

She gave a hiss. "Are you saying that you did not?"

"Would it be a great disappointment to you if I haven't?"

Elayne gripped the towel between her hands. "Oh!" She flung it down. "You are the Devil's creature!"

His dark lashes flickered. "I can be when I so choose," he said. "Be glad you have not seen that face of me yet. As to your maidenhead, I thought it courtesy to wait until you were wakeful and prepared. But that omission can be remedied without delay, if you wish. It will be before you leave this chamber, in any event."

She drew back a step, coming up against a tall pile of chests. Her heart was beating in her ears.

He shook his head. "Unwilling still? I wonder how you would have fared with Franco Pietro. He is not known as a man of tender gestures."

"And you are?"

He gave a slight shrug. "I will try to please you. I have not made much study of the skill."

She turned aside, plucking the damp silk of her chemise away from her skin. She did not feel cold at all now, but shivered anyway. "I suppose you required no particular study for ladies to incline to you," she said tartly.

"Why?" he said. "Do you think I buy their inclinations?"

She blushed and waved a hand in his direction "I meant—a man of your countenance."

"Ah. For my face."

"Indeed," Elayne said.

"Some have inclined," he acknowledged. "More than

some, by hap. But I am a manslayer, not a gallant. I don't know if you will ever wish to write me love poems."

She drew a deep breath and closed her eyes. She opened them again. "What things you say."

"Aye. And soon all those eager ladies changed their hearts and fled."

Elayne frowned at the chests before her, stacked to the height of a table, where a gilded pitcher sat atop the drapery of a fringed rug. She was not suffered to flee. He claimed her as if she were a bounty, some battle prize fallen into his hands. Raymond had courted her for weeks before he kissed her; the pirate thought it a great courtesy that he did not violate her in her drugged sleep. Raymond had called her a diamond, an extraordinary woman. This manslayer merely said he was not a lover. But he would try to please her.

She thought she must be as impure in her nature as Cara had always accused her, for she could not swallow the tight ache in her throat, the sensation in her skin, the awareness that he stood so near, tiny beads of water gathered on his chest and shoulders. To share the small room with him was like to being caged with a lazing black leopard, his claws sheathed, but not harmless. It seemed as fascinating, and dangerous, to reach out and touch him as it would be to stroke a wild beast she had discovered asleep in the forest. Even knowing what he was, she felt herself drawn to his mortal beauty as a salamander was drawn to fire.

"Are you afraid of me?" he asked suddenly.

She faced him. "Does it matter?"

He turned his head. With a sound of disdain, he shrugged.

"I will tell you this. I'm afraid of you. But more than that, I am angry. I'm angry that you force me, by guile and trickery, when I thought you might stand my friend. I'm angry that you are not my guardian, or my angel, but just an evil man, with deceit and blood on his hands, and still you come and save me when I'm in need. I'm disgusted that you make my heart feel hot as Raymond did, when you are not worth the ground under his feet. I should hate you, and I do not. It is intolerable!"

He lowered his lashes. "Haps you will write those lines in your book, as your love poem to me."

"My journal!" she exclaimed, realizing suddenly that she had left it in the storm.

"I found it at the stone head, when I went looking for you," he said.

She lifted her face in swift hope. "You brought it?"

"I tossed it off the cliff," he said, crossing his arms. "I did not like the text. I'll give you another, and you can scribe my poem there."

She glared at him. "I was mistaken. I do hate you!"

"Nay, that is the line I regard with most favor. You cannot be mistaken." He came closer and lifted his hand to caress her throat. He slid his fingers up into her hair as the towel fell free. The last tatters of her net gave way under his hands, and all her rain-soaked hair dropped loose, curling and twisting to her hips.

Elayne trembled, outraged by the ache of excitement that traveled down through her body. "Everything I care for was in that book."

"It is gone now," he said.

She closed her eyes. "I hate you." But he drew his hands down her shoulders and caught the neck of her chemise, pulling it open across her back, the buttons popping free with gentle tugs.

A memory of Raymond's fervent grasp flashed in her mind. She held herself stiff, refusing to yield if he tried to seize her with the same zeal. Instead his fingertips played on the curve of her skin, a mere teasing. When she opened her eyes, he was watching her, the black depth of his gaze almost lost beneath his lowered lashes. She could feel him breathing.

"If you had a poison ring, you could kill me now with a scratch," he said.

She gave a faint sob, almost a laugh. "A poison ring!"

He smiled. "You see I am not accomplished at love-prate. I expect this Raymond did not say such things."

"No," she said.

"Haps he did not put his life in your trust, as I do now." He slid his hands down her arms and slipped his fingers between hers.

"I have no way to harm you."

He guided her hands behind his back. "I have no shield if you do." The move brought her into an embrace with him, as if she held him close. Her wet smock drooped from her shoulders, only clinging to her by the damp. When he spoke, his breath skimmed her forehead, his words vibrated beneath her cheek. "This is wholly alien to me. To linger in close embrace this way. I dread to be defenseless."

Strangely, standing near enough that she felt his pulse against her breasts, she understood him. Another man might have said she was beautiful, or made tribute to her blushing lips. He locked them together in a cave, behind a door with no key, and put his daggers outside his close reach—in faith she would not kill him.

"I cannot imagine the life you have lived," she whispered.

His fingers tightened on hers and relaxed again. "You smell of rain."

"Not roses?" she said, nervous mocking.

He took a deep breath in her hair. "Nay. Windstorm." He released her hands and slid his palms up her bare arms.

She found that she did not draw back, but only let her fingers rest on his hips. She felt outside herself. Her skin was cool and hot at once. There was nowhere to escape; behind and beside her the heavy chests stood one atop the other, their straps gleaming dull metal.

He held her arms lightly, and moved his mouth in a whisper down her temple and cheek. "Fruit," he murmured, drawing breath at the corner of her mouth. His tongue tasted her skin. "Ripe plums."

She lifted her chin. "I stole them of you."

His body was a feather-touch against her, all down the

length of her, a sensation more of heat than of contact. "Good," he said against her lips. "You are a practiced sinner."

Cara had always said so. Elayne knew it was so now, for she was not struggling. She was not even pulling away as she had from Raymond. She was leaning faintly toward the pirate, toward an unredeemed outlaw—her shadow angel turned to living man.

He felt it, for he drew her closer, skimming his hands over her body beneath the thin damp silk. Her hips and her back, and then a single rough motion that tore the last buttons free. She heard one button hit a metal chest with a faint chink, and then drop upon the carpet.

He spread her hair against her bare skin. "Now I will know the scent of you." He took up a fistful, inhaling deeply in it. "If you are near, I will know it."

The promise was no light flattery. He said it as if he branded her. He pushed his fingers deep into her tangled hair. The faint tug and twist sent a sweet pain down through her throat as he forced her to lift her face to him.

"He made your heart feel hot?" the pirate asked, tightening his fingers in her hair.

"Yes," she said, a last defiance. One last piece of herself withheld, while her body submitted as he drew her against him, a gentle kiss upon her mouth, almost like a token between courtiers.

"Someday I may find this Raymond, and kill him." He bent his head, trailing his mouth down the curve of her throat, and closed his teeth on her skin.

Elayne drew a sharp breath. He hurt her, but an instant afterward he pressed his lips to the place softly, as if to soothe it, and the flow of his breath on her skin was like thin fire.

From the corner of her eye she could see the pendant that dangled from his ear, a blurry gleam that lay against his neck. The smooth curve of his bared shoulder was before her, the outline of graceful strength. She was angered by her own desire, by how his beauty alone lured her close to him.

It was not the love she felt for Raymond, nor the conjugal duty she would have owed a truly wedded husband, nor anything but simple, sinful, lust. Her fingers curled, drawing her nails across the hard plane of his back. He pulled her to him with a deep growl.

She knew herself then, fully. Everything Cara or Lady Beatrice had ever said was true. She was a wanton, unchaste creature, without even constancy. She might have resisted him, for her fidelity to Raymond, or for honor, or at least for the sake of her pride. But she let her lips touch him. The taste of rain and heat mingled with his quick reaction. He kissed her throat hard and drew her earlobe between his teeth. She met him with a fierce reply, opening her mouth against his shoulder, a willing she-cat to his leopard, biting him as viciously as if she could draw blood.

The sound he made went down her spine like a panther's hiss in the deep forest. He flung her from him without effort, holding her at arm's length. They were both breathing hard.

Red marks burned on his shoulder. He glanced down at what she'd done and then slanted a look at her from under his night-black lashes. With a faint menacing smile, he said, "That is what you like?"

"What weapons I have," she said breathlessly, "I will use."

"To what end?"

She did not know. She only knew that she was full of angry ferment, and he was beautiful and flawless and arousing, and claimed her body for his. She was ready to fight with him, her heart beating hard. Hot. He put his palm at her throat, his thumb pressed into her vein. It made her pulse throb in her own ears, a casual threat that turned to something else as he drew his fingers down to her breast and made a light circle at the tip, dislodging her shift. The touch of him there made her suck in her breath. He smiled, made a little cruel prick with his nail and then another circle of the lightest tenderness.

The sensation seemed to burst in her, in parts of her that

bloomed with flowing heat. She whimpered, pulling back. But he followed her, pushing her slowly until her hips pressed against the rug-draped chest. She felt the golden pitcher topple, a hollow clatter in the silence of the chamber. Her smock dragged downward to her waist with the tow of the rug, binding her arms at the elbows.

A bolt of real fear seized her. She was trapped, bared of any modesty, as he leaned over her. He had warned and threatened, assured her of her fate, but until this moment she had not believed it. Somehow she would be saved—as her guardian angel had always saved her—but the edge of the chest cut into her hips; the more she struggled with her elbows bound awkwardly behind her, the more she arched to meet him. With a spurt of panic, she felt him pull her shift above her knees and then higher.

He leaned on his arms, holding her confined, as if to imprint her helplessness on her. She could not reach him to bite or scratch now. Deliberately he lowered his head to her breast, closing his teeth on her nipple. Elayne jerked against the bright pain, felt him suck hard, sending fire and torture through her whole body. She threw her head back, trying to thrust him off.

He made a rough sound and held her pinned easily. For an instant she felt his hand search between them. She threw herself wildly as he came between her legs, his naked member pressed to the place he would take her.

"Yield!" he said between his teeth. "You are my wife."

She twisted her head back, impossibly ensnared, panting. He pushed into her, and it hurt. It hurt and burned, and he did not stop. He thrust against her hard, lifting her toes from the floor while she squeezed her eyes shut. He drove again, invading her deeper with each shove until with one fierce pang he forced himself wholly inside her; as she dug her fingers into the rug she could hear his animal breath. The throbbing in her body grew into an ache that numbed the pain, dampened and smothered it. She felt as if she were dying for air.

With a fierce effort to heave him off, she lifted herself on her elbows. His arm came under her head, pulling her face against the smooth hard skin of his chest. She scored him savagely with her teeth.

He made a brutal sound, closing his eyes, his head thrown back. His hands gripped her head, pulling her closer even as she hurt him. His whole body convulsed, driving into her as if he could not get in deep enough. She closed her teeth. His muscles bunched like a man in torment; his throat worked as if he tried to weep and could not. For an instant he held rigid, his fingers tight in her hair while Elayne bit him again, tasting blood. She heard his frantic breath as he lost himself. His body gave a violent jerk, a shudder as he arched. He pulsed and throbbed and burned inside her.

He tore her away from him by her hair. "Jesu," he growled, thrusting into her roughly once more. "Have mercy, sweeting."

"Mercy," she cried, trembling under his absolute domination. She could not move one inch without his compliance. "Damn you!"

He withdrew, releasing her and moving back with such quick grace that she could not kick him before he was out of reach. She rolled aside, dragging her smock up over her breasts as she sat up. She pushed the skirt down, seeing blood on her thighs and garters—her own this time, real.

"God curse you," she said, sitting hunched with her arms about herself. Then with a wild move she flung herself off the chest and grabbed for his dagger—but he had her wrist before she was anywhere close to the thing.

"Do not," he said softly. "Do not make us live in fear of one another."

Elayne gave a raving laugh. She stepped back, holding up her shift with her free hand. "Oh, of course not! What should we fear?"

He caressed the underside of her wrist with his thumb. "My lady, you have nothing to fear from me. From this night, your protection is all of my ambition."

There was a bruise and a trickle of blood near his shoul-

der blade, where she had assailed him. She felt wetness
sliding between her legs. She knew what it was—his seed
mingled with hers. He watched her with a faint wariness,
but no anger. There was even the trace of a smile in the tilt
of his mouth.

"We are wedded now, vows on a church step or no," he
said.

She sat back on her bridal bed of a lead-bound chest in
a locked cave. "It hurt," she said between her clenched
teeth, as if that were the worst of it.

"That did not please you?"

She looked at him. "No!"

He put his hand on his shoulder. His fingers came away
bloody. "Ah, I understand. Only to hurt me pleases you."

She felt sticky and achy and hot. But she would have
lied to say that there was no deep kernel of angry lust for
him still locked in her belly. It was amazing to look at him
and know it had been her teeth that bruised him. She had
made her own mark on him. Her own brand. She narrowed
her eyes and felt a moment of powerful pleasure in it.

She heard him draw in a slow breath. She met his eyes.
The leopard was there, watching her from between the trees
of a nightmare forest.

"You may hurt me, if you take delight in it," he said
softly. "Only never outside of bedding, or with a weapon
beyond your body."

Elayne wet her lips. She looked away from him, at the
books and the candle on the floor, letting her hair make a
curtain to hide her face. "A most obliging bridegroom," she
said bitterly.

He came to her, put his hands to her head, pushing her
hair back with infinite care. "You will find that so," he said.

He drew her into his embrace, holding her cheek against
his chest. She did not kiss him, but she tasted his blood on
her tongue and smelled the male scent of him and his seed
blended with the odor of her own rain-dampened skin.
There was nothing of delicacy or courtliness or high-
minded spirit in this joining. It was all of the earth, like this

cave. Something deep and hidden, never to be spoken of in the light. She pressed her lips to his shoulder and ran her tongue over his wounded skin with a malevolent satisfaction. She felt him grip her closer. He rested his head on her hair.

From where they stood, through her lashes, she saw the daggers' hilts agleam in the faint blue light. She would not attempt them; she had no will to murder in her—that instant of pure fury was passed. But she saw that she could not get to them if she wished. And she understood that even now, as he held her like a lover, his breath in her hair, he knew to a fine degree how far away they were and what she could reach.

She stood back a little. He released her easily. Elayne lifted her eyes from his boots to his black hose, his man-parts in shadowed half-concealment that still made her blush, his elegant form: fine shoulders and straight height, his face like fallen Lucifer from Heaven.

He knew she looked. He stood and let her. "Franco Pietro," he said casually, "is said to resemble a loathsome toad."

"A loathsome toad is in the eye of the beholder," she replied.

"You think so! And who taught you that?"

"Libushe."

"Your wisewoman?"

Elayne nodded.

"Still," he said, "I think you would prefer me, between the two of us."

She gave a little shrug.

"I doubt he would let you bite the hide off of him, at any rate," he said darkly.

Nine

———∞∞∞———

THE BLUE SPHERE suddenly grew fainter, its peculiar light dying away. Elayne started up as the shadows closed, but before the chamber was completely enveloped in blackness he struck a spark. Flame burst from the pile of charred linen in a small brass tinder bowl. For an instant, as the little fire flared, his face was hued in red like a youthful demon bending over his inferno.

He drew back from the smoke spiraling upward and quickly lit a candle, snuffing the tinder bowl with a metal lid. The candle made a brighter, warmer light—trading smoke and unsteady illumination for dyeing everything in more comfortable and human hues.

Outlined by dancing shadows, he clasped the belt again about his hips, girding himself with swift skill. As he moved away from her, Elayne found herself growing deeply chilled in her damp smock. He handed her one of the towels.

"Bind up your hair."

She glanced at him as she took it, shaking her hair back over her shoulder. He watched her, holding the candle, as she lifted her arms to coil her hair. She felt as if she were on indecent display, as close to naked as it was possible to be while wearing a garment. But they were in this secret place. He had made himself her bridegroom here, by force and blood. No witnesses, no banns, no Christian troth-plight or vows. He simply declared it, and ravished her. A pagan wedding between heathen beasts.

She damned him, despised him, but she thought wildly that it suited her. Somewhere there was a paper, full of high clerks' seals, assenting to her betrothal to Franco Pietro of the Riata. In dreamlike despair, under Lancaster's daunting eye and Lady Melanthe's chill acquiescence, she had put her hand to it in England on the day after the May.

She broke that contract now, with contempt. No one had tried to spare her, beyond mere weeping and regret. Not her godmother, nor her sister—not even Raymond. They had all bowed unquestioning to the Duke of Lancaster and flung her to the wind of fortune, until this pirate caught her up.

From this night, he said, *your protection is all of my ambition.*

She submitted to his study as he had allowed her to look at him, dipping her head to wrap the towel about her hair and then lifting her chin when she had the linen secure. If she were a wanton creature, an unfettered, unchristian harlot with too much learning to be modest; if she could never have the man she loved—wella, then she would take a beautiful murderous bandit instead, and read his books and learn his wiles and live with him in wickedness.

He threw open a chest and dragged a folded robe from inside, shaking it out in the dim light. "Wear this."

It was scarlet, cut full like a long tunic, embroidered about the hem and throat with astrologic motifs of indigo thread. The sleeves draped down over her hands. The hem fell in a voluminous puddle about her feet, measured for his height and breadth. But it was dry. She turned her back and divested herself of her chilly undergarment by wriggling free of it from within the capacious folds.

She kicked the wet smock out from under her feet and

faced him. He was daubing a cloth on his shoulder, scowling at the smudges of blood as if he had never had a cut upon him before.

"Do you think it will leave a scar?" she asked with light malice.

"Nay, I do not scar," he said. He gave her a half-smile, almost an apology.

It was true that he had no flaw on him. But for the place her teeth had scored, now turning black-and-blue, the skin of his chest and face and arms was perfect in the candle-light, unscathed by any injury. He blotted at the abrasion again, hissing air between his teeth.

"Leave it be," Elayne said.

"It stings."

"Of course, if you will pester at it like a child."

He flicked the bloodied cloth away. But still he had that odd ghost of a smile.

"It requires an herbal compress to take out the bruise," she said.

"An herbal compress," he echoed in a bemused tone.

"Have you never heard of such? I suppose you have no books of simples among all these weighty treatises."

"No," he said. "I prefer to confound my brain with arcane wisdom only." From beside the cot he took a box, bejeweled and enameled, lined with silver, and held it open to her. "But spare no compassion for my battle wound. Will you indulge in a gentler pleasure?"

Elayne peered inside. She expected jewels, or some other hoard, but it was full of many-colored grains, their hues reflecting in the shiny lid. When she hesitated, he dug his fingers into the mound and lifted them, the grains clinging to his skin and falling through his hand. He took some from his palm onto his tongue and savored it. "Confetti." He raised his hand to Elayne's lips.

Some of the grains on his fingertips clung as he touched her mouth. She licked her lip in spite of herself. The rich flavor of candied seeds of coriander and spices filled her mouth, bitter and sweet at once, drowning out the lingering taste of his blood.

"A particular specialty of Monteverde," he said.

She sat down on the carpet-covered chest, biting the sticky grains from her lip, each seed a burst of aromatic spice. "Yes. My sister repined for such."

"Poor damsel," he said. "Breaking her heart over sweetmeats, is she?"

Elayne glanced at him. "She's mentioned often how she missed it."

He poured more confetti into his palm, shut the box with a snap, and set it aside, as if the topic bored him.

"She never spoke of missing you," Elayne said, with the same intent she'd felt when she had scored him with her teeth.

The shaft did not seem to touch its mark. "I'm certain that she didn't. She was acutely pleased to be rid of me. Are you jealous that I loved her once?"

"No!"

"Alas," he said lightly. "Will I never win a lady's heart?"

"You can hardly expect to win my heart by the manner of your courting!"

"'Tis fortune that all I require is the use of your body." He lifted his chin and tossed the confetti into his mouth. Then he offered his open palm, covered with a frost of the glistening grains. "Wound me again, hell-cat," he said, holding it to her lips.

She turned her head. "Don't call me that." It was too close, too near a twisting of Raymond's endearment into this underground mating like barbarians.

He dusted the seeds away between his palms. "My graceless love talk!" he said. "I beg your pardon, most worshipful and obedient wife."

"I have made no vow to obey you."

"Nay, I place no dependence on vows." He reached out and brushed a clinging grain from the corner of her mouth with his thumb. Elayne wet her lips, tasting sugar; tasting his blood. "They are easily made and easily broken. I don't aim to direct your whole existence, but when I require that you obey me, you may be certain that you will."

He spoke with such simple ruthlessness that she could find no way to defy him that did not seem merely weak and peevish. Instead she drew the scarlet wizard's robe close and looked about the little chamber, where candlelight danced on gold and pearls and his bared skin. "Demon!" she said sullenly. "I must be halfway to Purgatory."

"Aye, it is a desolate place," he said, disregarding her insult casually. "I've felt so myself, banished here, but we will not be condemned to this island for long."

Elayne glanced quickly at him. "You are condemned here?"

"Did you suppose I live in exile by choice? You named me outlaw, and it is the vile truth. I am a declared felon."

"Fie, if you will turn to piracy—how else?"

He flicked the little silver clockwork with his finger and made the bell ring. "I was cast out for who I am, not what I do. If I prey upon Riata commerce, 'tis not robbery, but justice."

"Blessed Mary, all this?" She lifted a hand toward the riches that surrounded them. Her fingertips barely showed beneath the overlong sleeves of his robe. "Only of the Riata?"

"Your province is great in trade, Princess," he said.

She looked aside at him. "Did you build this castle?"

"I had the walls and towers raised. The foundations lay here in ruin before I came."

"That strange black stone, and the fine porticos, and the Moorish tiles, and the frescoes in your chambers?"

"I brought the stone from the mountains of Atlas. The porticos and chambers, and my observatory and study and—other things—aye, I caused them to be made to my desire."

"And the bridges?"

He smiled. "The bridges are ancient, like that great sculpture on the headland."

"A curious exile! I do not believe you rob only the Riata."

He looked at her with a wicked gleam. "I have certain friends. Sometimes they make me gifts, in return for—dispensation—from pillage on the seas."

"An opportune arrangement!" she said. "From your pillage, I conceive."

"How you rejoice to abuse my character!" His brows rose in a pained expression. "Can you not believe that I do my friends an honest service?"

"No doubt you serve them as honestly as you have served me," she snapped, with a lift of her chin.

He shrugged. "You will be more satisfied when we return to Monteverde."

"Monteverde." She looked away uneasily. "Depardeu, I would rather by far live banished here."

"Pah, this barren island?"

"It is not so unpleasant. Your castle, and the clear sea." She surprised herself, to realize that she meant it. "In truth—I think it somewhat beautiful, though the climate is too sultry," she said.

"Nay, you've forgotten the sweet airs of your own home. The passes of Monteverde are protected, but the breeze still comes cool from the north. The mountains give such shelter to the lake that it's warm in winter and refreshing in the summer. There is no finer climate in the world."

"With no doubt rainbows every eve!" she said mockingly.

"No, but I will order it for you if you like," he said, with a slight bow.

"Certainly—when you are ruler there—*Pirate*."

He leaned over her. "I think you prefer me as a pirate." She tried to avoid him, but he caught her wrists in his hands as she pushed away. "I think you are half-brigand in your heart yourself."

"No." She could feel the dust of the confetti still on his fingers, a faint sandy grit, a scent of spice between his skin and hers. Her body ached where he had forced himself upon her. But when he touched her, leaned close to her, the pain seemed to turn and twist into an unspeakable throbbing sweetness. She stared into his beautiful dark eyes.

"Do you claim your sister made you into such a tame rabbit as she? Or did she only succeed in teaching you to fear the place that belongs to you?"

Elayne jerked, but could not free herself. "You speak as if there is nothing to fear there."

"No more than here, or your freezing English mud pit, or anywhere that men live and die by fortune and the will of God Almighty."

"What lies! When you say you are a murderer yourself by trade."

He let her go and stepped back. "I am."

Elayne released a breath. "And you profess I have nothing to fear?"

"There is much to fear," he said quietly. "Everywhere."

She thought suddenly of what he had said, that he dreaded to be defenseless. She lifted her eyes and met his. "Are you afraid, then?"

He tilted his head, watching her. "It is foolish not to fear," he said, "but it is a grave error to give way to it. So I have learned to keep my wits and countenance in the face of any fell thing."

"And your weapons always within reach," Elayne said. "We did not have to live that way at Savernake."

"Not you perchance, my lady. But someone did."

She opened her lips to make a denial, and found that she could not. There was always a guard on duty at the gates of Savernake, and through the night the familiar calls and clatter of men changing watch upon the parapets. Even there, they had seen smoke from the property of the King's tax collector when the peasants revolted. Sir Guy had ridden out with men-at-arms to block the rebels on the road to the castle, while Cara had wept and prayed for two days and nights in succession. Even at peaceful Savernake.

He crossed his arms and leaned back, looking down at her through his heavy lashes. It was as if her grim angel had come to earth, and instead of holding back the shadows, he pulled them toward her and bade her not to flee.

"But you are banished by law from Monteverde?" she asked with faint hope. "You may not travel there?"

"I am declared dead if I enter there, or any allied country. I cannot come into most of the Tuscan provinces, nor set foot in the lands of the Holy Roman Empire. I am outlawed in Aragon and the kingdom of Sicily." His hair fell over his shoulder, shadowing his one-sided smile. "The Pope of Rome has excommunicated me, and the anti-pope has, too, though it must be the only matter those pious jesters have agreed upon yet."

For several moments she stared at the flawless line of his jaw, his face, his mouth—absorbing the full force of what he said. Easy to say to herself in a moment of wrath that she would live with him in wickedness, but she began to comprehend the depth of what she had fallen into.

"When they sort out who is the true pope," he said, "I'll go and throw myself on my knees to beg for absolution. But pray do not expect me to do it twice."

"And you mean to attempt to claim Monteverde for yourself?" she asked incredulously.

"For both of us."

"Do me no such kindness!" she exclaimed.

"Providence has done it for you. My father meant to unite our blood. Princess Melanthe denied him that prospect once, but fate bestows it now again."

"An evil fortune," she said. "Bound by rapine to a man outlawed from church and home!"

"Better by far than if you had married the Riata, my beloved." He smiled at her as sweetly as a fallen angel. He reached out and touched her hair, brushing his hand tenderly over her cheek and her lips. "You have me now for your sword and shield—instead of your assassin."

IN THE SILENCE of the tunnels, in the space between innocence and iniquity, she had near forgotten that the storm still raged above. They ascended by his secret ways, turning and climbing in the light of a common lantern. A deep sound began to grow as they mounted a set of spiraling steps, a rumble that became a howl. The dim light cast flailing shadows on the back of a tapestry, highlighting the uneasy motion of the woven folds. He shoved the hanging aside.

Beyond, the gale lashed the castle, raging through the open galleries and whistling in the shuttered windows. The lantern's fitful light showed his bedchamber, the great arcade doors creaking and straining ominously. Elayne realized that driven rain was seeping over the thresholds.

"Mary and Joseph," he muttered, gripping her elbow. "On guard."

He pulled her into the chamber. As they ran across it, the wind rose to a yet higher scream, as if it boiled up at the very hope of reaching them through the walls. An ungodly cracking rent the air. The lantern flame vanished into utter blackness. She heard wood strike stone, the deafening thud of timbers collapsing. The arched doors burst open as if smashed by a battering ram. The explosion of wind threw her back, tearing her from his hold.

He shouted at her. Elayne had no time to cry out. She groped for something to cling to against the invading whirlwind; in the dim confusion she found his arm reaching for hers. He gripped her elbow with an agonizing clench, dragging her with him through the roiling darkness. She could feel the whoosh of wind at her back, heard the scream of air rushing past into hollow passages. He yanked her forward; she knew not where. With a deep boom, some unseen door closed behind them. The storm receded to the faint bellow of a distant beast.

Elayne drew in a gasp of air. "God defend us!" She had never experienced a tempest of such savagery, that pounded and screeched and attacked like a living thing. She crossed herself in the blackness. "God spare us."

"You are not hurt?" His grip on her arm did not lighten.

"By mercy, no." She had a moment of vast gratitude that

he had led her from the headland when he did. The force of the tempest had increased a hundredfold; she would have been carried long since into the sea if he had not brought her away to shelter.

Abruptly he plunged on, finding his way through the tunnels without a flicker of light, pulling her along behind him. She tripped over the hem of the robe, stubbing her toes and cracking her elbows until he stopped so suddenly that she collided with him.

Light poured into the tunnel as he opened a door. She heard the storm again, though not so loud, along with human voices. There was a peculiar geometry to the corridor before them: corners and ceiling that did not seem to meet in the expected places.

He glanced aside at her. He released her arm, sending prickles to her fingertips, and slid his hand up behind her loosened hair to the nape of her neck. She felt the strength of his fingers in her hair. With the faintest pull, he drew her toward him.

Elayne resisted. Standing in the half-light, he smiled at her. A dark smile, as if there were a mortal secret between them. He curled her hair about his fist and bent his face into it, drawing a long breath. Her lips parted on a silent whimper, a secret moan of bitter pleasure.

Abruptly he let her go. With a decisive move, he turned to face the blank stone of one wall. To her shock, he walked right into it.

It seemed to disappear as he did it; become an opening that she had not realized was there. He looked back at her.

"Come."

Elayne stepped forward, almost expecting to find the stone spring up before her. But it did not. For an instant, from the corner of her eye, it seemed as if a red figure leaped at her from behind. Elayne jumped ahead in startlement, but the figure disappeared as if it had never been. With her heart beating hard, she saw that they stood in the gloom of an unlit gallery overlooking a huge stone-walled kitchen. Wind whistled in the chimneys. The smell of smoke and cookery hung thick from the activity below.

A deep-voiced dog barked, and at the same moment a young man shouted joyously, "My lord!"

The multitude of faces below turned up toward them. In the clamor everyone pushed forward. The white puppy came bounding up the stairs, leaping on Elayne's damp robe with frantic exuberance.

Il Corvo stepped to the rail. The dark mantle he had thrown about his shoulders flared, showing a blood-red lining. Talk ceased instantly. All in his household fell to their knees. The sound of the storm rumbled beyond the heavy walls like a hidden breath that made the torches shudder. Elayne saw Margaret's yellow head, and even the Egyptian magician's bald pate, lowered deferentially among a throng of boys and girls. The great dogs roamed between the tables and cook-pots, pure white, the size of wolves.

"Rise," their master said. He spoke in the quicksilver tongue of Monteverde. "I have contrived to recover my bride, as you see."

"God is great!" the young man exclaimed, and a chorus of other voices echoed him. He wore an infidel's headpiece, a turban topped with a scarlet cap, fancifully embossed with brightly hued patterns. "My lord, we have been fraught with dread."

"No one has gone out in search?" the pirate asked softly.

"No one, my lord!" The youth lifted his chin, a handsome, dark-eyed Ottoman with the forceful look of a man full-grown, though he was yet beardless. "We have bided here as you commanded, though it was painful to check ourselves."

"Well done, Zafer," Il Corvo said.

The young man exhaled a visible breath. He nodded. "My lord."

"Make a place for us. Dario—see to a meal laid. Fatima, set your pretty feet to bring us claret wine. Zafer, Margaret, come up—I desire your attendance."

The assembly burst into motion. Behind Zafer, who

mounted the stairs three at a time, Margaret hurried up to Elayne. The maid's blue eyes brimmed with tears. She fell to her knees at Elayne's feet, holding the damp scarlet hem to her lips. "Your Grace, I was so frightened! I never meant to displease you so, that you would depart from the castle and stay out in such a storm!"

"It was no fault of yours," Elayne said, misliking the apprehension in the young girl's voice. She reached down and raised the maid, fending off an eager puppy. "'Twas another entirely who displeased me."

Margaret's eyes widened uneasily. "Not Fatima, my lady?" she whispered, bending close.

"No," Elayne said firmly. "Not Fatima."

"Who then displeased you, Princess?" The maid was urgent. "Any fault should be remedied."

Elayne picked up the excited puppy, hefting it in both arms. She looked over her shoulder at the pirate.

"I'll order myself tossed from a cliff," he said cordially. "Go down now, and dispose yourself in comfort as you may. Zafer—make ready to depart."

The pup squirmed and twisted. Elayne looked down, struggling to hold it and disengage its scrabbling paws from her deep sleeve. As she did, a flash of light burst in the smoky room—a flare that threw everything into blinding relief, a sizzle like lightning had struck inside.

She pivoted. Through the vivid after-shapes that danced in her eyes, she saw no one behind her. The pirate and Zafer were gone.

There was a moment of full silence, and then the others went about their business without any sign of bewilderment.

Elayne blinked. She looked along the whole length of the gallery where they had been standing not moments before, up the curved ribs of stone to where the ceiling vanished in smoky darkness. The walls stood solid—or seemed to. There was no other stairway. The black stone gave back shimmers and shadows in the erratic light of the torches below.

Margaret courtesied with perfect serenity, as quickly turned to smiling as she had been frightened a moment before. Elayne realized how young she was; how young they all were, the assembly of this castle.

"Will you let me help you down the stairs, Your Grace?" the maid asked.

Ten

———∞∞∞———

TO MOVE FROM the underground darkness into a cheerful throng required a stretch and twist of spirit that left Elayne feeling remote from her very self. She could not seem to connect the easy mirth and chatter of his household with what had happened to her deep in his hidden chamber—with the person she had become there, violated and violent in return.

She descended the stairs beside Margaret, with the puppy still in her arms, hardly knowing how she should conduct herself. No one offered any guidance. The pirate had assembled a strange court in his island exile. Not even with Queen Anne's youthful entourage had Elayne bided among so many young people at one time. Not one of Il Corvo's household seemed to have more than twenty years, and most of them were much younger. The guard that greeted them on their first night had been of middling years, but she had seen none other such since.

While they seemed handy enough at their kitchen tasks, with no elders to hold high spirits in check the atmosphere of merriment bordered on glee. A troupe of boys and girls decorously bore a multitude of tablecloths into the cavernous chamber, under the distracted eye of a young man who was directing the setting-up of the single trestle. When he turned his back, the children began covertly pinching one another. A squeal broke out. The group hurtled past Elayne trailing a sail of damask cloth. The puppy barked, scrambling free of her arms to join the game. Its sharp teeth closed on the cloth.

"Softly!" Elayne said, reaching out to catch the damask.

They all halted, five or six wide-eyed faces turned to her, as startled as if a tree had spoken. The pup tugged and shook at the cloth.

They were just of an age with her sister's child Maria, nine or ten years, except for one young boy who could not have been more than six. But having checked them, she hardly knew what to say. It was herself who was usually the object of a scold—Maria had always been the best of children, docile and eager to please.

Elayne felt a moment of exquisite longing for her home, where Cara's reprimands were the worst fate she'd had to fear. This brood looked as scared of Elayne's disapproval as she had been in awe of her sister's reproach.

"For pity, 'twould be a shame to injure this fair cloth," she ventured, uncoupling the puppy from its fervent assault on the rich fabric.

She received a series of ragged bows and courtesies in reply. The children edged away from her, folding the damask with more care to keep it from the floor, and then hurried off with a sudden burst of giggles. The pup danced away after them and then bounded back to Elayne.

"Ach, they are rude babes, my lady, forgive them!" Margaret whispered in English. "My lord has not yet taken that company in hand."

Elayne's glance passed over the Egyptian. He instantly stepped forward, sweeping an extravagant bow. His age was impossible to guess, but he was by far older than anyone else in the chamber. He fluttered his long fingers and opened them, presenting a coil of golden cord and a jeweled collar. "A leash for the noble whelp," he said. "If Your Grace will honor my poor conjuring."

Elayne gave a regal nod, as she had seen Queen Anne do when she received presents of her courtiers. The majestic effect was somewhat spoiled by the puppy's vociferous objections to finding itself curbed when she fastened on the collar. The dog flew about like a hooked fish, fighting the leash, and then sat down and tried to bite through the cord.

"Come here, then, little witch." Elayne knelt and untied the leash, knowing too keenly herself the sensation of bejeweled confinement. She rubbed the pup's ears and set it free. Perversely, it stayed at her side, licking her fingers and jumping on her hem when she rose.

"Margaret—where are the elder folk?" she asked.

"Oh, Dario is here—" Margaret waved toward the young man who had finally placed the carved bench to his satisfaction in front of the vast, blackened hearth. "My lord took Zafer with him. Fatima has gone to the cellar. She will return in a moment with refreshment for my lady."

Neither Zafer nor Dario appeared to have more than a year or two beyond Elayne's own seventeen.

"They are the eldest?" Elayne asked.

Margaret glanced at her. She gave a shrug and lifted her hand. "Your Grace, I know not. I believe so. Will you take this place of honor? Here is Fatima with your drink."

Elayne recognized the same comely Moorish maid who had served Elayne and Countess Beatrice in their captivity. As Elayne sat down at the trestle, Fatima approached with great deference. She knelt before the table, placing two goblets. "Will you take wine, Princess?" she asked.

In all the days that Elayne had nursed Lady Beatrice, this maid had not once seemed to understand her French, nor Latin, nor Italian. But Fatima spoke now in the tongue of Monteverde with more fluency than Elayne owned in it herself.

Elayne gave a short nod. Fatima beckoned a young boy to her side, one of the merry crew that had sailed about the chamber with the damask cloth in tow. He made a deep bow, serious now, rubbing his fingers quickly on his shirt before he took the jar. His hands were barely large enough to hold the heavy vessel as he poured an unsteady stream of rosy liquid and placed the goblet before Elayne. He stepped back with another nervous bow, kneeling down to one knee.

Elayne gave him an encouraging smile and reached for the wine.

"Hold!" Il Corvo's voice froze her, ringing harshly in the great high chamber. Elayne let go of the goblet. He strode forward from nowhere, his hair dewed with moisture, the dark mantle flaring. "Taste it, Matteo!"

He stopped beside the table, glaring down at the kneeling boy. The child had already dropped his face to the tiled floor, quaking. "Matteo," the pirate said in a voice of ice. "You fail me. Drink of what you poured. Discard the rest. And then I do not wish to set eyes upon you again."

The boy raised his pallid face. Still on his knees, he crawled forward. He lifted the goblet and took a sip.

"Drink deeper," the pirate demanded.

The child took a full swallow, and then another. The entire household watched in silence. Matteo appeared as if he might retch, his mouth screwed into a tight, unhappy rose. Elayne watched with horror. It was an undisguised tasting for poison, credence without the pleasant rituals she had seen at court that made it seem only ceremonial.

For long moments everyone stared, but beyond the grimace, Matteo seemed to take no ill effect. He sat upon his knees, very still, his head bowed in disgrace.

Il Corvo turned his brutal look upon Elayne. "Never . . . *never* . . . take food or drink without credence."

She had forgotten. Lady Melanthe had warned her of such; this pirate himself had taken advantage of her trust to stupefy her when he pleased. He sat down, dismissing Matteo with a disdainful motion of his hand. The boy backed away on his hands and knees, in full health enough to rise and run when he reached the wall.

The pirate watched him go. He looked around at his petrified household and narrowed his eyes at the maid. "Fatima. Matteo's life is in your hands. If you allow him to make such a mistake again, you will be the one to put a poison cup to his lips yourself. Replace the wine."

Fatima went to her knees. "You command me, Your Grace," she said breathlessly.

She rose and turned, hastening after Matteo. Elayne gripped her hands in her lap.

The Raven looked aside at her. "Remember this, my lady. You, too, are responsible for their lives. Do not allow yourself to be imprudent, or to be served carelessly. If there is any injury to you, those who caused it—by mistake or by malice—will suffer an ill fate."

She tried to appear composed, sitting with her back rigid to control her trembling limbs. "He is but a child," she said faintly.

"The better to do murder unobserved."

"Do murder!" she echoed. "The boy cannot yet have eight years to his life."

"I had but nine, at my first," he said. He took the seat beside her, throwing off his red-lined mantle. "I do not ask so much of Matteo yet, if it comforts your gentle heart. But they all know the price of an error in my service."

Two of the littlest boys bore his cloak away, their faces solemn and scared. At his order, Margaret brought a golden dish and set it upon the table. Stiffly Elayne offered her hands to be rinsed from the pitcher of perfumed water. The fragrance did not mask the scent that lingered on her, the scent of lust and coupling—the scent of a manslayer.

The one called Dario came forward. He was a thick-muscled, broad-shouldered youth with blunt strong features, but he bowed with a precise elegance, taking the napkin from his left shoulder and drying Elayne's hands.

"Your pardon for this crude meal, my lady," the pirate said gruffly. "It is not what I intended. We will have a proper feast in Monteverde to celebrate our marriage."

" 'Tis no matter," Elayne said in a stifled voice. If she never had a feast in Monteverde, she would be pleased.

"Pour into three cups," he instructed Dario, and watched as the youth performed a careful ritual, tasting deeply at each before he served it.

The Raven took a slow sip of one goblet, and offered it to Elayne from his own lips. She drank a convulsive swallow, assured at least that this was safe. He lifted the next cup and held it out to her. But as she raised her hand to steady the goblet, he drew it sharply away.

"Do not drink of this," he said. "Be careful. Smell it."

She lifted her eyes in mistrust. He met her look under his black lashes, a steady stare. Elayne drew in a breath over the cup.

"Do you smell it?" he asked.

She shook her head. "It smells of spice."

He offered the first goblet again. "Look in it. Observe the color."

Elayne looked at a claret wine that seemed ordinary in its honey-red color and sweet scent of spicery. "I see nothing."

He held up the second cup. "What of this?"

She frowned down at the silver goblet so close to her nose. He tilted it—and she saw the thin film that threw transparent colors across the surface.

"Oh—" she said. "I see it."

"At last," he said in a tone of great congratulation. " 'Tis fortune that it's only a drop of olive oil." He pushed the third goblet over the cloth toward her. "This one contains bane enough to kill us both. Smell it."

Gingerly Elayne sniffed at the last goblet—one of the cups that Dario had tasted not moments before. He stood by, erect and unconcerned, bowing his head when she glanced at him.

The faintest odor of burnt syrup, of almonds blackened beyond mere roasting, tainted the scent of the last cup. It seemed to go instantly to the back of her nose and linger there. She pushed the cup hastily away. "But he drank of it!"

Il Corvo looked up at Dario with a slight smile. "Enlighten the princess to what passed."

The youth bowed to his waist. "Your Grace, there was no bane in it when I drank. My lord diverted you with the second cup and envenomed the last one while you were distracted with looking at what he showed to you. It is a common ruse."

"Common?" she repeated weakly. Her voice rose. "This is common in Monteverde?"

"No doubt they are clumsier about it," the Raven said, "and easy to detect. But you make a credulous target. You must learn to take notice of what happens around you."

"Helas," she cried, "God forfend that I ever came here!"

The pirate scowled. "By Christ, can you not yet see what true profit it is to you?" He waved his hand for Dario to remove the cups. "Madame, you were bound for Monteverde and certain death in your innocence. Whatever I have done, whatever I may be—there is no one alive who can school you better in the wiles of murderers, nor keep you more surely from any human menace. Do you doubt me?"

She stared at the white tablecloth before her, where a cup of the claret had left a mark like a bloodstained new moon—a mark of poison, or of sweet safe wine; she knew not which. Once she had trusted her dark angel to keep her from all harm. But that happy illusion was broken now; it was an assassin who proclaimed himself her protector with such forbidding certainty.

There are a hundred dangers, Lady Melanthe had warned her, in a voice of anguish. *There is no time to teach you.*

Her godmother had known this pirate.

Elayne could not reason that Lady Melanthe had somehow sent her to him. To her family's enemy. To the same assassin who declared that he would have killed her himself if she had wed Franco Pietro of the Riata.

She could not reason it, and yet she remembered Lady Melanthe's cool ruthless demeanor, her own sister's awe of the countess, the respect tinged with dread that was never spoken. And she knew that her godmother was closer in spirit to the Raven than to anyone else Elayne had ever encountered.

"I am yours," the pirate said to her. Softly. Simply. He watched her out of shadowed eyes. "To my death."

She took a deep breath, staring at the shape of the half-moon stain. There was yet the hot soreness inside her, where he had taken her, left his man's seed in her body. Black mystery and pain, and she wanted it again—she wanted him before her, his head arched back, at her mercy. The strength of what she felt, the power he gave her to hurt him—her desire for it shocked her. Thunder cracked and rumbled overhead. Sullen smoke curled from the chimneys, the tempest exhaling like a living thing from the darkest corners of the lofty kitchen. The grave faces of children gazed at her from the shadows.

"Do it, then," she said, lifting her eyes. "Teach me what arts of malice that you will. I am certain that you know them all."

His lip curved in dry mockery. "I could not teach you one-tenth of what I know of malice," he said. "But I can put you on your guard against it."

Zafer appeared at that moment, emerging from the smoky shadows, his tabard and exotic headpiece darkened and dripping with rainwater. As the Raven looked toward him, the young infidel made a bow, but no words passed between them. There was only a glance, a moment that seemed to convey some grim meaning between the youth and his master as the storm wailed outside.

"Attend me well, then, my lady," the pirate said, turning back to her. "Place no faith in such useless concoctions as the powdered horn of a unicorn or the color of a moonstone—such false alchemy is for fools. Open all of your senses. Each poison has a character of its own. Each murderer has a nature that betrays him, if you observe closely enough."

She lifted her chin. "And what is yours?"

His gaze lingered on her hand upon the table, then

moved upward to her face. No more than she could fathom a panther's mind could she have said what was in his.

"Let that question be your ultimate examination," he said. "We will discover if you are cunning enough to solve it."

FOR THE NIGHT he took her to sleep beside the great kitchen fireplace, a captive within a close embrace, held against his chest as he leaned back on the hearthstone. Zafer stood silent guard. The rest of his servants lay ranged about the chamber in what comfort they could find, shapeless lumps of shadow in the ebbing firelight.

All night the storm whistled and shrieked. Elayne slept only fitfully, plagued by uneasy dreams. She woke once to find the white pup's chin resting on her calf as the young dog lay sprawled on its back, belly up and paws all askew within the wedge of space between her leg and the pirate's. Dario had taken up guard, his face lit faintly by the pulsing red ember glow. She could feel the Raven sleep—strangest of all, for she had come almost to believe that he never did. But the soft touch of his breath was slow and even in her hair, his arm across her waist an insensible leaden weight.

He had a name, such a deceptive, unapt name that she could not bring herself to employ it with him. Allegreto, he claimed to be called. The English tongue had no such word, but in the Italian and the French it meant something cheerful and light—even joyous.

He did laugh, but only in mockery. He smiled as a cat might smile while it toyed with a mouse. She wondered if he had ever in his life had a fit of honest mirth, the way she had laughed sometime with Raymond, both of them falling into hilarity, piling one childish jest upon another until they could not draw breath.

She doubted it. Those who knew the Raven used a title more apt than his own font name. Fitting enough, to call him after the black-winged harbingers of death and war.

She had learned to distinguish the scent of three poisons

since supper, and watched Zafer empty a vial of powder, hidden in his napkin, into the salt. She had watched him do it four times, and never once detected the faint turn of his wrist until he slowed the motion and lifted the cloth for her to observe each step of the action. Then Margaret—composed and determined—had demonstrated how to apply venom to a cloak pin and stab Zafer as she aided him to dress. She was not very accomplished at it, and apologized profusely to my lord and my lady for her inexperience while Zafer held a dagger to her heart, having turned off the maid's assassination attempt with a move as quick and simple as a striking snake.

The pirate had watched his apprentices with calm attention, remarking quietly on their work in the way a good master would appraise his students' efforts and offer methods of improvement. He recommended that Margaret attempt a scratch instead of a stab, as less likely to arouse suspicion, and equally effective with the proper poison. He advised Elayne to cause any sharp fastener to be dipped in water and wiped before she touched it, and to place it in her clothing by her own hand. He slipped the daggers he wore from their sheaths and showed how poison subtly discolored a blade—the one for his left hand was always envenomed, he warned her, the one for his right was clean.

Despicable it was, to put children in the study of such evil things. And yet they all—girls and boys, from the youngest up to Dario and Zafer and Fatima—looked to him eagerly, vying to show the degree of their scholarship in his deadly arts. In his own manner he treated them with a grim sort of kindness. When Margaret's babe had begun to wail from its basket slung on ropes near the hearth, she was granted quick reprieve from any further mayhem in order to attend her child. Matteo, skulking miserably in a half-lit corner, was called forward to make another try at a proper poison tasting. After a multitude of attempts, he possessed himself sufficiently to pour a full cup without shaking so that he spilled drops all over the tablecloth, and performed the credence. When at last the Raven, without praise or censure, simply lifted Matteo's offered goblet and drank from it, the boy's face broke into a glow of tear-stained relief and pride.

Elayne could see the pirate's fingers dimly now, entangled in her loose hair, intertwined with her own black and rain-washed curls as if he had woven them together by design. Like enough he had, to be vigilant of her every move even while they slept—and yet a stray lock coiled across the back of his palm, lying softly against his skin, like a black lamb curled there in innocent affection.

His hands fascinated her: their swift ease with the blades, on the wine cup, the rough jerk in her hair as he had yanked her away when she bit him. He had smiled then—smiled—and the thought of it sent an ache all down her body, a liquid pain that seemed like bliss.

He drew her to him, a lodestone against her own will, as if all she had been taught of good and right, all she knew of joy and mirth, held no strength against the beckoning darkness. She wanted to wound him again. She craved to do it. Just that way, that shocking moment of power, to make him hurt and shudder and lose himself in her again.

With a shiver, Elayne pulled the wizard's robe close around herself in the night. She felt the pirate come instantly alert. Dario stood straight.

She shifted a little within the wider space the Raven made as he lifted his arm. When she was still, he lowered it again, holding her entrapped. The puppy turned over and heaved a sigh.

HE GAVE HER scrolls to study. They were nothing like the texts that Lady Melanthe had provided for her education. As the storm still slashed and rumbled overhead, she read a Latin compendium of toxic substances, divided into sections, first those natural and then those made by the hand of man: their manufacture, their modes of delivery, their effects. Dry mouth; rapid heartbeat; hot, dry; agitation and delirium . . . certain death.

In the margins were notations. Other effects—large pupils, muscle spasms; the names of men, some of them scratched through.

She might have been sitting in the kitchen at Savernake, on a bench and trestle borrowed from the great hall, with the smells of bread and cooked onions and soot, the watery storm light falling down from high window slits onto the parchment. She might have been studying her notes of Libushe's herbs and potions. Except she was not. She was reading how one man might kill another, or make him impotent or blind, while children sat about her chopping dates and talking cheerfully and Dario pumped the wheel of a whetstone, making a pitched whine above the rumble of the storm as he sharpened their proffered daggers and little knives, sending sparks flying to the tiled floor. Margaret's baby played at her feet while she mended buttons on Elayne's torn shift.

Il Corvo sat midway up the stairs to the kitchen gallery, dressed in black velvet, one leg extended—like an illumination in a book Elayne had seen once, of a nonchalant fiend overlooking the souls in Purgatory, lounging between the curves and struts of the letter E.

His languid glance came to hers as she lifted her eyes. Heat suffused her, dread and pleasure. She would have looked away, looked down, but it seemed as if that would be weak—an admission that she even noticed him. That she remembered—vividly. Between them now there was potential; he spoke of Monteverde and taking power there, but closer and more real to Elayne was the babe that tumbled at Margaret's hem. Libushe had explained it. Elayne knew it well enough; she had seen the animals at Savernake couple, seen the foals and lambs come spring. In her fondest dreams, she had seen herself picking wildflowers in the woods with a bright-haired son of her own and Raymond's—but somehow the gap between chastity and that vision had not seemed to invite very close examination.

He held her look. With a slow move, like a lazy caress, he touched his fingertips to his shoulder, to the place where she had bitten him. Instantly she felt a spring of hot sensation, a violent dream of her power to mark and wound him as he arched under her hands. He smiled at her, a mere hint in the greenish light of the storm.

Elayne looked down, snatching a quick breath, as if the atmosphere had closed upon her.

Perchance it was a spell he had laid on her, that made her blood run in a tangle and her breath come strangely when she thought he was remembering as she was. She had never in her life before wanted to hurt any creature. It was not anger, though anger was a part of it. But it was more than that, more—it was all twined and twisted with the way he looked beneath his lashes and smiled as if he knew.

Perhaps it was a curse to make her foreign to herself. He would perceive how to make such a thing, and not bungle it with mismatched feathers.

He rose from the stairs and came down in one graceful bound, scooping up one of the youngest ones as the child was about to reach for a newly honed knife that Dario had just laid aside. With a flick of his wrist, Il Corvo sent the blade spinning end-over-end above them. It reached a zenith and flashed downward; Elayne's heart stopped as the little boy looked up at the weapon descending toward his head.

An arm's-length above the child, the pirate plucked the dagger from the air.

"Hot," he said, holding the blade before the boy's face. He set the child on the floor. "Don't touch it too soon."

The boy shook his head vigorously.

"It's cool now," the Raven said. "Take it."

The little boy reached for the knife, but the pirate moved it. Instantly the child assumed a stance, his short legs spread, rocking forward on his toes; an echo of Il Corvo's agile pose. For a few minutes they feinted and sparred for possession of the blade. Fifty times the cruel edge came within a hairsbreadth of slicing the child's soft skin, but he ducked and twisted, moving in under Il Corvo's arms.

Somehow the pirate made it appear as if the boy really did dispossess him of the weapon, emitting a suitably foul oath and dropping the knife when the child cracked him on the knee-cap with a sudden, awkward kick.

"Well-placed," he said as the student bore his prize away. He sat down next to Elayne, rubbing his joint, and gave her a sideways smile. "A promising brat."

She did not return the smile. "Would not grown men serve you better?" It came out like an accusation. "Why children?"

He leaned back, his elbows on the table. "Because they are wholly mine."

Elayne turned her face away from his faultless profile. "They seem a frail force."

"Do they?" he asked idly.

She rolled the edge of the scroll under her finger. Her heart seemed to pound in her ears when he was so close to her. "Would you bring up your own child in such a manner?"

She felt him look at her. Before he spoke, she added, "And you need not enlighten me—I am certain it is how you were fostered. Would you make the same of your own blood?"

The sound of the whetstone wailed, searing metal to stone. His body was perfectly still beside her. She thought he was more frightening when he was motionless than when he wielded any weapon.

"Tell me what choice I have," he said softly.

Elayne wet her lips. She had not expected him to give her a serious reply. But he waited, as if he meant it. She frowned down at her knuckles, finding that mere admonitions to do good and not sin seemed foolish. She could not give a sermon on it. It seemed utterly wrong, to corrupt children, to bend them to such service, and yet she could only offer platitudes about abandoning his iniquity and seeking rectitude. Platitudes to the man who swore to guard her from such murderers as himself.

"I asked your sister the same once," he said. "And she had no answer for me either."

She bent her head. Then she took a deep breath and looked toward him. "If you desire that I will bear your children, then you must find one."

He never moved. His lashes flicked downward and up again. He remained gazing at Dario's back as the youth pumped the grinding wheel.

"Libushe taught me many things," Elayne murmured, barely above a breath. "Even if you force me, I can prevent a child."

It was a lie; Libushe had taught her herbs and methods that might prove successful at preventing a conception, but the wisewoman had not promised certainly, and warned her it was a deadly sin to use them. But Elayne thought even a wizard might not be sure of what a woman of knowledge could impart.

He looked at her then. Instead of the cold fury or disgust she had prepared for, it was a mystified look, as if she had spoken some riddle that made no sense to him. "Why?"

"Because it would be mine, too," she said, "and I will not have any child of mine brought up to be what you are."

His fine mouth hardened. "A bastard?"

"A murderer. Like these." She inclined her head toward the others.

"You wish him to have no defenses?"

She paused at that. "No," she said. "But . . ." She put her palms together, trying to find words for what she meant. "No more than other people. Not corrupted and trained to slay as if it is a game."

She thought he would mock her and call her foolish. He only frowned a little, then sprang up. He walked to the foot of the stairs, put his boot upon the lowest step, then turned and came back. He looked down into her eyes, still with that faint frown. "If I swear this to you, then you will not resist me?" he demanded in a low voice. "You will conceive?"

She felt her cheeks burning. His word could hardly be

trusted. She did not want to be his wife. The idea of bearing him sons and daughters was horrifying and frightening and exhilarating all at once. "If God wills it," she heard herself say, in a voice that barely whispered in her throat. But it did not seem that God's will could have any link to what she felt.

"Then I swear," he said at once. "Man child or girl, their education belongs to you. I will not teach them what I know."

THE STORM LASTED two nights and swept past, leaving wreckage and a crystalline atmosphere, a chill that made these warm-blooded southerners shiver and chafe their hands. The air felt revitalizing to Elayne, but even she huddled close in her mantle as they toured the storm-clawed rooms and loggias. She felt as shattered as the beautiful carved doors that hung askew on their hinges—as if she were someone unknown to herself, born of the destruction to a new and harsher spirit.

The white puppy trailed behind her, endowed now with the name of Nimue, for the Lady of the Lake who had bewitched the love-sotted Merlin and sealed him in his cave. The young dog cared for nothing but play and theft, investigating the debris with a sportive glee—the only cheerful presence amid a grimly silent household.

The castle stood, but the open arcades lay in ruins, their heavy beams torn askew and flung into the shuttered chambers. Elayne doubted if Amposta's ship could have survived such a tempest. She said a prayer for Lady Beatrice, but the countess's fate seemed distant now, in God's hands.

Her own pressed much closer. The Raven appeared unconcerned about the damage to his castle, the smashed tiles and drenched hangings. The gleaming horizon seemed to trouble him more—he stared out at the empty blue sea and posted watches at all the corners of the fortress.

Elayne thought of the fleets he had said might come for her. She'd thought he spoke in dry jest, but he surveyed the water with such intensity that she knew he expected something to appear. Before he had made no effort to constrain her to stay within the castle. Today he spoke sharply if she lagged more than a few steps behind him.

"Is there danger of attack?" she asked when he had sent Zafer away to discover how the town had fared.

He glanced down at her. For an instant the flash was there, that promise of fire and pain that bound them now whenever he met her eyes. Elayne forced herself not to look away.

"Attack is always a prospect," he said.

"Might you bring yourself to utter just how large a prospect?"

He gave a short laugh. "It is not attack on this stronghold that need alarm you, my lady. I maintain defense of the island by sufficient means." He looked back out to sea. "My comrades are to gather a fleet here, in preparation for our return to Monteverde."

"A fleet." She pushed back from the marble parapet, startled. "So soon?"

"The time was appointed many months ago. When first I had news that Franco Pietro was to take a bride—and her name was Princess Elena."

"A fleet," she said faintly.

"A great fleet, of sixty ships and four thousand men-at-arms, to bring about the absolute destruction of the Riata. It has taken me five years to assemble it."

"Depardeu," she whispered. She looked at him, and then at the empty horizon. The sea was fresh and running high. Huge waves crashed far below, rolling in under the precipitous castle wall. Nothing else interrupted the expanse of vivid blue.

"Yes," he said, "they do not come."

Veiled by the wind-tossed mass of her hair, Elayne looked down, twisting the band on her finger. She had wished with all her heart to depart on Amposta's vessel for England and home. But she did not believe anything could have kept it afloat in such a storm. Even if his comrades were marauding pirates, she could not wish so many such an end. Her throat felt tight and queasy.

"Haps they did not all perish," the Raven said evenly. "Some might have made shelter."

"God defend them," she said, signing the cross.

"No one will set this at God's door," he said. "They will blame me."

"You? For a storm?"

"Aye. And the Devil. They will say I tried to command the wind by diabolic means, and lost control of it."

The puppy broke into shrill barking, scrambling after a gull that had the temerity to land on the marble edge. The bird took off in a clumsy flap of wings, then hovered and wheeled in the updraft from the cliff. Having accomplished her adopted duty, Nim trotted importantly back to Elayne, skirting broken tiles and jumping over the smashed pot of a palm tree. She grabbed a branch of the palm in her sharp white teeth and shook it vigorously, sending dirt flying from what was left.

"Peace, little witch," Elayne said gently, pulling the plant away.

The pirate reached down. He grasped the whole of the shattered palm. He swept it up, as Nim skipped backward, and heaved it over the parapet in one great arc, flinging clods of dirt.

His face held no expression. He began to seize pieces of broken clay, hurling them one after another in graceful flights that soared and tumbled and fell out of sight. He moved with methodical calm along the railing, bending to grasp a piece of wreckage—any piece, large or small—rising in one swift motion to launch it from the cliff. Shards of tile and smashed members of wood sailed from the parapet and disappeared into blue oblivion.

When the floor was cleared, he put his boot to the edge of a pedestal that had survived the storm and toppled it, sending Elayne and Nimue cowering back as the stone smashed down. Chips of tile and stone went flying. Jagged cracks shot across the beautiful tile floor.

Elayne snatched up the puppy and turned her back as he moved toward a sculpture of a griffon atop the parapet. She squeezed her eyes shut, expecting another impact, but none came.

She turned hesitantly. He stood still, an ironic tilt to his mouth. The breeze played with his black hair and lifted the dark cloak, flashing wings of bloody red. He might have been the Devil indeed, standing there deadly and alone in the dazzling sun. He cast one look at the empty horizon and turned away.

"We leave tonight," he said. "Take what you want. We will not return here again."

Eleven

⋙

THE CITY OF Venice seemed to rise from the green water like a glistening dream: a silent place, where voices drifted from unseen windows and the faint splash of the boatman's pole was the only sound of passage.

"Case d'Morosini," the Raven had murmured to the boatman as they pulled away from the Egyptian's galley in the harbor. On the quays and the Great Canal there had been many ships and boats, but here in the narrower streets of water there was no bustle, not of wheels nor hooves nor footsteps. The peaked windows of the buildings all were shuttered. Exotic pointed arches and striped columns, their foundations awash, reflected plays of brilliant sunlight and darkness from the water.

The long, peculiar boats they called gondolas were like slippers with turned-up, pointed toes. Elayne sat in the small silk-draped cabin with Margaret, both of them leaning to stare about through their veils at the mysterious facades that glided past. The boatman swung the gondola in a graceful turn, guiding the bow into the cave-like water entry of a great mansion. Stripes and diamonds adorned the walls in bright colors. Painted leaves entwined the shapes of heraldic beasts. It seemed as if the silent city had been bedecked for a great celebration that no one had attended.

Without any signal of their arrival, the mansion door swung open. Il Corvo stepped lightly onto the wet landing, flanked by Dario and Zafer. None of them wore their blades; the customs officials had taken them into strong-boxes and handed back paper receipts. The youths stood by, their faces grim and alert, while Elayne and Margaret climbed onto the steps with the aid of pages in extravagant livery.

Elayne felt again the strange sensation of standing upon solid ground after so long at sea. It seemed as if the world slid past her for an instant, then stabilized—but if she turned her head suddenly it slid again, an instant's dizziness that made her glad of the pageboy's arm beneath her hand.

"My master begs you attend him upstairs," the pageboy said in an accent of the Italian tongue that she could barely understand. He ushered them through a humid hall, so dark that torches were lit in the middle of day. Elayne laid back her veil, glad enough to be rid of the smothering gauze. Iron chests and wooden tuns lined the walls. As the servant led them out into a courtyard, she shaded her eyes with the change from light to dark to glaring sunlight again.

They entered the mansion on the upper story. Beautiful inlaid designs decorated the smooth stone floors. The chamber where they waited was large and cool, freshened by a faint breeze through the tall shutters. As servants brought sweet wine and a tray of spiced cakes and tarts, the door opened and closed with a soft boom. A tiny man has-tened into the chamber, his abundant robes and sleeves trailing behind him.

Signor Morosini lifted a wizened face and gestured to the carpet-covered benches. "Be seated, be comfortable, eat! I will stand. I do not like to be looked down upon." His eyes were lost in wrinkles as he laughed. He waved at his one attendant who remained in the room, a heavyset man with the sad expression of a weary hound. "Federico here is to be trusted, you may be sure."

The Raven glanced at Dario and Zafer. They bowed and withdrew, not appearing pleased to leave their master and mistress alone with no one but Margaret for protection. But the pirate seemed relaxed, ignoring their host's command to be seated, leaning instead against the frescoed wall beside Elayne, not quite near enough to touch her.

He had not touched her since they left the island. He had barely spoken to her. And yet it seemed as if his presence saturated the very air she breathed.

Signor Morosini took up a position behind a carved and gilded podium, like a priest about to give a sermon. Federico placed a volume bound in iron straps before him. Morosini opened the book, turning pages while his attendant sorrowfully tasted wine and sweetmeats. Having demonstrated the repast to be harmless, Federico offered the refreshment.

Elayne carefully waited until the pirate gave thanks— her signal that she could trust the food upon the silver tray before her. Before they left the ship, the pirate had warned her that his dealings with the Case d'Morosini hung in delicate balance. She and Margaret had been cautioned to be courteous and agreeable, so as to cause no undue offense. They shared the entremets, a pleasing selection of little molded cakes and marzipan wafers that reminded Elayne of Lady Melanthe's fine table, and kept quiet, as was proper.

After a few silent minutes Morosini wrote, his quill scratching busily as he spoke. "The sum that you are owed . . ." He paused, glancing from one page to the next. His wrinkled brow wrinkled into even more creases. " . . . is substantial," he concluded.

"Sixteen thousand, four hundred eighty-five ducats and four ounces of fine gold," the Raven said, smiling. "I shall not cavil about the grains."

Morosini laughed. "Nay, I think not. I calculate some four thousand ducats fewer."

The pirate took a sip of wine. "Let us talk of happier

things, then. I pray that your affairs go well, by the grace of God. I recall that galleys carrying Morosini goods ply the waters from Candia to Cyprus. It's a fine trade—indigo and pearls—I often receive reports of their movements and cargo."

Signor Morosini looked down at his book. He tilted his head like a wise old squirrel contemplating a winter cache of nuts. "I do not think I have miscalculated," he said reluctantly. "But—let me examine the figures again." As he bent over the book, he said, "It is an excellent thing to see you free to journey abroad without persecution."

"I rejoice in the opportunity to visit my esteemed friends once again," the pirate said agreeably.

"But I am pained to hear that God saw fit to destroy so many in the recent tempest. I fear your colleagues lost many of their fine ships of war."

The Raven looked surprised. "Nay, we were blessed to be unscathed, St. Mary be praised. My captains are wise in the way of storm, and went to ground before it struck. I heard that Masara and Susa were obliterated, and many died in shipwreck in Agrigento. Morosini lost nothing, I hope?"

"Two round ships," the old man said. "God rest the souls of our sailors."

Elayne felt as if she were watching a game of chess, with plays and counterplays that none but the opponents themselves could fathom. The pirate lied and exaggerated with a frightening sincerity. After days on this journey, drawing closer to Monteverde with every stroke of the oars, she still had no notion of what he intended. They voyaged as common travelers, leaving all of Il Corvo's riches and most of his young household behind on the island, his warships smashed on the rocks or scattered to the storm winds. Only the Egyptian's leaking vessel had stayed afloat—protected by spells, the magician declaimed grandly, to which the pirate had replied merely by smiling and dispatching the surviving crew from his wrecked galleys to commandeer it.

The voyage seemed to be a matter of money and business, stopping at ports along the way to visit merchants and collect payments in gold. But it was evident enough, listening between the polite words, that these payments were in return for the unspoken promise that the Raven's brigand warships would not attack the merchant galleys. No one seemed to comprehend that he did not command any fleet or allies now. Or that if they seized him here, there would be no retribution on the sea.

She felt as if she were walking on water that the pirate made solid by brazen invention and falsehood—that any one of these sharp merchants might have sure news that Il Corvo's fearsome navy was destroyed, and know enough to see past his ruse.

The merchants were all exquisitely courteous to the Raven and his party. But Elayne could foresee that the price for detection would be death.

"I weep with you," Il Corvo said, in response to Morosini's lament about his poor circumstances since the storm. "I see now that my visit is inopportune. I have no wish to burden you with my demands at this time. Let us not dwell upon such things."

The old man's reaction to this sudden generosity was profound. Instead of becoming gladdened, his face melted into deeper caverns of sorrow. He groaned as if some angel of lamentation had touched him. "Nay, but I owe you a sum, and you demand it," he said unhappily. "I will not have it said that the House of Morosini does not honor its debts."

"We agree upon the lesser sum, then," Il Corvo said. "If you can spare me the first half of it, I shall send my envoy—let us say, at the Christmas fair, for the remainder. The galleys from Constantinople will have returned then, by God's grace. Will that lighten your burden?"

Morosini gave a deep sigh. "You are a saint among men, Il Corvo."

Not a flicker of mockery or humor altered either of their faces at this avowal. The pirate bowed his head courteously. "It is ever my object to serve you, Signor."

"But it is I who can serve you—there must be some errand I might perform on your behalf. Some pitiful return for your immeasurable generosity."

"I am in need of nothing, thank God. We are on pilgrimage in very gratitude for the fortune that spared my force and brought me great good chance."

Morosini nodded, showing no sign of shock at the idea of an ex-communicate pirate on Christian pilgrimage. "The merciful Lord be praised. I should do the same. I will, when my health allows it, I swear I will go to Compostela, or even Jerusalem! But your lady—I have some pretty things that you would enjoy to adorn her beauty." He glanced up at Federico, lifting a finger. The burly man turned and left the room.

The pirate looked at Elayne as if a sudden inspiration had come to him. "Nay—Signor, a small favor does enter my mind, if you might be inclined to please a lady."

"Be certain that all the powers of my household and my strength are at your service in such an agreeable endeavor!"

"My beloved Elena here is the scion of a great Lombard house. We are but newly wed, since several weeks past."

"Excellent!" Morosini swept a deep bow toward Elayne. "I had not yet been honored by this great news. All of Venice rejoices in your happiness! What Lombard house?"

Il Corvo lowered his voice. "She is the last *principessa* of the green and silver," he murmured.

The old man drew in a slow, audible breath. Elayne held her hands still in her lap. She felt him look long at her. *"Spirito Santo!"* he whispered. "We had heard that she perished on her journey."

"She was saved from the sea," Il Corvo said calmly. "By my men. She was brought to my island, and by the grace of God she has recognized and returned the ardent love and affection that I conceived for her."

Elayne bit her tongue between her teeth, lowering her face.

"Was she not betrothed to the house of Riata?" Morosini asked very softly.

"Was she?" the pirate said. "Verily, it was not made known to me. Ours is a love match."

The old man began to chuckle quietly. He washed his fingers together, laughing like a child. The cool room picked up the sound and echoed with his smothered mirth.

"What favor could be done?" Morosini said at last.

The pirate smiled indulgently at Elayne. "I can dress her and adorn her like a queen, but I have no power to make her great again in name and rank."

"Nor I. I have no power to restore that throne."

"Of course. You will understand—I have enemies." The Raven gave a shrug of apology, as if this were a personal flaw in his character. "I do not yet feel safe for her to be known abroad for who she is, in truth. But while we travel, I should like to clothe her with some likeness of the eminence of her rightful titles. To present her by letters that assure she is treated with due reverence, according to her high station among ladies."

Morosini nodded slowly. "I believe I comprehend you. A designation of honor. Letters of introduction, from trustworthy friends who know her merit."

"The Case d'Morosini of Venice is a name of respect and power in all lands. The honor of such a family would assure my dear Elena is not ignored or mortified on our journey."

Morosini's bony little hands plucked at a corner of his account book. "May I be honored to know the object of your blessed pilgrimage?"

"I would be remiss to hide it from you. We are bound for the north. The place we seek is not far from the city of Prague—it is called Karlstein."

Elayne lifted her head, looking quickly toward him.

"That is a fortress." Morosini squinted at the pirate. "Do not the Imperial regalia lie there?"

He smiled slightly. "Aye, in a sacred site. The Emperor's chapel of the Holy Cross."

"That can only be a place of pilgrimage for the chosen Emperor himself!"

"My lady had a dream." The Raven reached for Elayne's hand—a light touch that made her feel as if the floor beneath her feet stood in sudden danger of collapse—and held it between his. "As she floated half-dead, before her rescue from the waters, she dreamed that the Holy Virgin bade her seek out the thorns and nails from our Savior's crucifixion. She was shown a white castle in a deep forest, and a cross of gold." He looked down at her as she stared at him in outrage at this falsehood, and then back at the Venetian. "We sought counsel of the hermit at Leukas, and were told we must go to Karlstein. You may comprehend our amazement."

These lies were so bald and blasphemous that Elayne started up from her seat to object, but his fingernails dug deep into the back of her hand. She remained on her feet, glaring at him.

"A wondrous vision," the Venetian said, with a smile that suggested he did not believe a word of it. "Let us retire to my closet, and speak of what aid might best speed you and your bridegroom, my lady."

IN A CHAMBER on the highest floor of the mansion, Morosini swept about closing shutters, sealing off the breeze, leaving only thin watery reflections from the canal below to dance on the ceiling for light. He did not invite Elayne or the Raven to sit.

"The house of Morosini will lend no assistance to any attempt to steal the Imperial regalia," he said straightly.

"Signor," Il Corvo said, "you know I am no such fool."

Morosini stood very still, his bright eyes fixed on the pirate. "It is true I do not know you for a fool."

"I am the son of my father. My chief object is no secret to you. The Imperial jewels are as dust to me in comparison."

The Venetian nodded. "I do not quarrel with your ambition. The Riata are poor friends to Venice—they sit astride their mountain passes too greedily and try to cheat us of the silver we've contracted from the mines. But all men are subject to error in their judgment." He paused. "There were rumors of some alarm in Monteverde in recent weeks."

Il Corvo lifted Elayne's hand and bowed over it. He smiled down at her, his face strikingly handsome, under-lit as it was by the cool glow from the water's reflections. "I can well believe that this fortune given to me has caused unease in certain quarters."

"You are fortunate indeed to receive the favor of such a virtuous and illustrious maiden!" Morosini said, bowing also to Elayne. "But it was of more warlike motion that we had intimation." He sighed regretfully. "I suppose that it is not so."

"Rumors!" Il Corvo said with an apologetic opening of his hand. "How often they mislead. If the common knowledge whispers that I am poised to make war on Monteverde, you may be sure that is the unlikeliest of my intentions."

The Venetian seemed thoughtful. Elayne did not think he entirely accepted the pirate's vague account, but he did not press further on the subject. "Indeed," Morosini said, "it would confound the gossips to hear that Il Corvo is upon a pilgrimage of devotion."

"None would believe it," Il Corvo said simply.

The old man chuckled. "Forgive me, I must confess to doubts myself."

"I take no offense. For my lady, it is a pilgrimage of devotion. For myself, a pilgrimage in search of knowledge."

"Commendable," Morosini said. "What variety of knowledge do you seek in the Emperor's chapel?"

"Nothing in his chapel, of course; I could hardly expect to enter there. But among the old Emperor's collections—" He wriggled his fingers. "Charles was a fool for any holy relic. He would buy a tanned goat's udder if he thought it was one of Mary Magdalene's breasts." He gave a bland smile. "So I was moved to sell one to him, having no use for it myself."

The two men appeared to find this irreverence against God and Crown to be a fine jest. But Morosini managed to stifle his glee, offering an effusive expression of regret for offending Elayne's goodness. The Raven only flicked her cheek carelessly and said no doubt his wife would make him a better man.

"A task of staggering proportions," she said tartly.

Morosini had been about to speak—he closed his mouth and looked as if he had just seen her standing there. Elayne knew that in spite of his accomplished courtesies to a lady, until she spoke he had not given her personally any more thought than he would to a bedpost. She stared back at him in a manner that Cara would have certainly labeled as the behavior of a deplorable strumpet.

The Venetian's brows drew together. She could almost see into his mind: he would not tolerate his own wife or daughters to speak so bold. At that look she felt her eternal impulsive willfulness take hold of her tongue. "Do you think I can accomplish it, Signor?" she asked mildly.

Il Corvo gave Elayne a shameless flash of heat beneath his lashes. With one of his wicked lazy smiles, he touched his shoulder. He smoothed his open palm over it as if he only brushed a wrinkle. "'Tis certain no one else can," he murmured.

Elayne felt herself grow crimson at this barefaced intimation. He had warned her sharply against any discourtesy, but he did not seem dismayed now at her impudence. Nay, he looked at her as if he would take her up against the wall where they stood—a thought that made the air seem so close and hard to breathe that she thought she might well smother of it. "If you do not make me far worse instead," she replied, spreading her skirts in a mocking bow, looking down to hide her desperate flush. "My lord."

"'My lord pirate,' you mean to say! But the goodness of your nature prevents you."

The Venetian grew distressed, fluttering his hands. "Let us not speak too much in jest, I beg you!" He had recovered his civility. "Indeed, I have been remiss to keep her here, wearying her with our business trifles, when she ought to be entertained by my wife and her attendants. Do forgive an old fellow, Lady Elena."

"I have not been wearied at all," she said. "I find Il Corvo's explanation of our affairs to be—amazing. What is it that we seek in the Emperor's collections, besides a goat's udder? I'm greatly agitated to discover."

The Raven bowed to Morosini. "My wife is uncommonly learned for a woman. She delights in diverse knowledge."

Morosini did not commend her for that. "I pray she does not become overly excited by such activity," he said seriously.

Il Corvo took an impatient step, leaning his head against a window shutter and gazing out. Light from the narrow slats made bright lines across his face. "She's made of stronger fiber."

"Nay, but heed. The physicians are united in their advice on this topic! For a woman of advanced age, or a nun, it may do, but it is not healthy for a young maid of—of nubile years—to engage heavily in mental exercise."

The pirate lifted an eyebrow, looking toward Elayne. He might have been smiling, but in the laddered strips of sunlight she could not be sure.

"We can only hope that my husband will reveal his object before my poor brain is overheated," she said, with another courtesy.

"It is not your brain that concerns me, my dear," Morosini said kindly, turning to her. "It is the diversion of life fluid from the womb. The ladies of the green-and-silver have often made this mistake, I fear, allowing mental exertion to weaken their bodies for breeding. Princess Melanthe herself spent her vigor in too great study, and bore only one sickly daughter, you must know. It was a great tragedy for Monteverde. You want to please your husband with a fine son, do you not?"

"Very true!" the pirate said, before Elayne could respond with a heated denial of Lady Melanthe's inability to bear sons. He stood straight. "Madam, from this moment you are forbidden to read anything but recipes for lasagna."

Morosini nodded. "Wise of you. It would not do to create too abrupt a change in her habits."

The pirate smiled serenely at Elayne. "Certainly not. We will decrease her by degrees to instructions for sweetmeat," he assured their host.

The old man's face wrinkled into a deep smile. "Excellent. But we have kept her standing too long, I must insist. You have had enough exertion for this day, my lady." He rang a bell, and in a few moments two young pages hurried into the room. "Inform the Signora that we have an honored guest. Quickly now! Quickly!"

IL CORVO'S BUSINESS had not made her brain boil, but an hour in the company of Signora Morosini and her devout ladies was enough to make Elayne fit for a lunatic. The Signora in particular was liable to take offense at trifles, the pirate had warned her. He had cautioned her to take great care. Elayne knew she had already skimmed dangerously close to the behavior of a deplorable strumpet. So she sat in an upright chair next to Margaret's stool in the dim, shuttered room, enduring the slow conversation. It seemed to consist entirely of ponderous commentary on the imperfect morals and lewdness of young women in these latter days, and the punishment that awaited them in the Inferno.

Margaret kept her face lowered. Elayne did not hide, but held her hands still in her lap, saying nothing, thinking of the Raven, thinking of the underground room, thinking thoughts so immoral that they were near beyond comprehension.

There had been no opportunity for confession since the night in his secret room, and no repeat of the act—in the stifling, close quarters of the magician's galley, it was Zafer or Dario who kept watch over her as she slept, while the Raven seldom came into the cabin at all if she were there.

But the return to utter chastity between them had merely

closed the door on a hidden furnace. Elayne labored in a
state of sin that would have astounded the Signora. On the
galley she had sat in the place prepared for her under a
swaying canopy and pretended to occupy herself with gazing at the dolphins that escorted them. But when the Raven
was not looking, she had watched him stand beside the
deck rail, taking the motion of the ship easily, his hair tied
back under a knotted sash. She thought of the sound he had
made as he shuddered inside her; she felt his arms about her
and the taste of his bruised skin on her tongue.

He kept a distance from her: a deliberate, taunting distance. Elayne affected not to notice him. She watched. She
relived it again and again in her mind. And she knew that
he was conscious of it, that he knew every moment where
she was and what she was doing, as he knew the reach of
his daggers. She held her breath and thought that when next
he touched her in that way, she would shatter like a glass
vessel into a hundred razor-edged shards of desire.

Signora Morosini lifted a pale hand, turning her beads to
tell an Ave on her lady's Psalter, then launched a measured
discourse on the tortures to be meted out to unchaste
whores who lured men into fornication and adultery for
money. Concluding with a remark on the blessed sanctity of
marriage, she nodded at Elayne with an air of compliment.
A tiny motion caught Elayne's eye. She glanced aside at her
maid and saw that the girl was weeping without a sound.

Signora Morosini noticed it also. She looked at Margaret
with a faint, satisfied smile. The girl's quiet tears were a
clear betrayal of her history, but instead of showing pity, the
Signora resumed her sermon with renewed force, raising
fresh specters of the agony in store for harlots. Finding a
victim to address seemed to give her slow voice new energy.

When the Signora heavily advised Elayne that it was a
peril to her own chastity to keep a servant who had sinned
in such a way, Elayne came to the limits of her fortitude.
She reached over and took Margaret's hand, rising without
a word. Without taking leave of the Signora or her ladies,

without even a courtesy, she led Margaret from the chamber.

The pages leaped to open the doors and close them on the shocked silence that Elayne and Margaret left behind. The maid clutched Elayne's hand. As soon as they were in the hall, she turned her face into Elayne's shoulder and began to sob in earnest.

Zafer stood on the far side of the hall, his white turban gleaming in the dim light. He took an involuntary step forward, lifting his hand, then stopped. He looked up at Elayne, his dark eyes wide with question.

"They were cruel," she said briefly, holding Margaret's trembling shoulders. The girl turned her head, saw Zafer there, and put both her hands over her face. She shook her head violently and pulled away, hurrying to the farthest corner of the hall and turning her face to the wall. She huddled there as if she could hide from sight.

Zafer scowled. He held himself very straight as he bowed to Elayne, a little taller than she, but not as tall as his pirate lord. Then he waited.

"Il Corvo is still with Signor Morosini?" she asked.

"Aye, Your Grace," Zafer said. "I can have a message carried to him if you wish."

"Yes. You tell him that I have offended the Signora past redemption and await his further instructions," she said, with a light wave toward the closed doors behind her.

ELAYNE COULD NOT tell if he was displeased. He asked for no explanation, but she gave a stiff description of the Signora's denunciations of corrupt young ladies anyway, daring him to say she should have borne it. But she kept her chin lifted and avoided his eyes as she spoke, gripping her hands in her lap.

"She is a scourge of prostitutes, is she?" was all he said. He leaned down and flipped Elayne's veil over her face, then gave a quick a command to the pole-man of their gondola as they glided from the small river out into the teeming great canal, saying no more of their swift departure from the Case d'Morosini.

Elayne rearranged the folds of gauze so that she could see through the haze. She did not care for it; it obscured her vision and choked her breath in a way that she could not grow accustomed to, but she could comprehend that in Venice it was the proper attire for a modest woman. After the Signora's spiteful lecture, she did not care to be taken for an immodest woman here. Even if she was one.

Margaret still sat huddled, her head lowered and her face thoroughly hidden. She said nothing. Zafer stood behind her, in the rear of the little silk pavilion, his legs spread apart, his knee touching the maid's back with each rock of the slender vessel. Beyond the pirate, Dario also kept guard, his foot resting on the curved bow of the boat, his gaze sweeping over the passing quays.

Though she had known them but a few weeks, Elayne found an unlikely comfort in their little company. On the island she had thought it wicked of him to train up youths and children in his vile craft, but in the midst of this foreign city they seemed suddenly to form their own intimate band. None of them, Elayne knew, would scorn Margaret for her sins, and any one would spring to defend her safety with their life—as Margaret would do in return, if she could only manage to be quick enough with her poisoned cloak-pin. None of them would judge Elayne for the black desire she felt for their master, nor think it strange and sinful. They hardly knew what sin was, she thought. If he countenanced a thing, they would accept it.

Elayne greatly feared that she was learning to do the same.

"Come, I'll give you a turn around the sights of La Serenissima," Il Corvo said, as the gondola bumped gently ashore beside an imposing wooden drawbridge. A multitude of bells began to ring. Serene Venice was not so peaceful here: the gondolas vied for space at the quay and figures in long robes brushed past one another, men of light skin and dark, sloe-eyed faces of the east outnumbering the red

beards of Europeans; a hundred different colors in the
clothing and wildly diverse headdress. Many paused to pay
toll and then disappeared onto the covered bridge, their
footsteps creating a brisk rumble of sound on the wood, as
if the bells urged them to greater haste.

Somewhere to the north and west, across the flat islands
and the calm lagoon, lay the princedom of Monteverde.
Ever the uneasy ally of Venice—source of the famed
Venetian silver, guardian of the mountain passes; as Venice
sent her northern trade through Monteverde, the ships of
the green-and-silver sheltered in the lagoon and sailed in
the company of Venetian galleys to Constantinople and the
east. The hurried lessons in alliance and trade that Countess Melanthe had imparted to Elayne seemed more real
now. As Monteverde itself began to seem more real, and
more threatening, a storm just beyond sight, the sky darkening with menace on the horizon.

The Raven flipped a coin to the boatman as Dario helped
Elayne onto the mossy steps. She looked up through her
veil at a forest of peculiar chimneys towering above the arcaded facades, their tall, narrow necks crowned by upended
funnel pots, as if stone flowers raised their blossoms to the
sky.

The pirate took her hand, his thumb sliding across the
back of her palm. He bent his head close. "And are you in-
corruptible, my lady?" he asked beside her ear.

With so little, he set her to thinking of his body coupling
hers, hot thoughts in the public way, corrupt and lust-
haunted. She pulled away. He made a soft sound of amusement and put his arm at her back, guiding her into a
shadowed passage under the nearest building. Elayne had
to lift her veil to see where she was walking. The bustle of
the canal receded. The pavement and walls sweated damp-
ness, their surfaces stained black and green by mildew.
Footsteps echoed in the corridor as Margaret and the others
came behind.

They emerged from the quiet passage onto a small piazza lively with people. Elayne pulled the veil down over

her face again. She was glad of it now, glad that he could not possibly see that her lips parted, that she closed her eyes for an instant when he rested his hand deliberately on the curve of her back. To gain composure, she turned her look upon the arcades that lined two sides of the square, where knots of men gathered near carpet-covered counters, dealing loudly with one another.

The pirate stood a moment, his hand still on her, watching the trade at a table nearby. Amid bowls of gold and silver coins, the man wrote in a ledger while his assistant counted money into a triangular tray. He funneled the coins into a bag with a rush of silvery sound. Their patron lifted the bag high and turned with a shout, rushing toward another table to cast the coins down there.

Il Corvo smiled. He lifted his hand away from her. "The music and song of Venice," he said. "The island of Rialto."

Twelve

※

ELAYNE GAZED THROUGH her veil at the moneychangers. She had read of such in the Bible, of course, and once or twice perused, without much understanding, letters concerning matters of bullion and exchange from Italian merchants, passed along by Lady Melanthe for Elayne's further education. But the quick fingers and rattle of wood against metal, the open piles of gold spread across the Turkey carpets, the coins that moved so rapidly and assuredly from hand to hand, almost as if they had an end and will of their own—it was far more alive than the dry lists of silver rates and wheat prices she had read in the letters.

Two boys hurried past, pelting over the pavement with scraps of paper jutting from their caps. In one corner a half-dozen of armed guards gazed on the throng with narrowed eyes. A lady—unveiled—with a train longer than she was tall, moved across the center of the square, causing considerable hindrance to the traffic. She leaned on the arms of her maids, tottering strangely, as if she were on stilts. Over it all stood a plain church wall, inscribed with a cross and words in Latin. *Around this church may the merchant be fair, the weights just, and no false contract made.*

"Look you there, Margaret." Il Corvo glanced down at the shrouded maid and nodded toward the lady dragging her train step-by-step. "What profits that one, profits Signora Morosini."

"My lord?" Margaret asked in a small, muffled voice.

"Venice taxes her whores," he said, reverting to the French tongue. "Morosini makes the assessments and collections, and takes the first one-fourth for his trouble. I believe he sells most of the slave girls to the houses. It is a copious revenue."

Elayne drew a faint hiss. "Does she know?"

"The Signora? Doubtless she does not inquire. Let us pray that she's not too astonished when she finds herself immured alongside the other harlots in Hell."

The maid lifted her head a little. "I hope she may repent then, as I have," she said bravely.

"Indeed, we might have warned her of her danger ourselves, had we known!" Elayne said.

"Helas," the pirate said. "And abbreviated my very fruitful interview with Morosini even further, no doubt."

"Only for the sake of her immortal soul," Elayne murmured with innocence.

"Just let me collect my debt of him before you sink us entirely." He touched the empty sheath of his dagger and flicked his hand. Instantly Zafer and Dario moved, closing near as the pirate took Elayne's arm and started across the square.

He had chosen to dress simply, in a black tabard over voluminous sleeves of white. The sleeves swayed easily as he walked, nearly covering his hands. He nodded to the guards, who stared at them and received only thin-lipped replies. Elayne could not tell if they knew him, or only watched more closely because he was a stranger.

Their hard stares made her feel uneasy. As he paused before one of the tables and handed Dario a sealed document, Elayne's fingers tightened on his arm. She began to fear

that the guards' interest was more than a passing curiosity.
But the banker, a stout man with a fine fur cap, only looked
up from reading the document and gave Il Corvo a brief examination, bowing from the waist over his counter. "Good
day to you, Signor. You have a voucher from the Morosini?"

The pirate opened his palm. A large jasper bead, broken
in half, tumbled onto the rug.

The banker picked it up. He pulled a drawstring bag
from beneath his robe, shaking a little collection of shattered beads from inside. With a brief, skillful rotation of his
forefinger, he sorted out a black one, fitted it with the pirate's half, and nodded, satisfied. He barked an order to his
attendant, who ducked into the room behind and emerged
with a strongbox. Together they began to weigh bags and
count out the coin into bowls. As the golden piles grew,
several guards drifted closer. The crowd around them began
to thicken with onlookers.

Elayne was glad of her veil. She did not think she could
match the pirate's composure. Elayne had never handled
any money in her life, not even small coins—the amount of
gold that mounded up in neat stacks across the table was
unnerving. Finally a dozen fat sacks of coin stood waiting
on the rug. The banker looked up. "You are in agreement?"

The Raven requested them to empty one bag and weigh
out the coins again. The scale came up short by four
ounces.

The banker turned crimson. "My carelessness! I beg
your mercy." He quickly tossed three more coins onto the
scale, sending it tilting to the other side. "Niccolo! Transfer
only the demand from Morosini, and enter a debit of two
and a half from my own account into the ledger. My gravest
contrition, sir! Pray accept the gift, to amend my embar-
rassment. You are satisfied?"

Il Corvo gave the attendant a look that lasted just long
enough to make the man stand back, with his hands open
and well-removed from the bags. The crowd about them
quieted expectantly.

"I accept the tally," the pirate said.

An audible sound of relief stirred among the onlookers. Before the banker poured from his funnel tray into the bag, Il Corvo took a generous amount into his own purse, counting aloud to two hundred as he slid the gleaming gold across the table, coin by coin. With the rest of the money bagged, he nodded at Dario. The youth quickly began to tie the leather sacks together. He fashioned them into a pair of slings and handed one to Zafer, hefting the other over his shoulder with a grunt.

"You require escort, Signor?" the guard captain asked.

The Raven stood back. "Accompany them, if you will," he said. "I have further business."

The captain bowed his head and set about assigning his men. Elayne would have been pleased to return to the galley along with the coin and a pair of stout guards, but the pirate caught her elbow when she started after Margaret and the others.

"Let us take the air, *carissima*," he murmured softly. Elayne's limbs went weak at the timbre of his voice. After the weeks of distance, his every touch now seemed fuel to the flame between them.

Margaret turned back, too, but he gestured for the maid to continue. She paused, then took two steps back toward Elayne. "But—should I not remain with my lady?"

"Do not question me," he said coldly. "Your service is not required."

The girl drew in a sharp breath, curtsied deeply, and hurried after Dario and Zafer, holding her arms crossed under her breasts. She had begun on the ship to wean her babe, but Elayne knew that after the entire morning away, she must be in some fretfulness to return.

"That was unkind," Elayne said, trying to keep her voice steady. She took a step away from him. "She meant to do well."

"Which is more than I can say of you, beloved," he said, leaning close. He brushed his body against hers, so lightly and hotly, a touch of his thigh at her hip, a dark presence at her shoulder. "If I order you not to look at that man beside the second column there, in the white tunic and gray cap, will you stare at him only to gainsay me?"

Elayne found herself looking toward the man he described, unable to help herself.

"Well done!" he murmured. "Nothing could be more fatally obvious." He lifted his hand, as if he were pointing out an item of notable decoration on one of the buildings. "Now fathom, that you can look five paces to his right, without turning your head. Don't nod."

She bit her lip, checking herself from doing exactly that.

"Green hose, red slippers. When you see him, take my hand."

Without moving her head, she slid her glance to the right. Though the veil colored everything to a dim haze, she saw a young man in green hose and scarlet slippers with long, pointed toes. He talked animatedly with a banker, rubbing one foot up and down the other leg. She lifted her hand and slipped it into the pirate's palm. His fingers locked with hers, closing swiftly.

"Who are they?" she whispered anxiously.

"I have no notion," he said, lifting her hand and pressing it to his lips, smiling down at her in such a way that it seemed he could see right through the veil.

Elayne snatched her hand away. "I thought there was some danger."

"Of course," he said, "there are three of the Riata hounds watching us right now. But they will be dead by Vespers, so do not concern yourself."

She closed her eyes and opened them. "Benedicite."

He turned and began to stroll across the square, smiling pleasantly, as if they were lovers in a garden. "I knew you would not like it. I almost didn't tell you."

"Not like it!" she said faintly.

"You see that I was not so unkind to Margaret," he said. "It's not my gold they want."

"What do they want?" she breathed.

"They want my death. They want you in their power. They will have neither. It is them or us, beloved."

Elayne made a little moan. She could not believe she was promenading in a public street, hearing such things.

They had crossed the piazza and reached another shadowed passage that passed under a building; a damp, black tunnel with an arch of brilliant light at the far end. Even Elayne could see that it would make an excellent trap. She wanted to protest his firm hold on her arm, steering her toward the passageway, but she feared now to make any move outside his guidance.

She stepped under the decaying archway. An odor of fish wafted from it, growing stronger as she moved forward. Through the veil, she could see almost nothing. She kept walking toward the arch of light at the other end. A figure was silhouetted there for a moment. With an echoing shuffle, the person came toward them. Elayne tensed. The Raven kept walking. They passed, with a brief word of greeting on both sides.

He paused, turning toward her. He lifted her veil and looked down at her, his face lit faintly from the side. He was the only thing she could see. With a light push, he moved her back, and she realized there was a stairway behind her now instead of solid wall.

He smiled, resting his arms about her. "A kiss, *carissima*," he said aloud, pushing the veil back and leaning to her mouth. He breathed lightly against her skin, not quite touching her. She could not comprehend that he wished to make love to her now—here—in this dank, public passage with his enemies lying in wait. But he kissed her, his fingers closing on her arms, his lips hard and quick as the pulse rose in her throat. Someone else passed them with a discomfited mumble of salutation. From the corner of her eye, she could see more pedestrians at either end, black outlines against the strong light.

"They are coming," he muttered beside her ear. "Scream loudly when it happens."

Elayne's breath stuck in her throat. He kissed her again,

blocking all her air, holding her from turning her head to see anything.

"Courage, Elena," he whispered against her skin, and suddenly flung her back hard.

She felt herself fall, tripping backward on the step. He vanished from her sight and sound as she went down on the stone stairs with a painful yelp. She heard a scuffle of feet, a loud crack and a heavy thud, as if a thick branch had broken. There was another shuffle, a sound like a deep hissing gurgle. Then nothing more.

Breathing frantically, she held frozen, her hands on the slippery steps, staring into blackness.

"Scream, curse you!" he muttered from somewhere in front of her. His sleeve made a dim flash. He reached for her, his face and hands pale in the dark.

Elayne's throat worked. Only a faint high-pitched squeak would come out.

"Thief!" he bellowed, his unexpected roar discharging a thunder of echoes in the passageway. He pulled her upright into the passage. *"Thief! Help! Robbery!"* Then he squeezed her arm. "Will you scream?" he muttered.

She tried. She wanted to. Over the fish-market scent she could smell fresh blood; she felt something wet and slimy squelch beneath her feet. When her toe touched a form, heavy and lifeless, she gave another huffing squeak. The pirate made an exasperated sound.

"Thief!" he shouted. "Here! Help us!"

An invasion of people at the entrance blocked the arch of light. Their raised voices added to the echoes, creating a confused din. He put his arm around her shoulders in the disorder, walking her toward the entrance through the incoming throng of excited people. She was bumped and pushed in the dark, but finally they broke out into the light again. It seemed everyone in the square was crowding toward the passageway, craning their necks to see.

"They cut my purse!" the pirate shouted angrily. He held Elayne very close as attention turned toward them. "Tried to carry off my wife! God curse their souls! What evil is this in Venice?"

Shouts came from inside the passageway, cries of murder. People craned their necks. Orders and scuffles filled the damp air as the crowd inside began to back up, making way for men struggling to bear a body out.

Elayne stared. She had never seen the man before. He wore simple clothes of black, soaked to his waist with blood. His arms dragged limp across the pavement, his head bumped. Blood steeped his beard and flowed in a river of crimson from his throat.

She put her hand over her mouth, trying not to retch.

"I know him!" someone exclaimed, pointing at the bearded man. "Marco, he is called."

"He's dead!" another cried, as if no one could tell it.

"Who killed him?"

"It was a robbery."

"Go after them! Is the guard after them? Don't let them escape!"

"Nay, they're killed. Look, they're killed!" Another gap opened by the passageway. They pulled a second body into the light. He had no blood on him, but he was dead, his mouth lolling open, his lifeless eyes staring at the roof of the porch.

"Those are the robbers? Are the robbers still loose?"

"He says they robbed him! Abducted his wife!"

"Stay by your banks! Don't leave the counters!" someone shouted. The crowd washed back, leaving some space as a few hurried away toward their tables.

Someone caught the sleeve of the guard captain as he came out of the passage behind his men. "It's not murder. They were vagabonds. I saw them watching this Signor withdraw his gold!"

"They tried to seize his wife!"

"Murder! They've been murdered!"

"They're thieves. They're not of Venice."

Amid a general clamor that the dead men were Genoese, or Pisanos, or possibly Neapolitans, the captain shook off his eager informants, as if it were no fresh news to him that they were foreigners. He looked up at Elayne and the Raven. "Your gentle wife is unharmed?" he asked.

The pirate turned Elayne in his arms, lifting her veil and holding her back from him a little. "You are not hurt?" he asked warmly.

At the edge of his jaw, there was a drop of blood clinging to his skin. She pulled away, freeing herself. "You killed them." Her voice came out like a bird's peep. "You killed both of them."

He gave a slight shrug, as if the mention of it embarrassed him. "By the grace of God. It seems that I did."

"You had no aid, Signor?" the captain asked incredulously. "No man at your side?"

"I sent my attendants back with the money and your guards, Captain. They will be at the quay by the Grain Office."

The guard captain frowned. He held up a long knife, covered in gore. "This is yours?"

"Nay. I have no license. I deposited my weapons at the Customs this morn." He scowled down at the bodies. "Had I not wrenched it from that fellow, it would be in my heart, and my wife—the saints only can say where she would be by now."

The onlookers murmured and sputtered, not a few in disbelief. The pirate drew her veil over her face again. As he pulled her close, against her resistance, she felt his fingers slide up under the gauze and press against the skin of her throat. It hurt. It made her heart beat dizzily in her head. She tried to protest and wrench away, but to her horror a swift darkness was rising in her brain. From a distance she heard him speaking to her, as if he were not stifling the very pulse in her throat himself. "Madam, are you well? Are you—"

The next she knew, the darkness opened to the hard pavement under her shoulder and a multitude of feet in her hazy vision. The pirate was bent over her, cradling her head.

"Move away!" he snapped as the crowd pressed in. "Move back!"

Elayne sat up, aided by many hands. She struggled for air through the veil, bewildered, trying to remember who she was and where.

"Take her to the church!" the guard captain said.

"Nay, let me take her to my galley," the Raven said, kneeling beside her. "She's half-dead with fright. Escort us, keep me in your eye, but let her be made comfortable. Then I'll return with you to make a deposition."

"Well enough," the captain said. He turned. "Who has the Signor's purse? Count the coins. What should be in it, sir?"

"Two hundred ducats!" several voices chorused at once.

"Two hundred," the pirate agreed dryly. He looked up at the wall of the church across the square. "Let it be given to San Giacomo, in thanks for our deliverance, and restitution for my soul."

ELAYNE RUBBED HER throat, still trying to piece together what had happened. Her neck was sore and bruised from his fingers. Inside the stuffy little cabin on the galley, Margaret fluttered about her, trying to apply compresses which Elayne removed as soon as the maid pressed them to her forehead. The pup grabbed the cloths from her fingers and shook them vigorously, flinging drops of rose water into every corner of the small space, which made Margaret's baby laugh and struggle in its swaddling. Matteo stood at the portal, his fingers curled anxiously about the ragged curtain as he held it open.

"I am not faint," Elayne said for the tenth time as the maid tore yet another strip of cloth to soak. Her voice was hoarse. "I am perfectly well."

"Yes, Your Grace," Margaret said, soaking the cloth in her bowl of rose water and stubbornly wringing the cotton to fold again.

Elayne wiped a drop from her eyebrow. They had taken

away her blood-soaked shoes, but even attar of roses could not seem to cleanse the smell of butchery from her nostrils. "He is a demon," she said.

"Yes, Your Grace," Margaret replied, lifting the compress to Elayne's forehead.

"I can't live this way," Elayne said, pulling off the cloth and resting back on the pillows. "I refuse to do it."

"Yes, ma'am." The maid nipped her compress from Elayne's fingers before the pup could steal it and prepared to soak the cloth again. Nimue bounded out onto the galley's deck, looking for easier game.

"Margaret!" Elayne cried faintly. "He killed those men. In the dark. He could not even see them!"

"Yes, Your Grace. I am so glad."

Elayne sat up. "As if they were brute animals. As if it were no more than slaughtering pigs."

"They were pigs, my lady. Riata pigs."

Matteo dropped his wide-eyed gaze and looked down at his toes. He stepped back and let the curtain fall closed.

"But—in the dark," Elayne said, staring after him at the swaying drape. "Two of them. He had no weapon."

Margaret put the compress to her forehead again. "Do you lie down, my lady, please."

"He told me he was a manslayer," Elayne said, closing her eyes.

"My lord is very skilled," Margaret said. "Zafer says he can kill anyone he pleases, Your Grace, no matter how well-guarded they believe themselves to be."

"God shield." Elayne slumped back on the pillows. Rose water dripped down into her eyes. While she had been craving his touch, dreaming of his kisses, he had been planning how he would cut a man's throat. He had choked her pulse until she swooned, there in front of a hundred people, and none had seemed to know the difference. "He is a demon."

"Yes, Your Grace," Margaret said.

"And he has bewitched the whole lot of you!" she exclaimed. "I believe he can make the entire city believe he killed those men because they tried to rob us."

"I pray so, Your Grace." The maid's brow creased. "I pray so."

Elayne plucked off the compress. "What would they do to a plain murderer?" she asked the ceiling of the cabin.

"A murderer would be hanged, I think, Your Grace."

"Hanged and beheaded and drawn and quartered," Elayne said.

Margaret stopped soaking the cloth in the rose water. She made a little frightened whimper. Elayne stared at the planks above her. He had caressed her that way, made her tremble with desire for him, in full knowledge of what was to come. She thought of the long bloody knife and felt a furious revulsion in her throat. She could hardly say if she was more terrified for him, or of him.

She sat up. "Do not fear." She dipped both hands in the bowl and splashed cold water over her face. "They won't execute him," she said angrily. "They could not. They can't kill one of Satan's own fiends."

HE RETURNED IN the night. Elayne sat on the stern of the galley, hooded and cloaked in the cool air, watching a great harvest moon rise over the domes of San Marco and the glimmering roll of the water. She did not hear him come aboard; she only heard Dario's soft salute, in between the magician's snores, and a stir in the water below the ship as a gondola poled away.

Against the huge moon she saw his silhouette, moving over the cabin and rigging like a cat over rooftops. He landed silently on the deck before her. Elayne exhaled deeply, feeling as if she had been holding her breath for hours.

"The third Riata will not trouble us," he murmured.

"You have killed him, too?" she said. "What a comfort."

She could not see his face, only feel the warmth of his body near her in the night air. The Egyptian's snoring filled the silence.

"Drowned," he said after a moment.

Elayne folded her fingers tightly in her lap. She could feel his bridal ring press into her bone.

"Did they accept your deposition?" she asked at length.

"In large part. They could not believe I had no weapon on me. The Quarentia voted to banish me from Venice for a month, as a precaution. But I have a day's grace to absent myself."

"Fortunate," she said. "Just enough time to drown someone."

He leaned against the rail beside her, a blacker shape against the black night. "Elena. You did well."

"Grant mercy. Of course I am glad to satisfy you with my conduct."

"Even if you didn't scream."

"I never scream. I merely swoon when I am strangled."

He paused. "I regret that," he said. "I ask your pardon."

"Why should you? I am at your service to poison or throttle as you please, am I not?"

"I will not do it again," he said. "I swear."

"Ah, now I will sleep easy."

"You're angry," he said. He touched her cheek with his knuckles. His hand seemed warm against the damp breeze off the water. "My hell-cat."

"Don't call me that."

"She-wolf," he said.

"Demon!" she hissed.

"Aye. Ex-communicate and unshriven, too," he added. "Unless two hundred ducats can buy me relief."

She shivered in the night air. Margaret's babe began to cry, a muffled sound inside the cabin. It wept and then quieted at the maid's soft hushing.

"We must leave now," he said. "This galley will sail east at dawn, with Zafer and the others. You and I go west, under darkness, as fast as we can travel. Can you ride?"

"Yes," she said.

She did not move. He stood beside her. She thought of his hand at her back, the heat of his body so close to her in the Rialto. She hated the desire that rose in her yet, at his very presence. Silence fell again between them.

A great silence, a dark silence.

"Are you afraid of me?" he whispered.

Elayne rose. She pulled her cloak closer about her shoulders and turned away, leaving him in the dark.

Thirteen

SHE MUST FIND a priest, she thought. There was but one answer now. She could not go home; she could not live in such a manner; she could not go to Melanthe or Lancaster or Raymond. She had never been a devoted admirer of the clergy, the reproving deans and plump-fingered rectors who had come to dine on eels and venison at Savernake, but she could not turn now to anyone but the church.

They left Venice behind far across the lagoon, its domes and walls a black mass like a lion crouched upon the waters in the moonlight. The clouds towered up overhead, tumbled radiance, glowing at the edges with the silvery light. Morosini's man poled along a muddy bank, where there seemed to be naught but reeds and waterfowl making sleepy hoots in the darkness. Elayne said nothing. She let the pirate direct her. He meant them to travel by land; surely they would sojourn at some monastery—but then she was not certain if a man ex-communicate from the church would be suffered to remain in a house of God. But somewhere, soon enough, she would find someone ordained, and tell him she was abducted, and throw herself on the mercy of the church.

She could not live with him. The lies and ravishment, the study of poison and murder, the children left behind without mercy—all of that, she had borne, carried along on the tide of his will, drawn by his mystery, entranced by the way he moved and the thoughts he dared to entertain. Her other choices had seemed vague and distant, only leading to worse fates.

But she saw clearly now. She must get away from him. He killed so easily, so naturally, without mercy or regret. He lied as if angels commanded his tongue. It was his nature, as the leopard would stalk the nightmare forest and strike when it pleased. And a part of Elayne—a deep, hidden, wild and dreadful part of her—reached toward him. A part of her wanted to take that power to herself.

In truth, it was terrifying, the desire she felt for him. She was as blinded and besotted as Margaret and the rest. She had to get away.

The boatman bent to his pole, holding them against a low bank where reeds bowed and whispered in the night breeze. The Raven jumped onto the bank. Elayne stepped out as the boat tilted precariously. Her leather boots sank a little, water pooling around them.

A silent ostler brought two horses forward, their hooves making sucking noises in the soft mire. Elayne could only discern their size and outline—a stallion, she guessed, and a palfrey with a white blaze. The familiar smell and warmth of their big bodies permeated the damp air.

The pirate looked at her. He had changed into finer clothing, a dark houppelande and white shoulder cape with long indigo dags. He wore a hat like a hunter's, the folded point pulled down over his face, but she could see the line of his cheekbone; the shadowed curve of his mouth. Behind him, luminous clouds and sky glowed with midnight blue and silver brilliance. The light gave him form and substance, the graceful shape of her murderous angel of the dark. She hugged her arms around herself and turned, trying to give nothing of her thoughts away.

She had but a simple plan. Find a church, find a cleric. It seemed that it must be painted upon her forehead in burning letters. He stayed near her while the ostler threw saddlebags over the horses. She could feel his attention on her.

He had asked if she could ride. She could ride near anything, and had done it at Savernake, from the feral colts to the half-tamed breeding studs.

The ostler stood holding the smaller palfrey. The pirate reached for the stallion's saddle and put his foot into the stirrup without hesitation, without even testing the animal's girth. The big horse stood tense, head lifted, its eyes rolling white in the dimness.

Elayne paused, listening to the stallion's uncertain huffs, a sound that proclaimed it was ready to stand but happy to bolt given the smallest pretext. In the moonlight it began to turn, spinning in a circle, the hoofbeats growing more rapid and uneven. Il Corvo, the terror of the Middle Sea, hopped on one foot as the horse circled faster. He dragged on the reins. The stallion stepped aside, throwing its head in the air, its hindquarters coiled for an explosion.

Too late, the ostler lunged for the animal's bridle. Moonlight gleamed on the stallion's haunches and shoulders as it reared. Only the pirate's quick balance kept him from falling as he kicked free of the stirrup and landed on one leg, his dagged shoulder cape fanning out wildly. He bumped up against Elayne as he caught himself.

"Hang Morosini," he muttered. "One of his whores would be easier to mount."

Elayne chewed her lip. She moved back a little, reached down in the darkness, and pulled her back hem between her legs, knotting the silk shift up to her waist with a quick loop that she had made a thousand times. "I know a little of horses," she said. "I think you alarm him."

"Is it so?" the pirate asked dryly. "We are of one mind, then. He alarms me."

"Perchance . . ." She took a step forward, then back, not

wanting to appear overconfident. "I could try. If the man will hold him while I mount."

"And break your neck, my lady? Why would I allow that?"

"You are anxious of him," she said, rather than declare the truth outright—that he was evidently nothing of a horseman. "He senses it. I don't think he will be unruly with me."

He stood silent, looking at the horse. "You brought no other mount?" he asked the ostler.

"Nay, signor," the man said uneasily. "I was not told to bring another. Two good horses, steady and fast, for a gentleman and a lady, I was told."

"Steady!" Il Corvo said. "Bah."

"He is not often disobedient, signor," the ostler muttered.

Il Corvo snorted. "How long to bring another?"

"In haste—I might be back by Matins, signor."

The Raven made a sound of disgust.

Elayne gave a little shrug. "Let us wait for a gentler mount, then, if it wounds your pride that I might do it better."

He blew air through his teeth. "Oh, I am certain that you can ride him the better. Anyone could. God curse Morosini. We cannot stay till dawn. If this evil creature harms you, I'll see the man in Hell."

SHE COULD HAVE mounted from the ground, but she let the ostler help her. The horse stiffened under her, waiting for a reason to object. She gave him none, and after a moment the animal heaved a sigh and lowered its head.

In the dark the palfrey stood patiently as the pirate swung himself into the saddle. She could see the black stretches of the marsh and his silhouette clearly in the light of the great moon as it hung near to setting. The palfrey's white blaze nodded as the horse champed its bit. Elayne suspected the pirate was beleaguering the animal's reins for no good reason, but it bore his interference tolerantly. It ap-

peared to be a good mount for a green rider. She hoped it
was just such a sturdy slug, even though the ostler claimed
it had some speed.

"This track will lead you to the canal-side, signor," the
ostler said. "There is a road along the bank."

The palfrey's bit jingled as Il Corvo clucked to the animal, shaking the reins. It broke into a sedate trot down the
only path visible in the night. Her stallion followed willingly, a steady thump of hooves in the sandy muck.

Elayne had no notion of where they were or where they
were going. She could see smooth, silvery expanses of
water out across the flats, and the lumps and shapeless contours of vegetation beside the track. The moonlit clouds
shed such radiance that the horizon was a sharp black
boundary between sky and land. In some places she thought
she discerned the mass of a hut or a weir, or even the towers of a distant town, but she could not be certain what they
were. It seemed an empty place, given only to the night
breeze and the water.

It was so bright under the full moon that she could see a
tuft of downy white caught on the thumb of her glove.
Nimue had barked and cried, scrabbling to climb over the
railing as their boat had pulled away from the ship. Elayne
had not even been able to say a real goodbye to the pup. Or
to Margaret and her baby, or Matteo, or any of them. She
had not dared.

She rolled the white puff of hair in her fingers, and then
pushed it inside her glove. The sudden moisture in her eyes
magnified the horizon for an instant. She caught a clear
glimpse of a tower in the distance before she blinked and it
became a blur again.

The path widened to a cart track, pale marks between the
windswept reeds. A meandering canal gleamed between
low banks. Just ahead, the palfrey paced kindly along, following the road. The horse was a true ambler; a fine
smooth-gaited mount that even the pirate ought to bestride
with small discomfort, the sort of horse that Sir Guy would
have been proud to offer to Lady Melanthe for traveling.

Elayne did not intend to keep to an amble. Her heart beat harder as she realized she was gathering herself; the stallion responded immediately with a lifting of his back, coiling under her.

She gave a little false shriek, digging her heels into the animal's barrel at the same time that she dragged back on the reins. He danced in protest. She begged silent pardon of the confused beast, driving him again, and again, still holding him back on taut reins until he twisted and reared in frustration.

Elayne made an effort to scream. It came out as a yelp, but she hauled the horse around, prodding him cruelly again as his forefeet hit the ground. He squealed in anger. She sat back as she felt him duck his head. His body rose under her, a buck and hard kick. She rode the jerking motion twice, then saw the track and the palfrey standing before her. She released the tight reins.

The stallion sprang forward. She managed a resemblance of a frightened shriek. It bucked again, aimed a kick at the palfrey as the other horse shied hard away, and began to run.

She leaned forward, letting the reins slip through her fingers. The horse moved powerfully under her. She could not see more than the faint double track between silhouettes of weeds, the black lumps of hedges that vanished from the corners of her eyes. The wind tugged at her hood as the stallion's stride lengthened, his hooves pounding on solid ground now, his great body coursing forward in familiar rhythm.

Night air rushed past. She let the horse have full rein as it stretched into a true gallop. She put her hands against its muscled neck and let its cadence and power bear her blindly into the night. She felt suddenly freed, as if she might ride forever, as if the stallion were a magic beast that could fly across mountain and water to carry her home.

At the moment of that willful thought, the horse surged ahead. The gallop that had been free and wild suddenly transformed. The stallion began to drive in earnest, flinging its forelegs out into an enormous stride, ears pinned back, body flattened into the hammering stroke of a horse in full charge. She could hear the drum of hooves behind them—the palfrey bolting, too, and fast. Startlingly fast, for an ambler with a poor rider. In an instant of guilty exhilaration, she knew that the pirate must have fallen off as the stallion plunged past them, and freed his horse to sprint at speed.

The palfrey came on with incredible swiftness even as the stallion's gallop hurled her through the night. She spared a glance over her shoulder, wind and mane beating at her cheek, thinking to see the horse riderless against the bright horizon. With a heart-deep spurt of alarm, she realized it was not.

In the other cart track the palfrey pursued them like a horse out of Hell itself, the moonlight gleaming on its blaze as it drew even with the stallion's hindquarters. Wind tore her hood from her head, sending her hair lashing around her face. The stallion increased its effort as the palfrey challenged it, pulling forward while the track curved and the bushes hurtled past, their branches whipping her leg. She could discern that someone rode it, but she could not believe it was a man who did not even know how to mount.

He was a wizard. The idea seized her. Sorcery it seemed, as the palfrey's breath blew hot on her knee, as the lighter horse overtook them in spite of the stallion's exertion. With sudden terror she urged the stallion to greater speed in its wild race into blackness, but the palfrey gave no ground. It drew even with her shoulders as she bent over the stallion's neck.

Through blurry eyes she chanced a look aside and saw the pirate nearly abreast of her. In the darkness the palfrey's reins flew free; its rider was a black shape, one hand gripped in the horse's mane, half-standing and half-suspended from the saddle at a blood-chilling angle that seemed impossible to maintain as he reached toward her.

"Do not do it!" she screamed, realizing that he meant to grab her rein. "Do not!" In an instant all thought of sorcery vanished. He had no concept of what would happen if he succeeded. He was riding on will and dexterity, barely holding to his seat.

The horses hurtled together down the uneven road. There was no stopping the palfrey—it was one of those beasts that lived to race, to stay ahead, and the stallion flung itself into the contest. Both horses were beyond control now; a tiny stumble would send them down in a bone-breaking tangle. She hid her face in the stinging mane, praying that they could see their way at such speed. When the pirate reached again for her rein, she struck out at his arm.

"Lunatic!" she cried. He grabbed her elbow, as if that could stop her. She felt him drag her down as he lost his balance. "Let go!" she screamed, jerking free by throwing her weight to the other side. The move sent the stallion into a wild collision with the palfrey; as she nearly lost her seat she felt the heavy jolt and rebound. The palfrey swerved out of the track and made a leap, clearing black reeds.

For an instant he held on. In the moonlight she saw the arch of the horse's neck, saw the pirate grab mane with both hands, and then the animal hit the ground, throwing him free. In a flash of half-seen motion in the dark, he went down between them.

He was gone, left behind before she could even realize it. With no unwieldy weight on its back, the palfrey plunged full ahead, but in the universal manner of horses, it quickly seemed to realize that it only wanted to stay by the stallion instead of bolting past.

She could feel her mount flag. Elayne let it slow at its own will, paced exactly by the palfrey. The horses dropped to a trot. All of them, including Elayne, were breathing with explosive huffs. The stallion's ribs expanded and contracted between her legs as it fell into a walk.

She took the palfrey's reins. It halted willingly, a plain, gentle horse that reached over to nibble at a weed between pants, its mad race forgotten already. No trace of magic clung to it, no hint of the extraordinary speed that had overtaken the stallion's lead. She could feel her mount's exhaustion, but the palfrey seemed merely a little sweaty in the cool night air.

Elayne turned the animals, looking back down the cart

track. She could see nothing but the black marshland under the moonlight. A deep shivering possessed her. For a moment she could not seem to find her breath at all. She pressed her hands down on the saddle-bow and bent her head, trying to overcome the tardy wave of faintness.

It was certain he would be injured, if not killed. He was a great fool, a murderer, and agile beyond measure, to have held on as long as he had. She had no sympathy for him. She wanted to escape him. Over her shoulder the steeple was clear now in the distance. She was free, with sanctuary within her grasp.

She moaned, twisting the stallion's mane around her fingers. She closed her eyes, willing herself to turn and leave him there.

She opened them. "Damn you!" she whispered. "God curse you. What have you done to me?"

She drew a trembling breath and began to walk the horses slowly back along the track.

She found him at a clump of reeds, the sand around him gleaming with pale, deep scars from the horses' hooves. He lay halfway on the cart track, his shoulder lifted as he supported himself on one elbow.

Elayne dismounted. He rolled onto his hands and knees, then stood. He swayed, not seeming to see that she was there, and went down to his knees.

She watched him as he lowered his head over the ground. She knew that sensation from many a hard fall—the wind knocked from her chest and a wave of sickness in her throat.

"Don't try to rise," she said.

He lifted his head abruptly, saw her, and then leaned again over his hands splayed in the sand. His nose was bleeding. He gulped air. "You are not—hurt," he said, between gasps.

"Not I. Are you?"

He did not reply. She waited. After a few moments he sat back on his heels, putting his hand to his temple. He was panting softly. "Not—skilled—with horses."

"Verily!" she snapped. "You near slayed us both."

He looked up at her then, his face a little angled, squinting, as if it were an effort to focus upon her. He tried to stand again, and failed. *"Che cazzo,"* he said coarsely, and collapsed to one knee.

"Lie down," she said. "I believe your head was struck."

"Aye," he said, and tried to stand again.

Elayne dropped the horses' reins to the ground and went to him. "Lie down, you great fool." She pulled off her mantle and made a pillow of it, kneeling in the damp sand.

He resisted her, taking a reeling step. He reached for the palfrey's reins and leaned against the horse's shoulder, his face in its mane. His hand groped for the stirrup. As Elayne watched, he sank slowly to the ground beside the palfrey's leg.

She made a sound of vexation and went to him, leading the horse a few steps aside, where it was happy to graze on the marsh grass. The pirate was dead to awareness as she pulled off her cloak, but he came awake again, wincing, while she arranged it beneath his head.

Elayne pulled the laces of his cape open at the throat. "What did you think you were about?" she said angrily. "Did you think you could stop me?"

He closed his eyes and opened them. A lock of his loosened hair lay across his forehead, trailing over his bloodied nose and down his cheek. "Save you," he murmured.

"Save me!" she cried. "Depardeu. *Save* me!"

"Bolt," he said between his white teeth. "Vile . . . beast."

"He wasn't bolting with me."

"He wasn't?" he mumbled, in the meekest tone she had ever heard from him.

"No," she said fiercely.

"Flaming hell," he said, and closed his eyes.

THE PIRATE INSISTED upon traveling onward. Against her strong counsel, he had managed to mount, hauling himself onto the long-suffering palfrey by the power of will alone, for his body seemed to prefer the ground. She did not think another man would have been able to stand at all. In the early light there was blood smeared all across his perfect nose and lips. His cape was full of dirt and his eyes were turning blackened. He had lost his headgear, and his dark hair tumbled loose and tangled down his back. He looked like an escaped prisoner from the Abyss.

As dawn came up behind them, a silvery haze obscured the horizon and the steeple tower. She led the palfrey at a slow pace along the bank of the canal, watching the light spread gray and green color to the reeds. He was too unsteady to do more than hold on, but the sluggish progress greatly displeased him, as he made known in the most crude language, muttering low words in French and Italian and tongues she had never heard before. Often enough he put his head down on the palfrey's neck and lifted it again, looking about as if he did not fathom where he was. He asked her once why they were riding, and seemed to have forgotten that he had arranged for the horses himself.

She knew he had money and bread and papers in the stallion's saddlebags; she had searched them. She could have trotted away and left him now, with ease. The steeple had begun to resolve itself from the morning mist; she saw that it was not a church at all, but a small tower with a broken windmill at the peak. Salt ponds gleamed flat and white under the rising sun.

She halted the horses, brushing back her loosened hair. Strain and lack of sleep dulled her mind. She had hoped for a religious house, or at least a village large enough to have a priest. Though when she envisioned her plea—that she had been abducted by a man who could hardly lift his head and speak sensibly—it now seemed a feeble claim.

She ought to leave him. The saltworks appeared long deserted, the thatched roofs of a cluster of huts falling to ruin at the base of the windmill.

"Let us rest here," she said, turning in the saddle.

"No," the Raven said, his hand in the palfrey's mane. "No. We press on."

She looked at him. "You are in no case to ride."

"I can ride," he said grimly.

With a flick, she threw the palfrey's reins over its head and dismounted. "Ride, then. I must rest."

She led the stallion toward the windmill, guiding him between overgrown bushes. Little white castles of salt grew in the flats, like tiny fortresses scattered over the pale mud. The sluice carried only a trickle of water, its wooden gate crusted closed by glittering crystals of brine. She prodded with her toe at a lead salt pan lying overturned beside the sluice gate.

"We cannot tarry," the pirate said. "We must make our rendezvous."

She looked back. He was gazing toward the east, frowning vaguely at the distance. If he was to meet someone, she must leave him and find a refuge before it happened.

"Rendezvous?" she asked. "When is it?"

"Morosini did not tell you?" He looked around and blinked. "We are on the lagoon."

"He told me nothing," she said.

Under his slack reins, the palfrey took a step and reached down to lip at grass. "You brought us here," he said, with a faint insistence.

"Nay," she said. "You brought us. When is this meeting to be? Where?"

He wet his lips. He stared at her. Then he tilted back his head and laughed dizzily. "I cannot remember when." He shook his head in wonder. "I know not where!"

He looked about as if the answer might lie in the reeds or the misty horizon. In the early light he was apparition enough to inspire nightmares with his bruised visage. "We took wine—he was to arrange for it. . . ." He blew a sharp breath and groaned. "I recall nothing else."

"It must be the fall," she said. "Your head is shaken."

"My head is like to combust." He held his gloved palm over one eye and slid his fingers carefully down his blood-ied face. "Christus. I fell?" He seemed uncertain even of that, making a grimacing frown at the palfrey. "From this animal?"

"Indeed. And you will fall from it again, do you not give yourself a moment's succor."

"I don't remember." He drew a deep breath. "But no matter. I can ride on."

Elayne opened a saddlebag, drew out a loaf of bread and a flagon, and sat down on the overturned salt pan. She did not know why she even lingered with him, but that she was a besotted fool. Even with his eye blackened and swollen, he looked like an angel that had fallen down some rock-strewn cliff to earth.

"Ride on to where?" she asked, breaking the loaf. There was enough provision in the bags that she could guess the intended destination was at least a day's ride distant, but she made no mention of it.

He leaned forward and dismounted, standing with his hand on the palfrey's shoulder for a moment to steady himself. Then he pulled off his gloves and unlaced the bags behind the horse's saddle. He searched through them, reading each paper one by one.

He left the palfrey grazing with its reins about its ears and came to the stallion that waited stolidly beside Elayne. When he had finished examining the contents of the stallion's saddlebags, he gave a curse and sat down heavily beside her, dusting and flicking at the mud-smeared hunter's hat she had recovered from the ground.

"Nothing useful," he said. "I would not have written down such a thing."

Elayne stood up and retrieved the palfrey's reins before the horse stepped on them. She untied its fetters from where they hung on the saddle-bow and bent to secure the animal's forefeet.

"Nay," he said as she released the grateful palfrey's girth. "We cannot stay so long here."

"If you know not where you mean to go, then let them rest and eat." Elayne pulled the saddle free and loosed the horse to graze. The pirate said no more as she released the

stallion also to his hobbles. He watched her. She sat down
again on the salt pan, the only accommodation available beyond the muddy ground.

"You know something of horses," he said.

She tore off a bite of bread, well aware of his dirty sleeve
brushing her arm, his soft boots, his knee bent close to hers.
"More than you, 'twould seem." She did not look at his
face, uncertain if he would remember or recognize her design to flee from him in the dark.

"It appears docile enough," he said, watching the grazing horses. "Did it vault me off, the wretched animal?"

She let her hood fall forward, shielding her. "Yes, I think
so. I did not see."

He tapped her leg with his knee. "You are a poor liar,
beloved. What happened in truth?"

Elayne bit her lip, glancing down at where his knee
rested against the folds of her knotted skirt. She brushed
down the hem of her green surcoat to cover several inches
of bare stocking and her garter that showed above her boot.
"The stallion ran away with me. You came after and tumbled from your mount when you reached to stop us."

"Is that so?" he said vaguely.

Elayne pushed back her mantle and ate a piece of dry
bread. She offered him the rest of the loaf. Sitting so close
beside him, he did not seem inhuman, not the devil's spawn
she had been certain he must be. He seemed a man, be-
grimed and bruised, hazy-eyed as he watched the horizon
and broke plain bread with her. On his thigh there was a
long streak of grass stain and mud. He touched his face
again, running the pads of his fingers over his blackened
eye and his swollen temple, frowning a little, as if to make
certain of the pain.

She felt her soul slipping back down into his net once
more.

"We must return to Venice, I think," he said, tearing
bread for himself.

"Nay, you are banished," she said, suddenly afraid he
would do some stupid and bold and foolish thing.

"Banished? From Venice?"

"For thirty days," she said.

"God rot!" he said with a hiss. "What did I do?"

"Killed two men." She paused. "Or three."

He made a grunt, and then nodded. "The Riata spawn, I expect." He ate a piece of bread, wincing slightly as he chewed it. "Only thirty days? I must have bespoken myself well."

She gave him a hot look. "Oh, most ably!" she said in a bitter voice.

He stopped chewing and squinted at her through his straggling hair and blackened eye. "You would have preferred otherwise?"

She tilted her face to the sky. A breeze touched her cheek, carrying the tang of the salt marsh, the musky whiff of the horses. She noticed such things now, such subtle things as a trace of a man's scent. "I know not what I prefer any more," she said. "I hardly know who I am."

The windmill creaked, its ragged arms stirring as ripples fanned across the skim of water on the salt pond. She felt the warmth of his body, a few inches from hers, even through the weight of her mantle.

"The horse didn't bolt, did it?" he said softly. "You were running from me."

He did not seem angered by it. He said it as if it were a simple statement, ever able to fathom her mind.

"What am I to do?" she said to the sky, to the soft morning clouds, holding her knees and rocking herself. "I cannot stay with you."

"What did you plan? A bishop? A magistrate?" He stood up unsteadily and walked a few feet away, turning his back to her. "Why didn't you plead haven of Morosini?"

She had not thought of it then. She had been too occupied with the brazen play between them, with the way he had looked at her as if they were locked together alone in the dark, instead of trading lies with an elderly and respected councilman of Venice.

"Elena," he said, when the silence stretched, "I cannot

be other than I am. I would not live out the year, and I have no wish to see Hell any sooner than I'm obliged to."

She made a little sound of anguish. "How can you speak of Hell so lightly?"

"Because I'm afraid of it," he said.

She wet her lips, gazing at his disheveled figure. He caught his balance as he turned, standing with his legs apart.

"I know that is my fate," he said. "There is not gold or mercy enough in Christendom to pay for what I've done in my life, and will do yet."

She folded her gloved hands together and pressed them to her mouth.

"But I have thought," he said, "if I could make a place in the world, if perchance I could forge it well, and strong—strong beyond any hazard, beyond any enemies—if I could do that and leave a child of my own blood there. . . ." He locked his fists behind his back and looked up at the horizon. "Even twisting in Hell, I'll have that. I'll have that much." He shrugged. "And perchance it could be as you said—he would not have to be what I am. He might be a good man. He might even be taken up to Heaven when he dies."

Elayne lowered her hands. He smiled derisively, a harsh shadow in his battered face. The fleeting instant of wistfulness when he spoke of Heaven vanished, so that she was not certain if she had heard it, or if he only meant to mock himself.

"Do not the priests say that anyone might enter Heaven, if they repent and do penance?" Elayne said.

He shrugged, scanning the salt flats. "Doubtless." He reached down for the palfrey's saddle. "I place no dependence on what priests say; they contradict themselves once an hour. We must move inside, if we linger here. This place is too exposed."

As he began to lift it, he stumbled a little. He recovered himself and stood swaying, the saddle sprawled against his leg. Elayne rose. She hefted the hind-bow to her hip. Together they carried the burden to the base of the windmill. The pirate stopped at the doorway of one of the salt houses, leaning hard against the jamb.

"In truth, 'tis as you say." He took a deep, shaky breath. "I am not fit."

She pulled the saddle inside herself, where the deserted brine baths were still whitened with fans and icicle-pendants of salt. "Rest here," she said, shoving it into a position he could use for a pillow. "I'll bring the other, and tie the horses between the walls.

He stood leaning against the doorframe. As she made to pass him, he reached up and touched her shoulder. She paused.

He smiled at her, a drowsy, faraway smile. "Hell-cat," he said softly. "Will you stay with me in truth?"

Elayne drew a breath, looking up into his dark eyes. They were half-hidden by black lashes, encircled by purpling skin. His fine lips were swollen at one corner, his cheekbone scraped and red. It was not his beauty now that made desire and pain sink down through her.

"Yes," she lied. "I will stay."

THE STALLION HAD not wandered far. She bridled it hurriedly and led it back to where its saddle lay, looking over her shoulder often at the empty doorway. The bags were still tied to the hind-bow; they held a purse of coins, enough to buy food, she hoped, if she could not find a religious house soon. She would be leaving him with nothing but the bread and watered wine.

She heaved the saddle over the stallion's back in one great effort, pulled up the girth, and wondered if a liar and thief would be allowed into Heaven. With a glance over her shoulder, to make certain again that the doorway was empty, she swung herself into the saddle.

As she gathered the reins, she remembered the tuft of Nimue's white hair that she had saved. Carefully she drew off her glove, to make sure of the keepsake. It was there still, clinging to her palm beneath the ring. Elayne turned around and slipped the tuft into a safe corner of one saddlebag. She took a deep breath, frowning fiercely at the horizon. She would not think of Nimue and Margaret and Matteo and the others. She could not.

She started to pull on her glove, and paused. In the soft morning light the engraved ring on her hand gleamed.

With an effort, twisting and rotating it, she tried to remove it from her finger. It was tight about her joint, a painfully close fit over the knuckle. She spit into her hand and worked at it, whimpering in frustration. But she wanted to leave it with him; it did not belong to her; she did not want to abandon him injured and outlawed and utterly without resource. There was at least a little gold in the ring. With more saliva and a painful rush of air through her teeth, she managed to work it off at last.

She hesitated, her finger throbbing from her efforts. She had left him as he was easing back against the saddle, propped up on the lambskin pad, with his arm across his forehead. She was unwilling to go back into the salt house now.

She held the ring in her palm, looking down at it. When she turned it in her hand, she saw for the first time that there were letters engraved on the inner curve as well as the outside. She tilted it to the light.

A vila mon Coeur, it said in French.

A vila mon Coeur. Gardi li mo.

She closed her eyes, curling her fingers tight around the ring, and bowed her head with a whimper of despair.

Here is my heart. Guard it well.

Fourteen

—◦◦◦◦—

"ALLEGRETO," SHE SAID.

He had lain in a dead sleep for the whole of the day, propped against the palfrey's saddle. When she had returned to the salt house, when she had tugged the stallion's gear inside, when she had noisily overturned a heavy tub to sit upon and sent crystals of salt flying across the dirt floor, he had not stirred. It was a little frightening, for she had never yet known him to fail to wake alert at the slightest sound.

She had called him "pirate," and shaken his shoulder as evening came on. She had given him a rousing lecture on just how it felt to be abducted and dragged away from all she knew by an assassin and murderer who was afraid to go to Hell. She had shed tears of hot annoyance and pain as she struggled to push the ring onto her finger again—it was too small, and her joint was inflamed from pulling it off; she informed him in no uncertain terms that it was his fault if she could not wear it. But she shoved it over her knuckle in spite of how it hurt, and there it was now, hiding his secret words.

He breathed steadily. Untroubled, as if she were on watch over him, like Zafer and Dario. As if he trusted her.

She had napped a few hours in the quiet afternoon, while the horses munched outside. No Riata killers came to slay them. No one came at all but the water birds stalking slowly through the reeds and a pale, speckled frog that hopped to the door, sat there for a lengthy time contemplating her with round yellow eyes, and then hopped leisurely away.

She pulled all of the papers from the saddlebags, but they were only brief letters of introduction to men she had never heard of, and lists of words that made no sense. The only thing she found of value among them was the contract that betrothed her to Franco Pietro. She had hardly glanced at it when she had signed it, but she read it now as if the words were written in flame. *Make known that when I give my consent, I will take the most puissant and excellent lord Franco Pietro of Riata and Monteverde to be my wedded husband . . .*

When.

When she gave her consent. It did not say that she gave it yet.

She had no vow to Franco Pietro. In truth, by all that she had ever read of the ecclesiastical courts and marriage suits in the documents that Lady Melanthe had provided for her education, Elayne was not betrothed at all.

She remembered her godmother in fierce negotiation with Lancaster—the long hours of argument over dowries and gold and this paper, while Elayne stared out the window, deaf to it all. She thought of how the pirate had faced Countess Beatrice and smiled at the mention of the contract and its words.

"Allegreto," she said again, because when she called him by that name, his eyelashes flickered a little, and he turned his head and sighed.

It sounded so strange on her tongue.

She did not want to become attached to him. She tried to think of Raymond, tried and tried. She loved Raymond. For this pirate, this dark and beaten angel—she felt desire and sin, but not love, or anything like it.

"Allegreto," she said sharply.

He swallowed and smiled a little, then made a faint groan. "Awaken," she said. "The night comes on."

He winced and let go of a slow breath. He closed one fist, bending his arm upward. "Mary and Jesus," he muttered, without opening his eyes.

He spread his fingers. He closed the other fist, as if testing it, and then he sat up all at once, exhaling sharply.

"God bless," he said, leaning on one arm. "I can scarce move."

"It will be worse tomorrow," Elayne said.

He blinked at her with one eye. The other had swollen shut completely. "What promising news," he uttered, his voice slurred.

She offered him the wine flagon. With a painful effort, he sat up against the saddle and drank. He remained still, staring at the floor for a long time. Elayne ate a few bites of bread and left the rest in the rumpled crown of his hat for him.

"How long since we left Venice?" he asked abruptly.

Elayne frowned, reckoning. "Not yet a full night and day," she said.

He looked up at her, then toward the door, where the reeds and bushes cast long shadows. "The galley—when did it sail?"

"They were drawing anchor as we disembarked it," she said.

He made a soft curse and tried to stand. On the second attempt he made it to his feet with a sound of agony. "We must move on. Without the rendezvous. I'll have to conjecture what was arranged. But we must be at Val d'Avina before they reach it."

Elayne rose. "Val d'Avina? Where is that?"

He gave her an odd look, and a short laugh. "You don't know? Depardeu, is there nothing they taught you of Monteverde?"

Her eyes widened. "It is there?"

"In the mountains," he said. "High up the valley, at the mines." He lifted the wine again and drank deeply. "Zafer and Margaret are bound there, in guise as Il Corvo and his new bride, that fine unknown lady who carries Morosini's letters of introduction for her comfort." He wiped his mouth. "With Franco Pietro hot at their heels, if God wills."

"Franco Pietro!" she exclaimed, taking a step. "No! I thought we were bound for some castle in Bohemia!"

"Nay, Princess. We go to Monteverde." He smiled at her, his face an evil mask of bruises. "And I do not intend to meet your betrothed with honey and sweet affection, of that you may be certain."

SHE HAD NOT realized they were so close to Monteverde lands. A dread grew on her as they rode steadily all through the night. She looked toward the dark masses of villages under the rising moon and feared them now, instead of hoping for sanctuary. The marsh and canals and water were not under the hand of the Riata, but they led inevitably to rivers and towns as dawn broke, a rich province of ordered fields and vineyards, of dogs that barked and roads with loaded donkeys and early travelers upon them. She barely remembered the vellum maps that Lady Melanthe had unrolled, so full of unfamiliar names and drawings of castles and churches and hills, but she thought these must be the tributary lands that lay between Venice and the mountains of Monteverde.

The palfrey paced rhythmically ahead of her, tireless as the leagues and hours fell away. The land was flat; the highways dry. When full day came, she could see a precipice in the far distance, a serrated wall of crags that seemed to spring up from the level horizon like dragon's teeth against the sky.

The pirate did not stop to rest. Their pauses were brief, only long enough to let the horses drink in the swarming marketplace of a walled city, and take a loaf and cheese from a hawker to eat while they were still astride. Though he pulled the unkempt hunter's hat down low, people noticed his battered face and blackened eye, offering witty condolences and advice to stay out of street fights. He only returned a hellish grin, shrugging.

She could not imagine what he must be enduring. Even she began to feel the soreness of hours in the saddle after all her months afoot. But his palfrey was a smooth-gaited beast, well-suited to its task. It held the steady pace all the night and full into midday, the sweat darkening its shoulders and neck and flanks, the stallion trailing gamely behind. Just as Elayne was near to begging that they rest the animals, Il Corvo pulled back on the palfrey's reins and brought it to a halt in the midst of the open road.

The sharp mountains were close now: sheer, jumbled faces of gray rock mantled by dark green brush. And they had begun to seem like mere hills, for beyond them rose peaks such as Elayne had never imagined, massive slopes that faded into clouds and misty distance, robed in green and blue. They were startling, so near to the flat lands of Venice, looming unexpected and majestic.

The pirate looked forward and back along the empty road. Here, the neat vineyards had been abandoned to brush and undergrowth. Weeds bloomed in the derelict hayfields and gave way to overgrown ravines. He made a sound low in his throat, like a man not happily surprised. Slowly he walked the horse along the edge of the road, looking down at the ground.

"This way," he said. He pulled the uncomplaining palfrey onto a smaller track, through a gap in a rotting wicker fence. The trail led down into a heavily wooded vale.

"Let us pause for midday," Elayne said as they descended a path among the trees. A cool breeze touched her cheek. "The horses must rest."

He nodded, lifting his hand. The path rose, and the horses labored uphill. She realized that there were flat paving stones among the weeds, and a terraced edge. A road had once climbed the rise. Against the hill, a wooden hut with a poorly thatched roof stood aslant, as if it might at any moment collapse onto itself.

A woman, holding her face covered up to her eyes with a black mantle, looked out the doorway apprehensively as they approached. She watched them silently. Then her eyes widened, and she dropped the veil. She stepped into the path.

"Saint Agatha's blessing on you," the Raven said.

"My lord!" she whispered, and then seemed to recall herself with a start. "Commend you to her goodness!" she responded, bowing down to the ground.

He watched her a moment. "I was not expected, then," he said softly. "You had no message."

She lifted her face, young and quite pretty. "Nay, my lord! Nothing!" She looked toward Elayne, and stared as if she were a ghost.

He made a gesture with his head, up the hill. "Bid Gerolamo attend me there."

"Aye, my lord. But God comfort you! You are hurt."

"I heal," he said. "Be quick now."

She nodded and bowed hurriedly, turning to run down some hidden track among the trees. The palfrey heaved itself up the hill, its head lowered.

Elayne let the stallion follow on a loose rein. As they reached the top, she saw sunlight sparkle ahead through the brush. The view opened suddenly, blindingly . . . a vast lake, with the sun dazzling across its shimmering surface, a lake so huge that vapor nearly obscured the mountainous shore on the far side. The horses stumbled and lurched down a sharp incline. Their weary hooves sank into pebbly sand. Small waves washed the shoreline, water as crystalline and clear as the Middle Sea, darkening to blue and purple at its heart.

A peninsula ran out from the shore, a low saddle of land thrusting into the lake. At the end of it, like a crown set upon the water, stood a castle—four tall towers and a fifth that surpassed them, strong and beautiful, soaring upward against the mountains and the sky.

A castle—and broken—its crenellated walls breached, its stone harbor torn open, its inner courtyard empty and exposed to the lake's shimmering reflections.

• • • •

THE PLACE WAS deserted, given over to doves and echoes. The towers stood untouched, but no contents had been left within the pale walls. The pirate walked through it silently, without expression. They had left the horses tied on the shore and waded knee-deep, barefoot among reeds and grasses, to reach the arched water-entry. The breached iron gate still lay visible under the crystalline lake, growing streamers of vivid green moss.

Elayne curled her muddy toes, rubbing them clean on a sprig of grass that poked up through sun-warmed pavement. The frescoes on the inner courtyard walls had been spoiled by hammers, the faces of graceful ladies and proud mounted lords hacked and gouged away. The pirate seemed uninterested, passing the great hall and the towers; instead he led her down a stone stair to another water-gate, this one choked with plumy reeds and grasses. Little fish darted between the sunlight and shade, startled by their arrival.

He reached up to a huge lion's head boss of lead set in the stone. He put his fingers behind the snarling teeth, set one foot against the wall, and with an effort that made the muscles stand in his neck and shoulders, pulled outward. The lion's head grated away from the wall a tiny distance. He let go, drawing a deep breath, and turned to the water.

At first Elayne saw nothing happen. Then she realized that a dark line was growing at the edge of the small quay. As the water level dropped, a wall appeared, separating the lake from the pool under the arched gate. The reeds at the edge bent and laid down in mud, but the bottom of the pool was deeper. With a gurgling sound, the water line fell, revealing a stair and another arch.

Just inside the arch, under the wall, there was a door.

She recognized it instantly, though the metal had turned black with age. In the relief, the dogs and bear, the shepherd; tarnished but defiant, like the words engraved down the center. *Gardi li mo.*

Elayne followed him down the wet stairs in wonder. At

the bottom he cast a glance at her, a half-smile in the dim water reflections. "Do you remember?"

Elayne pressed the first letter. She remembered that much. The shepherd's staff, then the last letter. She reached for the bear. But the pattern had been irregular after that; she could only guess. The darkened bronze gave beneath her fingers as she tried the sheep.

"Nay," he said, stopping her hand. "Watch again."

She felt a little ashamed that she had not recalled it correctly. She watched intently as he made the pattern, repeating each letter to herself under her breath. The lock clicked, the panels came apart, though they required some pushing to force them fully open. This door did not give so easily as the one to his island strong-room. He had to put his shoulder against it and shove, wincing as he did it.

A stone stairway lay before them, dry and empty, turning up and up the inside wall of a square tower, a dim, echoing well of stone. Light entered from arrow-slits at each landing, bright beams slanting across the dim height. Doves cooed and rustled somewhere above her, but the floor and stairs were strangely clean.

He closed the door and began to mount the stairs. Elayne hefted her boots under her arm, took a deep breath, and started up after him. Halfway to the top she had to stop and catch her breath, leaning on the plastered wall, looking out the narrow slit through a wall nigh as thick as a man's height. She could see only a sliver of the lake below.

This was a Navona stronghold. It must have been, with that motto upon the secret door. Though the walls were breached, the gates torn down, it had not been destroyed. Only made unfit for defense. She had read of such, in some of the copies of royal writs among the papers she had studied. It was an insult, a deliberate mark of disdain, to slight the walls in such a way.

He passed from her sight above. She forced her aching legs to mount the stairs. Her knees were trembling by the time she climbed past the beams that supported the upper floor. She expected to emerge into a guard room, or outside, but instead there was a tiny landing, with no protection from the giddy drop, and another door: bronze again, embellished with the dogs and sheep and bear.

He waited beside it, looking at her expectantly. Elayne leaned her hand against the wall, still panting from the climb as she repeated the secret pattern. This time she made it work. The lock made a familiar sound, and the panels slid open smoothly. She turned the latch. The door swung full open on silent hinges.

Rich colors caught her eye, and a flutter of motion as birds took off, shadows on the outside of the shuttered windows. There was a great bed hung about with red-and-gold damask. A soft, fringed carpet beckoned her bare feet. A large chest and a throne-like chair and stool, a cupboard—even a mirror the size of a woman's face, framed in a gilded sunburst and hung on the frescoed wall.

"Hold," he said, catching her arm before she could enter. "Let me make certain of it."

With a quick move he sent one of his daggers spinning across the chamber. It stuck hard in the window shutter, rattling the wood. He stepped inside the door and looked up, running his hand all along the frame. Then he made a slow circuit of the room, his other knife at ready, as if some attacker might spring from the walls.

He reached the far window and pulled his dagger from the wood.

"You are sure that the galley sailed as we left Venice," he said. "One day and half another past now?"

She wet her lips and nodded.

"Come in," he said. "We'll be safe here. Use the bed, but touch nothing else. I'll return as soon as I've seen Gerolamo."

Safe here. He said so. As the door closed behind him, she dropped her boots and went straight to the bed. She climbed onto it and fell back against the pillows with a great sigh, asleep almost before she let her eyes fall closed.

• • •

ELAYNE AWOKE WITH a sneeze. In the first moments of fathoming where she was, she saw half-open shutters with a sky glowing vivid blue beyond. The doves cooed and rustled on the sill. She lifted her head from the pillow. Dust motes made her sneeze again.

There was a startled move beside her. She looked around as the pirate rolled upright in the bed, hand reaching for his dagger. For one perilous instant he stared at her, a stranger with murder in his grip, and then his hand relaxed and he made a groan, turning over into the pillows.

His face was not so swollen, but colored now in shades of blue and violet and green that would have done justice to an artist's palette. Dried smears of blood still marked his nose and jaw.

"I loathe horses," he said, half-muffled in the pillow.

Elayne sat up. She smiled wryly. "They served us full well," she said. "I hope your man took good care with them."

"Aye, I told him all you said to do." He turned on his back with a stiffness unnatural to him. "My own servants don't get better treatment."

"That palfrey is a rare animal," she said, crossing her legs carefully. She was a little sore herself. "I've never seen a finer pacer."

"It is yours, then, and welcome." His gaze drifted down to her lap. "God knows I hope never to mount the vicious beast again."

She felt herself flush at the way he observed her. She moved quickly to close her legs and rearrange her skirt over the rumpled damask bedcovering. "We are not to ride further? Is this Val d'Avina?"

"Nay, d'Avina is leagues from here yet. But we will go by the lake, when Gerolamo arranges for it. Until then, we wait here. We have two days of grace, if I told Zafer what I meant to tell him."

"You do not remember still?"

He stared at the bed canopy. He squinted, as if he were looking far into the distance, and then shook his head. "It is maddening!" he said. "I recall the wine with Morosini . . .

then nothing. Nothing after. I know what I intended—we can only pray God that is what was arranged. But I thought they would expect us here, and they did not."

Elayne slid from the bed and curled her toes in the rich carpet. She went to the window, pushing the shutters full open. The setting sun blazed just above the mountaintops. The air was so clear that she could pick out valleys and deep ravines on the far side of the lake, miles away. Angled shafts of golden light played through parting clouds and onto the water, like a perfect vision of Paradise. "What is this place?" she asked in wonder. "Is it yours?"

He laughed, a bitter sound. "Ask that of the Riata."

She looked back at him. He sat propped up in the great bed, a lithe shadow in the richly appointed room. It was clearly the residence of a wealthy man, but there was an air of austerity to it, a graceful simplicity, as if the owner had chosen the finest of each thing he wished to have, and no more.

"This chamber was not violated," she said.

"Aye. We kept some secrets, it seems." He scanned the room with a cool glance. "I've never been in it before. It was one of my father's chambers."

She remembered that he was a bastard son. He had called Gian Navona a devil; he had said that his father had tried to drown him for disloyalty. She looked at the room and its furnishings with a new perception, but still they only seemed to speak of subtle elegance, not evil.

"It is not what I would have expected," she said.

"Did you imagine a torture chamber? He did not like blood on his own hands." The pirate rose suddenly, swinging his long legs off the bed. He walked to the mirror and peered into it. "Mary, look at me!" he exclaimed with a harsh laugh. "He would have been revolted. And I cannot even remember a simple assignation! Forgive me, my sweet sire. Have mercy. Don't kill me in my sleep."

He stared at himself for a long moment. The late afternoon shadows made a dim reflection of his face, a rippled distortion in the mirror.

"Don't kill me," he whispered.

Elayne stood up straight. "Your father is dead," she said firmly.

He closed his eyes, his lashes trembling, and blinked them open.

"Yes," he said. He took a breath. "Yes. I brought him back and buried him in the duomo at Monteverde. Haps I'll take you there, hell-cat, in time—and you can light a candle to keep him dead."

For once, she did not object to his name for her. "Do you fear a mortal man's memory? You told me that you could keep your wits in the face of any fell thing."

"Did I!" He turned from the mirror. "I must have neglected to mention my father." He looked about the chamber. "We should be cautious here. There will be things even I don't know."

"You are ever comforting! What things?"

He reached out and touched the sunburst frame around the mirror, running his fingers along each gilded tip. "There," he said, holding his forefinger behind the frame. He tilted his head toward the bed. "Watch."

As she glanced toward the bed, there was a snapping sound and a flash of motion from the canopy. A needle the length of her hand stood buried in the bedclothes where the pirate had been lying. It wavered for an instant and then toppled.

"The poison will have long since lost effect," he said. "But it would hurt."

Elayne put her hands over her face and sighed through her fingers. "Do you know what is unspeakable?" she said, drawing her palms down and looking at him over her fingertips.

"My murderous family?" he asked lightly. "Or my murderous self?"

"I am not even discomfited anymore."

He smiled in the gathering gloom, as if it pleased him. "I'll disarm everything. I know my father's mind well enough to find what is here."

"Of course," she said.

"Close the shutters now. We want no sharp-eyed fisher-man to notice such a change." He nodded toward a large sack that lay upon one of the chests. "There is meat to break fast, if you want it," he said. "And then we will go down to bathe." His lip curled. "I cannot bear myself. I reek of horse."

"Is it safe here?" Elayne asked, looking down the little beach in the last of the silvered light. Rosemary and citron trees grew along the base of the castle walls, and even palms, a strange sight against the dark background of snow-capped mountains.

He paused, holding a pair of robes he'd taken from his father's chest over his arm. "You are learning to ask," he said, with approval. He moved ahead without giving an an-swer to her question, barefooted still, a soft shadow in the dusk. They followed a faint path that wound between the water and the castle walls. As he passed by one of the cit-ron trees, he yanked down three of the yellow fruits from a low-hanging branch and carried them in his palm.

The air was warm even as the sun set across the lake, but the water looked chill. Elayne carried a linen bag with soap of olive oil and herbs. She could smell the faint heavy scent of it, mingling with the rosemary, as familiar as Cara's cof-fer where she stored her Italian treasures.

Beyond the castle, a row of arches stood, black silhou-ettes against the day-glow. He led her along the ancient pil-lars that lined the shore. The lake seemed to be all around them now, at the farthest end of the peninsula. A faint white mist rose from the water ahead, a citron-scented haze that drifted through the trees.

There were steps carved into the rock. In the fading light she followed him down to a bathing grotto. Antique columns and marble tiles formed a spacious vault, the clear blue water reflecting and shimmering against pale stone. Wild rosemary bushes grew among blocks of stone and broken friezes. The trunk of a huge olive tree overhung the entrance, its twisted branches and silvery leaves shielding the grotto from the lake. Steam rose from the smooth surface, drifting and vanishing into the evening air.

The pirate dropped his burden onto the carved and fluted capstone of some ancient fallen column. Without hesitation he released his waist-belt and laid it out over the flat shelf edge, with the daggers' hilts turned toward the water. He pulled the loose volume of his doublet and cape over his head, tossing them aside, revealing vambrace guards of leather and metal strapped to his forearms, and another knife sheathed along the inner side. He turned his fist up and unbuckled the straps.

While she stood wide-eyed on the last step, he untied his hair and released his breechcloth. His back was to her as he stood for a moment, then lowered himself with a soft groan and a stiff move to sit naked on the edge, his bared arms and chest and loins awash with shadowy blue light—flawless, each muscle and limb formed in perfect harmony, the skin of his back and shoulders smooth and unscarred under the black fall of his hair. He paused only an instant, watching the steam, and then slid into the water.

He went fully under in the purple depths, and then rose like some lost water god, sending waves and ripples to the walls as he shook back his head and swept his hands over his face and hair.

He caught the shelf with one hand, turning to her. His blackened eye gave his face a strange asymmetry in the failing light, as if half of a pagan mask had been painted upon his temple. He tilted back his head and opened his arms on the steamy water with a fierce sound of pleasure.

"Heaven," he said, with the vapor rising around him, his voice echoing in the vault. He looked toward her, unsmiling. "Come join me. This is as close as I will ever come to it."

Fifteen

SHE STOOD FROZEN on the stair, clutching the linen bag. It was not fear or shame that held her. It was not modesty or shyness. If she could have claimed even an ounce of shame, she would never have followed him here.

She turned away, to hide her face, to compose herself. The vision of him standing for that one moment on the open shelf was like a revelation. She had not seen him so since that first night. The pure, unbridled force of her will to join him and wound him and sink down in that dark combat with him again caught her breathless, like a blow to her chest. This place, this pagan place, haunted by ancient columns and arches that no Christian hand had raised—he seemed a part of it, the very voice of it, calling her to the shadows with him.

She glanced back. He floated with his shoulders just above the surface of the water; the faint shade of the mark she had made on him still visible. He had sometime touched it and smiled that knowing smile at her, as if it were a sign between them. As if it were a token.

He grew still as she watched him from the ledge, return-

ing her steady look. That memory rose before her; between
them: that she had made her brand on him—that he allowed
her one means to violate his guard.

One means, to put him at her mercy.

A hundred times, a thousand, she had thought of her
teeth on his skin, his body shuddering with ecstasy as she
marked him.

His mouth curved a little. "Hell-cat," he said, as if he
were amused.

She thought distantly of Raymond. But that was so far
away, another world. Not this world, where a part of herself
that she had only glimpsed now sprang to vivid life.

He let himself drift backward, pushing away from the
ledge. His hair spread around his chest and shoulders.
There was just enough light left to see the smooth strength
in his arms, the graceful line of muscle, like a fine hot-
blooded animal as he stretched. He winced as he moved,
opening and closing his arms, and gave a long sigh. *"Helas,*
I hurt all over."

The ache of desire swelled open in her like a flower
blooming in the night. The thought of raking her hands
across his wet shoulders made her dig her fingernails deep
into the bar of soap through the linen bag. She moistened
her lips, turning her back again.

"Do not come in, then," he said, mocking her. "If you
are afraid."

Afraid. Oh, she was afraid.

She stepped to the water's edge without looking at him.
She knelt, skimming her hand into it. It was warm, near to
hot, as if a spring from the brimstone depths of the earth fed
it. Blue and purple and indigo swirled and broke with silver
under her fingers.

He ducked beneath the surface. She could just barely see
the length of his body, a wavering shape as he swam un-
derwater to the far side of the vault. He came up and drew
air, tossing back his hair. With a twist, he sat upon some
ledge beneath the water, turning toward her, barely visible
now in the darkness and steam.

With that much of distance between them, she pulled at the laces of her surcoat with trembling fingers. She hardly knew if it was dread or eagerness. She hardly knew what she intended to do until she sat down and put her feet in the water, yanking her chemise loose over her head.

She slid quickly into the warm lake, taking a block of soap with her. The depth was uneven, but smooth; her toes rested on curved surfaces of rock. The water enveloped her naked body like silk, slid against her breasts like softest velvet on her skin. She turned her back to him and ran the soap along her arm. The apple-scent of chamomile and almonds rose around her.

She bathed herself, vividly aware of her body, of every touch of the soap and the water and the smooth stone beneath her feet. Aware that he was there, watching her.

"Your hair," he said, from close behind.

Elayne paused. Her hair was still bound up, though the water caught at loose tendrils falling at the nape of her neck.

She turned her head a little, looking aslant. She could not see him, but she felt the water surface move and break just behind her back. Her breath, already uneven, left her completely. She lifted her chin.

"Take it down," she said, as if he were her servant.

Her own boldness amazed her. She watched the faint steam rise, holding her breath.

"My lady," he murmured, with a compliance that sent hot agitation surging up into her breasts.

Water splashed softly. He touched her hair, dripping warmth down onto her shoulder. With practiced skill he found the band and pins that held her braid, as if he had done such things many times before. It fell heavily onto her neck. He tossed the pins onto the dry ledge and tugged gently at her hair, unbraiding the strands as she held her place, until the loosened mass of it floated about her shoulders.

He came close behind her, took one deep breath against the side of her throat, and pushed back, floating away.

Elayne turned sharply, her hair coiling about her. "Do not," she ordered. "Unless I wish it."

He stilled, an arm's length from her. She could no longer see his face clearly, only the planes and shadows of it. Her heart was beating hard. She did not know if she wanted him to contest her or obey her; it seemed as if she wanted both. She clenched her teeth as if in anger, but it was hot and melting anger, full of black desire.

"Tell me what you wish," he murmured.

A deep thrill of excitement sank down through her. "You know what I wish. Do you know it?" It was half a question, half a cry.

His lips parted. She saw his chest rise and fall. "Tell me."

"To give you hurt again!" she exclaimed, with a tinge of panic. "God save me."

He made a sound like a muted growl. "Hurt me, then."

She was panting. She turned away, in recoil from her own self. "Nay," she breathed.

"I want it," he whispered. "I have lived in dream of it for days."

"Allegreto," she said, closing her eyes.

The water swirled as he moved. "It is so sweet to hear you say my name."

She wanted to weep and to wound him at the same time. "What is this? Is this a spell?" She let go of a sharp breath. "What is this you have done to me?"

He gave a strange laugh. When she looked again, his head was tilted back to the sky, the strong, bare column of his throat exposed to her. "Only told you the truth, for once."

As she watched, he let himself sink below the surface. The water shifted and stirred. He rose at the far wall again and settled there, no more than a shadow, like a lonely spirit curled against the back of a cave.

"Elena . . ." The water and the vault brought his hushed whisper to her as if he spoke in her ear.

She leaned against the ledge, her feet finding a shallow

bench, some ancient seat carved for bathers from time lost. She rested her hips on it, her hair flowing around her, tangling in her arms and encircling her waist. The longing in his voice cut her like an exquisite blade. Excitement possessed her, sharp as black polished glass. He gave her this. He wanted it.

She ran her tongue over her upper lip.

In the growing darkness the water seemed to take on its own faint glow. She could see him as he came to her, a strong movement in the depths; the sleek beast from the nightmare forest, his face awash as he broke the steaming surface. She laid her head back, hardly able to look at him for anticipation. She stared at the fading sky beyond the vault, the rising steam, her heart beating in her ears where the water washed against her.

"Allegreto," she said.

"I am here," he whispered.

She raised her head, her hair lying heavily on her neck and shoulders. He was very near, kneeling before her with the water to his chest. She leaned toward him, lifted her hand, and opened her fingers. She set them against the side of his face, just touching, resting gently on his injured temple. "I will not be taken again as you did before. Against my will. Do you understand that?"

He stared into her eyes, unmoving, as if her light touch held him like a leash. She pressed one fingernail into his bruised skin. His lashes flickered; she saw the instant of reaction. Then he reached beneath the water and grasped her waist, pulling her hard toward him.

"No." She twisted away, drawing her nails violently across his cheek, scoring his injured face as she jerked free. She heard his hissed intake of breath. He let her go with a curse and a half-laugh, shaking his head back and spreading his arms with a deep shudder.

She had not intended it, to ply her fingers so hard where he was already hurt. But he said her name again, a low voice of hunger. And she felt the hunger in herself: she wanted the way he looked when she did it, the way it broke his inflexible control. The dim glow showed him under the water, full ready to mount her, but he kept his distance. They were like combatants now, circling . . . assessing one another.

She wet her lips again, and saw his glance fix there.

"Be still," she commanded softly. "Do not touch me."

He smiled, a faint curl, almost scornful. But he did not reach for her again. He drifted in the water, half-kneeling, watching her as she slipped from the bench. She did not allow her body to contact his. Instead she slid close around him, to the side. The water swirled between them, as intimate as a caress. She bent over his shoulder, not touching, letting her breath heat his skin. Her hair tangled with his.

He turned his head a little, as if he would face her.

"No," she said, lifting her hand to his jaw, the sharp tips of her nails pressed against him in warning.

He laughed strangely, closing his eyes. A shiver ran through him.

She could feel the light roughness of new beard on his cheek, yet still his skin was smooth and hard. She let her fingers trace the elegant outline of his face. She slipped behind him, drawing his wet hair aside as she bent to the back of his neck. She pressed her fingers into his jaw, holding him as she closed her teeth softly over his nape like a she-animal in heat.

He made a low sound. She could feel a tremor grow in him, bone-deep. With her hands on either side of his face she drew his head down. She licked the skin under the dripping fall of his hair, taking cool drops on her tongue, tasting him. She felt him move; his hands came back for her, searching, as if to pull her close.

She drove her fingernails into his face and bit him hard. His back and shoulders contracted. "Do not touch me," she said, her lips on his neck.

He was breathing roughly. He gave another laugh, short and husky, a vibration against her breasts. He could have thrown her off with one move. His daggers lay within his reach.

He opened his hands wide under the water and closed them into fists. But he did not pull away. A wave of dreadful delight suffused her, driving off all reason.

She slid her hands down his shoulders, down his arms. She caught his wrists and drew them behind his back.

"Do you understand?" she asked ruthlessly.

His fists closed hard. He had begun to tremble; she could feel it in his taut muscles where she held him with the lightest touch.

"Be still," she murmured. She circled her fingers around his wrists, binding his hands crossed within her hold. She kissed his back and shoulders, opened her teeth against his skin. He tasted of sand and salt and water. His skin felt hot. He shook under the gentle stroke of her tongue and made a sound like a waking dreamer.

She drew away, leaving one hand resting on his crossed wrists. She stared at his bent head, his exposed neck, the taut line of his shoulders swelling as if he were truly bound. Her leopard, black and deadly and magnificent, surrendered to her will.

The first moment she had seen him, in his full power, armored with mystery and magic and command, he had seemed as perfect as any creature formed in Heaven or earth. But wounded and kneeling now in the blue-lit shadows, he was beautiful beyond comprehension.

He panted as if he had been running a far distance. "Elena," he said, shaking his head.

I dread to be defenseless.

She could see it in every muscle of his body, in the way he closed his eyes and opened them wide, water dripping down his jaw. He could have killed her before she drew another breath. And yet she held him with her fingertips, in utter submission.

She did not free him. She kissed the nape of his neck. She slid her belly against his closed fists, deliberate taunting. In the place below, in the tips of her breasts, she was burning, all sensation.

She ran her tongue over his shoulder and leaned closer,

feeling his hands work as if against bonds. The water supported her as she spread her legs and lowered herself so that his fists were against her nether curls, near the place Libushe had warned her was a woman's greatest danger and weakness.

His hand opened against her, and she knew then it was a weakness beyond resistance. His fingers slid in where he had forced her maidenhead, probing and exciting her now. She kissed his shoulder and his throat and his ear, and closed her teeth on his earlobe. Her body moved of its own will, finding a hot pulse of delight. She was panting in his ear, pressing her breasts against his back, making little whimpers in her throat as the sensation grew toward a crest of joy.

He moved so suddenly that she cried out, breaking free in one swift twist, lifting her as he rose from the water. He kissed her, his tongue plunging deep into her mouth, driving her head back. His fingers slid down her back and into the curve of her buttocks, dragging her roughly against his thrusting cock.

Elayne tilted her head aside and kissed him greedily, drew his lower lip into her mouth and bit down until he fell to his knees again. He tore away as the water engulfed them, grinning with his teeth bared.

She laid her head back, resting lightly against his arms, her hair drifting about her. "Hell-cat," he said, his voice harsh and breaking. The muscles of his shoulders swelled beneath her palms as he sat back, cupping his hand around the nape of her neck.

Floating in his hold, she let one hand drift down to his chest. When she brushed his nipple, he drove his fingers into her hair, gripping it hard. She abandoned every wisp of shame and drew her heels up, floating, supported by the water and his arms at her back, suspended in the swell and ripple. His member slid over her, pressed hard at her opening, exposed as it was to him by the wanton position she took.

Sensation bloomed irresistibly, like nothing she had felt

before. She gave a gasp and held his arms. It made her breasts ache and swell and tingle. She held him off, would not let him closer, but rubbed herself gently against his shaft, reaching up to clasp his neck and shoulders, letting her head fall back. She could feel the quiver in his muscles where he knelt, the checked motion in his body. He made a groan deep in his throat, as if she hurt him.

Before, he had thrust himself into her by unyielding force. She lay open now. Without words, without teaching, she knew that this was torture for him. She knew by the way he looked down at her, his dark eyes hot and his teeth bared in the shadows.

Under her lashes, she gave him a taunting smile, pleasuring herself with deliberate leisure.

He held still. He closed his eyes, breathing hard and unevenly. For a few moments she was gentle, as soft as his hands in her hair were rough. His skin was smooth and hard and slick, as warm as the water. She slid her hands down his chest and passed her fingers in and out of the liquid surface, just touching his nipples, and then closed her nails sharply on him.

He sucked in air, a harsh sound. He pushed himself against her, asking for entry.

"No." Her fingernails dug hard on that sensitive place, so hard that he jerked back, uttering a soft curse, sending water rushing in waves around the vault.

"Not yet. It will be when I please," she said, her fingertips still resting against him. She moved leisurely, lying back, using him for support. "Only then."

He was panting between his teeth. With a feral smile, he pushed his shaft against her again, purely defiant. She hurt him in response, cutting him, punishment until she was sure it must draw blood. But he leaned into it, close to her, heavy on her. His hoarse sound of desire carried and resonated between the water and the walls. Elayne made an answering whimper as her body arched and met his of its own accord.

She let the head of his shaft come inside her, just inside her, stretching her a little. He sank down over her, his arm locked behind her back, his breath discordant in her ear. His hair tangled with hers across her breasts. He twisted with a groaning gasp, pushing halfway into her, fighting her as she gave back pain for each sweet burst of sensation, allowing him nothing without that price, until he was shuddering in all his limbs and she thought her body would disintegrate in torment and bliss.

She could not bear it. She cried out and drew back, sliding free, panting, fearing she might drown of this merciless pleasure—though the water never came above her chin.

They stared at one another. He made a pleading growl, his arm taut under her, his breathing racked and painful. Even in the dimness she could see the angry marks of her fingernails on his bruised face, his chest and shoulders. And yet he was so beautiful. She could not endure the way she felt, wanting to rend him, wanting to kiss and comfort him as if he were a child. She touched the marks, stroked them, overcome with a rush of tenderness and shame. He closed his eyes, his long black lashes tangled with drops.

"I am sorry," she whispered, tracing down his cheek-bone and his jaw.

He lifted her up, taking her backward with him in a flood of warm waves into deeper water. He kissed her throat. "Hurt me," he said fiercely against her skin.

Elayne rested her cheek on his hair, stroking her palms down his back, her eyes hazy with steam and sudden tears. "I don't want to hurt you."

"Hell-cat," he said into her throat. "Sweet Mary, take up my blade and I'll let you kill me."

"Oh, no." She gave a little sob. It was no light love-speech with him, no pretty words of praise or fondness. "Don't say such things."

"I am yours," he said, lifting his face to her.

She kissed his forehead; she cupped her hands around his jaw and pressed her lips to his bruised temple. Her hair wrapped them together, swirling around his body. He could have impaled her; she felt him ready for it, but he held her floating in the water above him.

"Whatever you will," he said, inhaling deeply, carrying her up and down with each breath. "Whatever you will."

She cut into the skin beneath his ear, catching it between her fingernails, pressing slowly, gently, a terrible delight as she felt him quiver beneath her. His lips parted. He closed his eyes and moaned. Every muscle in his body seemed to thrill like a bowstring, but he did not move. He waited, controlled explosion at her command. She delayed, hurting him until he was shaking, until she could feel his will to have her rise to the shattering point, until he was uttering faint sounds of desperation with each panting breath. She waited until his fingers pressed and kneaded her buttocks with a rhythm that lost its cadence in jerky motions. She waited until he had no dominion over his own body. Until he had no defenses.

"Now." It was barely a word, barely a murmur. "Take me now."

He ran his tongue over her lips as he let her slide downward. "Say my name," he whispered harshly.

She bent her head and closed her teeth on his shoulder. Water washed into her mouth as he pulled her down onto his hard shaft, pain in return for his blunt pleasure. He gripped her hips, going deep in one swift thrust. She wounded him with savage guilty joy, power over him as he took her, water and blood as he made a sound of agony. He filled her, dragging her against him. He shoved hard inside, his fingers spreading her buttocks to bring her closer. It hurt her, too, pain deep inside at the limits of her body, but a brilliant wave of sensation coursed up though her. She gasped, throwing her head back, rocking against him again and again. "Allegreto!"

He answered, driving his seed into her, desire and pain and hot elation at her bidding.

THE SCENT OF citron enveloped her as she rested in the darkness with his arms about her, the warm water cradling them together on the bench. She held his hands, his beautiful hands, his fingers entwined with hers. She was infinitely gentle in her touch, afraid of her own self.

"I am ashamed," she said, bowing her head.

He turned her cheek against his shoulder, spreading his fingers over her skin. "Beloved," he whispered.

She pressed her face to him, swallowing a sob. "How can you say that now?"

He drew his hand through her hair. "How can I not?"

She bit her lip. "I must have a demon in me."

"Nay, only a small imp," he said, holding her tighter. She could feel his mouth at her temple. "A little fallen seraphim, to harrow and torment me."

She lifted his hand and kissed his fingers. "You are hurt?"

"Elena," he said, "I am wounded beyond any hope of healing now."

She whimpered and turned in his embrace, her hair drifting and floating all about them, mingling with his. She leaned her head against his shoulder. In the silence, the lake made faint ripples and murmurs of sound. He brushed his fingertips across her cheek, outlining her lips and her chin.

"I nearly left you," she whispered. "I thought to find refuge with the church."

He tapped her cheek. "The church. Foolish hell-cat. You make me fear for you."

"Where else could I go?"

"Even Morosini would have been better," he said. "He might have held you safe till Advent, before he made a bargain with Franco Pietro to see that you died of some opportune fever. I would have had a hope to steal you back."

"But the church—"

"Elena, you would not be safe within the church. Do you suppose any bishop in this province was not invested with his mitre at the Riata's whim? Do not attempt it, I entreat you. Franco Pietro will see you dead now, if he fears that you carry a Navona babe."

She was silent. Such black thoughts had not occurred to

her, but she did not doubt him. She curled her arms around her waist.

He held her closer. "Do you think it might be so?" he asked, his breath light in her hair.

She felt as if she were falling from a high cliff. "I know not," she said.

"You have done aught to prevent it?"

She hid her face against his throat. She could feel his chest rise and fall. "Nay."

He was silent and still for a long moment.

"What comes, Elena—what I intend . . ." His voice was suddenly grim. "You must obey every instruction that I give to you. Do not cross me or forestall me. Our lives will depend on it, and Zafer's, and all the others, too."

She lifted her head. "What do you intend?"

In the dimness she could see his eyes narrow. He looked beyond her, staring into the blackness of the lake. Elayne closed her fingers into fists.

With a faint shake of his head, he put her away from him, turning her gently to the water. "Let us not tarry longer here. It is not wholly secure."

Sixteen

—⚙—

"STAY BY THE bed," he said as Elayne stood garbed in a man's robe again, this one luxurious, pure white damask silk with an ancient scent of lavender. She shivered in the cool night air, her wet hair still trailing in a tangle down to her hips.

He shielded a small oil lamp and moved about his father's chamber, his fingertips searching the frescoed walls, tracing the patterns of red diamonds and painted vines and flowers that ran in perfect geometry around the room. He wore only laced hose and breeches now, his chest and feet bare, his black hair tied back roughly. He paused, flipping his dagger into his hand, and probed delicately at a spot on the wall.

Elayne watched. His skin bore red marks where she had scored him. She felt unnerved by what they had done, as upset and distressed as if she had caused some calamity. And yet she loved to look at him. He moved with such confidence and grace, like no other man she had ever seen move. She felt a deep possessiveness of him now, so fierce and raw and tender that it was almost like despair.

He placed his shoulder against the wall and pushed. Elayne leaped, recoiling onto the bed at the sound of a huge wooden crash behind her. An arm's length from where she had been standing, the carpet sagged over an open trapdoor, the knotted fringe trailing down into darkness. Cool air flowed up, carrying the warble of anxious doves. She realized with horror that the trap opened to the full drop of the tower.

"Look," he said. "Here." He tapped the wall and held the small clay slipper lamp near it. "When you see this—a diamond with a tooth at two points. Draw a line between, then an arrow in your mind, from that line. In the perpendicular direction, five paces distant. It will happen there."

"What will happen?" she asked faintly.

"Something unpleasant," he said.

Elayne closed her eyes and opened them.

"Attend me, hell-cat. Do not forget these things, as you forgot the door."

She nodded, twisting his ring around and around on her finger.

"I am going to kill Franco Pietro. I can't reach him while he remains in Monteverde, in the citadel in the city. He must be drawn out. So I have made sure that he knows we are abroad, that I have you. If I killed three men in Venice as you say, then there was a fourth that I allowed to live, so that he could send the news to Franco Pietro and set him on our trail."

"We are followed?" she asked uneasily.

"I think not." He strode across the chamber and kicked back the sagging carpet from the hole. Kneeling, he reached down and under the floor. The muscles in his back and shoulders worked strongly. As he sat up, the floor creaked and squealed, and the trapdoor sprang back into place. The boards vibrated with a hollow crash.

He leaned hard on the trap, testing. Then he rose, taking up the lamp. "We will hope that Zafer leads them a fine chase," he said. "But Franco Pietro has men enough abroad in the Veneto. They will be caught by the third day ashore, by my reckoning, and Hell itself to pay when Franco's men discover they have the wrong company. Zafer will betray me to Franco Pietro, to avoid their torture."

She drew a sharp breath. "Nay, Zafer would not betray you!"

He glanced up at her with a faint smile. "You think not? How little you know of Riata torture!"

"Oh God, you have not planned this! That the Riata will capture them!"

"Aye, that was my intention. Zafer knows it to the last detail; and you adjudge well, that he would not betray me. Not for torture—even the Riata will guess that much. But to save Margaret from it, he will do it."

She shook her head. "Nay!" she protested wildly.

"It is what we planned, beloved. It is a ruse, but they must believe him, that he turns on me."

"But there might be some misfortune, some misstep—" Her fingers gripped a handful of the scarlet bedcover, twisting the damask silk. "How can you know?"

"I cannot. But I trust Zafer's cunning as I would my own." He gave a short, harsh laugh. "Nay, the misfortune is here," he said, touching his bruised face. "In my own wits. There are things I have not remembered, that I must know. God rot your beloved palfrey."

She drew her feet up, hugging her knees close. "It is fiendish! Margaret is with them. And her babe. And Matteo!"

"It is Margaret's choosing. I meant it to be Fatima," he said, "but Margaret beseeched me to allow her to take the task. And she will serve the better. It will be easier for Zafer to make them believe what he does, for he loves her anyway."

She lifted her head quickly. "He told you that?"

"I have eyes," he said. He leaned down, searching again in his father's coffer. He tossed an ivory comb toward her onto the bedclothes. With a little bitterness he added, "Why would he tell me? She won't let him court her, because he is not Christian."

Elayne knew it. Margaret had never spoken of her feelings, nor of Zafer, but the truth of it shone in her face whenever she looked toward him. To such degree, now, that she begged to be the one who accompanied him into hazard in the service of this lethal scheme.

Elayne watched the pirate as he leaned on the bedpost. She had thought it painful before, impossible to stay with him, because he killed men so easily, because he lied so well. Now she felt as if her mind and heart were tearing asunder.

"God curse you!" she exclaimed. She stood up from the bed, turning on him. "Do you not heed what happens to them? Why must you do these things? Why do you have to kill the Riata?"

He leaned back on the bedpost with his profile to her, his blackened eye and the livid marks of her fingernails hidden from her view. Only his lower lip was a little swollen; it gave him a sullen aspect as he crossed his arms.

She grabbed up the comb he had tossed on the bed. "Monteverde!" she hissed. "I hate the very name!" She sat down on the edge of the bed and yanked at the tangles in her wet hair, making an angry whimper at the pain. She ripped out a knot, wincing.

He turned away, the shadows from the tiny lamp playing on his bared back and elegant form. As he moved around the bed she did not turn, though she tensed at the prospect of some new trap or hidden trick. She jumped when she felt the mattress sink under his weight behind her. He took the comb from her trembling hand. His fingers brushed her throat as he drew the mass of her hair back over her shoulder, leaving a coolness on her neck.

He began to comb it out as gently and skillfully as the kindest maid, so that she felt nothing but the soft damp sweep of her hair as it moved. She sat still, halfway to tears.

"I do not understand you," she said.

He said nothing, working at the tangles.

"For Zafer—if it is his choice to serve you, then God absolve his soul. But Margaret. And her baby," she said painfully. "What have they done, to risk so much for you?"

With infinite care he pulled the comb through her hair, the faintest of tugs at her scalp.

"And Matteo! A little boy! He is so frightened of you, and even still he loves you."

He paused. He ran his hand down the length of her hair. Then he resumed his task in silence.

"At least you could have left Matteo in safety," she said roughly. "Why did you bring him from the island at all? What can a child do in this fell scheme?"

"He is Franco Pietro's son."

Elayne jerked away from him, sliding from the bed as she turned. "He is what?"

He knelt on the rich scarlet coverlet, holding the comb. He looked at her, expressionless. "Surely you knew that, Elena," he said quietly. "Did you inquire of nothing about the man you were to marry?"

"I knew there was a wife—she died in childbirth. I—" She had not asked more; had not wanted to. Had not known nor cared. "Matteo is their son?"

"He is."

"Your hostage?" she moaned.

He inclined his head. "I told you I protected the island by sufficient means."

She had thought he meant magic, or his pirate fleet. She thought of how Matteo's young face had been so anxious; how much he wished to please; how he had stared wide-eyed whenever someone spoke of the Riata with hate and disdain. "God save him," she breathed. "He loves you."

Something flickered for an instant in his black eyes, a shadow under the long lashes, as when he had stared in the mirror and asked his father not to slay him in his sleep. She thought of the training, the poison, a boy's fear and pride as he tried and tried again to serve Il Corvo's wine.

"If you mean for him to kill Franco Pietro," Elayne said, lifting her chin and speaking softly, her lip curled, "if that is what you intend, I swear before God I will see you into Hell myself. I will slay you any way I can."

He gave her a long, unblinking look. She was trembling with the force of what she felt. She would push him through the trapdoor or spear him on one of his own daggers—she was terrified of what he would reply.

He smiled darkly. "I said I would kill Franco Pietro. That is not a pleasure I wish to forego to any child."

She let go of her breath, blinking. Her eyes were suddenly blurred, and her nose stung.

"I am not sure that is a great advance in merit," she said. "But I am glad to hear it."

"Come here," he said. "Hell-cat. Let me comb out your hair. Comfort yourself that Dario took charge of Matteo and the babe. He brings them by another route to meet us."

She wiped her hands across her eyes quickly, then turned and sat on the bed. He gathered a thick mass of her hair and resumed his work.

"You would have slayed me in truth, I think," he said, his voice pensive. "Or made the attempt."

"Yes," she said fiercely. "And will yet, if I must."

His hand stilled. He leaned forward and put his mouth to her hair. His hands rested on either side of her throat. He could have strangled her or caressed her, but he did neither.

Elayne blinked again. She swallowed, pressing her hands together.

"God grant you mercy," he said quietly.

She wet her lips. "For what?"

The bed sank as he sat back. "I was Matteo once," he said.

No more than that. He pulled the comb through her hair, working gently in the tangles, awakening the damp scent of rosemary and citron. His knees were spread, just touching her hips.

"A hostage, do you mean?" she asked shakily.

"A hostage, though none so valued as Matteo. A weapon in my father's service."

"It is evil," she said.

"Is it?" he said. "I know not." He drew his fingers downward in the waist-long strands, parting them. "But it would have heartened me, to think I had a champion to curb what he asked of me."

"Let Matteo be heartened, then," she said grimly. "And all of them."

"Will you be my conscience, hell-cat?" He sounded amused.

"I do not jest," she said.

He held back her hair and traced his forefinger along her temple. "Nor I. I am in dire need of one."

No doubt the priest at Savernake would have despaired—if not laughed—at the idea of Elayne set to guard anyone's conscience. She thought of all her small trespasses and sins, and how she had never been repentant for them, never in truth.

She thought of the steamy lake, the water dripping from his face, his head bent before her in submission . . .

"What could I hope to tell you of conscience?" she said in a painful voice. "Belike asking an imp to tutor a demon in virtue."

He kissed her throat. She tilted her head back and closed her eyes, feeling his warmth amid the cool fall of her hair.

"I would listen," he said softly. "I would try."

She lifted her hands and spread her palms over his, slid her fingers down to his wrists and held them, pressed them to her jaw and her cheeks. "It cannot be stopped now, can it?" she said. "There is no way to withdraw from what you plan."

"Nay," he said quietly. "It is set in motion."

She shook her head within the compass of his fingers. "Then there is no question, is there? We can only go forward, and carry it through without fail."

He released a harsh breath at her ear. "I will not fail. Not this time." He drew his hands downward and shaped her shoulders and her breasts. He pulled her back down onto the bed, her tangled hair around her. She stared up at him,

the dim golden light on his bare arms, the black queue of
his hair falling down over his neck, her marks on his skin.

He kissed her mouth, her chin, the line of her throat, so
gently that she could have wept.

"I will not fail you," he whispered.

She lifted her lips and opened them against his kiss,
spreading her fingers in his hair and dragging him hard and
close. She tasted his tongue and the swollen cut she had
made on his lower lip, refusing his gentleness, seizing his
mouth greedily.

She drew his tongue between her teeth, raking the tip
and the sides of it. A deep vibration hovered in his chest. He
gave a low laugh and broke away sharply, his face flushed.

"You think to master me that way," he said, breathing
deeply.

She wet her lips, looking up aside at him under her
lashes, tasting the flavor of him on her skin. She lifted his
hand clasped in hers and held it to her cheek. Then she
could not help herself; she nipped hard on his thumb and
his fingers, and watched the heat in his black eyes, the little twitch of reaction with each bite. "I own you," she said,
her breath on his open palm.

He laughed and blinked, searching the room as if he
awakened from a sleep. "Aye, you do," he said, shaking his
head slightly. "The Devil give me strength, Elena. In this
you do."

SHE DID NOT own him at chess, though, or in any other
way. With a guarded amusement, he did not quite come
near enough for her to touch him, but prowled the chamber
until she had set up the pieces that he had found in his father's coffer. At Savernake, Elena had been the leading mistress of the game, able to vanquish her sister or Sir Guy or
even Raymond. But she was no match for the Raven. She
sat upon the stool, her damp loose hair brushing the carpet
at her feet, frowning at her position. For the fifth game in

succession, he held her king mated in check within the space of a dozen moves.

She tossed her hair back and looked up at him. "Dice?" she asked, pressing her hands between her knees.

He smiled. "You prefer chance to cunning?"

"Verily, what choice have I? I did not know I was so poor a player."

He reached over and completed the only move open to her, then caught her pale king in his hand. He set it lightly in the center of the painted board. "You are not the worst of players," he said. "But then—my reason is not yet wholly lucid, either. That was three moves beyond what it required to best you."

Elayne gazed at the ivory figure, the finely carved crown of an elegant set, still a little disconcerted to find that she possessed far from as great a skill as she had supposed. His courier and knights glistened in the lamplight, cut from a blood-red crystal stone.

"I learned to play against my father," he said. "I never won." He sat back in the chair, draping one leg over the carved wooden arm. "But I could take Franco Pietro in five games of seven."

She looked up. In the glow of the small lamp he looked like a great black cat resting across the chair, watching her. "You've played him?"

"Many times, before he exiled me."

"You were friends once?"

"Nay, we were never friends. My father let the Riata have me in hostage when I was seven, in surety for some pact between them—I know not what. Franco was a few years older. And he was not fond of a slinking Navona bastard." He looked into the darkness and smiled. "When I would not attend confession with his puling priest, who wanted more than confession from me, he had me stripped before his whole family—the women, too—and led about like a dog on a leash. So I took out his left eye with my blade."

She drew a breath between her teeth. "God save."

He looked at her steadily, the shadows carving his face in ebony and gold. "One of us will kill the other, Elena. It is certain."

She shook her head with a small, sad laugh. "I must suppose that as your new-appointed conscience, I cannot hope to persuade you against it."

"And wait until he comes for me?" He gestured toward the board with a faint smile. "It is no wonder that you lose at chess, Princess."

Elayne rose. She pushed her hair back over her shoulder. "You said the Riata kept me, also. I marvel that I survived it."

"Aye. But you had a use. You were surety that Cara would kill Melanthe for them." He lifted his lashes, looking up from the chair as she stood frozen above him.

He meant to shock her, she could see. She felt helpless, still unable to fathom such things. Her sister—her *sister,* to kill Lady Melanthe? To kill anyone. It seemed absurd. And yet Elayne turned away, as if by squeezing her eyes closed she could blot out the sound of Cara's begging, the frantic look upon her sister's face, the cold flat calm in Lady Melanthe's voice as she said that Elayne must wed the Riata and there was nothing she could do.

"Cara tried," he said. His voice held a softer note. "But she was hopeless. She had not the skill for it, or the heart."

"Thank God for that, then." Elayne bowed her head. "I would not have had her commit murder for me."

"No? But you have just sworn to kill me on Matteo's behalf, if you must."

She looked aside at him. She frowned.

He returned a half-smile. "But that is different, I suppose."

Elayne pressed her lips together. She lifted her eyebrows. "What thorny questions you do pose your conscience."

"I have a lifetime's hoard of them," he said, "set aside for your deliberation."

"I used to read of such things." She thought of the long

texts in Latin, the dilemmas and careful weighing of reasons in the documents that Lady Melanthe had sent to her. "Of the jurymen and the advocates and assizes. I would read the writs and decisions, and think of what I would do if I were to judge."

She thought he would laugh and dismiss her as a foolish woman. But he said seriously, "I never thought to study such." He leaned on his fist, as if considering, and then made a dismissive gesture with his hand. "I would have supposed all the judges bought and paid for. Did the decisions seem just to you?"

It had never occurred to her that the ecclesiastical judges and the king's justices would be anything but honest as they struggled to find the truth. But she could easily recall cases that had not seemed to end equitably at all. He leaned his head back on his chair, awaiting her answer, challenging her. She made a rueful face. How green she had been. Of course the judges could be bribed or coerced.

"Often they seemed fair," she said slowly. "Not always." She pulled her hair back into a tail and drew it over her shoulder, shaking her head. "But in truth, even when the choice was difficult, I believe they were mostly honest men, and wise. Sometimes—what I was certain of before I began to read, I understood differently by the end. They asked questions. They made me think." She lifted her chin. "If you believe that a woman can think for herself."

He laughed aloud. "I served in Melanthe's chamber for enough years of my life, sweeting. Do you suppose I could believe otherwise?"

Another shock, to find he had been so close to her godmother. But she feigned to ignore it. "Some men do not."

"Some men are fools. As are some women. I should not like to have been in your position, for example, and have my life depend on your sister's cunning."

"I seem to have survived," she said, a little offended by the implication that her sister was a fool, though indeed Cara's mind was not overly given to sharp wit.

He watched her, tilting his head. "I wonder what you would have done in your sister's place."

She turned full toward him, her loose hair swirling around her. "Tell me this," she said. "Why was I with the Riata at all, and not with my sister and Lady Melanthe?"

"We thought you in safekeeping," he said. "Prince Ligurio knew he was dying—we all knew it, for months ahead. There was time to prepare. You were too important to be unprotected and too young to be usefully wed, so he saw that you were dedicated to the holy sisters at his abbey; the one he provisioned in Tuscany, where he meant Melanthe to go after she buried him. You set off before he died with an escort of ten knights, and word came back that you had arrived. Do you have any memory of it?"

She blinked, and shook her head. "Nay—of a nunnery?"

"No memory of a seizure, of a fight?"

She shook her head. "No."

"You were young," he said. "Four years, at best. I know not how they stole you, then, by hap an abduction, or treachery within the abbey itself. But once they had you, they had Cara's will. She kept it secret—even I did not guess, though the devil knows I suspected there was something. By then we were bound for England, while Melanthe played all sides false." He gave a dry laugh. "Even my father. Melanthe was ever daring beyond reason in her dealings. I think that was half of why he loved her."

Elayne frowned. "My sister told no one?"

"No one," he said.

She sat down, gazing at the red and ivory chess pieces, twirling a lock of her hair around her finger.

"Who would she have told?" he asked. "We knew there was a Riata agent among us. My father had set me to protect Melanthe. Cara well knew that I would kill her in a heartbeat if I discovered she was their tool to murder his betrothed."

Elayne looked up quickly. "I thought you loved her."

"I did."

She curled her hair around her fist, stroking her thumb

against the smooth strands. She gave a short, uneasy laugh, staring at the black-and-white squares on the board, thinking of her sister, of the silence around Monteverde. "Poor Cara."

He showed his teeth in a sneering smile. "Aye. Poor Cara."

She took a deep breath. "I know not what I would have done in her place. The same as she did, I must suppose."

"Make the attempt, but be certain that you bungle it? Spare your own soul at the price of what you love?"

She raised her eyes and met his dark steady gaze. He tilted his head a little, inquiring.

"Is she so much to be blamed for that?" Elayne asked. "It was murder they asked of her."

"With your life at stake." He regarded her, resting his cheek in his palm. He smiled so faintly that it was barely visible. "The silly Monteverde rabbit, she never had the steel to commit murder, not even to save you. The Riata's besetting weakness; they misjudge the temper of their weapons. You were doomed from the moment they took you."

"I live," she said.

"Aye," he said, "it is a miracle worthy of a saint."

Or worthy of an angel. A dark and potent angel, equal to the task.

She looked down at the chessboard, where her defenses stood in disarray under his swift attack. She was alive, and it was not Cara's doing, or Lady Melanthe's. All her life she had trusted in her guardian, felt him standing in the shadows to protect her. She bowed her head.

"I thank you," she said, "for what you did for me. For bringing me out of their hands—when no one else could do it."

He glanced up at her, his dark eyes half-concealed by the lazy black lashes. Then he shrugged and stretched out his leg, looking away. He kept his gaze averted, swinging his foot lightly over the arm of the chair, and gave a soft snort of disdain.

"You do not like to be thanked," she said.

He opened his palm and frowned at it, as if there were some mystery there. "I hardly know. You are the only person who has ever done it." He closed his hand and then flicked his fingers wide, and suddenly there was a blossom in his palm, one of the tiny sweet-smelling flowers from the citron trees. He held it out to her between his fingers. "For your hair," he said brusquely.

Elayne reached for the flower, holding it cupped in her palm. It was slightly bruised, the petals creased, giving off a heady scent.

"Cara never thanked you?" she asked, taking a breath of the tiny blossom.

"I did not linger to speak to her," he said.

Elayne had no image of him in that single memory of her arrival at Savernake. Only snow, and Cara big with child. *I can't believe she never once spoke of you,* Elayne wanted to say.

He rose, a move as elegant and sure as a dance step, all of his stiffness vanished. "As well she married her English swineherd after all. I'm sure I would have killed her eventually, when we required a goose to pluck at Christmastide."

Seventeen

—◦◦◦—

"HAVE YOU PLAYED morra?" he asked as he returned the chessboard and pieces to the coffer. The room was growing cooler. A night breeze had risen, a low sighing in the shutters.

For a moment she did not understand him, and then gave a startled laugh. "Morra! Not for years."

"Nor I. By chance we would be more evenly matched."

"At a child's game!" she said ruefully.

"Nay, I've seen fortunes won and lost at morra," he said, dropping the chest closed. "Is it only for children in England?"

Elayne tucked the little sweet-scented flower behind her ear. She saw him watch the move, and felt herself grow warm. "Cara taught us when we were young. I've not seen it played since."

He held out his fist. "Two fingers or four?"

She frowned a little, recalling. "We played only two. You can play it with four?"

"We can play it as you like," he said. "Ten rounds, two

fingers—and a fist for zero? Call the sum of all fingers. One point for each win."

Elayne gave a little shrug. It seemed quite a descent from the strategies of courier chess, but he stood before her with a serious look, one hand behind his back. She held out her hand and faced him.

"Count of three," he said. "One . . . two . . . three . . ."

"Four!" they said simultaneously, and Elayne looked down at their hands. They each had two fingers extended.

"A tie," she said.

He nodded. "One . . . two . . . three . . ."

Elayne blinked, caught without having considered how many fingers she would show. *"One!"* she said as he said, *"Two!"* She looked down and realized she had held out two fingers. He had extended one.

She rolled her eyes. "Stupid of me." The total sum could hardly be one if she held out two of them herself.

"Tie again." He frowned downward. "One . . . two . . . three . . ."

"Zero!" she exclaimed, holding out her closed fist as he flicked out two fingers. "Oh, Mary, you—" She almost said he had won, and then looked up at him. "What did you call?"

He scowled, and cleared his throat, and then said with an embarrassed look, "I forgot to call."

She giggled. "'Tis more difficult than I remembered."

"Aye!" he said, with a shake of his head. "Ready?"

They stood facing. She could see that he was pressing a smile from his lips.

"One . . . two . . . three . . ."

"Three!" Elayne exclaimed to his *"One!"* He held out one finger and she two.

"I won!" She felt an absurd rush of pleasure to be the first to triumph. "What round is this?"

He tilted his head. "The fifth?"

"Avoi, I am ahead."

He bowed, his black hair falling across his shoulder. "You are ahead, my lady."

She stared down with concentration at their fists, nodding faintly in time with his count. *"Three!"* she cried, and almost forgot to hold out her fingers. She scrambled to extend two a moment after he made his show of one.

"Oh ho! Cheating!" he said.

"No, no—I lost my concentration," she said. "Do not count it."

"Very well," he said, "but you should know that I have cheaters tossed down that trapdoor."

She glanced up, but he was grinning. "Loser must carry the chamber vessel down the stairs!" she said, flicking her tongue at him.

"A cruel fate! Ready?"

She nodded, tensing, trying to hold her two numbers in her head while he counted. *"One!"* she cried, thrusting out her closed fist as he snapped out two fingers.

They both looked down.

"You forgot to call again!" she said.

"God's blood." He shook his head with a startled laugh. "You start the count. It seems that I cannot do both."

Elayne bounced on her toes as she counted. "One . . . two . . . three—*four!* No, *three!* I meant three!" They were holding out three fingers between them. She looked up. "I did! I swear it!"

He put his hand under her chin. "You are a cheat, hellcat. A born cheat."

Elayne took an excited breath as he leaned over and kissed her mouth. She sucked quickly at his lips and then broke away. "Ready? I'm ahead."

"I will not allow you that last point."

"I'm still ahead. What round is this?"

"Six. Because you cheated," he said.

"Ready?" She drew a deep breath, her body taut with anticipation, planning to call three and show two, trying to remember which was which. "One . . . two . . . three—*five!*" she yelled.

He paused, holding out his two fingers near her two. "Five?" he inquired mildly.

Elayne blushed. "You confused me!"

"How?" he demanded.

"By—standing there." She gave him a wounded look. "And kissing me."

"Where shall I stand? Over the trapdoor?"

She held up both palms, and then pressed them together. "Round six. One more time. We must compose our minds."

They stood with their fists out, nearly touching. Elayne closed her eyes. For some reason the simple act of choosing two numbers and causing her mouth to produce one and her fingers to show another was quite strenuous, particularly when she seemed to want to laugh every time she met his eyes. She looked at him. He was watching her with a comical expression of inquiry.

"Are you sufficiently composed, Princess?"

She made a face at him. "You are distracting me."

"You are beautiful."

"No, sir, *you* are beautiful, and know it far too well for any man's good. One . . . two . . . three—*three!*" she cried.

"One!" he shouted at the same time. She held out two fingers, he held out one.

"Ha!" Elayne jumped like a child. "Two points for me now. Seventh round."

"Your hair is like silk." He reached out to touch it, but she caught his hand.

"Round seven," she said, holding his wrist steady before her, preventing him. "One . . . two . . . three . . ."

"Four!" They both shouted at once. Two fingers showed on each hand.

"The Devil," he said. "I'm going down to a tie."

"I'll win." She gave him a smirk.

He caught her around the waist and pulled her against him, burying his face in her throat. Elayne gave a shriek and pushed him away, laughing. "Now who is cheating?"

He stood straight. Elayne began to count. "Wait!" he said.

She stopped.

"I must compose my mind," he said.

"One . . . two . . . you are a loathsome toad . . . three . . . *zero*!" Their voices united as he yelled, *"One!"* When she looked down, he held out one finger against her closed fist.

She thrust out her lower lip. "A point for you."

"You'll never win," he growled. "I won't abide it. Last round, hell-cat."

They leaned toward one another. Elayne counted. "One . . . two . . ." She held her free hand against his shoulder, holding him off as he pressed toward her. She could not look at him; she would have burst out in hilarity for the ferocious look on his face. " . . . three!" She flung out her hand. *"Three!"* she cried, while he shouted *"Four!"* at the same time, almost in her face.

They both looked down. He held two fingers extended. She had one.

She shrieked again as he took her down against the bed, falling in a shower of hair and his body tumbling beside her. "I won!" she mumbled against his palm over her mouth. "Sound and fair!" She yelped as he rolled her over and muffled her head down in the pillows. "I won! I won! Ow!"

"Say my name," he ordered, holding her into the pillow by the nape of her neck. He was nearly on top of her, his weight pressed warmly against her hips and her back.

"No!" she cried, then gave a stifled scream and a buck as he put his arm about her. "You *lost!* "

"Aye," he said beside her ear, "but you think I'm beautiful."

"A loathsome toad!" She giggled and gasped for air. "A great . . . toad!"

She found herself turned over and pulled atop his chest as he lay back on the bed. He held her tight, their legs tangled amid the white robe and scarlet bedcover.

"Allegreto," she said, and he closed his eyes and leaned his head back and smiled.

She had not known he could smile so. She had not imagined he could laugh. And he was beautiful—a far vision beyond beautiful—he was her pirate, her angel, his cheek and jaw and throat a perfect form, shadowed with roughness, his lips parted. She could feel his breath rise and fall, the strength like a hunter's longbow drawn taut, easily held, as his arm curled about her to pull her close.

"When I saw your eyes," he said, "I thought of that lake out there."

She ducked her face into his shoulder, taking a deep breath of his warm skin. "At home some said I had the Evil Eye when I looked on them."

"Fools," he said. He twined his fingers in her hair. After a moment he tugged it and said, "This is your home."

She did not answer. She had no answer. Monteverde still seemed unreal to her, a place of foreboding and violence. And yet this lake was Monteverde, the dark mountains, the water so dazzling under the sinking sun and radiance that it almost made her mind ache. And he was a manslayer, without any sense of right and wrong that she could fathom— and when he laughed with her . . . just once, laughed with an open delight in the moment—she felt as if some long-lost part of herself had been completed.

"You should not have to come home this way," he said. "Like a thief. I should have held it for you."

"Not for me," she said, shaking her head.

"Look what is left of Navona." His mouth tightened, the smile gone. "I knew they had pulled the walls down—but I did not realize—until I saw it . . ." He let out a long breath. "I have not done well."

She rested her hand on his chest. She had a strong desire to deny it, but there was not a single thing she knew of him that she could say with a whole heart was well or rightly done—except that he had saved her life. She traced the line of his collarbone with her forefinger. "You defeated me soundly at chess," she offered.

He gave a short laugh. His mouth relaxed into an easier curve. "We have two days safe here."

"Time enough to play morra again. I prefer it."

He caught her hand in his fist, running his thumb up and down the inside of her palm. "I might have other amusements in my mind."

She lifted her head from his shoulder and looked into his eyes. He raised his elegant eyebrows. She smoothed the tip of her finger along one of the scratches she had made on his skin. With no more than that, she felt his body grow taut. His lashes lowered. He ran his tongue over his lower lip.

"I won," she said in a low voice.

He turned over and lay atop her, spreading her hair on the pillows around her head. "Be cautious of me, hell-cat," he said. "Be careful. There is a brink there—and I don't know where it is."

She felt herself as if she had long passed some precipice, and walked on thin air in this tower above the dark lake. "Do you fear it?" she whispered.

He ran his hands up behind her ears, his thumbs caressing her cheeks. "The galley drew anchor two days ago," he said. "You are certain."

"I am certain."

He closed his eyes briefly. "God help me, I cannot keep it in my head."

"In the small hours of the night, two nights past," she said.

He looked aside, frowning. She could feel his hands tighten in her hair. "I should know the names of Franco's men in d'Avina."

"You do not?"

He stared down at her, shaking his head slowly. "No." He lifted his head abruptly, as if he remembered something. "There should be a message tonight." With a quick move, he sat up on his elbow.

Elayne sat up also, watching him. The moment of play had vanished; he had nothing of pleasure or ease in his face now.

"I must go," he said. He started to rise, and paused. He leaned very close to her, just touching the corner of her lips. "Rest, beloved," he murmured. "Do not leave this chamber. I will return before morning."

He kissed her deeply, pressing her hard down into the pillows. As Elayne lifted her arms around his shoulders, he

pulled back and turned away, his bare feet hitting the floor
lightly as he left the bed.

THERE WERE NO books in Gian Navona's chamber. If he
had been a scholar and wizard like his bastard son, he left
no sign of it in this tower haven. Elayne spent some of the
long hours of the night in searching through his coffer and
the cupboard, being careful to touch nothing that Allegreto
had not examined and declared safe. She pulled the musty
bedding from the mattress and replaced it with sheets from
the cupboard. The scent of ancient herbs filled the room,
their dry skeletons scattered across the carpet where they
fell as she shook out the folded linen.

A wealth of fine tapestries lay rolled in the bottom of the
cupboard—winter dress for the chamber, their rope cords
coiled neatly by the hand of some long-vanished servant.
Elayne looked up at a row of gilded wall hooks shaped like
the heads of mastiffs, running the whole length and breadth
of the chamber under a ceiling painted with silver stars.
Gian Navona had not spared his comfort or expense here.

She made a pile of the old sheets. To occupy herself, she
shook out Allegreto's indigo doublet and tried to brush the
dried mud and sand from the collar. She had an idea of
hanging it, to ease the wrinkles, and even managed to toss
one of the tapestry cords over a hook before she looked
again at the stains and deemed it a hopeless task. She laid
the garment over his chair instead, feeling an unfamiliar
moment of housewifely enjoyment as she arranged the
cloth.

She punched and poked his felt hat into shape again, too,
smiling a little as she hung it over the chair, thinking of his
discolored eye and criminal look from under the pointed
brim. She braided her hair when it was dry, standing well
back from the sunburst mirror to see as she pinned it around
her head.

Raymond had called her a remarkable woman. She
looked at the shadowy face in the glass, only able to discern

the line of her nose and cheek and the shape of her eyes in the weak lamplight.

Everyone said she resembled Lady Melanthe. But she did not see it. Perhaps their eyes were a similar color, and unusual, and that accounted for the likeness. Her godmother looked like a queen—Elayne did not think her own face and bearing even fitting for the princess that they said she was. There was a softness to her features, a wideness to her eyes, and an upward curve to her mouth that made her appear more like to a mischievous pup. She had hoped it would disappear as she grew older, but in the dark mirror she thought she looked no more regal than Nim.

She tried to make her face severe, and only succeeded in looking as if she were pouting. She tried to envision herself giving orders, dispensing justice. Even young Queen Anne looked more imperious.

It was no wonder Raymond had thought her a foolish girl. No wonder Il Corvo thought her naïve.

A vision of him came to her, a clear image of his body, his back to her at the edge of the lake, that moment that he stood poised before her.

She imagined him on his knees.

She stared at herself. And even she could see that her face changed, that the pouting mischief transformed into something . . . different. It was the same face, and yet it was as if the shadows grew sharper and finer, more dangerous, and the lips no longer held a curve of mischief, but some secret unspoken knowledge.

She twisted her hands together and turned abruptly away. She did not recognize that face. It did not look like Lady Melanthe or Cara or anyone that she knew.

He warned her to be careful of him. Well she knew it. He was simply a killer, born and bred and trained to it, as an alaunt was made to take down its prey. A wolfhound might roll and sigh under an affectionate hand in the kennel, but an hour or a moment later, it would rise to hunt again.

She took up the tiny blossom from where she had laid it carefully by the comb as she braided her hair. It was but a

fading thing now, a soft, broken star of petals. She closed
her fingers on it and rolled it in her hand, crushing it until
the heady scent rose up and filled her nose with sweetness.

IN THE DAWN he stood by the open window embrasure,
leaning his elbow on the stone wall. He looked out, his face
and body lit with brightness from below, a half-silhouette in
the dim room. He wore no shirt still, but black hose and
boots of undressed kid softly wrinkled about his ankles and
calves. The vambrace guards were strapped to his forearms.
His daggers hung from the leather waist-belt, resting gently
against his thighs.

"The message came?" Elayne asked, from within a nest
of pillows and fragrant linen. She had put off the white robe
when she went to sleep, and lay naked now within the
sheets, a strange and delicate feeling. She had been in a bed
unclothed only once before. In his bed. She could feel every
place where the linen touched her.

He looked over his shoulder. "Not yet," he said. "But
word came to Gerolamo to expect us to arrive here." He
gave a soft derisive snort. "Morosini took his good time."

She hugged a pillow to her, watching him. She had not
slept much, and when she had, she had dreamed of playing
morra in a dark lake where the water would not let her
move her fingers.

The leather buckled to his arms gave him the look of a
fighter. He leaned at ease on the wall, his hand propped behind his head. Against the pale skin beneath his arm,
against the smooth taut muscle, the sight of the dark gaunt-
let straps made heat rise in her throat.

He turned onto his shoulders and crossed his arms, resting his foot up against the wall. "So we will wait. Though I
fear there is little to provide diversion here. I brought food
and drink, if you want it."

She did not want food or drink. She wanted him.

"I thought of a game," she said, turning onto the pillow

on her stomach, keeping the coverings up over her to her neck.

He lowered his chin, looking at her from across the chamber. "Another game?"

Elayne flipped a bit of sheet over her nose. "By chance it is more of a story than a game." She pulled the sheet down a little, just enough to clear her mouth. "It is like . . . feigning the people in a tale."

"Is it?" he said.

"Yes." She lifted her head, resting on her elbows. "An amusement, to pass the time. You said you delight in games. This is a game of human character."

His mouth curved up a little. "You remember that."

She rolled over, examining one of her fingernails, the sheet draped over her arms and breasts. "My game . . . it is something like a play. I have one part, and you have another."

"What parts are these?"

She gave him a sidelong look, holding the sheet up to her throat. "I thought in haps I would feign to be a great queen."

He smiled openly then, tilting his head aside. "Not a minor one?"

"A great queen." She flushed. She sat full up against the pillow. "Like to the Queen of Sheba. All-powerful, with many lands."

"I see," he said dryly. "And no doubt Your Majesty requires a humble servant to serve you in this game."

"Oh, no," she murmured. She slipped down a little in the bed. "I do not require a servant."

His glance drifted downward, along her body beneath the bedcovers. "A Solomon, to share your throne?"

She shook her head. "No," she said.

"A lover?" he asked.

Elayne drew breath more quickly. "I am told you are a manslayer, not a gallant."

"It is true, my lady." He bowed his head.

"Then haps you will play the part of a warrior." She looked up at him. "A prince."

"Will I?"

She caught the covers in her hands and sat up fully, holding them to her breasts. "Aye. A warrior and a prince, I think. From a far land, that has been—" She hesitated, burying her hands into the bedsheet. "Conquered."

A long silence followed her words. She did not look at him; she could not. She blinked rapidly, aware that there was an excited blur of moisture in her eyes, as if she had just heard some terrifying tale of goblins and hauntings. Her body seemed to grow warm all over, sensitive to every touch of the linen.

"Brought—" She cleared her throat. "Um—brought before me as a prisoner," she said in a failing voice, when he did not answer. She leaned over her knees, hiding her face.

"Do you think I would abase myself?" he asked.

She looked up. He watched her from the dimness, obscured now against the growing light in the window. She could not see his expression clearly. Only his bare muscular arm crossed over the other, strapped in leather.

"I don't know," she said unsteadily. "It is play."

He made a soft laugh. "I fear you do no justice to the role of a great ruler—with that squeaking voice, and fortified among pillows. As your defeated enemy, I am not much impressed."

She drew herself up. The disadvantage of her nakedness was palpable between them. The white robe lay across the foot of the bed.

With a regal move, she threw aside the bedcoverings. She folded her knees in the most graceful and queenly manner she could contrive and took up the robe as she rose. She imagined a host of handmaids and pulled it on with proud leisure, not deigning to close it from neck to toe, but only fastening one button across her breasts. She looked up, but still she could not discern his face against the glare.

She swept forward a few steps and sat down in the large

chair, placing her hands on the arms. "Let me see you," she said. "Come into the light."

For a moment she did not think he would. Then he moved, one step that swung him away from the wall into the growing sunlight, standing with his legs apart and his arms still crossed, a little curl of scorn on his lips.

He made a very good likeness of an enemy prince. But he did not appear conquered, not at all, though his eye was blackened and his shoulders bore scratches and bruises like fading battle marks. With some effort, Elayne kept her face composed. She found it necessary to imagine guards—a number of them. She met his faint smile with a narrow look.

"You are insolent," she said. "Lower your hands."

He looked down at her. His glance drifted in clear boldness to where the robe opened to reveal a curve of her bare thigh and knee. Elayne stared at him, unblinking. Guards, she reminded herself. If she were a queen, there would be guards enough to cause him to do what she pleased. She leaned back in her chair with a casual move, careless of the robe, not taking her eyes from his. No challenge, no contest; a simple assumption that he must obey. It was a game, though it did not entirely seem so.

He drew a slow breath. Then he gave a low toneless laugh and raised his look to the wall above her head, uncrossing his arms, his hands not quite at his side, but open, resting lightly on his thighs. It was the stance of a man who might draw his weapons in an instant.

"Disarm," she said.

His faint smile of contempt vanished. He glanced at her. A long moment passed, with a new guardedness in his look. Elayne felt the tiny hairs on her neck and arms rise. He was truly splendid, standing half-naked like a royal savage, gazing at her now as if she were a stranger to him.

"Do you fear me so much that you must have your blades at ready?" she murmured.

He put his hand to the buckle of his waist-belt. Then he dropped it away and shook his head just slightly.

"Perchance you are afraid to play this game," she said.

He turned back his head and gave a raw laugh. "Aye. I am. Hell-cat."

She stood, walking to him, and put her hand on his chest. She felt him draw a deep uneven breath. He closed his eyes, then opened them when she passed her fingers over his nipple.

"You are insolent again," she said. "Disarm."

He seemed taller than he ever had to her, standing so close—tall and barbaric and unpredictable. She gave his nipple a sharp flick.

He drew air between his teeth. He reached again for the buckle and pulled the leather loose, standing straight, staring over her head. As the belt came free, Elayne caught it in her hand. He resisted for an instant, and then let it go.

He stood looking beyond her, utterly still.

She let her gaze pass over him, from his waist to his hips and up again to his chest and shoulders and throat. She could see that beneath his breeches there was a thickening in his body, a growing readiness. Another prickling wave of sensation raised the secret tender places on her skin. It made her feel warm and damp beneath the robe. She paused, drinking in the sight of him. He was such a pleasure to look upon. And hers. Her captive, her prisoner—she lost herself in the fantasy of it, that he was under her command; entirely at her will.

She dropped the waist-belt on the table and touched him again, reaching up to his shoulder, running her palm down his arm. He turned his forearm up and moved his hand abruptly, as if to reach for the vambrace strap and release it.

"No," she said. She slipped her fingertip just under the leather, tracing the well-fitted edge. His skin was firm and silky at once, the blue veins showing on his inner wrist. She rested her fingers there, feeling his hard pulse. "No. Wear these. I like them."

She lifted his hand between hers. He submitted to it, his lashes lowered, making no resistance as she spread his fingers and explored the perfect masculine shape of his hand.

The metal bands on the arm guards gleamed dully. His third blade, bone-handled, lay in a tight leather sheath inside the length of his forearm. When she put her hand over the hilt, her fingers slipped easily into spaces molded for them.

He made a warning sound in his throat, not quite a word. Elayne closed her hand and drew the knife, looking up at him slantwise. "Is it poisoned?" she asked coolly.

He breathed deeply, his eyes on the blade. All distance was gone from his look. "No," he said.

She nodded down toward the others. "Only the left-hand dagger."

His left hand opened and closed, as if he could feel the hilt of it. He never took his eyes from the knife she held. "Aye."

"I remember," she said, taking a step back. "Do not move." She picked up the waist-belt and walked apart from him, taking his weapons away the whole width of the chamber. When she was on the far side of the bed, she turned and stopped, watching him.

He stood still, but he flexed his hands with a motion that showed all through his body, as if he pressed against a great weight. The muscles in his shoulders and neck grew taut. He swallowed, staring at the empty space before him. "Elena," he said hoarsely. "Take care."

She ran the tip of her tongue over her teeth. Take care with the blades, perchance he meant, but a fine sweat had broken out over his skin. She could see it in the morning light streaming now from the window. It was as if she held his very life and heart in her hands, in these glimmering shafts of steel.

She was well-cautious with the daggers, placing the bone-handled knife gently on his father's coffer and leaving the others sheathed as she slid them free from the belt. His girdle was plain, made of fine strong hide, dark and well-worn, the inside lined with kidskin as soft as a lady's glove and stitched in small even seams. The leather was still pliable with the heat of his body. She curved it around her fist, pleased by the feel of it next to her skin.

She walked slowly back to him.

He turned his head. "What have you done with them?" he asked sharply.

"Whatever I like," she said, holding her hands behind her.

"Hell-cat." His voice held a fierce warning, though he stood rooted in the place she had left him.

She looked aside at him speculatively. "I am your queen now, warrior," she said softly. She clasped her hands modestly in front of her, the belt entwined and dangling from her fingers.

He glanced down at her hands. For an instant there was something like relief in his face, and then the curl of derision came again to his mouth. But she could see the pulse beating hard in his throat.

"I will do what I please," she said in a quiet voice. "With your weapons. With you."

There was the shadow of the nightmare beast in his expression, the hollow stare of an animal caged, as if he would have his daggers and be upon her but for invisible bars between them. Somewhere far deep inside, she was frightened—appalled—at what she did, but overlying it was the dark game between them, that depth of pleasure, the thing that kept him standing imprisoned before her without any bonds at all.

"Put your hands behind your back," she said.

He turned his head a little aside. "Elena," he said low, "this is dangerous. This is too . . . difficult."

"Shall I go, then?" she asked. "I can leave you."

"No!" he said quickly.

"Then do not tell me what is too difficult." She walked beside him. "Come, I will make it easier." With a light touch she drew his wrist behind his back, thrilling to the faint angry sound he made while his shaft answered with a swell of desire. "Sweet warrior," she whispered, lifting his hair and kissing his back, running her tongue over the tight muscles between his shoulder blades. "So well-made. I wish to make best use of my vanquished foe."

"Ah . . . damn you," he said, shuddering as she drew his other hand into place.

"You are impudent." She used the end of the belt against him, a light slap like a tutor with an unruly student. But the leather had a solidity that magnified the flick of her wrist. It struck his skin and the inside of his wrist with a crack that made them both jerk.

Elayne drew back. She stood an arm's length behind him, startled. She'd felt the sting of punishment across her own hands often enough as a child—Cara had never had the heart to do it herself, but Elayne's strict Italian duenna had known just how to apply the rod, for the little good it ever seemed to do in recalling Elayne to proper behavior. She wet her lips.

His held his hands crossed behind him in rigid fists, the tendons and muscles standing all along his arms. She walked beside him. A slow drop of sweat made a trail below his ear. He stared straight at the wall before him, his member straining hard at the black cloth and lacing.

She lifted the belt softly, tracing the inside tip of it down his arm, barely touching him. He flinched. And she could not help herself; she loved him when he stood so, like a man braving fire and Hell, and then made that tiny spontaneous jerk under her touch.

She turned the belt and snapped the outside leather hard against his skin. His chin came up. He stood sweating and taut, like a stallion worked into obedience that might yet explode at any moment. Yet it excited him—he was full and stiff, heavy with desire. She put her hand on him gently, outlining his shape. He sucked in his breath and took a step backward.

"Do not move," she said. She struck him, the tip of leather like a nip across his ribs, his flinch like a brand to the torch lit inside her. It left a reddening mark on the pale skin under his arm.

She stepped before him. He swallowed, blinking at her, with a glancing look down at the belt and back up again.

She lifted her hand, and he took another step back. One

pace behind him, dangling from the tapestry hooks, was the silk cord she had thrown there.

"Stand still," she said softly. "I want you still."

She reached toward him again, and she could see that he tried to keep his stance. But he took one more step back as she moved closer, his lips tight together, breathing like a winded animal. His fingers touched the wall behind and he stood stock straight, yanking his fists apart. He brought his hands up as if he would seize her and shove her back.

Elayne used the belt on him, full across his chest. He froze; they both did, at the sound. He stood with his hands open.

"If you will not be still, I will have my warrior bound."

He made a sound deep in his throat as she grasped the cord. He must have known it was there—he would have noted anything, every small detail in the room, she was certain. And yet he looked as if the sight of it in her hand stunned him. She had never before seen so much of his feeling show in his face; he looked near to some encounter with the Devil himself. But his body was flushed; hard and ready for coupling, the red line of her strap glowing across his chest.

"Your hands," she said firmly, before he could find his sense and refuse. "Cross them before you."

"No," he said, his voice grating. "Elena!"

It was a plea. She answered by touching his face, stroking him as she would a frightened beast. "For me," she said tenderly. "I want to use you, sweet warrior."

All the breath seemed to leave him in a rush. He turned his head under her touch, as if she had struck him across the face. "Oh, God and Mary," he whispered.

"Do it," she said gently.

He put one hand across the other, breathing as if he might begin to weep.

For a moment she looked down at his arms—his strong wrists crossed, the dark leather guards and gleaming metal, his hands working faintly, rhythmically, like a heartbeat. Inside the robe she felt as if her body thrummed some deep answering note of sensation, as if she were the very string upon a harp.

She drew the cord about his wrists, holding it lightly. She could feel that he was nearly frantic, though he held himself rigid and did not break away. The twist of fine silken threads felt soft in her fingers, a luxury, the tassel a fan of creamy elegance against the hard-tanned leather and steel of the vambrace guards.

She looped the cord twice around his wrists and tied it as she would have secured a horse's lead, a knot that would not loosen, but draw tighter with any pull or struggle. He watched her work with a glazed look, as if he did not believe she did it.

"Raise your arms," she said.

For an instant he stood motionless. He blinked, and she could see the glitter of moisture in his eyes, that spontaneous wetness of fear and pleasure that she'd felt herself, imagining this moment with him bound before her.

She lifted the belt and ran it over his shoulders, down his arms, up again beneath his throat. She snapped a cruel flick against the smooth silky skin beneath his ear, and then across his nipple. He sucked in his breath and closed his eyes, his body racked by faint shivers, his full member pumping. He lifted his hands above his head.

Elayne drew the slack cord taut and leaned up and kissed his mouth, because he was so beautiful and helpless and exposed to her this way. He opened his lips, half-turning his head away from her, and then bowed down and sucked and strained against her mouth, his breath mingling with hers as she pulled his arms higher. It was a desperate kiss, like a battle in which she would lose if she released the hard tow on the cord in her hand.

She broke away, feeling her grip on the silk slipping.

She held it with both hands, searching out the anchoring cleat in the wall. With a quick loop, she made the cord secure and stood back, staring at him, her palms heated by the slide of the silk in her hold.

He was trembling all over, standing with his legs spread

and his head tilted back to the wall, his blackened eye like a painted design in the half-light. It was not a game now. She was not certain that it had been from the start. Her mischievous reverie of a warrior prince faded before the reality: dark murderous perfection bound before her, and he had let her do it.

"Allegreto," she whispered, her voice filled with wonder at herself, at the sight of him. "God save, I love you."

It was as if the words had come from someone else, some other place. He grew utterly still—for a long moment she could not even see him breathe. He squeezed his eyes hard shut and gave a tiny sound. He dragged his hands down so that the cord went tight and straining all along its length. The muscles in his arms swelled. His chest heaved with his sudden effort to break free. The silken cord drew taut, squealing against the hooks.

He went abruptly still again, panting. "Kill me," he said in a broken voice. "I can't bear it. I can't—bear it."

She stared at him. She hugged herself, shivering.

"Please," he said, the one word an ache in the room, an echo of torment.

She went to him and put her arms around him and laid her head on his chest. He jerked the bonds when she touched him, and then the tension in his body seemed to crumple; he swayed against the cord and pressed toward her, rubbing his cheek on her hair like a child seeking comfort.

"Elena." He breathed a laugh. He put his head back and yanked at the cord that held him. "Christus, do you know how much I fear you? I'll die like this."

She let go, standing away as he hauled and fought the bonds. "I love you," she said again, as if some evil angel had her tongue.

He gave a bestial groan and lowered his face, looking at her with his teeth bared. "I'd like to ride you until you can't draw breath to beg or squeal."

The sudden raw threat hung between them. Elayne felt it like the sting of the strap, the crude recovery of his power.

But it brought something vital between them, an armor against what had been in his face and in her voice.

She gathered herself, took refuge in the game. She paced slowly, observing him as if he were a piece of merchandise displayed for her pleasure, trying to drag her mind back into safe imagination.

"But you cannot, can you?" she asked. Her words at least came out with something that resembled cold confidence. "My so-fierce enemy. You cannot."

He was silent, watching her like a chained demon glowering from the shadows. Elayne stopped, facing him. He raked her with a look from head to toe, and she realized for the first time that her robe had come unbuttoned and fallen open. He meant to intimidate her with that devouring stare, but she tossed back her head and shoulders and let the gown slide from her body. She held it delicately, as if she were about to step into a bath. Guards and handmaids and a queen . . . she conjured them for courage and banished them in the same instant, leaving her alone in this chamber with him.

"I have use for you, warrior," she murmured, pulling one pin at a time from her hair. The belt dangled from her hand as she did it, the kidskin soft on her cheek and shoulder. "I could give you to the guards, or have you enslaved—but I do not." She shook her head, feeling the weight of her braids tumble down her back and brush against her naked buttocks. She paused and let him look at her as she fingered the plait and worked her hair free, reveling in his hot dark stare. "I find you well-formed and favored. A worthy sire of princes."

He pulled down slowly on the bonds, his arms flexing. "If you be a mare in heat," he said coarsely, "then set me loose, and I'll service you without mercy."

"Oh, no," she said demurely. "I need not set you loose."

Eighteen

———∞———

HE WAS ANNIHILATED. Utter destruction. His reason was a void. He wanted to rip the anchor from the wall; panic and terror and fury and longing all at once, while she went naked and sat down on the stool, turned a little away from him, with the rippling black fan of her hair all down around her like a swaying scarf.

She looked back at him, her hair parting over her white shoulder, her blue eyes vivid beneath long black lashes, a face like a woman-child, like Heaven and Hell to him. Insults and rage and pleas for mercy were all the words he could form. He gritted his teeth together and swallowed shame, unable to find himself, lost off the brink and falling, falling; with no refuge but brute silence.

She huddled on the stool and gazed at him as if he were some curious marvel that had caught her attention, holding her arms around her breasts, her fingertips resting lightly on her own bare shoulder as if she covered herself modestly. It was no expression he could fathom or predict, though he had spent a lifetime learning to read the hearts of men on their faces. He could not fathom it, he knew not what she would do next, only knew with awful certainty that it would cut him open to the bone.

He had let her play this game; he had all but begged for it, giving himself away inch by inch, unheeding of the risk. But he had never known what it would be to find a woman who did not fear him. He could have laughed and wept to see himself eviscerated so utterly by a violet-eyed maid. He wanted her; he wanted this; he suffered it with a frenzy beyond any measure.

She rose slowly. He backed himself against the stone wall, gripping the cord above his fists. He had seen men on the rack with more courage than he could summon.

A faint smile touched her lips, as if she knew his thoughts. His guts went to liquid inside him. He tried to imagine her as a quarry, to find his cold shell, but she had taken it with his daggers and returned with his own strap to scourge him, to make him burn for her the way his skin blazed under the sting. All his shield obliterated, forfeited like a scrap of beggar's cloth before he fully understood his jeopardy.

She pulled her hair together and drew it forward in one shimmering midnight tail over her shoulder. It fell down between her breasts. He had seen her do that, over chess, and adored it like a smitten boy, like a calf-head, the way he adored every move and thought and feature and limb of her. But he had had charge of himself then; he could conceal the depth of what he felt. Now her hair slid apart around a full pink nipple, split in rivers of sable down to her belly, and he could not move of his own accord to touch her. He heard himself make a sound that had no humanity in it, a groan like a simple beast.

He wished that she would raise the strap. He would have bowed down like a sinner at a whipping post; he had committed sins enough. He could bear that easy torture at her hand. But he realized what she intended too late to find any protection; he was raw skin and lost soul when she came to him, smoothing her palm down his chest to where the cloth pressed and chafed his erect rod.

With gentle fingers she drew the laces. No dream or night-sent climax, no succubus or angel could have made him impassioned as she did. He could not move away from her; he refused to swing and twist on this gibbet for pride or humiliation; he stood frozen with his boots planted apart as her hair fell down between them.

She was going to use him. She said so. He could hardly comprehend it. In her playing at queen, with him as her sport—in her game she said she loved him, a taunt that left him reeling with no defense against it.

She lifted her face and looked up at him with such a strange innocence. Such eyes like the depths of sweet blue Hell. He thought of flinging her onto the floor and ramming himself in, thought of it just as she released him to her hands and he could do nothing to prevent her.

She curled her fingers around him. White-hot bliss arced through his body; she held him between her open palms and he clung with both fists to the cord above his head, the only solid thing in existence beyond her.

She leaned on him, kissing his chest. He did not think any whore in Christendom knew the things she seemed to know; she bit and pulled on his nipples, sweet painful tugs that brought him to the edge of extinction. He clenched his teeth, enduring it, half-dying with furious pleasure in it. And then she let him go.

Shudders washed over him. He opened his eyes and looked down, panting, blinking at her bare feet and calves and her thighs. He did not dare lift his eyes any higher. The dark triangle between her legs was like some glorious secret, half-glimpsed, worth his life to reach. He would have slit the throat of the Pope himself only to see it, but her long hair swirled across it as she turned away. She left him hanging. Powerless. He made a silent moan, held inside himself, his eyes shut and his head resting back against the hard wall. His arms ached, but he was no more now than his sex, desperate to couple her even like this.

Wood scraped and thumped near his feet. He lifted his

lashes and found her before him, at his height, her wide eyes on a level with his.

Without a word she kissed him hard, her mouth spread open. Her breasts pressed against him. Her hands searched and held his shaft. As he thrust his tongue in her mouth, she made a delicate feminine lift of her hips, pulling him in, sliding down on him hot and wet. The feel of it sent him almost to oblivion. She broke from the kiss and pushed back, her arms braced on the wall beside his head.

He could not move, forced to the depth of her in blind sensation. She stared into his eyes, her lips parted, rocking her slit against him, softly at first, and then harder, taking her pleasure of him while he was utterly subjugated. He could feel his seed leaking into her. She tilted her head and shoulders back, her womb sucking at him with hot sweet greed.

Her breasts rose before him. He lowered his head but he could not reach, he could only arch up into her as she kneaded his shoulders with soft cries, spreading her legs open and pushing her hips at him roughly. He surrendered to it wholly, lifting his head back to the wall, powerless while she clung to him and used him as any night imp would use a man; without reserve, her body pressing on him, careless of what pain or satisfaction she gave. Used him until she jerked and cried out wantonly, bursting around him.

His mind exploded with her peak. He had no thought. He had white nothingness in his vision, like sun-dazzle. He dragged down on the bonds, ramming up into her, pure pleasure as everything he was blew apart and fell away, beyond any hope that he could find it again.

She held tightly to him while he shuddered; her arms and body squeezing and throbbing around him. She rested her forehead on his bound and upraised arm, their bodies joined. Both of them panted for air. She kissed his skin, making small delighted noises. Then she lifted her face and looked up to his hands.

He was completely broken; he did not care that his wrists burned within the cords, or his shoulders ached with

strain if she would stay leaning against him so that he could
feel every breath she took. He turned his face and kissed her
ear and her cheek, searching for her lips.

But she lowered her head and drew free, stepped down
and away, leaving him. She released the cord with a suddenness that was bright pain. He rested his arms on his
head, the only move he could yet make, letting blood flow
into his joints.

She hurried away to the far side of the chamber. He
slowly let down his arms before him, his wrists still bound
together. He stepped away from the wall, found the end of
the knotted cord around his hands and freed it with one tug.
His fingers burned with blood returning. He held his wrists
and flexed his fingers, breathing through his teeth. He fumbled at his breeches and still felt stripped naked even after
he'd laced himself.

She came to him, her loose hair all about her like a veil.
She held his belt, with his daggers sheathed on it again, and
the stiletto in her hand.

"Careful," he said, his voice cracked and harsh, a grasp
at recovering himself.

Bowing her head, she knelt at his feet. As if she were a
pageboy, she lifted the waist-belt, her hair a black waterfall
over her hands and arms. He looked down at her in amazement as she girded it around his waist, her moves graceful
and lovely at the humble task. She buckled the leather and
smoothed it with a reverent touch.

He could not find words. In wonder he let her open his
arm and slide the dagger into the bracer's sheath. She
pressed her forehead to his wrist and his open palm and
then kissed it.

He sank to his knees before her. He took her face between his hands and lifted her chin and stared at her. Her
lips were shell-pink and soft, a little reddened and swollen
from violent kisses. She looked into his eyes steadily, that
open marveling look she had, as if the world were as new
and fresh as dawn to her; the blue-violet depths of lakes and
oceans and infinity beneath her lashes.

"You are my queen," he said roughly. "I have no other sovereign."

She smiled a little, like a pleased child. She nestled her face against his hand and closed her eyes. He felt the mingled touch of their breath, the brush of her hair, the confiding press of her cheek in his hand.

Conquered. Beyond the force of armies.

AT TIERCE ON their third day of waiting, she rolled over in the bed and lay against him, her hair in her eyes. The bells were faint; they had sounded each morn and None and Vespers every day since he had brought her here. He could see that she was listening, as if she had just heard them.

"We should make confession," she whispered, staring at the canopy above.

He understood her. The things they had done together must be mortal sin. Any priest on God's earth would judge them acts against nature—for a man to submit to a woman, to take carnal pleasure in the pain and shame she gave him.

He could not repent, but he did not want her to be in danger. He brushed the hair back from her face. "I'll ask Gerolamo if he'll take you in secret," he said, tracing her cheekbone with his finger. "I think it can be done."

"And you," she said quickly.

Her eyes slayed him yet, each time she looked into his. Immeasurable depth of blue and purple, gazing up at him with unguarded honesty. He shook his head with a faint smile. "I cannot, beloved."

"In secrecy . . ."

"I cannot," he said again softly. He saw her remember, and realize. He could take no sacraments, nor wanted to. He only felt sorrow for this to come to an end, these brief days of serving her at any ruthless delight or sin she desired. When she was cleansed of it, and penitent, he did not think she would command him again that way. As well for that, too, for he had no defenses left to him if she did, and the world outside would make no games of weakness.

She lowered her lashes. He leaned on his elbow, watching her, taking pleasure in animal sensation; in their legs entangled warmly under the sheets, in her hand resting in light possession on his waist. She was thinking, and he could expect some unforeseen slant to her thoughts when she spoke them—he would be amused or confounded or alarmed, he did not know which.

She had discovered things in him. Things he had not known himself until she touched them.

"You fix my penance," he murmured, burying his face in her shoulder, his arm across her breasts. "Your punishment is like bliss for me."

She turned her body full toward him, so that he could not hide his face in shame for what he wanted. She wrapped her arms around his shoulders. Her eyes were very close; he could feel her lashes on his skin when she blinked, the brush of butterfly wings.

"Is it so for all men?" she asked shyly.

"No," he said. "You know it is not." He heard the trace of helpless anger in his own voice.

"Only you?"

"Oh, God." He turned away onto his back. He stared upward, looking into the abyss of himself that he had not known existed. "I know not. Haps all the angels despise me, and give me pain for pleasure."

She raised herself over him, her hand splayed across his chest. He bore her contemplation like a blade against his soul. Even her position, subtly governing, her light touch a mastery, made his body stir again. "I love your pleasure," she said.

"Jesu," he whispered, tilting his head back, his bare throat exposed to her, his rod growing stiff against her hip.

She slid her hand down and covered the tip. He stilled, with fear humming through his veins. She pinched the tender hood between her fingers until he panted, gripping the sheets beside him. Then she drew down his sheath and scored fire across the head with her nails. He made a hoarse sound, arching to her.

They both knew, they both had learned these small cruelties and delights quickly, as if demons whispered instruction in their ears. His body wanted to roll and take her down and cover her, but she would kill him then, she would tie him to the wall and he was more afraid of that than of the pain. The vision of it sent him near to spending in her hand.

She let go, the only thing that saved him. But she rose over him, sitting across his chest. Her hair fell down in waves over his throat. The scent of their couplings drowned him as she held him, his body pinned within the compass of her spread legs while she reached back with one hand and caressed and pinched and tortured his cullions and shaft with her fingernails. She made the tip of his rod slide over the velvet skin of her buttocks, exquisite pleasure as she hurt him. He thrust into her palm with a rough sob, his muscles working hard against the pain that was utter bliss.

Then she brought her body forward, releasing him just as he could no longer endure it, and knelt over him with her hands against the wall and her rosy slit to his mouth, allowing him to suck and worship her. He felt it like a gift, that he could taste the depths of her and make her tense and rock and arch back in ecstasy.

His shaft throbbed and burned for her, still sore from her hand. When she moved back with an eager panting he followed her, turning over, rising with fervent obedience as she commanded him to serve her. She took a stance before him on her knees and arms, to be mounted like a lovely she-demon. She had abused him so that it hurt to enter her, but he was lost in it, gloried in it, his mind gone near to roaring blackness as he looked down at the sight of her pale back and sable hair, her round buttocks and his rod plunging in. He held her hips and shoved deep; he heard her whimper and cry, but it was delight and demand, and he answered fully, commanded by her even as he spilled his seed in blinded ecstasy.

Afterward he lay with her close in his embrace, curled around her body. His pulse still beat loud in his ears. She was soft and warm and delicate. He felt it fiercely, that she was under his protection, and the idea mingled and twisted in his mind with the way he submitted to her rule, a strange and sweet confusion, hardly bearable.

Lethargy tried to creep into his limbs. He drew a breath, to deny it and clear his brain. He threw back the sheets, setting her away as he rose. She made no protest, only watching him from amid the dark tumble of her hair as he sat on the edge of the bed.

He looked across a space of infinity to where his daggers lay.

With another deep breath, he stood and dressed himself in clean breeches and gray hose of Gerolamo's provision, aware all the time that she observed him. He tied off the laces. His belt and bracers lay tangled in his father's chair. Without looking at her, he crossed to them and drew his stiletto, gauging the edge with a stroke across the back of his arm, shaving a patch of hair sheer as a razor. He sheathed the blade and took up the arm guards one by one, strapping them on.

"What manner were you punished as a boy?" she asked suddenly. "With scourging?"

He gave a slight laugh, like a harsh breath, and shook his head. "That is not punishment."

"Worse?" she asked.

"I was not punished," he said. He reached down for the waist belt. "Not as you mean."

She lifted her brows. "Never?"

"If I erred, he would have killed me," he said simply.

He felt her gazing at him as he drew each dagger and inspected their points. She hugged the pillow and made a grieving sound.

He had a sudden dread that she would shed tears for him. He girded on the belt and buckled it. "It was what I thought, at least," he said, sliding leather through the keeper. "Doubtless only a boy's fear."

"How well you lie," she said.

He strode across the room and caught her hand and gripped it hard in his fist, holding it up to his mouth to kiss

her fingers. "Dress for travel, my queen. The time has come
for me to prove it."

THE OLD PRIEST was loyal, a Navona himself, distant
blood-tie still clinging to this poor remote sanctuary in the
hills beside the lake. The house of Navona had been scattered and decimated, the castles razed, the villages burned.
It lived in hiding now, a veiled web of shared hate for Riata,
a promise of revenge and blood and fidelity to the bastard
son of Gian Navona.

But he did not let himself be seen; he wanted no eyes to
recognize him, no more acquaintance or complications than
he must have. Gerolamo had arranged it; the priest would
shrive a veiled woman of her sins and give her communion
and ask no untoward questions of who she might be or why
she sojourned here. For the character of the sins she had to
confess, Allegreto thought, it would seem plausible enough
that she came here because she dreaded to voice them to
any but a stranger and God Himself.

He stood with her at the water's edge, under a tangle of
reeds and overhanging olive bushes. The lake lapped softly,
rocking the little barque as he held it ashore with his boot
at the prow. What village had once clustered about the pale
stone church was deserted now, the houses burned, the
small piazza gone to goats and weeds. At the last moment,
as his man made a signal from the arched shadow of the
church door, Allegreto held her back. "When you confess—
do not say that we adultered," he said, leaning down close
to her heavy veil. "Do not mistake that we committed such
a sin."

She turned her face toward him. He could not see her
beneath the cloth. It had only occurred to him in that instant, that she might remember the island, the false bedding, and think she had fornication, too, on her soul. He did
not want any speculations or guesses of such a thing, even
by ancient silent priests, but mostly he found that he did not
want her to believe it.

"We are wed before God," he said. "You had no troth to the Riata, no free consent."

The moment that he said it, with such insistence in his voice, he wished it taken back. He could see her pause, and think of things that she had not before. He cursed himself for a sotted fool, that he had even spoken to deny it, to remind her that she had never given free consent to him, either.

She bent her head without reply. In full black, her face hidden, she could have been any widow from city or countryside, come to light a candle for her husband's soul. She carried a small basket of eggs for the priest, with a gold coin in the bottom of it.

He felt a wave of desire for her, a wild thought that he would go down on his knees and beg her not to go away from him into light and grace. She would return a stranger, made innocent again as she had been when she first came to him. She might even forget, or not want to remember. He thought of forcing her into the boat and back to the tower, a dream of locking her into it forever with him as her servant and defender; so satisfied with all he did for her that she would never want to leave.

Such thoughts were a blink in time. He did not touch her. "Go now," he said. "I will wait here."

He watched as she walked out into the sunlight. It was a small church, and old; bare white stone with blunt corners and a single slit for a window above the door. He knew it inside, knew what it would be to step from glare into the sudden murk, to pause a moment and kneel, accustom his eyes to the golden pinpoint light of a few candles. The odor of incense, the stone floor, the massive columns marching into shadow, painted with spirals of red-and-white that led upward to a few faded saints who smiled down at the center aisle.

He stood there exiled from it, with a longing at the back of his throat. As she reached the door that Gerolamo held open for her, and passed under the arch, he turned away.

She would come back. If she did not, he would go and

seize her, and the old Navona priest would be no bar if it came to that. Better in haps if he did seize her, for then none could claim that she bore his society willingly, or defied the decree to shun him from any Christian relations.

He stepped aboard the boat, making a final tally of their provisions—clothing sufficient to see them into the mountain passes, small coin and walking staves, a tinder-pouch. Clouds had begun to roll over the peaks to the north where the steep flanks plunged into the lake. Gerolamo stood guard by the church door.

It creaked open again, far sooner than it should have. Allegreto glanced up, looking through the tall reeds.

She appeared in the entry with the priest at her side. The old man held the basket. They paused for a moment at the door, the priest speaking urgently to her as Gerolamo drew respectfully away.

She shook her head beneath the veil and put her hand on the cleric's sleeve with a small reverence. Then she left him, her head bowed low, and walked rapidly across the open ground toward Allegreto, her feet kicking aside her skirts with determination.

He stepped back onto the sandy bank, signaling Gerolamo to retire with a jerk of his chin. "What passed?" he asked sharply, as she came under the tangled shade.

She put back the veil and looked up at him. "I will wait to confess," she said.

"Wait? Nay, there will not be another chance," he hissed. "I cannot vow safety elsewhere."

The priest was still standing under the church portal, looking after her. She could not have done more than tell him she would not make confession; there had been no time for more. Allegreto could guess that the old man's pressing words had been strong advice to clear her soul. He took her shoulder, reaching to turn down the veil again. "I know it is difficult," he said more gently. "But he does not know you, nor will ever."

She threw the cloth back. Under the black hood, her skin was like ivory, her eyes the hue of the deepest lake. The shadows of reeds and branches played over her face. "Nay, it is not for shame." She lifted her chin. "I will wait for you."

"Wait for me?" He stood with his hands on her shoulders.

"I know you cannot. Not yet." She wet her lips. "But I will wait until you can be absolved, too."

He let go of her abruptly. "Do not be a fool."

"I thought on it these many hours," she said. "By chance I am a fool, but I cannot say I am full sorry, or ask for pardon alone."

"Why not?" he demanded. "I thought it was what you wanted."

"Because I thought on it—and thought—" She looked away from him, toward the lake and the dark clouds rising. "What if something goes wrong? What if we are slain?"

"So much the more cause to be in grace!" He caught her arm, giving her a little shake. "These are deadly sins, you know it. You're in danger of damnation for such."

She looked down at his feet. "Aye, and 'tis pain of excommunication for me only to converse with you. I asked him, and he said me so."

"You asked him!"

"I did not say your name. I only asked it as a doubt I had, as if it were some neighbor."

He set his jaw. "And he answered rightly, but that we are wed, and so you may speak to me and such common things without penalty. I have inquired into all of those matters well enough myself."

She lifted her eyes to him. It was true that a wife need not shun her own husband—that much was certainly true.

"We are wed!" he exclaimed, with mulish resolve. "We will have it blessed in the church when we can." He looked toward the sanctuary. "But the other need not wait. Here is a confessor; you wished to repent and be shriven. It is foolish and . . . and"—he searched for sufficient words—"sinful to delay!"

She smiled then, as if she knew a secret that he did not. "I will wait."

"Elena!" Her easiness about it made him strangely angry. "It is your immortal soul at peril!"

She tilted her chin downward, like a wayward child, and looked up at him aside from beneath her lashes. "Are you a priest now, to be so alarmed for my immortal soul?"

He gave a huff of disapproval and stepped back. "Nay, I am no priest. But Hell is not a game of morra, for you to smile at me that way about it. I will not see you in danger of damnation; do not put that on my conscience, too."

"And neither do I wish to enter Heaven while knowing you could not. So I will wait."

"Elena! And risk—"

"Aye!" she snapped. "I understand what is at risk. And this is what I choose."

He heard her words as if they slipped through his mind without catching—sounds come and gone, senseless—and then their meaning struck him full, like a clout across his face.

The reeds bowed and rustled around them. An olive leaf fluttered down, a silvery thin shape, catching in a black fold of her veil. Her lower lip trembled as he gazed at her.

"I would miss you for eternity," she said. "I would grieve."

He shook his head, all the feeble movement he could summon. If she had held out jeweled cities, riches, towers of gold, all the stars and the sun and the moon offered to him in her hands, he could have spoken. But he could not. She would miss him in Heaven. She would grieve.

She did not know what she was saying, in truth. What she risked. He had read every poem and sermon and hymn about it; he had studied all the ghastly frescoes that portrayed the kingdom of Hell in terrifying and perfect detail. But that she would hazard the chance for an instant, or even think of it, for him . . .

He feared for a long moment that he would die where he stood, only from confusion. He put his hand on his dagger, for something solid, something he could understand in the roaring flood that engulfed him like water rushing from a broken dam of ice. "I pray you," he said helplessly. "This is madness. Go and repent. And then stay there. Stay away. Don't come back."

She did not turn. She did not flee to safety and grace and the priest still standing in his infinite beckoning patience at the door of the church. "No," she said. "I will wait for you."

Nineteen

ᴇʟᴀʏɴᴇ ᴋɴᴇᴡ ᴡʜᴇɴ she was in disgrace. She was familiar with the averted eyes and compressed lips after she
had not been sufficiently contrite over some misadventure.
He said nothing of it, or anything more of his brief perverse
command to her to remain with the priest. But he had desired her to be shriven, and she was not. And so the long
hours of the journey on the huge lake passed in a silence
that was more than mere stealth.

A cold breeze funneled out of the north, creating small
sharp waves that splashed against the prow. Clouds rolled
over the cliffs and tumbled down the sides like foam pouring from a vessel. Shrouded under the pointed hood of a
peasant's mantle, Allegreto took up oars, bending into the
pull in time with Gerolamo's efforts. His face was set in an
unchanging scowl. He never once looked at her.

He was armed now. She would not be suffered to touch
him. Unspoken, that pact held between them, and she had
no wish to breach it. Instead she looked at his soft boots
braced against the thwart, at the way the muscles in his legs
worked as he rowed, and the things that came into her mind

were sufficient cause in themselves to make the preachers spit and rage.

The boat seemed small, a mere chip bobbing and skimming below the terrible beauty of the mountains. The cliffs passed slowly nearer, closing upon the lake like the walls of some giant's castle. She craned her neck as the gray crags grew steeper, the summits taller, masses of rock pitching straight into the water without even a narrow shore for relief. Ledge mounted upon precipitous ledge on overhangs that no man could climb.

Gerolamo kept them to the center of the lake, far from any barges or boats or the towns and castles perched along the cliffs. It was darkening to late afternoon as they passed close under a vast spur of stone that thrust far into the lake. But the sun broke through looming clouds, lighting the water below the headland with a sheen of silver. The brisk wind dropped suddenly to a ripple over the surface.

A bright bay came into view. Across the water the sails of small boats drifted like white birds flocking toward the towers and walls and quays of a great city.

Elayne sat up. She knew it instantly. She had never held a clear memory, never been able to conjure it in her mind, but the sight of Monteverde was like a dream she had dreamed all her life.

In the midst of the towers rose an imperious rock, a high sharp promontory walled all around, crowned by a citadel that ruled the structures below. But the lower city pushed up toward it in proud challenge, a forest of towers reaching skyward, stone fortresses tinted in rose and cream and ochre with banners flying from their rooftops. Behind it the blue mountains lay in a circle of massive defense, cradling the smooth rich valley at the head of the lake.

Allegreto sat back on his oars. He glanced over his shoulder toward the city. Then he turned a sidelong look to her from under his hood, watching her face.

Elayne put her fingers over her mouth. She felt startled and confused, almost mortified by wonderment. She shook her head a little, as if she declined some spoken invitation.

He smiled. "Not yet," he said, like a soft promise.

Never, she thought—but it was only an echo of an idea, a distant sense of trepidation. She was fallen in love. Directly and straightaway in love with a place, with the reality of it as it lay before her, lit by sun-shafts that toyed with the citadel and the towers, sparkled on the lake and vanished in cloud-shadow.

She huddled in consternation at this unforeseen sensation, watching as Gerolamo let the boat drift and Allegreto worked with him to throw out a net. As the sun angled lower, the light breeze carried them slowly toward the wild headland, as if they were only casting for fish along the shore.

Elayne still stared across the bay. It was as unexpected as his laughter, this dazzling city. Hidden by mountains, guarded by cliffs and fathomless water. Another castle held the precipice above them, overlooking the narrows from the headland. Elayne could see a colossal chain that bowed down into the water, stretching from the rocks below the fortress across the throat of the bay, marked by floating fetters. She could barely discern the other end where the cable rose again from the water below a stronghold on the far cliffs.

Tiny boats such as theirs sailed across the boundary without pause. But the laden barges and bright-painted galliots seemed to be required to pass at the center, where a pair of sturdy guard ships awaited them. A warlike galley lay in wait beyond, the oars flashing as it made a leisurely circuit of the bay.

She thought suddenly of the fleet and army of men he had lost; realizing for the first time the magnitude of that attempt. To bring such a force—from the sea—up the lake or over the mountains, or both; what devices and plans he must have had, strategies laid out like the plays in a game of chess. Five years, he said, that he had worked for it.

She thought, too, of the way her journey might have gone. Should have gone. A regal procession; a cavalcade with the green-and-silver banner overhead and a man she never yet seen to be her bridegroom. Or perchance she would have arrived by water, in one of the glittering galliots, these pretty replicas of seagoing galleys made to ply the lake.

She felt very small, staring across to the walled towers. Someone else held it, Monteverde. Someone who could not be weak-willed or defenseless to rule this place. The citadel rose in unyielding splendor, a fortress within a fortified city. The very idea that from this little boat there could be any chance of unseating the possessor of that power was beyond her imagination.

"His ensigns fly at the water gates," Allegreto said quietly, standing beside her, his legs braced against the sway. "He means to conceal that he's left the city."

Elayne did not have to ask who he meant. "He's left?" she said under her breath. "Can you be sure?"

He gave a slight nod toward the distant walls. "The last standard by the western quay."

She squinted. The green-and-silver banners rose and unfurled in lazy waves in the fitful breeze. The last one seemed as the others. She glanced again along the line of banner staves that marked each quay, and only then perceived that the westernmost flag was not quite raised to the full height of its pole. The difference was so subtle that she would never have noticed if he had not told her where to look.

She released a breath and glanced at up Allegreto.

"One banner only," he said softly. "He left this day, by the western gate." He turned his bruised face toward the city, his teeth showing in a faint smile of mockery. "I knew he could not forgo to be in at the kill."

Gerolamo made a wordless grunt and jerked his chin toward the great chain.

"Aye, 'tis as Morosini told," Allegreto said. "He's beset with rumors. Full prepared for attack. I count at least two dozen masts inside the harbor walls. I want the number of his hired companies, and who leads them, and what he's contracted to pay—have our blessed saint send me certain word of it by way of the lamb."

The man assented, as if orders to saints and livestock were common things. The boat rocked as the two of them hauled in the empty net. With the push of an oar, they drifted into the deep shadow below the headland. Their small vessel rode up onto a tiny space of sand under the cliff. Allegreto leaped lightly ashore and turned, reaching for the bundles and staves that Gerolamo was already handing off.

Elayne rose, grabbing Gerolamo's shoulder, comprehending their haste to be out of plain sight of the city walls. She made the jump, propelled by Allegreto's hand toward an overhang of rock that was covered in brush. He came after, crowding close behind her under the thorny branches. When she glanced back through the leaves, she could see Gerolamo casting the fishing net again, the boat drifting slowly away from the shore.

"SLEEP." THE BUSHES shielded him as he sat on his heels, overlooking the lake and the tiny path they had ascended.

Elayne huddled back in the recess under an overhanging rock, where there was a flat space of ground and odd bits of rubbish, a wax stub and the torn and dirtied sleeve of an old chemise amid the litter of leaves. She had never felt more awake. "Sleep!" she whispered, as low as he had spoken. "I cannot."

He cast her a look from under the gray hood. There was a hardness about his face that she had not seen since the island storm. "Are you frightened?"

This cliff seemed wholly exposed, almost facing the city, with the castle directly above them so close that she could hear the sentries call their stations. "Yes!"

He nodded. "We will move after dark. I must see the sign that Gerolamo has entered the gates."

"Into the city?" she asked anxiously.

"Aye." He turned back, surveying the bay. "Try to sleep," he said to the lake. "I will not fail you."

SHE SAT WITH her eyes closed. She had not slept an instant, vexed by nerves and the stony ground and the prickle of dry leaves no matter how she tried to shift and sweep at the debris. It seemed that hours passed. Each time she looked through her lashes, the mountains were only a little darker, the clouds somewhat thicker, the sun rays fading slowly into a broad evening gloom.

He knelt a few feet from her in the drab gray clothes of a common man. The pointed hood had fallen back. She realized for the first time that his hair was now cut, rough curls hacked and twisting below the nape of his neck, a loose strand hanging down across his face. The colors about his eye had been fading slowly from their virulent purple to ugly shades of green. Even so, he was striking—not all of the unsightly elements together could conceal his rare looks.

In the silence of twilight the wind had gone to nothing. A deep chill descended with the shadows. From below, the lake made small clear sounds, water washing gently on the shore.

He turned his head abruptly. Elayne heard it at the same time—the slide and crunch of footsteps descending the path above them.

Thick brush covered their position from any view from the lake, but there was only a thin screen of thorn branches to shield them from the path itself. They were easily visible. As the descending intruder began to whistle an aimless tune, Allegreto moved back. He grabbed Elayne and pushed her down, his full length sprawled atop her.

Before she knew what he was doing, he had pulled up her skirts to her hip, exposing her hose and bare leg. He covered her mouth in a grinding kiss, tearing at her clothes. With a fully audible groan he dragged the gown off her shoulder and plunged his hand up her skirt. Elayne made a gasping squeal of surprise.

The whistling stopped. Allegreto nipped her earlobe hard. "Hush!" he whispered, quite loud enough for anyone nearby to hear.

She gave a scared giggle. He lifted his head, his hair falling down over his eyes as he looked toward the path. He reached up and put his arm and elbow at the side of her head, blocking her from any sight of the intruder, but she knew her naked leg and shoulder must be in full view. She could feel his other hand hover near his poison dagger.

"Pleasant eve," said a man's voice, with a hint of amusement. "Are you well?"

There was a moment of silence but for Allegreto's harsh breath. He looked out with a malevolent glare. "Well enough for my business," he said caustically, "if you will leave me to it."

The other man chuckled. "You need no aid?"

"And bugger you!" Allegreto hissed.

"I pray you!" the interloper said wickedly. "Spare the lady's ears!"

She felt Allegreto's hand close on the dagger hilt. Quickly she reached up and grabbed his face between her hands and pulled him down to kiss her. She made a moan and writhed against him. His whole body went rigid. He broke away, pushing her face toward the wall.

"But she is not discontented, I see," the man said. "I will leave you to your task, then. Take care on this path after dark!"

The lazy sound of footsteps receded upward. Allegreto lay over her, looking out, until they were vanished. Then he sat back, pulling her skirt down with a snap. "Dirty goat," he muttered.

Elayne rearranged her gown and brushed small pebbles from her sleeves as she sat up. Her fear had altered to something else. She felt mortified and breathless, a peculiar exhilaration. "He seemed harmless enough," she whispered. "I'm glad you did not kill him."

"I should have." Allegreto sent a dark murderous stare after the intruder. "He knows this is a trysting place. He should have turned back without speaking."

"You know him?"

"Nay, I don't know him. It is some lackey from the castle above, no doubt come down to do himself—" He stopped, looking conscious. "I pray your pardon. But he knows well enough. Everyone does."

Elayne looked at the torn sleeve among the leaves. She felt a mix of aversion and excitement. A sharp memory of her meeting with Raymond at the mill came to her. There was something deeply disturbing about the chance of discovery at wanton play in such a place, stirring and embarrassing at once. Allegreto's indignation only made her want to take him around the shoulders and thrust her fingers into his rough-cut hair and pull him back down to the ground.

Their eyes met as she thought it. At once his face grew stone and cold, as if he saw into her mind and rejected such things instantly. He sprang lightly to his feet. "Did you rest?" he asked.

"A little." She watched him walk to the edge of the cliff, a figure half-lost in the growing darkness.

"We should go," he said, "before he steals back to peer again, the harlot."

Elayne rose, shaking out her skirts. "Did you ever . . . make a tryst here yourself?" she asked, without looking at him.

"No," he said bluntly.

She took the stave he handed to her and slanted him a smile. "Good."

He put his hands to her shoulders. For a moment she thought he might kiss her, but instead he yanked her mantle up over her head and close to her face. "Keep your eyes down, and try to walk like a modest woman," he said, holding it together under her chin. "I don't want him supposing you will lie in the dirt and giggle for any yokel who passes by."

"Only you!" She smirked at him, tapping the side of his boot with her stave.

"Only me," he said. "Unless you care to leave a trail of dead men in your wake."

ELAYNE WAS THE straggler of the party. She sat with her head down, hardly able to distinguish the sound of a pouring waterfall from the ringing in her ears. The steep paths had become agony for her; she could not seem to find enough breath to fill her lungs. Her legs burned with exhaustion. She rested on a boulder beside the misting waterfall, panting, with sweat trickling down her neck and back and soaking her chemise. If not for the vision of Margaret and Zafer in the hands of Franco Pietro's men, there was nothing that would have made her stand up again.

What easy ground there was, they had covered in the night, under cloud-glow and a fading moon. A few hours of sleep in a thatched shed and then just before dawn the young shepherd woman had come to lead them. They climbed with a little flock of four ewes and a late-born lamb, taking paths that led upward, up and up past the vineyards and apple orchards into the fir trees, up until fingers of mist clothed the tall trunks in gray, up until Elayne's head was pounding and she could think of nothing but how to lift one foot in front of the other. A pair of the white guardian dogs ranged alongside, loping through the pine trees and up the rocky slopes, trotting ahead and returning like pale shadows in the woods.

Allegreto had long since thrown off the gray cape and hood. Though his hair clung to his neck and he had tied a band of cloth around his forehead to keep the sweat from his eyes, he did not seem to suffer from the wobbly legs and weakness that made every step a torture for Elayne. Their guide sat serenely, no more winded than the dogs. She was a lovely girl, with soft eyes and cheeks delicately touched with rose from the climb. She held the lamb in her lap, gazing up at Allegreto as if he were the angel Gabriel and she some haloed Madonna in an altarpiece. Elayne hated her.

He turned from an outcrop that overlooked the valley below. They were still within view of the city. Elayne could see it between the trees when she found strength to lift her head, a mass of red rooftops, the towers like tiny child's toys amid a patchwork of green. A river curved across the cultivated valley, running languidly to the silver slip of lake still visible beyond the city walls. The blue mountain crags sprang up to cloudy summits, white drifts that seemed to hang so close she could touch them if she reached up her hand.

"He's invested the eastern pass to Venice with his troops," Allegreto said in French.

Elayne could see scraps of color strung in lines along a white strip of road. They might have been tents or crowds of people, though she could make out no individual parts from this distance. The shepherd girl had brought details of the mercenaries in Franco Pietro's hire; fifteen company of foot soldiers and eight troops of horse—to Elayne it had sounded enough to conquer the entire north of Italy.

She tried to think through the pounding in her brain, blinking wearily at the peaks on the far side of the valley. "I should not mind to have an elephant to ride across this mountain," she said.

Allegreto leaned back against a tree trunk. "An elephant?" He frowned for a moment, and then raised his eyebrows in surprise. "You have read Titus Livy, then."

"Lady Melanthe sent it with some Latin texts by Petrarch. I liked the elephants. I was sorry Hannibal did not win." She gazed down at the city and valley laid before them like a giant map. "I suppose Franco Pietro does not study ancient history. It does not seem to occur to him that you might march from the north."

He gave a short laugh. "As well you were not here to suggest it to him."

"Was it your intention?"

He glanced toward the shepherdess, who had been gazing at them uncomprehendingly while they spoke in the French tongue. "In haps," he said with a shrug. "It is little matter now. How do you fare? We will move more slowly, if you wish."

Elayne lifted her face. "We must arrive in time. I can do it."

He observed her narrowly for a long moment. "I do not want you to expend yourself too far." He made a little gesture with his chin toward the shepherdess. "You are no peasant, to labor like an ox and then give birth in the field."

"'Tis only that I am not accustomed to climb so much," she said. "I swear there is no air to breathe here."

"Aye, 'tis harder to fill your lungs in the mountains," he said. "We will rest more often."

"I don't want to make us delay." She planted her staff among the fir needles and pulled herself to her feet.

"Sit down," he said.

"But—"

"Sit." He came toward her with such suddenness that she sat back on the boulder abruptly. "I wish to see you take more sustenance," he said. "You've eaten little." He grabbed up one of their bundles and began to pull out bread and apples.

In her exhausted state Elayne had no desire to eat. But she saw that he was determined on it. And in truth, if she was to go on, she had to find a source of vigor from somewhere. She took an apple and sank her teeth into it obediently. He laid before her bread and olives, along with a rosemary-scented sausage and cheese enough for two or three people, then knelt on one knee beside her. He examined and tasted each and cut off pieces and watched her eat until she could not take another bite. Then, when she would have risen to walk on, he bid her sit longer and rest.

She knew the source of this overbearing concern. She had seen Sir Guy insist on the same sort of indulgences to Cara when she was with child.

"Do not make foolish delay for me," she said to him. "You must be there."

"And leave you by the wayside?" He pitched an apple core into the roaring cascade.

"Aye, if you must!"

He shook his head. "There is time."

"How long?"

He looked away from her. "There is time." He tied the food bundle to the end of his stave.

"You cannot be certain," she said. "Think of Zafer and Margaret, and what you have forgotten—"

"I think of it every moment," he said curtly. "And other things, also. Waste no more of your precious breath on this, madam." He stood up over her. "Rest until I command you otherwise."

ON THE SUMMIT of a mountain pass they paused again at a tiny wooden shrine. They had climbed up out of the trees into blowing snow, where the only plants were grasses and lichen and a few miniature flowers clinging to the crevices of rocks, whipping in the wind. Elayne kept her head down, facing away from the gale and huddling within her mantle, holding her gloved hands under her arms. The rock she sat upon felt like a block of ice.

The shepherd girl, too, sat hunched over her lamb, with the dogs lying at her feet and the sheep scattered nearby, snatching at grasses or curled into windblown piles of wool. Elayne worked hard for breath. She knew they could not stay here long—already a deep shiver possessed her as the wind cut through her clothes to her damp chemise. She could see Allegreto's figure a distance away, where he stood alone on the broad open saddle of the pass, staring down into the valley that lay ahead. The wind whipped his hair and tore at his cape, but he seemed heedless of it.

The ridges rising to either side of them were almost lost in gray fog and snow, the landscape utterly barren. Elayne shook inside her mantle. She was too tired to stand, but the cold was sinking into her very bones, making her shudder helplessly. She gripped her staff, trying to force her unsteady legs to obey her, when one of the dogs suddenly looked up. They both hurled themselves to their feet, barking feverishly as they raced toward the dark shape of a man that materialized out of the blizzard.

Elayne made it upright, standing next to the shepherdess, squinting through the snow toward the stranger. He stood still, held at bay by the furious dogs.

"Call them back!" It was a young man's voice, shouted over the barking and the wind. "I'm here to warn you, fools! There are bandits in this pass."

Allegreto was suddenly beside her, blocking the snow as she leaned heavily on her staff. "Call the dogs," he said briefly to the shepherd girl.

She made a high-pitched cry, half-carried away by the gale. The two dogs paused. They looked back. The girl called again, clapping her hands. With reluctance their white guardians turned and trotted toward her.

"Look." The young man pointed up onto the far slope. He walked forward as the dogs retreated. Upon the rise stood another man, silhouetted in the fog. A second appeared beside him. Elayne held back her hood to look at the ridge above, and saw armed men there, too, stationed amid the clefts and rocks.

She turned to Allegreto, hardly able to close her shaking and frozen fingers on the walking stave. She could not run. If he had not put his arm about her waist, holding her back against him, she was not sure she could have stood. The boy—he was hardly yet a man—came up boldly, though he kept his distance from the dogs. He was tall, dressed in rags that could hardly have kept out the cold, his head wrapped in a dirty black cloth.

"I see we are well trapped," Allegreto said, bracing solid and warm against her.

"I know them," the tall boy said urgently. "They can be satisfied with enough gold."

"You are their emissary?"

"Nay!" The youth shook his head vigorously. "I live

below. I don't like to see folk hurt. I can talk to them. I might succeed, if you offer gold enough."

"And if they are not satisfied?" Allegreto asked. Elayne felt his low voice as a warning, like a growl from the dogs.

The young man looked meaningfully at her and the shepherd girl. He shrugged. "You won't leave this mountain alive. The women—well . . ." His words trailed off into the wind.

Elayne waited, shaking uncontrollably, half-expecting Allegreto to step forward with his poisoned dagger and murder the boy. She did not know what would happen then—if the bandits above would rush upon them. When he moved his hand downward toward his knife, she stepped away from him with a faint cry.

He restrained her by the elbow. He drew a single coin from his purse and flipped it to the young man. "Go and talk, then. Say that I send health and all honor to the dread and invincible Philip Welles, and this is how much I offer to see us safely through the pass."

"A piccolo—" the tall boy objected, his wind-chapped face turning redder still. "I dare not! This will only enrage him!"

Allegreto grinned in the teeth of the gale, the snowflakes wetting his dark eyelashes and collecting on his hood and shoulders. "Then add that the Raven invites him to take drink and meat with us this eve, for the sake of bygone adventures together."

Twenty

⎯⎯✼⎯⎯

THE LIGHT OF the campfires glowed on tall tree trunks, highlighting the white scars of cut limbs. Under a shelter made of pine boughs, Elayne sat on a log bench, breathing the sodden smell of smoke and wet forest. Rain dripped from two places in the makeshift roof and made puddles at her feet. She was still trembling with fatigue, but her clothes were new and dry and the fires gave out a cheerful warmth.

After a goodly feast, if rough, Philip Welles's men lay about under what cover they had, gulping large swigs of excellent Tuscan wine. A few women and children worked at clearing the meal, while the giggles of less industrious females sounded from unseen places.

Philip Welles was an Englishman. He had the strong laugh and pink cheeks of the northern isle, though there were deep lines engraved about his eyes and his hair had gone to gray. He held council under the pine boughs like Robin Hood, with a tree stump for a throne. It was difficult not to like him; Elayne had to remind herself several times not to blurt out her replies in English when he used his

painfully awkward Italian to address her. He seemed to
have some notion that she could not follow the general conversation in French, but his manner toward her was so fatherly and cheerful that she let him bumble his way through
his misformed Monteverde tongue, and only nodded and
smiled in reply.

Even Allegreto appeared to be in a congenial humor. His
face seemed relaxed in the firelight, his hair still damp and
his jaw clean-shaven. But when Philip dismissed most of
his men and turned to the pirate, demanding to know what
purpose was afoot, Allegreto's dark eyes came alight.

"I have need to penetrate a castle," he replied.

"Where?" Philip asked instantly. "What defenses?"

"Maladire. The old Navona fortress at d'Avina."

"Hah!" The outlaw sat back. "Let us take London and
Paris as well! I've thirty good fighting men!"

Allegreto smiled. "Nay, do you think I want a battle?"

Philip narrowed his eyes. "What do ye need us for, then?
I've no craft with your poisons and stealth."

Allegreto's smile vanished. "Such things are my office,
aye." He looked into Philip's face with no expression. "But
don't tell me you've not guile enough, old fox. I require a
diversion."

For a moment Philip seemed aloof, as if he had been offended. Then he grinned, the lines about his eyes creasing
deeply. "And how much would you be offering for this diversion?"

"One thousand marks of Venetian silver."

Sadly Philip shook his head. "Divided among thirty?
Hardly worth our time on the muddy roads, my friend."

Allegreto lifted his eyebrows. "The traffic through this
pass must be prosperous of late!"

The outlaw rubbed his lower lip with a stout finger.
"Aye, we've had some luck." He frowned. "D'Avina, you
say?" He glanced over at one of his men who had remained.

The man nodded, as if in answer to an unspoken question.

Philip ran his tongue over his lip. He jerked his chin. "Bring me those chests with the silver coins."

The man rose quickly and spoke to someone standing outside the shelter. In a few moments he returned with a companion, both of them lugging large metal-bound boxes. The chests hit the ground with a heavy chinking. Their tops were painted with the emblem of Monteverde, a castle upon a green mount.

Philip leaned over and slid a key into one lock. With a heave, he pushed the opened chest toward Allegreto. "Examine that," he said.

Elayne could see the glint of silver coin inside—a very great deal of it. She could perceive why the offer of one thousand marks had not been judged overly generous. Allegreto scooped up a few pieces and turned them in his palm. He shaved the edge of one with his dagger, then bit the coin and shook his head. He glanced at Philip, who said nothing.

Allegreto looked down again at the coins. He dipped a handful from the chest, sliding them one over the other with his forefinger. Suddenly he paused. He let the silver shower back into the chest and then picked up one piece at a time, setting them side by side on his open palm, rotating each as he looked closely.

He closed the chest, laying the coins out in even rows. He reached over and took a handful from the second box. Over and over, he compared coins, holding them close to his eye on the back of his hand. Finally he made a soft snort.

"All struck with the same burin. There is an extra prong on the crown." He looked up. "Did you rob these direct from a minter's bench?"

"Not I," Philip said.

"Who?"

"We escorted a fellow of Germany through the pass," Philip said innocently, as if they had been hired for the task. "This was the payment."

"Luck indeed," Allegreto said with a dry smile. "I'd expect an armed company to convey such as this, and no deal with the likes of Philip Welles, begging your indulgence."

"Aye." The outlaw did not take offense. "You would think so, eh?" He nodded slowly. "And yet he was a young man, with only two pack mules and a servant, and the coins hid among bags of onions." Philip shrugged. "Saint Mary, we wished the man no harm, and he went upon his way." He grinned. "Back home, I believe, as his traveling funds were a little low. Too liberal with their purses at every tavern, these young bucks, eh?"

Allegreto smiled dryly. "Take care how you spend these coins, my friend," he said. "The alloy is bad, as you know well enough. Now if you like good Venetian silver that will pass anywhere without a question—my offer stands. Make it fifteen hundred marks."

Philip seemed to ponder, as the firelight warmed his grizzled face and gleamed on the coins. He shook his head. "I am tired," he said slowly. "Tired of this life."

Allegreto said nothing. Beside Philip, he appeared timelessly youthful, as if age could never touch him.

"It is not enough," Philip said. "We' re thirty here. Three of us share half, and divide the rest by each man. Even with another fifteen hundred marks, after we split fair among us . . . not enough." He sighed heavily. He looked down at his open, callused palms. "I'm weary, boy. Weary of the rain in my bedroll and the weapon always in my hand."

"Tell me what you want, then."

The outlaw looked into the darkness. "Eh. A warm house in town. A plump merchant's daughter to soften the featherbed. And peace."

"You would be fatigued to tears in six months of such a life," Allegreto said.

"Nay, not I."

"What will you do? Eat and sleep and rut and grow fat. You're not so old. Leave that for when your mind grows dim and you can't think of a fraud to earn your breakfast."

The corner of Philip's mouth turned up. "A fraud!"

"Aye, a fraud. As your black heart desires, I well know.

Set aside the Venetian marks, then." Allegreto nodded toward the chests. "What is it you devise to plunder?"

The twist of the outlaw's mouth turned into a grin. "You are ever one step ahead of me, lad. You tell me, then."

"I don't know enough yet. There is an engraver's burin escaped from the mint. Where is it? Who has it? How often is this watered coin leaving Monteverde?"

"It was not leaving. The boy was headed in from the north. Claimed his father is the chief officer of the mines here, if you can credit it. Name of Jan Zoufal, or something like, he said. Seems to be a foreigner."

Allegreto turned his hand suddenly, flipping the coins and catching them in his palm. "It's extortion you have in mind, then?" he asked.

"Nay, I don't doubt the honorable Jan Zoufal would send me packing if I tried that. Who would believe an outlaw like me against Franco Pietro's head man?"

Allegreto looked at him a long time. His glance moved to Elayne, touching her like a leisurely brand. Even through her weariness, she felt it. He smiled at her and turned to Philip. "Still . . . there is promise in this," he said at length. "Much promise. I believe we can make an arrangement."

Philip grinned widely, kicking the chest at his feet. "I knew you would see it. Well met!"

Sudden shouts came from the darkness beyond the camp. The bandit instantly leaped to his feet, ducking outside. Allegreto followed. Elayne rose as she saw a big white pup run into the clearing, gamboling alongside a knot of men who emerged into firelight from the trees. They held a stumbling figure erect as they marched him forward.

She recognized Dario in the same moment as he looked up toward Allegreto. The youth's broad face held a wild expression; he seemed to find his feet and then fell on his knees when he saw his master.

Allegreto strode forward. Nimue ran to Elayne, leaping on her skirts with big muddy paws, but Elayne could only grab the puppy and hug her close, staring in alarm at Dario's bowed shoulders and look of agony.

"Matteo!" Allegreto demanded, standing over him.

Dario shook his head. He pressed his fists to his forehead, then bent over his knees down into the mud. "Escaped, my lord."

The bandits gathered mutely around. A silence spread over the entire camp. Even the women stopped their work, everyone held frozen, without sound but for the muted pop of the campfire and Dario's half-sobs of breath.

"What passed?" Allegreto's face had gone to a mask, his dark eyes to ice.

Dario sat up, his square jaw marked by slashes of mud. He spoke to Allegreto's boots. "At the cross trail to d'Avina, in the night. We took shelter at a farmhouse. The babe was weeping and I thought to warm him. We had time; we were well in time to pause and rest. The woman was kind. We ate." He bent his head and locked his hands together until they shook. "My dread lord—I fell asleep—without securing him."

Allegreto stepped forward and grabbed the youth's hair. He yanked Dario's head back and down. "You tracked him?"

Dario swallowed in his bared throat. "I tried. I tried. I lost him at the edge of the town. He's gone into it, I think. I left word with the cat to hunt him, and came here."

For a long moment Allegreto looked down at him. Time stretched to taut infinity, as Dario winced and panted.

"Are you confessed?" Allegreto asked softly.

The young man's face grew still. He wet his lips and clutched his hands together to his mouth like a man in desperate prayer, making a soundless whisper against his fingers.

Elayne let go of Nimue. The puppy dropped to the ground and bounded toward the remains of the bandit feast.

She saw Allegreto's hand reach for his dagger. He had a look of inhumanity beyond any comprehension. Dario ceased his prayer and crossed himself, exhaling, his face and body relaxing into peace as if he fell asleep with his head forced back and his clasped hands resting on his knees. For one instant she saw Allegreto's face too change; his eyes drifted shut like a man about to lose consciousness—then he opened them, his fingers closing on the dagger as he drew it with a swift move.

"Do not!"

Elayne heard her own voice ring like a bell through the clearing in the trees. She stepped forward.

Allegreto stilled, his knife poised to slash over the boy's throat, the blade gleaming in the firelight. She could see Dario's pulse pounding under his skin, but he made no move, no resistance.

"Let him go," she said.

No one spoke. Campfire smoke drifted slowly across the sodden ground in tendrils and rose into the trees. From the edge of her vision, she saw that the bandits stared at her, but she did not take her eyes from Allegreto.

He was like a statue with Dario kneeling before him. Not one flicker of emotion or expression crossed his face. When he raised his eyes, he seemed to look at nothing, unblinking.

Suddenly he shoved Dario's head forward, withdrawing the knife. The youth fell down with his face and his hands on the ground, sobbing openly.

"Princess," Allegreto said. He made a cold bow to her and sheathed the dagger. He turned and walked away.

"WHO IS SHE?" Philip asked.

No one had spoken to Elayne in the night, after Allegreto had gone out of the camp. But now in the chill morning he was returned, and the bandits stood in a circle around the blackened fire-pit, gazing at her with wary awe, with the same expressions she had seen on their unshaven faces as they had watched Dario crawl to her and kiss her mud-sodden hem.

"The one who can grant all your pardons when she takes her place in Monteverde," Allegreto said. "Or have your hands cut off and hung about your necks for thieves, while your bodies dangle at the city gates."

Philip walked to her and went down on one knee, baring his head, his mail chinking as he hit the ground. With a sound of creaking and muffled thuds, all his men did the same. "Princess," he said. "God and Your Grace forgive me! I did not know."

Such reverence disconcerted her. She looked down at his grizzled hair. "I thank you for your welcome here," she said. "There is nothing to forgive."

He remained on his knee, and Elayne realized that he was waiting.

"Rise," she said in French. "Everyone."

Allegreto had not knelt. He stood looking across the banked fire at her. She did not think that he was pleased. "Philip," he said, "we must speak in private."

The bandit turned a little, not quite facing away from Elayne. "Aye," he said gruffly. "I think it a wise idea."

He sent his men to the perimeters of the camp and escorted Elayne into the shelter of pine-boughs. He insisted that she be seated on the tree-stump throne. She did not know if it was because he had discovered her title and hoped for pardon, or that she had averted Dario's execution in cold blood in his camp, but he made it evident that he looked to her now as the higher power.

Dario himself hung uncertainly at the far side of the clearing, near where Nim was tied. Allegreto ignored him as if he did not exist. Elayne thought of calling him, of sending him to fetch Margaret's babe that had been left with the woman at the farmhouse, but she thought better of it. The blind coldness had not left Allegreto's eyes. The baby was likely as safe in a house as in this camp among women who drank more ale than the men. Better that they all feign Dario was invisible until his dark master decided otherwise.

"Pardon my bewilderment, donna—but you are Prince Ligurio's granddaughter?" Philip asked bluntly, standing under the shelter with the dry green pine needles brushing his balding head. He looked from Elayne to Allegreto and back to Elayne again.

She nodded.

"I see it well enough, now I look," the old bandit said. "Though you were but an infant when we took you to Tuscany. You have your father's eyes, Princess, and your grandfather's certain way with a command, God assoil them both."

"You took me to Tuscany?" she asked in astonishment.

"I was one in the escort," Philip said. "It was before—" He made an apologetic gesture, his palm stretching open in his fingerless glove. "It was in better days for my company." He drew a heavy breath. "He was a great man, Prince Ligurio. I admired him."

"Aye. He was," Allegreto said quietly. His mouth made the faintest hint of a curve. "He would have checked me last night."

Elayne looked up at them both. She had never thought deeply on her grandfather, only known that Lady Melanthe had been his wife, and he had been much older, and he had died.

"You knew him?" she asked Allegreto.

He shrugged, looking down at the rough-cut chips that scattered the ground. "Whatever of me is not my father's, Prince Ligurio taught me."

"It was the undoing of this state, when Ligurio passed," Philip said. "It was the ruin of this place, to fall into vendetta." The bandit leaned against a tree trunk, flicking needles from his sleeve. "And you and your father were no small part of that, my boy, let the Devil blacken both your names. You mean to try to overthrow Franco Pietro now again, do you? That's why Monteverde bleeds money to those French condottiere on the road to Venice, instead of fortifying against Milan, and Franco misplaced his betrothed. I should have guessed."

"If you'd rather Monteverde bled to you, old fox," Allegreto said, "I'm here to hire you to my side."

Philip shook his head. "You cannot win."

"I can," Allegreto said.

"You cannot. I see now who it was that escaped you—Franco's son, eh? Slay the father and you must slay him, too. And it all begins again. Give us at least the poor peace we've had these five years, to build something back."

"What is it to you?" Allegreto spat on his hand and jerked it toward the clearing. "You're naught but foreign condottiere yourself, or a bandit when you have no better prospect."

"This is not my land, aye. But I've lived here twenty years, and I'll find my grave here. Kill Franco, and you will have civil war."

"Not this time." Allegreto glanced toward Elayne. "We are man and wife."

"Navona and Monteverde! There are those who will not suffer that union, and well you know it." Philip crossed his thick arms.

"The people will rally to Ligurio's blood."

"If she survives it."

"Then help me make certain that she does. Or betray us to the Riata if you want his peace."

"You know I would not." The bandit laid his head back on the tree trunk with a heavy sigh. "But God and all the saints have at you, Navona. Give it up. Why not be satisfied with a little skimming of silver, and no more?"

Allegreto set his boot on one of the chests. "You won't skim more of this silver, watered or not. It's been sent in from Milan, to mix with our coin and shake the faith in Monteverde's currency."

"You say!" Philip stood straight.

"That's all it can be. Else why would it be coming in, instead of leaving? Why has Zoufal not come after you for it? Run your finger over the chests, you'll feel where the Visconti's viper has been painted out. Zoufal has some pact with Milan to mingle it with the good coin."

Philip made a rude noise, then glanced at Elayne contritely. "Your pardon, donna."

"Franco mistakes his men too often," Allegreto said.

"But no doubt Jan Zoufal would vacate a snug warm house in town, if you would care to take his place as master of the mint."

Philip wiped his hand over his mouth. He looked toward Elayne again. "What think you of this fellow, Princess? I suppose he's pretty enough for any woman's taste. But you saw him last eve—do you like a man who'll kill as easy as he breathes?"

"She knows what I am." Allegreto pushed off the chest. "And you are no bloodless saint, nor Franco either, when it comes to that."

The bandit fingered his lip thoughtfully, still considering Elayne. She felt herself growing warm under a contemplation that was almost fatherly, half-exasperated, as if Philip Welles had the giving of her hand and Elayne were a blushing maid too much in love to know her own good.

"When I commanded him to stop, he obeyed me," she said in a steady voice.

Philip shook his head slowly. "He did. But he did not want to kill that boy, my lady."

She knew it was so. As well as she knew he would have cut Dario's throat if she had not checked him in the instant before. Allegreto stood still while they spoke, impassive, looking somewhere out beyond the shelter.

"I'll wager he might even have a small idea that he ought to thank you for sparing him from it," the bandit said.

Allegreto turned and met her eyes. Nothing in his face changed. He only held her look for a long moment, his eyes as dark as midnight sky. She remembered his touch in the tower chamber, his hands in her hair, his lips at her throat. *I would listen. I would try.*

He had listened. Her fallen angel. Pirate, assassin, warrior prince.

"Mary save us," Philip grunted in the silence. "I believe they are in love!"

Allegreto smiled a little, glancing at the bandit. "Nay, I have no heart. My father hacked it of me out long ago, for his convenience." He nodded toward Elayne. "But she is my compass and measure now."

To hear him say it openly made her realize the depth of it, how much he gave up to her. *Love* was a light word, a plaything in comparison.

"Is it war, then, you want, my lady?" Philip asked. "That is the compass and measure of what he intends."

"No," Allegreto said sharply to her. "Once you take your place, they will yield. Why do you suppose Franco leaped like a hound at the chance to wed you?" He turned on Philip, scowling. "You know what Ligurio's memory means to the people. They revere it more every year that passes under the Riata's hand. Look what savagery it's taken for Franco to hold his place! You think my father ever managed worse? If I had not had Matteo, he would have killed us to the last woman and child who ever whispered the name of Navona."

"Because he is afraid of you," Philip said intractably. "If you would surrender to defeat, and let it go, as Princess Melanthe did, we would have no more of blood revenge."

"Englishman." Allegreto made a hiss of disgust between his teeth. "You do not understand."

"I understand that you and Franco Pietro are as like as one dagger point to another." He rested a heavy hand on the tree, turning his grizzled face toward her. "Do you understand it, Princess? You were betrothed to Riata. Now you gaze at Navona here like a moonstruck maid. Take your pick, they'll both have you for your name, and either one would tear apart all Prince Ligurio built to elevate their own. You were well out of this nest of vipers while they fought over his grave, my lady. God bless you, Princess. I am sorry you had to return, if this is all that will come of it."

Elayne hugged herself. She lifted her face and looked toward the old bandit. In truth she understood him better than she understood Allegreto, but she thought of Zafer and Margaret in Riata hands, of the child that might already be inside her, of Gerolamo waiting in the city and Dario on his face at her feet in gratitude for his very life.

"I don't know what to do," she said. "I don't know how to stop it."

"He's bedded you," Philip said gruffly. It was not even a question.

Elayne lowered her eyes. She bent her head down in a wave of mortification.

"Aye, and sent word of our marriage all over Christendom!" Allegreto took a sudden step toward her. "Look up and show no shame for it! I won't fail in this. I'll make you safe. I'll make Monteverde safe. I told you what I would do even though I burn in Hell."

She raised her head. He stood like dark Lucifer dressed in peasant clothes, daring hellfire in the gloomy light that filtered through the pine boughs. Elayne gazed up at him, helpless to find any way to leave or turn from him now.

The bandit heaved a sigh. "Forsooth, she is besotted! I see that it is futile to reason. Tell me what's your plan then, you black murdering bastard. Perchance we can see at least that she lives through it."

OF THE TWO dogs devoted to Elayne, Nimue was the least loyal. Whereas Dario would not allow her out of his sight, Nim was inclined to wander all over the camp, making friends and stealing anything that took her fancy. It seemed she had grown bigger even in a week, a bright-eyed beauty with the heart of a bandit, her brown eyes full of liquid adoration and her teeth capable of shredding chain mail. Or at least marring it beyond any reasonable use.

She was therefore banished along with Elayne when Philip Welles broke camp at word that Allegreto's designs bore fruit. It was a strange exile, a hiding in plain sight in the town of d'Avina. Elayne took up residence with Margaret's baby in a house built by Prince Ligurio himself, home now to a widow of strong Riata connections, childless and wealthy and pious, and devoted for years to supporting the cause of her late husband's family—so that it was half-forgiven and mostly forgotten that she was the relic of some ancient failed attempt at reconciliation from Ligurio's day, and had been a Navona before her marriage.

Elayne came in the guise of a young gentlewoman in some unspoken need of charity. The presence of a babe and her voluntary seclusion spoke their own tale for the gossips.

The widow herself was not ancient. Donna Grazia had no more than thirty years, to judge from her lovely face. All of the women loyal to Allegreto's cause seemed to be lovely, Elayne thought with some impatience. Lovely and silent. Donna Grazia delighted in taking charge of the baby, but there were no more than the most necessary exchanges between Elayne and her hostess.

Elayne was immured with Nim in a chamber fit for a prince, heavy with tapestries and lit by three leaded windows of glass that gave out onto the street. It still held objects provided to her grandfather for his comfort when he visited the mines: a writing desk and lectern, a silver goblet embossed with his initials and ringed with tiny emeralds. Dario kept watch outside the only door. By the end of a day both she and Nim were almost frantic. Nim at least was allowed to walk outside with Dario once every few hours, but Elayne had no relief, not even care of the babe. She could only stare into space and think of Zafer and Margaret and what Allegreto planned.

She knew only the outlines of it. Zafer was to betray a meeting with Allegreto somewhere in the mines, a time and a location—but that encounter would never be convened, if Franco Pietro did as Allegreto predicted of him and went first to the fortress of Maladire to command his garrison there. A counterfeit betrayal of a false rendezvous, all to lure the Riata into his own secure and well-defended castle—where Allegreto knew every secret hole and passage of its dark Navona past.

Elayne closed her eyes, thinking of it. Five games of seven, she repeated in her mind. Five games of seven he could outmaneuver his enemy in chess. Five out of seven, five out of seven . . . the numbers worked their way into her dreams, so that she woke from nightmares of blocked doors and broken mirrors with her teeth gritted together in a soundless chant.

He had never remembered his arrangements with Morosini. He had to deduce what signal he had agreed upon with Zafer, what spy Venice had on the garrison, what agents Franco Pietro had in the town. He had to expose himself just enough that the Riata would believe he was near, awaiting Zafer, yet give no hint that he guessed Franco would attempt to seize him. And Matteo was vanished like a young ghost, with no knowing what he might reveal if he could reach his father.

Elayne was afraid for Matteo. Allegreto's covert hunt through the town had found no sign of him. She imagined him alone in the mountains, or huddled in the mouth of some mine in the freezing night air. Elayne had extracted a pledge that the boy would not be hurt if he was discovered; it was her last word with Allegreto before they parted at the camp.

If she opened the window of round watery panes of glass, Elayne could see Maladire looming close, its blank sheer walls and single tower raised like a fist against the leaden sky. It had none of the elegance of the Navona castle on the lake. This fortress was a fierce and haunting silhouette, a barren challenge to the black peaks that encircled d'Avina, overlooking the green valley far below with a malevolence that matched its name. It had not been razed, but confiscated and strongly garrisoned: guardian of the mint and the mines, the silver lifeblood of Monteverde.

The smell of smoke lay heavily in the air. A strange grinding noise filled the street below, the sound of the miners dragging wooden tubs full of rock along the ground. The town itself clung to a ledge on the mountainside, its single street leading at one end to the castle and at the other to the slag heaps and gray landslides of the mines. Near the fortress, the steep-roofed houses were richly appointed, plastered and painted in frescoes, their gilded arcades and window casings agleam even under the threat of snow from the lowering clouds.

Bare-legged workers in white hooded smocks mingled with men and women in long blue robes, all of them hauling baskets and bags and bowls of broken stone toward the covered dais just below the castle, where men in opulent furs and brocaded gowns sat around a huge table and examined the ore set before them.

It seemed a busy and prosperous scene, like a vivid trance overlaid on the secrets below the surface. She leaned one knee on the wooden window seat, looking out, until she saw glances of notice from the people in the street. Then she played ball under the desk and over the bed with Nim until the puppy chewed the leather orb apart and fell into a happy nap amid the pieces.

Elayne paced the chamber. There were books inside the dark wooden chests, but she had not been able to concentrate her mind on reading. Finally she turned to the lectern that stood before the chimney, running her hand over a thick volume that lay wrapped in green velvet upon it. She pulled away the cloth and loosed the straps. The spine creaked as she laid the book open, as if it had not been used in a long time. She expected a Bible, or a book of hours, hoping there would at least be pictures that might distract her. But it was not a religious volume. Under a blank sheet of vellum, the first page was brightly illuminated, entirely covered in flourishes of green and gold and tarnished silver painted around the castle upon a green mount. Below the emblazoned Monteverde arms were Prince Ligurio's name and the title in Latin.

A History of the Glorious Republic and Principality of Monteverde.

Elayne turned the page with a dawning curiosity. She drew up the lectern stool and began to read her grandfather's words.

•   •   •

ALLEGRETO CAME TO her in the small hours. Nim gave one startled bark, waking Elayne from a drowse as she lay with her arms crossed over Prince Ligurio's book. She did not know how he entered; he was there as she sat up in confusion from a dream of war and houses burning.

The weak firelight showed a dust of snow on his shoulders, flakes melting and catching sparkles in his hair. He brought a scent of cold and smoke as he leaned close to her. He put his hand on the back of her neck and drew her into a fierce kiss, his fingers and his lips chill, his breath warm. She was so glad to see him alive that she broke away and held his cold face between her palms, running her fingers over the outlines and contours of his cheeks and jaw as if to be certain he was real.

"Is it over?" she whispered.

He kissed her again, deep and probing, as if he could draw the life from her into him. "Nay, it only begins," he said against her lips. Then he let go of her and moved abruptly away, standing in the shadows. "They are come. He holds Zafer and Margaret in the castle, and gave the signal that betrays me."

She slipped from the stool. "And you've sent a reply?"

"God grant that I answered it rightly," he said. He stepped back, moving subtly away from her as she came close to him, ignoring Nim's inquisitive nose at his boots. "But all is in train. I only came to tell you that if I do not return here by prime, in the dawn two days after tomorrow, Dario will take you to Philip, and he has the means to see you through the mountains to Zurich. There is a commandery of the Knights of Rhodes at Kusnacht; take refuge there and send to your godmother for aid."

"My godmother," she echoed.

"She has some pact with them about you, I'm sure of it. At the least they will spare your life from Franco."

Elayne gazed at him in dismay.

"It is only if I am slain or captured," he said calmly. "Send word to her from Kusnacht."

She drew a shaking breath. She put her hands to her

mouth and turned away and closed her eyes for an instant. But she did not want to let go of a moment with him now. She opened her eyes and went to him, lifting her face. But he stood unmoved. He looked at her, but she was not even sure that he truly saw her. She paused, clasping her fingers hard together.

He had already gone away somewhere beyond the reach of feeling. She saw it clearly—the firelight made a shadowed mask of his face, but it was the leopard that gazed out at her, not a man. Remote from her now, detached.

"Philip makes a show of hounding travelers on the road," he said. "They'll have to send out a troop to cover it. And guards to watch the mines. The garrison will be thinned. Once I am inside—sometime tomorrow or tomorrow night—and find where he holds Zafer, I can move on him."

She walked away to the farthest side of the chamber, to prevent herself from saying the words that sprang to her lips. The desire to fall on her knees and beg him to stay his hand fought with the knowledge that Zafer and Margaret would die horribly if he did. It was too late for arguments and pleas—she thought it had been too late from the first moment she had looked up into the black eyes of a pirate prince and seen the guardian angel of all her half-waking dreams.

"Do it well, then," she said. "What you must."

"I will," he said with soft certainty—with something nearly like pleasure. "It is what I am made for."

There was no warmth in that pleasure, only a keen energy, a force that delighted in the game of life and death. She was not sure if it even mattered to him in that moment what came of it, if Monteverde were won or lost—it was only the game itself that counted for him now.

And it was best that way. If she had frantic prayers and words of dread and love locked up inside her, she would keep them there, out of his sight and hearing. She stood straight and silent, committing to her mind the look of him, the shape of him, the stark curve of his cheekbone in the fire's red glow.

"I am yours," he said. He looked into her eyes, but it was like a chant, a motto spoken by rote, without tone or meaning.

"I know it," she whispered.

He turned from her to the door and left the room without farewell, so silently that it seemed he had never been there but for the scent of cold he left behind.

Twenty-one

THE ONLY THING that kept her sanity was her grandfather's book. It was called a history, but it was more. It was a voice that began in the mists of the past, in times that seemed as old as the lake and the mountains, speaking of the foundation of Monteverde in an assembly of all the people of the valley to elect a single ruler, because they were tired and sickened with quarrels and wars among themselves. It told of the choice of the green mount, where only a sainted hermit had ever lived before, as the impartial center of a new republic; it told of the building of the city and the discovery of the mines.

Elayne sat in one of the very chambers where Prince Ligurio had once written—reading of how he had studied and traveled the lands of Monteverde and collected the memories of his people and inscribed them on the spot, so that his work would be as truthful as he could make it. There were stories of miracles and amusing tales of animals; there were legends and facts, and her grandfather was scrupulous in noting which he believed true and which he thought were fantasy.

She felt as if she sat at his knee and listened to him, as if she could hear the very sound of him speaking to her. While the snow fell outside and she swallowed fear in every breath, it seemed almost as if he did speak to her, purposely—as if he had gathered here all that he might have taught her if he had lived to do it.

His history was not like most she had read, a long catalog of wars and generals. He wrote of the wars that had battered Monteverde, yes, the hard struggles to keep the republic independent of Frankish and Lombard invaders, but he wrote too of the achievements in laws and charity that had accumulated over the centuries. He wrote of the dissention and factions that grew as the noble houses began to war among themselves, of how the council disintegrated under pressure from outside and in. He told of how the first Ligurio—her own ancestor and his—had fallen on Monteverde in its weakness and conquered the city, the final destruction of the republic in favor of a Lombard tyrant.

"And if a kingdom is divided against itself, that kingdom cannot stand," Prince Ligurio wrote, in the words of Saint Mark. "And if a house is divided against itself, neither can it stand."

D'Avina was quiet outside on the Lord's Day, the grinding of the miners' tubs silenced, the houses and street mantled in snow. As she read, Elayne drank a cordial of hippocras wine, flavored and sweetened with spices. Dario had tasted carefully of it before she drank, then left it for her warming by the fire. She remembered the last snow she had seen, from outside the window of Lady Melanthe's solar. She had been in misery then over losing Raymond's favor—what a small childish hurt that seemed now, and yet she had thought she would never heal or smile again.

Raymond was good man, a devout knight, obedient to his liege and the church. There was not much chance, Elayne thought, that he would die unshriven and hellbound. She had a moment of intense longing for the sunlit days of Savernake Forest, for the heartaches of an untried

girl. For someone to speak to openly of all her dread and
uncertainty. In the night she had begun her monthly
courses, a sure sign, Libushe had taught her. She carried no
child, and the depth of her relief and sorrow for it filled her
with miserable guilt.

But she had only the book of Ligurio's words, and as she
turned to them again, and read, she slowly began to perceive the dream he had for Monteverde.

BY LATE EVENING Nim was in a mood of relentless
play, bounding from one corner of the chamber to the other,
up over the high bed, dragging the richly embroidered pillows to the floor. The young dog had been out with Dario
twice, but he did not like to leave his post for long, and refused to take her again. Elayne sacrificed one large gold-
threaded tassel that the pup had already chewed off the
bed—no doubt worth a year's living to one of the miners
here—and used it for a toy to save the fine carving on the
back of the door from Nim's raking claws.

Elayne threw the tassel and played tug until finally it
rolled under the bed. Nim was almost too large to follow it.
The pup bowed down as far as she could, her head and
shoulders under the bed-frame, her white plumed tail curled
up over her back as she struggled to reach the golden toy.
Then suddenly she pulled back, her eyes alert. She abandoned the tassel and bounded to a window, scrabbling at the
base of the wooden seat. Her deep-throated bark seemed to
rattle the glass lights.

"Hush! Hush!" Elayne sat down on wood as cold as
stone, trying to quiet the enthusiastic pup. Nim could not
decide if she were more interested in clawing at the base of
the seat or jumping halfway into Elayne's lap. Elayne finally let her scramble up, heavy paws sinking into Elayne's
stomach, a warm furry bulk in her arms.

Nim put her black nose to the open window crack, trembling all over as she sniffed at the cold air flowing in.
Elayne held her tight, to prevent her barking and just for the

comfort of holding an innocent living thing close in her arms. Nim bore it for a few minutes of time, and then thrust her nose again to the window, batting at it with her paw. The glass swung open with a draft of freezing air. Nim barked and lunged, bracing her paws on the sill and staring down into the street.

It was empty of people, but the snow had stopped falling. Under breaking clouds, evening light picked out the gold on the houses and glowed on the gray walls of Maladire. Nim barked again, the sound echoing in the street, taken up by distant dogs. A motion caught Elayne's eye—she looked across at the tiny alley between two houses and saw Matteo staring up at them.

He turned instantly away as Nim flew into a frenzy. Elayne jerked the pup back and locked the window closed. She ran to the door, but Dario was already opening it.

"Your Grace, you must not let the dog—"

"Matteo!" Elayne hissed, running to him. "He is outside!" She barely grabbed Nim back from flying through the door.

Dario froze. "Where?"

"In the alley across the way! Hurry! You'll see his tracks!"

The youth did not hesitate. He vanished out the door.

Elayne flailed about the prancing pup, trying to buckle the dog's leash onto its collar. She was pulling on her mantle, trying to keep Nim from grabbing the hem and make certain that she had the veil to cover her face, when the dog yanked free and ran back to the window, trailing the leash.

Nim jumped onto the seat, circling and sniffing at it. Elayne thought there must be a mouse behind the wood; she called the pup and started toward her, then shrank back, smothering a shriek as the seat bumped visibly under Nim's heavy paws.

The pup leaped free. Without a sound the seat rose like the lid of a chest as Matteo crawled out.

"Nim!" he whispered, falling on his knees while the

puppy leaped all over him and licked his face. "Your Grace! I didn't know you were in the town!"

"Matteo." Elayne could not find another word in her throat. She strode to the window and looked down into the hole that emanated cold air and the scent of rock and dust. She could see the rough stone inside the wall, a single stair and hand-hold—the rest was blackness.

"Oh, child," she exclaimed, "I've been so afraid for you! Where have you *been?*" Then she had a dread thought. "Did you find your father?"

"Not yet!" He looked up at her, a brown-haired, gray-eyed boy with rosy lips and a pointed chin that gave him a fey look. His sturdy soft-soled boots and leggings were damp with melting snow. "But I have been nearly in the castle!"

"You must not!" Elayne dropped her mantle on the floor. "Wait here for Dario."

"No! He won't let me go! He'll stop me! Please, Your Grace, don't tell him!"

Elayne paused on the brink of speech. She fell on her knees beside the boy and took his small cold hands into hers. "Matteo! I don't know how—I can't—" She could not find words to tell him what Allegreto meant to do. "You must not go!"

"I know I am Riata, and no one can trust me." He looked up at her with wide eyes, with a plea that tore her heart. "But please—Princess—"

"It is no shame that you are Riata," she said. "Never think so."

"It is," he said. "But I *can* be trusted. I have a plan that my father will not guess. Dario will think I can't do it myself," he said, lowering his face shyly. "So I didn't tell him. But I can!" He lifted his face with a childish excitement. "I found my way under the castle! I could even look a little into it, though I haven't found the way inside yet. This warren connects to that building across the street, where they keep the silver. I know all the Navona tokens—I followed them—they've tried to block some of the passages, but there are others they cannot see. I can do it!"

Elayne stared at him. "Do what?"

"I can kill Franco Pietro," he said, his rosy face intense. "I know I am not yet grown, but my lord killed a man when he was no older than I. I heard him tell you so. I'll kill my father for him. And then he will trust me."

She closed her eyes. "Oh, God save, Matteo," she whispered.

"Do not tell Dario, I pray you!" he said. "I only came because I saw you and Nim in the window, and I wanted—" He grabbed the puppy and hugged it to him. "If I should not return."

"Your return is not at issue. You will not go," Elayne said sharply. "Do not think it."

"Please don't tell!" He let Nimue go. "I must do this! It is my only chance."

"No," she said.

"I will!" he cried, pushing out his lower lip. He scrambled to his feet. Elayne had seen a child attempting escape often enough to reach for his collar, but before she could grab him, he kicked her, a blow that struck her just below the throat so hard it knocked her back to the floor, all the air escaped her lungs.

She gasped for air as she scrambled upright, but he was already into the window seat and dropping in one swift leap out of sight. Elayne gulped another breath and leaned over the black well. She ran to the door, but Dario was yet gone. She had no time to call on Donna Grazia. Nim stood over the opening, leaning her head down as far as she could reach, searching with her hind paw for purchase. With one light spring, she leaped into the hole, trailing her leash.

"Avoi!" Elayne muttered frantically. The candle lantern by the door was already lit; she yanked it from the hook and held it down into the opening. She could see a set of stairs between stone walls, barely wide enough to pass, descending into shadows. Nim and Matteo were lost from sight.

She gathered her skirts and put her feet over, sitting for

a moment on the edge of the window seat. With a deep breath she let herself slip down, holding the lantern before her. Through openings of glass and horn, her candlelight bobbed on rough steps that were so high she had to sit upon each one to slide down to the next. The space was narrow enough that she could not turn, only look straight up to see that the wooden cover was still open above her. When Dario returned, he would at least know where to follow.

By the time she reached the bottom, the rough-cut stone blocks had given way to a passage hacked into the mountain itself. Rock bulged from the walls, colored in rusty reds and strange vivid greens in the light of the lantern. The way led in three directions into utter blackness, one back toward the town and the others away.

Before she had to choose which one to follow, Nim came trotting out of the dark, tripping over her leash. Elayne crossed herself with a prayer of thanks and reached down to grab the trailing lead. She ducked her head, avoiding the overhangs and the distorted walls, making her way as fast as she could in the direction Nim had come, with the puppy dragging her avidly ahead.

It seemed an endless passage. She thought it led toward Maladire, but there was no way to trust her sense of direction. Sometimes she heard other footsteps, but she could not tell for certain if they were Matteo's or only an echo of her own. The boy had no light, but he had been taught to move silently and hide well, she knew. No doubt he could make his way swiftly in the dark.

At a fork, Nim did not pause but plowed ahead with her nose close to the floor. The pup stopped at a puddle, finding it a sudden fascination, but Elayne pulled her on and she sprang forward again.

A bronze gleam flashed in the darkness ahead. Elayne stopped, lifting the lantern, while Nim tugged insistently at the lead. She moved cautiously forward. A door blocked the passage, a solid buttress sealed in the stone. The familiar imprint of the Navona motto—and the dogs and shepherd and bear—glimmered dully in the lantern-light.

She drew a breath, set down the lantern, and crossed herself again for guidance. She was surprised that Matteo would know the secret key; she doubted Allegreto would trust the Riata boy with it. But Nim had pulled her unerringly down this passage. To go back now as far as the fork might mean to lose him entirely.

The panel slid back smoothly on her first attempt at the opening sequence. She reached for the lock and started to turn it—then had a moment's thought of all that Allegreto had tried to teach her of caution.

She closed the lantern, leaving only the light from the punches in the lead casing. Holding Nim up close on the leash, she slowly turned the latch and allowed the door to swing open. A quiet, eerie melody and chant made the hairs rise on her neck. In the faint thin line of candlelight, a set of stairs led upward. There were unmistakable footprints on them in the dust, as if someone had passed this way recently more than once.

Nim strained to go up. Elayne stood in the doorway, breathing a little easier as she recognized the sound of compline prayers from somewhere above. She did not think she was yet in Maladire itself.

If Matteo had come this way, she had fallen well behind him. There was no loose stone, no way to prop the door. She judged it best to return to the widow's house and Dario, who would have far better skill than Elayne at stealing through tunnels and walls in pursuit of a foolish and unhappy boy.

Nim ceased her pull suddenly and came down from the step, her tail wagging. She gave a deep bark. At the same instant something hit Elayne hard from behind, out of the tunnel. She stumbled forward, cracking her knees on the first stair as a child's figure lunged past her through the door.

Matteo scrambled up the stairs like a silent cat. Elayne threw herself after him, managing to grab him by one ankle. He kicked and squirmed, but Elayne held on with the strength of desperation. She rose just enough to fall upon him with her full length, pinning him to the stairs as they struggled in silence while Nim danced around.

The weak light winked out. With Matteo panting and wriggling beneath her and Nim snuffling at her shoulder, Elayne realized with horror that the door had closed behind them, with the lantern on the other side.

"Be still!" she hissed in Matteo's ear. "Matteo, Matteo, listen to me for the love of God. You must not go!" She wanted to scream at him, but she kept her words next to his ear. She wanted to plead with him to understand the hideousness of what he thought to do, but she had no time or reason to reach a child's heart that had been twisted so badly. Instead she whispered, "Do you want your father's men to catch Il Corvo? Do you care nothing for Zafer and Margaret? He is in there now to save them, and it will take every atom of his skill to do it. Every instant is a danger to him. To all of them. Do you understand? You cannot help, but only hinder. You cannot earn his trust this way, but you might be the cause of his downfall. He does not expect you, or know what you intend—Matteo, I pray you, I pray you, do not put him in such danger."

Her voice caught, for the unexpected strength of what she felt. Matteo ceased his fight, suddenly going limp beneath her. He lowered his head, his small shoulders shaking. "I want to help!" he whispered. "I only want to help."

Elayne sat up carefully, making certain she did not lose her hold on him. There was a tiny amount of light from somewhere above; she could barely see the pale shape of his face as she pulled him close into her arms. For a moment he resisted her and then pressed his face to her shoulder.

"I knew I couldn't do it," he said brokenly. "I c-can't do anything right. He'll never trust me now."

He does not deserve it, she thought fiercely. Allegreto never deserved such love, not for what he had made of this boy. But she did not speak past the ache of anger and fear and love in her own throat.

As she held him, there came a sound, a huge low boom

that seemed to reverberate through the very stone around them. Nim gave a nervous half-bark. The evening hymns ceased. Elayne turned to look up the stairs, clutching Matteo as the boy twisted to see. Above them was nothing but shadow. From a great distance shouts of alarm filtered down.

"We must go back," she said urgently. She pulled him with her toward the door. He did not resist—the depth and strength of that sound was warning enough that something beyond their grasp had happened above.

Elayne blindly explored the door, searching for a latch or carvings. But the metal was a blank wall under her hands. She could find neither handle nor symbols, and no way to force it open, not under all her strength.

FROM A SPY hole under the parapet walk, Allegreto watched the drawbridge and the outer gatehouse burn, pouring black smoke against the last glow of twilight on the snowy mountains. One jostle of the two glass vials that he had carried through the tunnels to the bridge, and he would have seen Hell himself far sooner than he wished. But he was not yet blown to pieces, and the arrows shot by Philip's best marksmen had ignited the powder of fulminating gold in a crack of thunder that echoed off the walls and soared instantly into flame along timbers anointed with resin and sulfur. The only known way out of Maladire was a sheet of unquenchable fire.

There were others, but he was already certain that the Riata had not discovered them. What secret ways they had found had been blocked or destroyed. Allegreto had spent the past day and night surveying passages and traps that he well-remembered—his father's exacting tests had burned the mysteries of Navona into his mind and his bones. He knew where Zafer and Margaret were chained; he knew where Franco Pietro slept with five guards around him and a mastiff at his feet.

He knew that Franco would comprehend at any moment

that he had fallen into a trap. Allegreto left the spy hole and slipped lightly down a set of stairs between the outer walls, counting his steps in blackness. At the first sliver of light above, he hiked himself up by handholds and found the opening at the peak of a storehouse roof. He squeezed himself through—not as easily as he had done in younger days—and felt his way down the slant of a beam to the heavy wooden column that held up the roof.

He was losing all light as he made his way across the trusses, landing off-balance and catching himself twice. But he had a cold exhilaration in him now, to move silently above the confusion he had caused below. He found the opening into the false ceiling as if the hidden ways of Maladire were drawn on some map within his blood. Crouching down on his ankles, he crawled between the double rafters until he could smell smoke again and see faint light between the planks.

He was near the courtyard—outside the shouts were louder and the fire rumbled. An orange-tinted glow illuminated the barred window in the door of the storeroom below. He could just see Zafer sitting on a bare floor, looking up, one fist gripped around the chain that held him to the wall, the other holding Margaret's arm.

Allegreto pushed a straw between the boards and let it fall. Zafer gave the clear signal and leaped to his feet, urging Margaret up silently. Allegreto laid back a sham ceiling plank and dropped through the hole.

IT WAS THE sound of evening service that befooled Elayne. When they could not return through the bronze door, she had guessed that they must be under the church that overlooked the piazza. The smell of bitter smoke began to fill the stairwell, ominous enough to drive her up toward the faint light and some hope of another way. The stairs ascended a great distance, but only led in the end to an arched cavern—a dark cistern full of water, strangely lit by reflections from the small drain above. The single ledge was so narrow that she had to pull Nim back from falling into the black water.

Matteo stood behind her, holding her skirt and peering past. "Don't let Nim go!" he said.

"No." She wet her lips. There must be some opening to this cistern—they could not be trapped here. It was impossible to judge the depth of the water, but she feared from the size of the pool that it must be deep. She could not see the far side well enough to discern if there were another ledge or door. The smell of smoke and the shouts were much stronger here, sounding almost as if they were overhead. She swallowed a rising sense of terror.

This must be the cistern for the fortress. She much feared that they were under Maladire itself, and the castle was burning.

"Your Grace," Matteo said. "Look at this."

She could barely see as he tugged her skirt, turning her back toward the stairs. But there were no stairs now. There was only wall, until he moved his arm quickly up and down. She nearly leaped backward into the water as she saw a pale shape in the wall move with it.

"Mirrors," he said. "Like the castle at Il Corvo."

Elayne stared at the wall. If he did not move his arm, she could make nothing of it but more stone in the dim shadows, but when he waved his hand in a certain direction, she could see the pale flash appear and vanish and appear again. She put out her fingers and found nothing where she expected wall to be. But when she took a step forward, and stretched, she found it an arm's length beyond, where she touched the silver reflection of her hand and her skirts in a series of small glassy plates set at angles in the stone.

"This way!" Matteo said confidently, and led her into a passage where it seemed no passage should be.

THEY COULD NOT discover a way that led back out of the castle. The narrow steps Matteo had found went into darkness again, the walls closing upon Elayne's shoulders as they climbed blindly. She began to feel smothered, as if the whole weight of the towers and fortress above pressed upon her throat and lungs; as if she would be trapped in this black maze until she screamed to get out. She gripped Nim's leash in one hand and Matteo's shirttail in the other, not to hold him back now but to know she wouldn't be left alone in this crushing darkness.

The boy stopped suddenly. "This is the end of it," he whispered.

"The end?" Elayne felt a spurt of dismay as she looked up, seeing nothing. The shouts had faded, more distant now.

"I think—" Matteo moved up a step. "I can see a little. There's a peephole. I think it is a church."

"Let me look!"

They stumbled over one another, trying to exchange places in the tiny stairwell, while Nim entangled herself between Elayne's feet. She found the crack and looked through into a tiny candlelit chapel.

They seemed to be close to the altar, opposite a pair of choir stalls. In the steady glow of the candelabras, Elayne could see painted frescoes covering the walls and the golden gleam of a large crucifix. She glimpsed no priest or congregation—the service abandoned while everyone ran to the fire.

She felt over the wooden barrier. Her fingers touched metal, and without a sound, the panel before her sprang open. The sensation of being freed was so strong that she barely glanced around before she gathered her skirts and crawled through.

She emerged onto the seat of another choir stall. The empty chancel and nave were small but richly decorated, tiled in black-and-white marble and painted over every inch of the walls with the saints and gilded halos of some biblical cycle that Elayne did not pause to identify. She only made certain that there was no one in the nave and then took a madly struggling Nim as Matteo lifted her through the open back of the stall.

Elayne wished now that she had her mantle and veil; in

the confusion of the fire, there might be some chance they could reach the widow's house without notice. The smell of smoke was dense and peculiar here, a sharp foul scent overlaid on the sweet incense of the candles. With Matteo and Nim close at her heels, she hurried down the vaulted nave and pulled open the door a crack.

In the last of twilight the tower of Maladire loomed directly over them, a turreted silhouette against black smoke that billowed across a rose and steel-blue sky.

Elayne stepped back and let the door fall shut.

They were inside the fortress.

Matteo stood looking at her expectantly. She had seen no one outside, only the tower and a snow-covered court that looked as wild as the mountainside, full of steep outcrops of gray rock, with the castle walls and buildings rooted into them as if the stone had grown up naturally into shapes of man's desire.

She was certain that Allegreto had caused the fire—he had made sure the garrison was lightly manned, and now diverted by the blaze. He was here somewhere, hunting Franco Pietro. If he succeeded—when he succeeded—he might see the open window seat in the widow's house and search the secret tunnels and find them.

She thought of the dark, and the walls pressing upon her. She could not do it. Nothing would make her go back into the narrow passages between the walls, trapped into the lightless tunnels by dead ends and mirrors.

"There must be a crowd of townspeople at the gate," she whispered. "We'll try to look as if we've come to gawk."

Matteo nodded, wide-eyed now and willing enough to take her direction. She grabbed his hand and pulled the door open quickly before she could be paralyzed by second thoughts and guesses.

They slipped and slid down uneven steps carved in the rock. The column of smoke and commotion of voices made it easy enough to head toward the fire; once they found the crowd, they would see where the townsfolk came into the castle and escape that way. Elayne went down the steep court, following a path of footprints in the snow, keeping her eyes on the ground to avoid twisting an ankle on the icy surface.

Nim had no such concerns. She ranged at the end of the leash, threatening to pull Elayne off her balance at every step. Elayne managed to keep her feet halfway down the courtyard, until the puppy lunged forward with a happy bark. Elayne slipped and skidded and shrieked as her feet flew from under her. She hit the cold ground hard, an impact that sent pain from her back to her teeth. As she sat stunned, Matteo slid past her, chasing the loose dog. A pair of men strode around the corner below, their torch flaring light over the court.

Elayne scrambled to her feet, trying to back up and turn away. Her heels slid without purchase; she was only saved from another fall as one man took her arm roughly, his mailed hand digging into her skin to hold her up. She kept her eyes down, watching Nim roll in submissive ecstasy under the nose of a great brown mastiff, her plumed tail flinging snow. The other man had caught Matteo.

"Lying bitch!" he roared, and reached to grab Elayne's jaw while he held the boy tight. "I'll—" He jerked her chin up, and then as suddenly let go.

She did not look up, but she had already seen the dark patch over his left eye. Her heart was pounding frantically.

"Nay, it is not the infidel's whore," Franco Pietro snarled. "God send they're still locked up, then." He made a gesture, as if to order his man up the court, and then paused. Under the glare of the torch, his face was distorted and puckered along a scar from his lips to the eye-patch, the shadows making it an evil mock of Matteo's delicate features. But they were frighteningly alike, the boy wrenching and struggling and the father who gripped him easily in an unknowing grasp.

"Hold her," Franco said to the guard. He caught Elayne's chin again with a brutal hand. "You aren't from the castle. Who are you?"

She kept her eyes down, afraid that even in the dark their color might betray her. She answered nothing.

"My lord," the guard said, his hand so tight on her arm that her fingers tingled with pain. He lifted the torch. "My lord—look at this boy . . ."

"He's my brother!" Elayne said quickly. "He ran away from me at the fire, chasing the pup."

But Franco paid her no attention now. He was frowning at Matteo.

"He was only following the dog, my lord!" Elayne said, her voice high-pitched with strain. "Let me take him home, and he'll suffer our father's wrath!"

Franco Pietro was staring hard, his big hand clutching the boy as he strained to pull away.

" 'Tis no child of the town," the guard said. "And they must have been inside before the blast at the gate. They're some of his."

"Nay." Franco's voice held a peculiar note. He grabbed the boy by both shoulders, turning him toward the torchlight. He put his mailed gloves on either side of the child's face and leaned close over him. "Matteo?" he whispered.

Matteo wrenched at his father's grip. "I hate you!" he cried. "I *hate* you!"

"Matteo." The Riata stared down at him an instant. "What miracle is this?" He looked suddenly more fretted than angry or amazed, glancing quickly around the walls. Then he glared at Elayne. "Your brother, eh?" He spit into the snow. "Are you another lying Navona whore?"

Elayne could think of no reply that could retrieve this disaster. She could think of nothing now but to struggle foolishly like Matteo, shrinking back as Franco Pietro turned his face aside, moving near her and jerking her by her hair. He looked intently down at her face with his good eye.

"Blood of Christ," he muttered. He let go of her as abruptly as if he had just seen a specter. He started up the court, hauling Matteo with him as his boots sank in the snow. "Bring her to the Turk," he commanded. "If they've swindled me, they'll all die for it, and curse the bastard of Navona to the lowest rung of Hell!"

Twenty-two

ALLEGRETO ROSE TO his feet at the creak of footsteps in the fresh snow. In the faint wavering glow from beyond the barred door, he stood alone in the storeroom, dressed in Zafer's infidel clothes. The youth had wound his own turban around Allegreto's head, tucked the tail of it with swift skill, then balanced upon Allegreto's shoulders to hike himself through the false ceiling and follow Margaret into the secret passages.

From the sound of the footsteps outside the door, there were more than two coming. Torchlight danced and twisted on the walls, but Allegreto kept his gaze averted from it, preserving his night vision. He placed the open manacle of the chain around his wrist and gripped the links in his left hand. As a key fumbled into the old lock, he turned aside in the corner, hiding the long length of steel that he held behind his leg.

The door scraped open. Allegreto did not turn. He staked everything on foretelling Franco's fury, that the Riata would not send some minion but come himself, fast and enraged, when he realized that Zafer had lied.

The shadow of a figure fell across the walls.

Allegreto ducked his head and lifted his arm, as if he hid his eyes from the glare of the torch. Over his sleeve he saw flickering light fall on the familiar torn features, the patched eye, while Franco Pietro shoved the smoking torch into a wall ring. In the instant that the Riata turned and took in the details of the room, in the moment before he would realize there was something amiss, Allegreto moved, dropping the chain and sweeping his sword upward, lunging to make the kill.

He seized short in the midst of it, barely driving aside the point of his sword as a woman stumbled into his path, shoved through the door by another man. Allegreto's body and mind froze as if he had been struck by a storm-bolt. Elena stood between him and Franco. And Matteo, his cheeks bright red, his small body resisting the soldier's hand with every step.

Allegreto did not drop his guard. Under the cruel discipline of a lifetime, he held still, taut, facing them with his blade at the ready.

No one spoke. Elena stared at him with her eyes wide and unblinking, terrified. Allegreto felt the wall and the corner at his back, all of his advantage evaporated in the instant he had hesitated.

Franco gave a sudden bark of laughter. "Of course!" he said, in a voice that was strangely mild. "It is Gian's godless bastard. I smelled the rot from your stinking fire." He drew his sword with a hiss, thrusting Elena and Matteo back toward the guard.

Allegreto made a slight feint, a twitch toward the wall, to draw him further from her. But Franco Pietro was no fool to run himself wildly on an enemy's sword point. They knew one another.

"Has your scheming gone awry?" Franco grinned, his lip pulled back like a dog's snarl, a distortion in his scarred face. "By chance you did not mean for me to discover Matteo, or this maiden with the pretty eyes. This *noble* maiden. This bride that you thought to steal from me!"

Allegreto closed one eye in the same instant that he
hurled a glass vial to the floor. A flash and a brilliant light
filled the room as Franco leaped forward in murderous reaction. But he was blinded by the flare; Allegreto slapped
the point aside with his blade and slipped past, heading for
the guard.

While Franco's man stood dazzled under the failing
torchlight, Allegreto slid a dagger between his ribs, thrusting hard through the links of chain mail, straight up into the
heart. The guard's head snapped back and struck the stone
wall. He crumpled to the floor, releasing his hold on his
prisoners.

"Elena," Allegreto hissed. "Get out! Now!"

"I can't see!" she cried.

He grabbed her arm. She scrabbled for the boy's hand as
Allegreto dragged them together and pushed them toward
the door. Already Franco had found them through the after-
images, still blinking, but he swiftly marked his target. Allegreto brought his sword up to guard, covering Elena's
escape.

"Bastard!" Franco lunged forward, feinting to the left
and then thrusting toward Allegreto's right side. Allegreto
made a backward leap over the guard's body as he parried.
He realized the trap too late as he collided with the wall, his
feet restricted to a narrow space behind the dead man. He
could retreat no further as Franco renewed his attack.

Allegreto made a sweeping parry, knocking Franco's
sword aside. He dived forward under the return cut, tucking
and rolling to his feet. In one unbroken move he pivoted toward Franco's back with a killing thrust. Franco just managed to turn and beat the blade aside.

Allegreto paused as his enemy did, both of them shifting
their footing, seeking advantage. There had been other
ways to murder Franco, simpler ways. But it was long since
they had fought in duello, well-matched as they had always
been, long enough to brood on every offense and dream of
taking retribution face-to-face, to count every insult in
blood.

Franco grinned and made a quick cut towards Allegreto's face. He blocked, but the Riata drew a long dagger and drove forward, forcing him to block again. Franco slid his blade along Allegreto's until the hilts locked, then tried for a disemboweling thrust with the dagger.

Allegreto swept his left arm down and caught the stabbing attack on his arm guard, but he felt a fiery sting as the tip of the dagger scraped along his stomach. He backhanded Franco with his left fist, knocking the man half off his feet.

As Franco staggered, Allegreto slid his own dagger from its sheath. He could feel sweat down his back. His throat burned with smoke and exertion. The shallow cut bled in profusion, soaking his infidel's sash. They had trained together under the same masters; they knew each attack and parry. It would be a match of endurance and wind soon enough if he did not alter his stratagem, and he had no aim to let such chance decide the outcome.

He made a quick, direct lunge, a common attack. Ever loyal to their teachers, Franco responded with the fitting downward parry. Allegreto spun suddenly away from the block and slashed with his dagger. The point slid across Franco's torso, scored through leather and cloth, drawing blood. Only Franco's good speed allowed him to avoid a serious cut.

"Gutter-born bastard," Franco snarled. His breath was coming hard.

Allegreto panted, letting his body slacken, feigning weariness. He held his arm across the bleeding cut and made a weak thrust. Franco's eye widened in triumph as he moved in to take advantage. Allegreto shifted his grip on his dagger, ready to finish with a thrust to Franco's undefended throat.

Something metal glinted at the edge of his vision. And suddenly, from nowhere, Matteo was lunging toward Franco with a naked blade.

Allegreto twisted wildly, pulling his thrust to keep from stabbing the boy. As he was thrown off balance, Franco

struck. In the slow crystalline moment of ruin, Allegreto
saw the tip of Franco's blade moving in a line toward his
heart. He brought his rapier up, just deflecting the thrust,
but the blade sank into his shoulder, an instant of numbness
and then pain as if a flaming brand pierced him through. He
sucked air between his teeth, jerking back, his sword hand
falling useless.

"My lord!" Matteo shouted, standing between them with
the guard's sword in both his hands.

"No!" Elena's cry came from the door. She stood panting, her skirts covered in snow and her hands on the frame.
Allegreto tried to lift his blade, but his arm would not obey
him. He could not feel his hand, but blood streamed down
his sleeve and he heard his sword clatter to the floor.

"Do you want him, Matteo?" Franco asked savagely.
"Do it then! Be blooded on him—a fine vengeance for
Riata!"

The guard's sword was almost too heavy for the boy to
lift but he raised the point to Franco's chest. "Stay back!"
he cried. "I won't let you near him. I'll kill you!"

Franco Pietro stood still, his gaze passing from Allegreto
to his son and the trembling blade at his heart. For a long
moment his scarred face held no expression. Then his
mouth curled down, his disfigured face grew stark and reddened. "Kill *me*?" he whispered in hoarse disbelief. "I'm
your father."

"I hate my father. I hate you! *I'll kill you!*" Matteo
leaped forward, aiming the sword's tip at Franco's heart.

His father easily slapped the blade aside, overbalancing
the boy and sending him sprawling. He turned on Allegreto.
"God destroy you and your cursed house! *Destroy it!*" he
roared. "What have you done?"

Allegreto stood glaring at Franco. His right arm hung
limp, his shoulder blazing with pain. Blood dripped from
his fingers to the floor.

"You've turned him from me!" Franco shouted. He
squeezed his one eye closed, raising his face, his teeth
bared in anguish. "Merciful God, let me kill you; let me tear

your heart from your foul chest—" He came rushing at Allegreto with his sword, flinging Matteo aside as the boy tried to stop him.

Allegreto brought his left arm up with a snap, releasing his poison dagger in a sidearm throw. Franco knocked the blade from the air with a sweep of his sword. As it hit the floor, Allegreto already had his throwing knife from his right bracer. He flung it hard, aiming low even as Franco raised his sword to protect his chest. The knife struck home, halfway to the hilt in the top of Franco's thigh. He gasped and stumbled, losing his grip on his blade. It flipped from his hand and clattered to the floor. Matteo leaped forward, brandishing his sword as his father lurched to one knee.

"Stop!" Elena yanked Matteo back by both shoulders, barely saving Franco from a sword through his throat. In the instant Allegreto knelt to retrieve his rapier left-handed, she set her foot across the blade. "You will not. Enough!"

He could hear voices outside, Zafer and Philip's men. He let go of the hilt, pressing his hand over his bleeding wound. He looked up at her, his vision hazed. "Philip comes." With an effort he made his feet again, turning to the door. "Here!" he shouted, without taking his eyes from Franco.

Philip entered first with a brace of his men at his flank. His glance took in Elena and Matteo and the Riata struggling to stand, his hands gripped over the blade in his thigh. "Bind him," the bandit ordered. "Secure the weapons." He gave Allegreto's wound a passing look and raised his grizzled eyebrows. "We've occupied the mint. The garrison is yielded. A messenger stands ready to signal the citadel that—" He paused, with a frown toward Franco Pietro.

"Signal them," Allegreto said. "He's as good as dead."

"Signal what?" Elayne asked sharply.

"To take the city in your name, Princess." Allegreto leaned against the wall to hold himself up. He cradled his arm, resting his head back on the stone as he smiled. "Monteverde is ours."

•   •   •

IN THE SPUTTERING torchlight, blood spilled down Allegreto's white sleeve and covered his torn tunic. It spread in a dark scarlet pool beneath the body on the floor. It dripped from Franco's leg. Even Matteo was spattered with it. Elayne turned toward the door, drawing a deep breath of the frigid night air to possess herself. She held the frame, and then reached down to grab Nim and the mastiff as they tried to nose curiously past her.

"Matteo. Take the dogs." She forced a tremor from her voice. The boy hurried to obey her, dragging the animals out into the snow. When she looked back, Philip's bandits surrounded Franco Pietro, holding him up as they made fast the bonds. He did not struggle, but his face was a hellish vision as he stared with his one eye at Allegreto.

In Zafer's clothes and white turban, Allegreto seemed a stranger; propped against the wall with his face half in shadow, a bloodied foreigner, as hell-born as his enemy. But he was alive.

She had seen the blade aimed for his heart, seen it pierce him.

He was alive. Zafer was alive, Margaret was safe.

Instead of relief, a rank fury boiled up in her. She closed her eyes, struggling to contain it.

"What do you want done with him?" Philip asked.

Elayne's eyes snapped open. He meant to address Allegreto, she knew, but she answered him instead. "Detain him," she said coldly. "And Navona, too. They are both under my arrest."

The old bandit turned around to her, his shoulders straightening. She saw Allegreto drop his bloody hand from his wound and look up.

"I am Ligurio's only living heir," she said, lifting her head. "I am Monteverde. And I will not let them destroy it like this. Take both of them."

No one moved. They all stood looking at her with a baffled horror, as if she had burst into flame before them. Elayne glared back, her eyes stinging with fierceness, with the force of her grandfather's vanquished dream.

"Take both of them," she said again. She did not look at Allegreto, she could not, but she felt him there, a motionless shadow at the edge of her blurred vision.

The Englishman made a sound, half a laugh and half a grunt. "Do you mean it, Princess? Because I'll end with my head on a stake if I follow you and you draw back from this."

"I listened to what you said in camp," she said. "I will not have war against ourselves. And that is what will come of it."

"She speaks true," Franco Pietro said hoarsely. "Kill me if you will, but all of Riata will rise against you for it. We'll never let a Navona sleep easy in the citadel."

Allegreto sprang upright from the wall, holding his arm against his chest. "Brave words!" His lip curled. "See what's left to rise when I'm done with you. And I've never slept easy since I could say my father's name or yours—that will be no great burden to bear."

"You won't sleep in possession of Monteverde one night, easy or not." Franco wrenched at his bonds and went halfway to one knee as he tried to step forward. "We'll burn it to the ground before we let you take it!"

Allegreto grabbed his throat, grimacing as he dragged him up. "I'll see you swing from the gates long before you can burn anything, Riata. Before morning I'll see it!"

Elayne reached down for the hilt of his sword. The handle turned in her fingers, slick with his blood, but she held it tight as she straightened. "Philip," she said sharply. "Arrest them both."

Allegreto dropped his grip on Franco and glanced at her as she raised the sword. "Elena," he said, almost below his breath. "Do not."

"Both of them."

Philip jerked his chin. One of his men moved hesitantly, lifting his hand toward Allegreto.

"Elena!" There was no fear in his voice, or even anger. It was disbelief.

"I will not hurt you. No one will hurt you or Franco. You

are both in my protection." She had no way to enforce her
words, no guard or garrison at her command, but she said
them. She said them with Prince Ligurio's will, from the
power of his vision of what Monteverde could have been.
Could still be, if she had the heart and resolve and good fortune of a thousand angels at her back.

She had bound him once in a game before her, a defeated warrior at her command. In stark reality he was
bleeding, and she was only a girl, untried and outrageous in
what she asked, the sword tip trembling in her hand. She
could not force him—she did not think all of Philip's men
could, or would, prevent him from walking out the door if
he willed it.

His mouth was set. With each breath the muscle in his
cheek drew taut—pain or fury, she could not tell. He looked
at Franco Pietro and Philip and bared his teeth. His dark
gaze passed to Elayne.

He stared for a long moment at her. His look held all the
truth between them, that he had trusted her, when she knew
he had never trusted anyone before. That he had let her take
his defenses and put his life in her hands and love him.

"Allegreto," she said. "Help me."

He blinked at the sound of her voice, turning his head a
little, as if he heard it from a great distance. And with the
same bewilderment, the same blank pain, he lifted his face
upward like a prayer. "Ah, God," he said in a helpless
voice. "Don't do this to me."

"For me," she whispered, serving him a betrayal that
went deeper than Franco Pietro's blade.

"Monteverde bitch," he said softly.

Franco made an incredulous sound as the fetters clattered in the bandit's shaky hand and closed on Allegreto's
wrist. The Riata looked up at Elayne, scowling.

"You will have what is rightfully yours," she said to him.
"Navona will have again what was his. As it was under my
grandfather. Will you accede to it?"

Franco wet his lips. He glanced at Allegreto and back at

Elayne. "I do not comprehend this." He thrust out his chin. "What of our betrothal?"

"There is no betrothal."

"You forswear it?"

"There is nothing to forswear. I have given no consent."

"That contract!" he exclaimed, instantly understanding her. "Damn the English pig, is Lancaster behind this?" He grunted as he shifted on his wounded leg. "Have you sold us to the English?"

"I have not," she said.

"Better the English than Navona," he sneered. He was breathing deeply, his face creased in pain and hate as he looked at Allegreto. "Has he got another bastard like himself on you?"

In the half-light Allegreto lifted his eyes from the fetters on his wrist.

"No," she said bluntly.

She saw the faintest brush of Allegreto's lashes, an instant of some expression that passed over his face, impossible to comprehend before it was gone. He stared at her coldly. Elayne felt her heart break inside her throat, tear into pieces that would never mend.

"What of my son?" Franco Pietro asked. His voice rose. "I want my son."

Elayne thought of the boy with a blade at his father's throat. "Matteo will stay with me, until I deem otherwise. He will not be in Navona's power."

"I don't trust you, that you come here this way," Franco Pietro exclaimed. "In secret, and at his hand."

"Then we must wait until you can," Elayne said. "I will do my best to be just. But Monteverde is first. Before Riata. Before Navona. Monteverde is what we all are, before we are anything else."

WITH A TROOP of bandits she took d'Avina. It all happened swiftly, like a spark in a dry field of corn. Philip held the mint, easily seized when everyone in town had run to the fire, and easily defended once his men closed the great outer doors in the massive wall. The fortress of Maladire was hers, the small remnants of the Riata garrison surrendered to Philip's men, cut off to anyone who could not pass the secret entrances.

The townspeople seemed frozen in doubt. They huddled in a mass beyond the burned-out bridge and guardhouse, shouting and milling without direction. They knew something momentous had happened, but none could cross to the castle over the smoldering remains of the bridge.

She ordered Philip to have the bell rung in the piazza.

In all of their blood and battle wounds, she took her prisoners. She allowed Zafer to bind up Allegreto's arm in a sling with his turban. Franco had to be half-carried, unable to walk on his leg. But Philip's bandits were efficient jailers. They moved their injured captives through the underground ways, up through the mint, and out onto the torch-lit dais in the piazza with speed.

She still carried Allegreto's sword. She stood foremost on the dais, overlooking the uneasy crowd of people gathering below. The freezing air burned her cheeks and turned her breath to frost.

Be clever. Lady Melanthe had said it. *Be bold if you must, and act on the edge of a moment.*

Prince Ligurio would approve it. She felt so sure that he would approve that it was as if he stood beside her and whispered what words to say.

"I have come here first!" she shouted, her voice a cry that died away in echoes in the night. "I am Elena of Monteverde, and you are my father's and my grandfather's people." She looked down into the eyes of a man who stood just below her, a young miner from his clothes. "And my people."

He stared up at her, his grimy face intent in the firelight. His mouth opened, and he gave a little bewildered nod as she held his gaze.

Elayne nodded back to him. She lifted her face. "Tonight in the fortress, while the bridge burned, the leaders of Riata and Navona fought." She gestured back to Allegreto and Franco Pietro with the sword. "Look at them."

The miner looked, wide-eyed. The crowd around him looked, murmuring, and saw what she wanted them to see—two men bloodied and torn by their combat.

Below her, there were richly dressed men in fur, and thin-clad miners mixed with women and children. They filled the piazza now, a sea of faces fading into darkness. She knew there were Riata among them, and others loyal in secret to Navona. She knew the Riata would lose from what she did, the Navona would rise. But there were others, too, all those who belonged to neither house, those her grandfather had written of who only suffered from the endless discord.

"This is what Monteverde has been," she said over the crowd, holding up the bloody sword. "A battleground for wolves! And I've come to put an end to it. I've come in the name of Prince Ligurio and my father, to rule in peace, and with equal justice. I have no allies. I am not of Navona, nor Riata. I have nothing to overpower you—only these few outlawed men who stand beside me." She raised her voice in fierce emotion. "But it is not *bandits* who have bled Monteverde of concord or peace!"

She looked down at them as her shout died away. There was utter silence in the piazza, only the hiss of torches and the soft groan of the snow underfoot as people stirred.

"By chance you will not have a woman over you," she said into the quiet. "It will be your choice. Tonight I hold the mint and the castle and these two men by my small force. Tomorrow, in the morning, you will each bring a stone, every man and woman of you, and place it in a pile. This is how you chose your leaders long ago, under the old republic. There will be one for each of us. Franco Pietro della Riata. Allegreto della Navona. Elena di Monteverde. So look at us here—at what we are—and think of what you want for yourselves and for your children."

She stepped back, lowering the sword, turning away. In

the silence Allegreto stood in the fetters, gazing at her like a man watching a comet cross the sky.

The young miner raised his fist. *"Monteverde!"* he yelled. Someone in the back took up the shout. People pushed forward, reaching their hands toward her. She felt a spurt of fear, but they were not enraged—they were smiling as they pressed and shouted, taking up the chant.

She dropped the sword and knelt down and touched their hands.

Twenty-three

———❧———

IT WAS NOT until the bells tolled midnight that she had a moment to stop and feel the magnitude of what she had done. To feel fear. Philip and Zafer and Matteo and Margaret and even Donna Grazia had demanded her notice. She had conferred with the bandit on where to place the prisoners, she had ordered Zafer to make certain no message was yet sent to the city, she had put Matteo and the dogs in Margaret's care, and exchanged a hard hug with the freckled maid that needed no words. Dario hovered near, standing over them with his blunt jaw set. He did not move away as a tearful Donna Grazia begged a moment that became near an hour to pour into her ears the story of how the Riata had killed all her brothers, and yet she had forgiven them for her late husband's sake, and how terrified she had been of Allegreto's plans, but she could not deny her aid to him for the sake of her brothers' name. She ended in a confused and joyful pledge to Monteverde, above any house, holding Elayne's hands in hers until they were wet with tears.

It was while Donna Grazia wept over her fingers that Elayne began to know her own fear. The woman was so grateful, and unquestioning, so afraid that Elayne would think her a Navona or a Riata and punish her for either—Elayne began to see all the peril of being caught between—of what could happen now. Dario already saw it, she realized; he had shadowed her from the instant she had left the dais, so close to her that he would not even allow Zafer near. He was afraid of her assassination, she realized with a jolt. Afraid that even Zafer might attempt it.

She sent them all away, but Dario. In the rich chamber that held her grandfather's book, she sat again on the stool and turned the pages, trying to read, trying to resurrect the feeling that Ligurio stood with her and guided her. The book itself was a guide—it held her grandfather's exact vision of the laws and functions of the new republic, and warnings of how to circumvent those who would pull it down. But there was nothing to tell her what to do in this moment, how to cross the yawning chasm before her. Nothing to give her the words to persuade Franco Pietro to relinquish his power, nothing to protect her, no plan for escape if the people voted tomorrow for Riata, and left her and Navona to his mercy. Nothing but what she knew Allegreto had meant to do—kill him.

"Dario," she said. "I must speak to your master."

"If you mean Allegreto Navona, Your Grace, he is no longer my master," Dario said. "My allegiance is wholly yours."

She glanced at him, a little shocked, though she knew he had devoted himself to her safety since the camp. "Grant mercy," she said. "I need you now."

His square, strong face was grave in the lamplight. "I would warn you of Zafer, Your Grace. I cannot say what is in his mind, or Margaret's. I watched them close when they were near you."

She could not think of Margaret as an enemy. "Surely not . . ."

"Zafer is dangerous, my lady; I beg you will never forget it. Il Corvo commands him, and always will. Margaret—" He shrugged. "I cannot say of her. She seemed to have true affection for you, but she is great in love with Zafer, and she is devoted to her master, too."

Elayne looked down at the book before her, rubbing the green velvet sheath under her fingers, more shaken by this division of loyalty within their small company than by anything yet.

"Philip Welles will stand by you, I believe, my lady. And I owe my life to you. I think the people will accept you. But the houses will not be broken easily. I beg you will be careful. Welles was right to warn you not to set them free of the fetters in their chambers. I am certain that Navona can escape the tower if he is not chained."

Of course. It would impossible to imprison Allegreto in a Navona stronghold.

Imprison him. She bit her lip and frowned down at the book.

"I must speak to him," she said. "Come with me through the tunnels."

SHE AND DARIO had an argument outside the door in Maladire's tower. He did not want her to enter alone, not even if she kept her distance from Allegreto. But she ordered him to stay outside with Philip's man on guard, leaving him red-faced and angry with her, his hand resisting the door even as she closed it behind her.

She stood with her back to it for a moment, holding the lamp against her skirt. She half-expected to find the chamber empty, after Dario's warnings of how easily he could escape. But Allegreto was there—he lay propped on a cot beside the rough wall, bare-chested but for the sling and a dressing around his torso, watching her through slitted eyes.

He did not move, or speak. When she saw the heavy chain on his ankles, she wished that he had escaped.

"I'm sorry," she whispered.

He said nothing.

"I cannot let it go as you intended," she said, and

sounded foolish even to herself. "I'm sorry for this. But I cannot. Do you understand?"

Still he did not reply, but turned his head a little, as if he could not look at her.

She held herself against the door, quelling a frantic urge to turn and fling it open and insist that they remove the chains. At least the chains.

"Put down the light," he said. "I can't see you."

Quickly she set the lamp on the floor and moved away from it. "Did they leave you no candle?"

He made a sound of bitter amusement. "I am a prisoner, Elena."

She stepped in front of a little arched wall shrine with a crude painting of Madonna and child inside it—the only thing in the room besides the cot. "I did not mean for you to be treated as a common criminal. It's near to freezing in here. I'll have them bring a furnace and some blankets."

He only looked at her, a lift of his dark lashes over his perfect sullen mouth.

"Dario thinks Zafer might try to kill me," she said, all in a rush.

"He will not," Allegreto said.

Elayne took a step toward him. He seemed to reject her without moving, a faint shift back against the wall, that subtle withdrawal from any contact.

"I am not certain what to do next," she said.

He lifted his eyebrows. His lip curled. "You do not expect me to help you."

She clasped her arms around herself and turned away.

"I could not help you if I wished," he said. "You said the truth. You have no allies. You must have none—most particularly not me."

"I know," she said desperately. "I know."

The simple Madonna had a blank, wide-eyed expression, as if a child had painted it. Elayne felt as stupid and stiff as the dull figure, with no words for the tangle of feelings inside her.

"If they vote for Riata tomorrow, I'll see that you escape," she said suddenly, with no notion of how she would do it. "You can go back to the island. And I can join you there."

She heard him exhale a long breath. The island seemed a paradise to her now, a distant vision of safety.

"That will not happen," he said. "They will choose you."

She made a little shake of her head, half-turning, afraid to look at him.

"The things you said out there—they love you for it already," he said. "Is it not what you wanted?"

She wanted only to go to him and touch him and make certain again he was alive. "Did Philip's leech see well to your wounds?" she asked, still not looking toward him.

"I will heal. I always heal."

"I'll give him a recipe for a compress," she said. "If the herbs can be obtained here."

She dared a glance at him. He closed his eyes and laid his head back with a black and ugly smile. "A compress."

She looked at the curve of his shoulder, the bandages lit by the soft gleam of the lamp. They had given him clean woolen hose, but his hands were still stained with blood. She went to him and knelt down on the floor before him and took his unwounded hand into hers. The fetters rattled as she pressed her forehead against his fist. "I could not do else!" she cried. "I know you cannot understand."

He let her hold his hand, but he did not open his fist. She turned his wrist and kissed his hard-closed fingers.

"It's not to take Monteverde from you," she said. "Can you believe that? I don't want to rule; I never wanted it. I don't know how. But I cannot let it be torn asunder."

She lifted her face. He looked down at her. An ironic smile touched his lips. "You know how to rule, my lady. If you did not, I would not be here."

She bowed her head and pressed his hand to her mouth. She tasted blood and smelled the cold scent of steel. "I thought he killed you. I saw his blade—I thought you dead then."

"Not yet."

She gripped his hand with an unhappy sound. "Why do you always speak so?"

He gave a heavy sigh and relaxed his fingers open. He let her kiss them. He lifted his hand and brushed her cheek with icy fingertips.

"I want to tell you something," he said. "I want to tell you about your grandfather."

Elayne looked up at his face.

"I knew him well, Elena. While I was still beardless, he used me to protect Melanthe. After your own father was murdered, and Ligurio was growing feeble, he made an accord with Gian for me to come into the citadel. I played the eunuch, so that I could sleep beside her, and act her lover." He had no expression as he looked down at her and let his fingers trace down her cheek. "She suffered me, because Ligurio said she must. But she despised me. Everyone in the citadel did. And feared me for what I could do."

Elayne held his cold gaze, pressing his hand between hers, trying to warm him. She could feel his ring still on her finger.

"Only Ligurio gave me welcome there," he said. "He taught me there was another kind of man beyond my father. That there was something in love that was not wholly dread. That there was reason in the world. And kindness. He taught me alchemy and astrology. He gave me a way to be something beyond what my father made of me." He scowled, his mouth hardening. "When Ligurio died, I went down in the pit under the citadel, where I knew no one would come, and wept until I was sick with it."

He sounded angry. He lifted his hand away from her and rubbed it across his mouth, the fetters clashing.

"I see him in you," he said. "I read his book. I heard what you said out there. We are all Monteverde first." He dropped his hand beside him with a chinking noise. "But you cannot do it while I live, Elena. Not I, and not Franco. There can be no point to rally around that is not Monteverde. Tell Zafer to slay Franco tonight, and then let the guard step away from the door long enough that a Riata can get to me. There is one somewhere now, awaiting his chance."

"No," she whispered in horror.

"You came to ask my help. That is all the help I have to give you."

She pushed away from him. "No."

"It will happen anyway," he said. "Do it now, and you will be safe."

"Safe!" she cried. She stood up and turned away. "Do you think I care so much to be safe?"

"I care for it," he said quietly.

She shook her head.

"It would be a favor to me." His voice grew harsh. As she looked back at him, he lifted his hand and gripped the chain in his fist. "I'll die like this. You know it. Let it be sooner than later."

"You will not die," she said fiercely. "It is only for a little while, until you and Franco agree that your houses will cease this vendetta. Then I will set you both free."

He laughed, an echo in the cold stone room. "Are you mad?"

She let out a deep breath. "By chance I am mad," she said. She walked across the small chamber, standing before the shrine. "You asked me once, what choice you had. You said Cara had no answer for you." She blinked down at the crude painting, the awkward child and misformed mother, the colors gray and chalky. She turned to him. "This is my answer."

He stared back at her. Then he closed his eyes as if he had seen something that he could not bear. He shook his head and sat forward, leaning over his injured arm with a deep grimace. He sat with his head bowed. When he lifted his face, he had a helpless look. "Elena, he'll kill me. I'll be in Hell and you won't be there."

Her eyes began to blur. She did not move. "I won't let that happen."

"How will you stop it?" He swung himself upright, standing with a clatter of the manacles, holding the sling against his chest. "Give me the ring." He reached for her hand. "You cannot be seen wearing Navona's motto."

Elayne covered her fingers, but he caught her arm, his grip hard and cold.

"You're Monteverde alone now." He dragged at the gold band, yanking it over the bone without mercy as she tried to pull back. She gave a cry of pain and dismay. The door flung open, with Dario standing in it, his hand on his dagger.

Allegreto glanced at him and stepped back, holding his hand away in clear withdrawal. He nodded toward the young man. "She is safe," he said coolly. "But do not let her from your sight again."

"WHERE IS MY SON?" Franco Pietro struggled from his cot and fell on his knee, clashing the fetters. He dragged himself upright against the wall, with a sharp breath between his teeth. The wound on his thigh still seeped fresh blood through a bandage. "Is he alive?"

"He is alive, and safe," she said. "Do not fear for Matteo."

He paused, breathing through his nose. The scar below his eye patch was livid purple as he watched her warily. He glanced at Dario standing behind her.

"Have you thought on what I said?" she asked. "That I mean to return to the houses what is rightfully theirs, as in my grandfather's day?"

"I heard what you said." He held himself on the wall with one hand. "You said more than that."

"Yes. And meant it. If the people elect you tomorrow, then I have no intention to gainsay them."

"And if they don't?"

She gave a slight shrug. "If it is Navona they choose, then I suppose you will fight him to the death, and let Monteverde bleed. If it is I—then there will be the same election in the city and all the towns."

"You are mad, girl," he said.

Elayne smiled bitterly. "So I am told."

He shifted, lifting his lip in a grimace of pain. "What is this hold you have on Navona?" he demanded. "I'd be dead by now if he had his desire."

"Indeed, you would." She made a dry sound, not quite a laugh. "But he appointed me his conscience."

"Madness!" Franco said, with a bewildered shake of his head. "If I had not seen it!" He squinted at her. "You do not intend to ally with him?"

"No," she said firmly.

Franco Pietro looked at her with doubt. "He abducted you."

"He did," she said.

"I suppose you can have no love for him for that."

"It was vile, what he did."

The cot creaked as he lowered himself onto it painfully, his injured leg thrust out before him. "Did he force you to bed?"

"Yes," she said. "But there is no child of it." She stared at him, refusing to lower her eyes.

"God succor you, Princess," he said. His voice softened a little. "It was ill-done. I should have sent my own escort for you."

"Perchance," she said. "I will bear the shame. You need not make it a public concern, but I tell you because I wish you to have such truth as matters."

He gazed at her, his head tilted a little aside. "You are a remarkable woman, for one so young."

Elayne wanted to laugh in irony. Her finger throbbed, aching, but she held to a perfect and cool countenance. "My godmother Lady Melanthe taught me a little of what is required to rule."

"To rule!" he said ruthlessly "You suppose you can rule? As a woman? A mere girl?"

She glanced down at his chains and up again. When she met his look, his one eye squinted and he lifted his eyebrow.

"Aye, you have me, for now," he acknowledged. "Unless Navona is behind all this in secret."

"What would it gain him?" she asked. "He had his plans, until I prevented him. And you know what they were."

He pressed his hand over the wound on his leg, shifting with a grunt. "It was you who stopped Matteo from—" He looked down at his hand. He began to breath harder. "My own son," he said viciously. "He set my own son to murder me!"

"He did not. Matteo schemed to do it himself."

He flung his head up. "Nay, that's a lie!"

"Matteo hates you," she said bluntly. "I will bring him to tell you to your face, if you wish. That's why we were in the fortress, because I had chased him to prevent him from such a deed, when he told me what he planned. Navona did not know of it. You know he would make no such stupid errors of his own accord."

"Navona. God wither him, and let dogs eat out his heart!" Franco's voice was shaking. "My own son!" he shouted, slamming his fist to his chest.

Elayne took a step forward. "Listen to me now," she said coldly and softly. "It is Navona's doing, but it is your doing as well." She stood over him, her jaw taut. "It is the sum of what Riata and Navona have come to. It is hate for the sake of hate, and fear for the sake of fear. You sit there and grieve and rend your breast for yourself, when it is Matteo who knows nothing of love but that he should kill for it! You will reap what you sow—did you suppose you could escape it? That you could hound the house of Navona to death and feel no retribution?"

He glared at her. "He stole Matteo from me."

"As Riata stole me!" she hissed. "An infant, from a nunnery. And well you know why."

He narrowed his one eye at her. "It was my father who did so."

"Happen that his sin is visited upon you and your son, then, by God's justice," she said. "I do not care. Leave that vengeance in His hands." She stood back, drawing a breath.

"It is time to leave such things and heal ourselves. I will bring Matteo with me to you, so he can see you and begin to know who you are in truth. His love for Navona is a child's devotion, because he was afraid, and too young to understand."

Franco's broad shoulders slumped a little. "You would bring him?" He touched the eye-patch and then gripped his torn tunic.

"Not now. Not like this. When I can. But I will keep him safe until then."

He sat looking down at the floor and shook his head. "In truth—it seems that I have some debt to you."

Elayne said nothing.

"So I live another day, Princess?" he said, without looking up at her. "By your mercy."

"I will do nothing to harm you. I will protect you from Navona if I can. I ask that Riata makes no move against him either. I wish to reconcile the houses, and have peace."

He lifted his head and gave her a curt nod. Without the scar and the patch, he would have been a handsome man, gray-eyed and fair-skinned like his son. "I will consider what you say. I promise you that much. I will consider."

THE PILE OF stones lay before the dais, under three boards, one roughly chalked with a castle, one with a dog-and-bear, the third marked with a crude dragon shape. The rocks nearly obscured the castle drawing, tumbling down from the steep sides of the pile until some of them joined the sparse stones under the other two boards. But there was no doubt that Val d'Avina had elected Elena di Monteverde to rule.

Elena. Not Elayne anymore. As she stood and accepted the oaths of the people, still dressed in the simple scarlet cote-hardie given to her by Donna Grazia and wrapped in a fur-lined mantle that had come from someone in the crowd, she felt herself altered—as if with each murmured pledge, each kiss upon her hand, she lost Elayne of the summer fields at Savernake, of the island of Il Corvo, of Navona's tower above the lake, and became another—a stranger— Princess Elena di Monteverde.

Her finger still hurt where he had taken the ring. She could feel it, a slight throb with each pulse, a spike at her heart.

Franco Pietro leaned upon a crutch, scowling while the stones piled up. Allegreto stood silently, apart, both of them under guard and still manacled by hand and foot. Dario held fast to Elena's side, scanning every person who came near, tense and alert to protect her.

Couriers had gone out to the city. D'Avina was but one town, there was still the whole of Monteverde before her that must choose. She had written out the message to be read in the streets, using Ligurio's words. She promised reunion, and a republic under her grandfather's laws. She used his name with brazen authority; a return to a dream of better days.

Philip had read it, and nodded once. "You are a sweet-tongued rogue, Princess," he said with approval, and set his men upon the road, escorting d'Avina's beadle to cry her words in the city. A message and a generous gift of her grandfather's emerald-studded goblet went also to the commander of the French condottiere lying at the pass to Venice, informing him courteously that Elena held the mint. Philip seemed to think that the Frenchman could reason from that information to the strings of his purse, and would do so with alacrity.

When she had greeted the people, down to the last broken beggar, she turned. "We will talk together now," she said, sweeping a glance over the two men under guard. "Come."

To a thousand cheers and balls of snow that soared in the air and splashed against the ground, they left the piazza and walked under the heavy archway of the mint. They passed through walls ten paces thick into the inner court. Around the perimeter were empty stalls with snow-covered counters and benches like the Rialto banks. Philip led them into the powerful mass of the mint itself, his keys jangling as he opened guarded, lead-bound doors. They entered a chamber lined with chests, supported by arches carved with leaves and flowers in soft white stone. The old bandit waited until Franco and Allegreto were inside, and then ordered his men out. Only Dario remained, standing behind Elena as Philip closed the door.

She sat at the head of the broad table. She was tired, her insides shaky from spending the whole night in conference with Philip and Dario over how to proceed. She had a document before her, and pen and ink set upon the board. There was red wax and a candle, and a seal of sorts hastily created from a Monteverde ducat attached to a stub of wood. She looked up at the two men before her. Neither of them had taken a seat at the benches along the table.

"I give you joy of your victory, Princess," Franco Pietro said dryly, leaning one hand heavily on his crutch. "May you not live to regret it."

Allegreto took a step toward him. The chain at his feet rattled. He stopped, staring darkly at his enemy.

"We are here because I wish to parley in private with both of you," she said, ignoring Franco's words. "I do not intend to release you until you have agreed to end the conflict between the houses of Riata and Navona."

They were both silent, looking at one another with all the fondness and reconciliation they would feel toward toads and worms and pestilence.

Elena allowed the hush to lengthen. She left them standing like a pair of refractory boys on either side of the huge cracked slab of tree trunk that formed the table. The light from a high slitted window fell down between the arches, as if it were a church, though the room was lined with the silver hoard of Monteverde. Finally she said, "What would be required, my lord, for Riata to agree to this?"

Franco Pietro turned his look on her. "I do not see how it can be done, Princess. I said that I would consider, but I do not trust him. Look to what he has just done, tried to overthrow and murder me. You did not know his father, but Gian Navona's malice bred true in his bastard whelp."

She looked at Allegreto. "And what would be required for Navona to agree?"

He curled his lip. "To drive every Riata from the face of the earth," he said coolly.

Elena put her fists together and leaned her forehead on them.

"Do not be naïve, Elena," Allegreto said. "This will not succeed."

"Not while you live, Navona dog," Franco said. "But it is a rare and noble hope she has. I do not fault her for it."

Elena looked up in surprise at Franco Pietro, but he was frowning at Allegreto.

"What gallant words!" Allegreto said, with a disdainful flick of his good hand. "Lying whore."

Franco took a noisy step, pounding his crutch on the tiled floor. "No more than you, you murderous harlot. What do you know of honor?"

"Nothing," Allegreto sneered. "I am Gian Navona's bastard, what do I know but iniquity? Kill us both, Princess, and be done with it. That will find peace for Monteverde."

She looked at him. "Do you want peace?"

He cast a look back at her, a grim and impatient demon. "*Avoi,* I would die for it, is that not what I'm saying?"

She gripped her hands before her on the table. "That may be, but I will not kill you for it."

He flicked his fingers toward Franco. "He will."

Elena tilted her head, looking toward the Riata. "Would you?"

Franco glanced at her with an uneasy frown. "Is this a game, Princess? What questions are these? Yea, I would kill him, for he'd serve the same to me!"

Elena spread the pages before her. "I ask you both to reconsider. I have written here an agreement between you. It requires that you swear your loyalty first to Monteverde—and whoever is the elected prince of it. It states that you will not spill blood in any contest between the houses of Riata

and Navona, or take hostages, or seek to overthrow the chosen prince. I would ask that you sit down and read it, and
sign it, and abide by it, for the good of Monteverde and of
yourselves and your own houses."

Silence filled the chamber. Elena could hear Dario
breathing deeply at her shoulder.

Franco Pietro moved first, banging his crutch as he
scraped the bench back and sat. He reached out his hand for
the documents.

Elena handed him one of the copies. She glanced at Allegreto.

For an instant, it almost seemed as if there was something besides derision in the shadowed look he returned her,
a contact like a passing touch of his fingertips on her skin.
But he set his mouth in a mocking smile and took the papers with a sharp sweep of his hand, sitting down across the
bench with his back turned to her.

She had lost to him at chess. She doubted she could have
defeated Franco, either. She watched their bent heads and
thought they could be plotting anything; laughing at her
feeble attempts to assert control.

After long moments Franco Pietro looked up, holding
the page open with his hand. "I can agree to this. If he will."

Elena felt a surge of surprise and hope.

"No," Allegreto said. He tossed the crisp vellum onto the
table. "Do not trust him."

Even to her, such an easy capitulation by Franco seemed
suspicious. "It is to be signed under solemn oath," she said,
trying to keep her voice steady and certain.

"He'll break his word before a fortnight has passed."

Franco lunged up over the table, his face red. "You question my honor?"

Allegreto made a move, as if to reach for his dagger. The
chains rattled over the edge of the wood. Dario stepped forward, his blade singing from the sheath. It came down between them, the point resting lightly on the tabletop.

Allegreto was frozen for a moment. He looked at Dario
under his eyebrows, and sat back. "I question how much

you relinquish by this," he said to Franco in a quieter tone.
"It is all sacrifice and no gain for you."

Franco grimaced as he lowered himself. Dario lifted the
sword from the table, but he kept it free and ready.

"She holds Matteo," Franco said. "And what is to prevent you from poisoning me in my bed? I see no assurance
at all to hold you in check!"

"Nay, I have nothing else to lose, do I?" Allegreto said.
He looked to Elena with a bitter smile. "Nothing."

Franco narrowed his one eye. "And I question what is
between you and the princess—these telling glances that
you give her. I would be fool indeed to sign this surrender,
only to see Navona elevated by some bedroom trick."

Elena pressed her lips together. She looked at the center
of the table, and then at the pale carving that arched above
the heavy door. She had been coming to this moment, inevitably. She had felt it like a great stone that slowly began
to turn and roll and gather speed to crush her. She thought
of the tower room, and the warm sheets; his body curled
and tangled with hers. She thought of him smiling down at
her as she counted for a game of morra. A fierce sweetness
seemed to break inside her, a pain that drifted down her
throat and settled in her heart, a dark silent crystal buried in
her own blood and sinew.

"There is nothing between me and Navona," she said, in
a voice that sounded calm, a little thin, peculiar to herself.
"I will be impartial between you."

She heard the words die away in the barren chamber,
amid the chests of silver. She could not look at Allegreto.

"Hang us both as traitors," he said in a vicious tone.
"That would be impartial."

She bore his anger. He had a right to it. He had seen this
true, before she had admitted it even to herself. Taken his
ring. Advised her to kill him.

"I cannot." She did look at him then, only for a moment,
so that she would not break or show anything before the
Riata. One moment, to brand his demon-beauty in her
mind. "But you will both remain under close arrest, as pos-

sible conspirators, until you agree to what I have asked. Dario."

The young man strode to the door, rapping on it sharply with the hilt of his sword. The great metal-bound barrier swung open to admit Philip and his men. Elena watched as they came with pikes and swords and clubs to surround the prisoners.

Allegreto paused, under the arm of a guard, and glanced back at her from the door. As his eyes met hers, it was a dread feeling, as if they both knew, as if he was fading from her through a mist, gone already far beyond what she could see.

The guard jostled him. He turned and went through the door.

SHE RODE DOWN from the mountains on a gray palfrey, with only ten of the bandits and Dario for an escort, now dressed in Monteverde's green livery. She left Philip to guard the mint and her prisoners, and approached the gates of the city alone.

But she was not alone, not quite. People from d'Avina had followed her out onto the road. They had cheered her as she passed the burned-out gatehouse and bridge, the gray tower of Maladire. She had thought they would fall behind, but a crowd of them came with her, walking and riding in her train. Some ran and galloped ahead, easily enough, for she kept the palfrey to a gentle amble. Among them she recognized the young miner who had looked up at her on the dais, striding along just after her bandit guard, his white hood thrown back in the sun. As they moved down through the pine forests and left the snow, they seemed to gather followers. By the time they reached the apple orchards and terraced vineyards, the procession was doubled in size, and people had begun to line the road in each village. In the warmth of an autumn afternoon, a girl ran out and offered Elena a sheaf of sunflowers, their great yellow heads nodding gaily as she kissed Elena's hand.

Elena felt no fear. She felt as if a trance held her, and everyone. Even when she came within sight of the city below, she was somewhere beyond fear, simply moving forward to a fate that seemed inevitable.

When she reached the gates at sunset, she had a great march of common people behind her. Her small banner, a green-and-silver pennon taken from the magistrate's hands at d'Avina, drooped in the shadow of the city walls. She could see the citadel, a white glitter of towers and crenellations on the mount, rising above the city. The drawbridge was up, and the smooth rapid water of the river coursed between her and the city, flowing blue and clear into the lake.

She waited. From the gatehouse, she could see faces peering from the windows.

She took the banner from a bandit at her side. She rode forward, into the easy range of arrows and stones, with Dario close behind her.

"I am Elena di Monteverde!" she cried, her voice almost lost against the massive walls. "Open the city! I have come home!"

Behind her, a swell of noise began to rise. She heard the miner's voice call out her name, and the chant become a bellow from the crowd.

Over the sound of the people came the creaking groan of wheels and chains. The drawbridge lowered, falling into place with a thunderous crash that grew to a roar as the crowd cheered.

With a sheaf of sunflowers, a troop of bandits, and a flood of shouting followers, Elena rode across the bridge into the city of Monteverde.

Twenty-four

⚮

IT WAS SUMMER, but Her Grace the Magnificent, the Prima Elect, the Most Potent and Just Principessa Elena di Monteverde, could not tell it from inside the council room of the citadel.

Within the huge chamber, it was still as cold as winter. Candles and torches barely lit the high ceiling blackened by decades of their smoke. While one of her grandfather's elderly councilors held forth with relish on his theme, she sat dressed in miniver and damask, her scepter laid at the head of a table. The board was twice as long as the one in the mint at d'Avina, polished black and carved on the legs. But it reminded her; it brought back that day. She did not think of it often; she tried not to, and the life of the Prima di Monteverde was a life of harassment, of meetings and writs and petitions and mercantile matters, judgments and decisions, careful arguments and piles and piles and piles of scrolls and records to be read and pieced together for their history and intelligence. She had no time to think of else, except at night in the moment she lay down to sleep, when she thought of Allegreto.

He was incarcerated within sight of the citadel. If she had walked out on the parapets, she could have seen across the city and the lake to the two castles that rose from the promontories and guarded Monteverde's harbor. Franco Pietro resided in one, and Allegreto in the other.

He haunted her today. The subject of this meeting was her marriage, and her councilors were fervent on the topic.

A number of prospects had been put forth. Princes and dukes from places as far away as Denmark and Spain. Men of high blood and power among the elite of Monteverde. Even one or two of the councilors themselves were proposed, causing them to blush and claim their unsuitability while they vowed they were at Her Grace's service if she should deign to consider them. The discussion had been intense and brutally blunt, day-long, the favored and disfavored alliances flying back and forth across the table like frantic birds unable to find a roost. The cherished possibility of one faction was deemed to favor the anti-pope; another was too poor a soldier, a third too ambitious for his own power to be allowed a great role in Monteverde's fragile new Republic. Elena sat and listened to a procession of names and disputes.

But I don't want a prince, she thought with a sad inward smile. Lost to her, the girl who had once said those words to her godmother. She had a letter from Lady Melanthe, of fierce support in what Elena had done. Lady Beatrice had returned to England safely—a miracle itself—with news of Elena's abduction. But no one had conceived that she would fly from Navona and establish herself alone at the head of Monteverde. Ligurio would be proud, Ellie. I am proud. Lancaster is confounded. *Be careful.* Overlook nothing. Trust no one.

Her godmother promised to come in the next spring and spend the summer. Elena longed for it.

But it was not in her character to trust no one. She trusted Philip. She trusted Dario. She trusted a great many things and people, because she had no choice. The houses of Riata and Navona were barred from the citadel, but no one else.

It was trust and not suspicion that Monteverde needed now to heal. It was faith that she restored possessions to their former balance, that she showed no favor to either side. It was a thin thread, liable to be broken by any whisper of treachery. She lived in daily fear of word of some murder or escape from the castles.

But there had been none. For his son, or for realizing the popular support of Elena's cause, or because she kept the French condottiere at hand, Franco Pietro yielded up his Navona holdings without direct opposition. But he would not sign any agreement to cease the blood vendetta until Allegreto did. And Allegreto would not sign.

Elena watched the old councilor in his fur cap and dragging robes. He seemed to be coming to the end of his words, looking toward her expectantly. They all were turning toward her, two long rows of faces, bearded and smooth, elderly and middle-aged and a few near as young as she.

Elena was hungry. She was tired. And she felt utterly alone.

She put her hand upon the scepter. The old councilor nodded around the table and sat down with a fur-trimmed flourish of his sleeve, as if he felt none could dispute his point that Monteverde was in dire need of an heir and the custody of a strong man at the earliest possible moment, and therefore they must not waste their breath in futile arguments. Let Her Grace the Principessa say her wise preference among the prospects put forward, and proceed from there.

Elena stood up. She laid aside the list of names that her secretary handed to her. "I do not intend to wed at present," she said quietly.

An astonished silence met her words.

Before they could burst into protest, she lifted her open hand. "Monteverde does not need an heir. We are a repub-

lic again, and will choose our leader by the laws we have
adopted, as set forth by Prince Ligurio."

The old councilor made forceful motions, requesting to
speak. Elena nodded, but she remained standing.

"Your Grace, it is true what you say, it is true. I misspoke
myself, perchance, to speak of an heir to rule, though it
would be great happiness to all to see the house of Ligurio
again bear fruit. And doubtless your prudence and modesty
has prevented you from considering a marriage before we
received the annulments from Rome. But the Holy Father
has given us surety now on that point; there is no question
of any betrothal or connection between you and Franco
Pietro of the Riata, or your—" He paused, with a slight gesture of distaste, as if he could not even bring himself to
speak the name. "Your abductor," he said finally. "But I
cannot countenance that Your Grace remains unwed. It is
dangerous. Milan takes notice, that we have no man to
order our defense."

"We have Philip Welles," she said, glancing down to the
gray-haired soldier at her right hand. "He is experienced
and loyal. He has dealt well with the condottiere, has he
not?"

She allowed them to sputter their objections. Philip was
old, he was English, he was a bandit. She stared them
down.

"Can you find fault with his ordering of our defense
against Milan?" she asked.

They could not. She knew they could not, for they had
approved it themselves in the last meeting.

"We would be fortunate to find some prince or duke
with as much understanding of matters of defense and
guile," she said. "We are repairing what was razed by the
Riata—all of the Navona strongholds are impregnable
again. For that, we hold the southern lake with greater
strength than we had before. We have expelled the traitor
Jan Zoufal and thwarted his intention to devalue the trust in
Monteverde's coin. I am in negotiation with Venice for a
fresh treaty of alliance, should we need further support. If

there is more that we should arrange in our own defense, put it before me for discussion."

The faces down the table looked unconvinced. There were low mutters. Another councilor asked to speak, and Elena nodded.

The man rose, keeping his face averted. He was one of the younger ones, heavy-browed under his fur hat. His name had been put forward as a possible husband for her. "Your Grace, what of your prisoners of Riata and Navona?" His voice had a heated edge.

"What of them?" she asked.

"Navona has already attempted to force himself upon you once, Your Grace," he said angrily. "Forgive me, but it would be disaster if it happened again, or some Riata malice found you. We would be plunged into chaos, as it was in the years after your grandfather's death, may God assoil him. A strong husband at your side will prevent such." He turned to her. "And as long as you remain unwed, there are those who will scheme for a union between you and Franco Pietro or Gian Navona's cursed bastard. It cannot be suffered!"

A loud chorus of agreement echoed in the chamber. Someone called for a vote of primacy, and instantly there were seconds from half the council.

Elena could not stop it. It was part of her grandfather's law, that eleven council members could call for a vote to override her decision, and force her to submit to it. While she stood and watched, they made a state resolution to bar the Prima of Monteverde from marriage to a man of Riata or Navona blood, on pain of death or exile for him. They further resolved to seek a husband for her without delay, the final decision to be made within a fortnight.

If Philip had not looked up at her, his plain, hard-tanned face concerned, she would have borne it better. But his fatherly glance knew her heart; knew where her secret lay in the castle beyond the lake.

She felt her lip begin to tremble as the votes added up. The cloak of power and control began to slide away. She felt again like the girl who had sat on a stool before Lancaster, young and overwhelmed.

The voices died down. The resolution passed. She stood before them.

"You cannot force me to marry," she said, with her voice shaking. "Not even with this. I will not consent."

The young councilman sprang to his feet without waiting for her recognition. "Nay, this is imprudence beyond bearing! What if you are murdered without protection?" he said loudly, all courtesy and formal practice forgotten. "What if you sicken and die?" He flung out his arm. "Do you want us to fall again to Riata? Or to fight among ourselves until Milan drags away the spoils?"

She narrowed her eyes. "It would only be what you did before I came," she said.

They shook their heads, disputing stridently. The eight months of her rule had been peaceful, even if it was like the peace before a storm. The people were pleased with her. The houses of Riata and Navona stayed their hands. But that was not enough now.

"If God sends that I do not survive, it is your task to continue what Prince Ligurio tried to do," she said, banging the scepter on the table as she raised her voice. As they turned back to her, quieting, she lifted the heavy jewel-encrusted staff, trying to hold it steady, to prevent her voice from breaking. "Choose what man you like for me, but know that I will never consent to wed him. This meeting of the council is dismissed."

She turned, walking away amid renewed angry murmurs, with the scepter clutched in both hands and Philip and Dario at her side. A guard leaped to open the door for her that led into the privy chamber. As the heavy door closed behind them, she made it as far as the grand desk where Prince Ligurio had signed his decrees in state. The scepter fell from her fingers, making a mark in the wood as it struck.

She went to the trefoiled window that overlooked the city. The watery green glass was open, letting a warm rosemary-scented breath of summer into the chill room. From here she could look down upon near all the city, the bannered towers, the river that wound to the lake. She could see the cliffs that plunged into the water, with the two fortresses mounted high on them—as high as the citadel stood above Monteverde, on a level with her gaze.

She stared at the castle on the eastern crag. Somewhere on the cliff below it was a hidden path, a lovers' trysting-place.

"They are right," she said helplessly. "I should marry."

The old bandit came behind her and set his hand on her shoulder, as if he were giving courage to one of his men. He wore fine studded mail now under a green tunic, his broad chest embroidered with the silver insignia of captain of the guard. But he was still Philip Welles of the forest and the camp, smelling faintly of wood-smoke and dirt. "Bless and keep you, Princess," he said brusquely. "It is a hard fate for you, I know."

She pressed her hands together, rubbing the place where the ring had been. She felt it like a ghost, like Allegreto's presence. "Sometimes I think he comes here," she whispered. "Sometimes I can feel him near, at night."

"I do not believe it, Your Grace," Dario said. "He could not enter here even to reach Franco. The citadel has no secret ways."

She gazed at the fortress across the lake. She only wished that he came, knowing he could not. Knowing that it was she herself who kept him bound there.

She looked back at Philip and Dario. She closed her hand over Philip's hard and calloused fingers, pressing them from her shoulder. "I cannot wed another," she said fiercely. "Not while he lives. Let them pass what laws they choose."

Philip shrugged. "As you will, Princess."

"We will keep and protect you, Your Grace," Dario said. His bullish face was set in stubbornness, his dark eyes serious. "You need no husband for that."

"Aye," Philip said simply.

They stood before her, solid and steadfast. Her mouth quivered. Philip gave her hand a rough squeeze. With a sudden sob, she turned into his deep embrace, weeping as he held her close and rocked her like a child lost.

ON THE MORNING after the council meeting, Elena had arranged for the first interview between Matteo and his father. It was not going well. The boy refused to speak, standing with his back pressed to the door and his arms crossed while Nim and the mastiff sniffed and played about Ligurio's desk in the privy chamber.

Elena contained exasperation. She had already suffered through a furious dispute with Dario over whether there should be a guard present. He had produced five new men to add to her protection, and insisted that all six of them were to squeeze into the chamber with Elena and Franco and the boy.

She would not allow it. Even Dario was too much—he and Matteo were bosom friends, and the boy's loyalties burned yet too fierce to have such competition present in clear suspicion of his father's intentions. After they had brought Franco Pietro from a search to his bare skin for any weapon or threat, she closed the door in Dario's face, leaving him near to tears of rage and frustration. He opened it every few minutes and insisted on checking inside, which did not aid the matter.

Franco was little help, either. He had limped into the chamber and stood in a state of gloomy silence, leaning against the wall opposite Matteo and looking like some fiend from a prayer book with his scar and eye-patch and scowl. He also had his arms crossed, a mirror image of his son's mute denial.

Only the dogs were friendly, meeting one another again on more even ground since Nimue had grown to her full size. She stood as tall as the table now, still a bandit at heart, but disguising it in the elegant face and stature of a downy white princess, her soft-lashed eyes full of nobility and joy.

The huge mastiff was instantly smitten, fawning over her and rolling onto his back in majestic submission, no doubt full of canine hopes of a high alliance.

"Let us play a game," Elena said, after exhausting the subjects of Matteo's tutors and how he had grown. Both of the Riata males looked at her without enthusiasm.

"Indeed, Princess," Franco said after a moment, standing straight and making a courteous bow. "What game do you propose?"

"What of morra?" she asked.

Franco nodded. He lifted his torn lip in something that resembled a smile. "If it would please you, Princess."

"Morra is for babies," Matteo said with vast disdain.

"Nay, it is a fine game for anyone. I'll play with your father, if you don't like to join in," Elena said, rising from the desk. She stood before Franco Pietro and held out her hand.

They played five rounds, very awkwardly. Elena won by three. She did not look around at Matteo, but from the corner of her eye she could tell that he watched them, petting his father's mastiff while Nim sprawled panting at his feet.

"We should play for stakes, Princess," Franco said. "That is what adds the relish."

Elena considered, tilting her head. "That is a fine gold button on your sleeve."

He nodded. "It is yours, if you win in five rounds."

"And what do you play for, my lord?"

"Another visit with my son."

"Done," she said, holding out her hand.

Their rounds went smoother this time. Franco Pietro won. Matteo had drifted closer, only turning back when Dario opened the door and looked in suspiciously.

"We are playing morra," Elena said to him. "All is well."

Dario hesitated, clearly misliking her proximity to Franco Pietro.

"You may close the door and leave us alone, Dario," she said pointedly. The great door swung closed. Elena gave Franco a small nod. "He is our watchdog," she said. "A little overbearing at times."

"I understand, Princess," Franco said. "It is more than wise to keep a close guard around you and Matteo."

"But I have not won my button yet," she said, avoiding darker subjects. "You are too clever an opponent for me, sir."

"I'm better than him," Matteo said, stepping forward with a proud, stiff move. "I can win the button for you, my lady."

"Excellent. I have a champion." Elena drew back and seated herself in Ligurio's high-backed chair.

Matteo's cheeks were burning as he stared down at his father's hand in a boy's ardent concentration. They played five rounds. Matteo lost.

"Curse you, Riata!" Matteo said, flinging himself away. "I hate you."

"Matteo," Elena said sharply. "You will not speak ill to your father."

The boy glared. But Elena had spent many months in gentle chatter, building a slender bridge to the heart of this high-strung child of hatred. Nim had helped, with her sweet tumbles and happy loyalty, gradually wearing away his desperate displays of what skills he had at deceit and murder. He no longer tried to show Elena how he could have killed both of the guards outside their door with a single thrust of the dagger she did not allow him to carry. He did not question Dario so often on what manner of poison would be best to slay his enemies. He even laughed sometimes.

She had sent for the rest of Il Corvo's island household and placed them with the monks and nuns of a double monastery within view of the citadel, advising the abbot that they would be wise to blunt their table knives. But she took Matteo as her own charge, slept with him and ate with him and spoke of her grandfather's ideas. At night she knelt beside the bed with him and said a part of her own prayers aloud, including Franco's name and Allegreto's in the same blessing, along with Dario and Philip and Margaret and the others that he loved.

"I am sorry, my lady," Matteo said sullenly. He spoke to Elena, not his father, but she let it pass.

"Another round?" Franco said to him.

Matteo gave him a seething glance. He had only a week ago added his father's name to his prayers. That was when Elena had sent to Franco, allowing him to leave his detention for a day and come to the citadel under a heavy guard.

The boy gave a contemptuous nod, as regal as any prince. Then he looked down and played the finger game as if ten thousand men were in fatal combat at his command.

He lost.

Elena could have hoped Franco Pietro would skew the odds a little, but morra was not a game that was easily thrown without being obvious. Matteo stepped back, his cheeks spotted with red. "I can't win!" he cried. "I never do *anything* right!"

He turned his back, marching for the door. Franco moved suddenly, his hand on the boy's shoulder. Matteo stopped, shivering. Tears glittered in his eyes. "It does not matter," Franco said.

Matteo shrugged his hand off. He stood and dashed at his eyes. "It matters! I'm not good at anything! No one will want me. I can't even win a stupid game for babies! I try and try. And I *can't*."

"It does not matter," Franco said. "You are my son."

Matteo drew a sobbing breath. His body stilled.

"My heart died when he stole you from me," Franco said roughly. "And then he made you hate me." He drew a breath between his teeth, as if he would say more, but stopped. He looked toward Elena. "You have no reason to trust me, Princess, and yet you have. It has been a revelation to me."

She lifted her face. He leaned on the table, still favoring his leg. She might have had him for a husband; a strange and difficult thought. "I have been fortunate, I know," she said. "By God's grace, I thank you that you have not—done what you might have done."

He gave his twisted smile. "I thought you plain mad," he

said. "I do yet, I think. But you hold Navona in check, it seems. I did not think it possible. You have kept your pledges to be impartial thus far."

"I am trying. If you have any complaint, then tell me, and do not brood on it."

"Oh, I have brooded. I do not care to be penned up at the hest of a mere maid. But my son would have killed me, and you stopped him by your own hand." Franco turned as Matteo made a faint sound. "You think you cannot do anything," he said harshly to the boy, "but you would have had a blade through my throat if the princess had not saved us both. You have courage, Matteo, and that does matter. Listen to her, and learn how to use it better."

He took one limping stride to the door and gave it a hard blow. Dario opened it instantly, his sword on guard. The other men surrounded Franco, swiftly penning him between his jailers. The mastiff growled, but Franco silenced it with a word. The dog trailed close as the Riata was escorted out.

Matteo held Nim's collar, watching until the door closed behind them. Elena let go of a muffled breath and sat down again at her grandfather's desk. She had a list of her afternoon audience; she opened it and pretended to read.

"Would you like to see him again?" she asked casually.

Matteo shrugged. "Nim likes his dog."

"By chance I will ask him to come back, and bring it."

Matteo made himself very interested in rubbing Nimue's ears. "I'll practice at morra. I can beat him, I think."

"Good," Elena said. "I have conceived a great desire for that button." She sighed and glanced down at the list before her. "Now I must put on my crown, and be courteous to a great number of very wearisome people. You may come if you like."

Matteo grinned suddenly, going on one knee with a flourish. "My lady, I beg your indulgence. I'd rather take Nim to the tilt yard."

"Desert me in my hour of need, then," she said, waving him out. "Tell Dario where you will be."

He promised it and left, calling Nim after him. As the

door swung closed under the hand of the standing guard, Elena looked down at the parchment. The Venetian ambassador, again. The representative of Milan, who would speak to her as if she were a three-year-old child who would not behave. A sainted envoy from the prince-bishop of Trento. And an emissary from His Grace the Duke of Lancaster, Sir Raymond de Clare.

"LITTLE CAT!" RAYMOND murmured in English, kissing her hand as he knelt before her. "What have you done here?"

"Don't say such things," she said below her breath. She pulled away, walking to the window of the privy chamber. In the public audience they had exchanged nothing but exquisitely courteous formalities and the Duke's letter, and even here Dario stood impassive by the door, a wooden guard on such virtue as she had left. "Rise," she said, speaking court French, turning from the view of Monteverde. "I am pleased to see you, Raymond."

He came to his feet with a familiar chivalrous ease and a little sideways smile at her. "It is beyond telling how I thank God for my fortune, Your Grace."

"I pray He grants you and your lady wife good health and gladness."

He lowered his eyes. "It grieves me to tell you that my wife Catherine returned after the spirit to her heavenly place, these five months since, may the Lord give her soul rest."

Elena was already discomposed, hardly knowing what to say to him. This news left her without speech entirely for a moment. He stood before her with his head slightly bowed, dressed fine in his black-and-red doublet and scarlet cloak, as if no day had passed since she had last seen him.

"God assoil her," Elena said, making a slight recovery. "It is grievous news."

He bowed his head further, and then looked up with an

expression that said it was not grievous news at all. "Grant mercy for your compassion, Your Grace. Her passing was quick. She did not suffer greatly. As my lord the duke knew me at liberty, and near enough to come with speed, he chose me to convey his greetings." He smiled openly then, the same playful grin. In English he said, "It was a boon to me!"

She found that he embarrassed her. She had loved him and hated him; all those rash and untamed feelings, with nothing left of them now. And yet it was like a comfort to see him, to hear English words, to speak to someone who had no part in the hazards that surrounded her.

She found her lips turning upward and heat in her cheeks. "Raymond," she said, keeping to English, "truly it is good to see you."

"Little cat." He did not move, but the timbre of his words was like a caress. "I never thought to have the joy again."

Elena flushed, afraid that Dario would hear the emotion even if he could not understand the words. The youth watched Raymond from under his heavy eyelids, a slow blink that belied the speed with which Elena knew he could move. "You came from Bohemia, then?" she asked

"As fast as my horse could carry me," he said. "I was not sorry to leave it." In English he spoke openly. "You know I hated that alliance." He cast a glance at the great desk. "But you—you spurned your betrothal! And now rule in his place! Elayne, I am struck in awe."

It was strange to hear her name in English. She gave a feeble laugh. "Oh, Raymond, I hardly believe it myself. It is not—what I intended."

"But even the duke congratulates you!"

"I'm sure he only wishes to know that his agreements on a dowry are not to be discarded," she said with a wry smile. "I hope he may not be too dissatisfied if they are set aside."

"I am here to speak to you on his behalf," Raymond said. He gave her an amused look. "I'm glad to hear you are set against his desires. God send that it may take a long time to persuade you, and many meetings between us."

"Raymond," she said, feeling her cheeks grow warm again.

"I never forgot you for one moment, little cat," he said low. "Never for one moment."

"You flatter me. Don't speak so." She was flustered in spite of herself.

"I know I can never have what I desire," he said, soft and fervent. "I gave up my hopes for that, though it tore my heart from my chest. But if you need a friend, let me offer all that I am to your service. How strange it all is, that we come to this! I love you still, Elayne, I will say it though you despise me."

"No," she said, "I don't despise you."

"But I speak too warmly," he said, lowering his head again. "I have no right."

She felt sad for him. He had only done what any man would do, obeyed his liege, as she had obeyed the duty laid on her. The dream of a safe home and this handsome knight seemed so faint and mild that she could hardly recall what she had wanted so badly.

She wanted something else now, even more unreachable, as impossible to possess.

They had that in common, that they both wished for things that could not be. And he was familiar, and faithful, and apart from all the burdens of Monteverde.

"I am in dire need of plain friendship," she said, holding out her hand. "I hope you will not hasten to depart too soon."

He took it between both of his and went down his knee.

Twenty-five

———∞∞∞———

ALLEGRETO DROPPED HER letter in the fire. He sat down before the great hearth, watching the wax melt in a sizzling red stream and drip to the stone while the parchment smoked and took flame. Her entreaties to him slowly vanished, marks of ink that blackened and curled and fell away to ash.

"No reply," he said.

He heard Zafer go to the door and speak to the guard through the barred window in it. There were vivid moments when he thought to kill himself, most powerfully when she wrote to him of how willing Franco Pietro was to sign her accord if Allegreto would, and urging him to put his head on the Riata's block for chopping.

He could find no way out. She had tethered and trapped him on all sides, and not with walls or guards. He could not leave, he could not remain, he saw no future. He could find no way to anywhere but Hell, by his own hand or by Franco's.

He had a set of chambers furnished as fine as a silver merchant's, with a featherbed and writing table, any books

he desired from Ligurio's library, a second room for alchemical work and visits from the steward appointed to ad-
minister Navona's reinstated properties. Zafer shared his
confinement, and Margaret seemed to have some lodging
somewhere in the castle; they both served him, faithfully
performing credence as if he cared whether he drank poison
pure from the cup.

With Zafer's contrivance, he would have been able to
leave this finely furnished prison easily enough in a trail of
blood. But he remained, watching the fortress across the
narrows for Franco to make his attempt, watching the
citadel, spreading a silent cordon of protection around her
as he could.

His endeavor would have been more effective if Dario
had not managed to discern every attempt he had made so
far to infiltrate a man to the citadel. Allegreto received
sharp chiding on the matter in his letters from Elena, as if it
were a schoolboy's trick. She seemed determined to be a
martyr to this cause, exposing herself in peril to everyone
but him.

Dario at least was there. Zafer was the best, but he was
stained too deep with Allegreto's taint to be suffered inside
the citadel.

The small fire in the hearth smoked and popped. Allegreto opened the papal dispatch again, holding the smooth
vellum between his fingers. The true Pope seemed to be
going mad; Allegreto's letters of supplication had chased
him all the way to Naples, where the holy father appeared
to have no business but to grab at some rich territory for his
fat and useless nephew, leaving Rome in disarray. If Allegreto would bring armies from Monteverde in aid of this
hallowed endeavor to wring more blood from the kingdom
of Naples, God's highest representative on earth would
consider Allegreto's humble petition to lift his excommunication.

Allegreto tore off the handful of holy seals and sent
them with scornful flicks one by one into the fire. He laid

his head back in the chair and thought of a girl with a bloodied sword in her hand and a dream of another way.

This is my answer, she had said.

It was not stone walls that held him here. Not guards or
blades or chains. It was her answer, that there was another
way, and even if he could not touch her or see her again, he
could at least stand in the shadows and shield her from his
kind.

"My lord," Zafer said, placing a goblet with the embossing of a stag toward Allegreto—signal that he had
some news. Allegreto took up the wine and rose, carrying it
with him as he ducked out onto the tiny parapet walk that
overlooked the lake.

Zafer stood in front of the low door, as if he merely
awaited his master's orders. "Franco was invited to the
citadel, under guard, to see his son and parley with her," the
youth said, softly enough that his voice was carried away
by the breeze.

Allegreto set his wine down on the parapet.

The lake glimmered, blue and purple depths, the color of
her eyes. She invited Franco. Winter and spring and summer, Allegreto had endured, his mind and body screaming
for release from this velvet trap.

She invited Franco. Allowed him inside the citadel.

He hurled the goblet, watching red wine arch through
the air as the cup turned and tumbled and fell. It receded to
a mere glint against the stunning drop of the walls and the
cliff, the huge surface of the lake. He lost sight of it.

"What else?" he said.

"Only the public audiences, my lord. After Franco departed, she saw Venice and Milan and Trento. And an envoy
has arrived from the Duke of Lancaster. She spoke to him
after in private."

"In private?"

"Dario was with them. The envoy is an Englishman,
Raymond de Clare by name."

Allegreto stilled. He turned his look on Zafer.

There was a nearly imperceptible flaring of Zafer's nostrils; a sudden wariness in his dark eyes. "My lord—he is an enemy?"

An enemy. The sanctified knight of her love poems. The gallant, charming, faultless Raymond. She saw him in private, that mud-stained offspring of an English pigsty.

Allegreto turned back to the lake. His knuckles grew white as he pressed his fingers into the rough stone parapet. He stood looking across to the citadel, containing the desire to cut his own throat and let himself fall, plunging downward like the cup spilling wine.

ELENA MADE PLANS for what she knew was an error. It was courting jeopardy past reason or defense. On the night before the council meant to choose a husband for her, she left the citadel.

She had Franco's words, that he recognized her as impartial—thus far. But he was only the head of Riata. There were those of his house who chafed under his surprising restraint, hating their lowered status and Navona's elevation. Her grandfather had warned of such things in his book. Elena was trying to follow Ligurio's counsel, working to bring them into some bettered situation, raising this one to new offices, bestowing a windfall on another, trying to make certain no one of the houses worked directly together, or worse, over one another.

But they were not wholly appeased. If any rumor spread of her destination, all was at risk. And her life was always forfeit if she failed.

She took only Dario, though he was loathe to do it, his obedience bought by the threat of being removed entirely from his post at her bedchamber door. Through the rainy night he rowed her across the lake to the eastern headland. Both of them climbed the path on the cliff, past the little trysting cave. Thunder rumbled above the mountains. By the light of a shuttered lantern, they came to the postern door of the castle, set deep within the rock.

A guard met them there, one of Philip's best men. Elena

wore the modest clothes of a maid, only a black shift with
short sleeves, her hair wrapped up in one long cloth like a
poor woman. But over that, she had a striped hood, the legal
mark of a prostitute in Monteverde.

She kept her face lowered as they climbed the stairs and
passed through the tiers of guards, walking between Dario
and Philip's man. Any murmur of interest from the other
soldiers was quelled with a cuff, or a gruff mumble: "It's
permitted to him for a night."

By the time they reached the last heavily guarded door,
Elena did not know if her heart was working so hard from
the climb or for the moment when she would see him.
There was a brief pause as Philip's man worked his key.
The door opened. From her lowered gaze, Elena saw that
someone moved into it, blocking the way.

"Out," Dario said briefly. "He won't want your company."

She realized it was Zafer who stood in the door. He hesitated, and then obeyed, leaving the doorway free. Dario
gave her a hard little push. Elena walked through. She
heard the lock and bolt made fast.

She stood a moment, lifting her face, her heart pounding
in her ears. At midnight several candles still burned, but the
chamber was empty, furnished with excellent comfort as
she had ordered, the table covered with parchment and
books. A pot of fresh ink gleamed black beside a sheaf of
new-cut quills.

One doorway led outside, standing open, the rain falling
in a steady splatter of sound. A peculiar scent hung in the
air over the fresh smell of rain, a sudden and intense reminder of his study on the island. She walked past the table
to another arched door that stood open. As she lowered her
head to go through, she saw no one beyond, though the familiar blue light illuminated a table crowded with glass
globes and vials and a mortar and pestle.

She was about to speak when her arm was seized and
twisted up behind her. The spike of pain would have made

her cry out but for the hand gripped over her mouth hard enough to stifle anything beyond a muffled yelp.

He held her trapped for an instant, driving sharp agony into her shoulder. Then he drew a deep breath at her throat and suddenly let her go.

Elena sagged with relief, turning. She rubbed her shoulder, looking up under the hood at Allegreto.

His face held no pleasure, no sign of any surprise or feeling at the sight of her. "I thought Franco might have sent a woman," he said without greeting.

She realized that he meant someone sent to murder him. It was not how she had hoped to begin.

"I was afraid to send word ahead to you. That it might be discovered."

He observed her impassively. "Your disguise is well-chosen."

Elena lowered her chin, doubtful of how to take his meaning. He was as comely as she remembered—more so, with all traces of his bruises long vanished. He wore pure black silk trimmed with silver and pearls at his cuffs. His hair had grown long again, braided now behind his neck in infidel fashion.

Raymond was a handsome man of even features and a charming smile. Allegreto was simply Lucifer made real, the lord of light fallen down to perfect darkness in the flesh.

"What is it?" he asked. "Why have you come?"

Now that she was here, facing his cool reception, she was hardly certain. She had wanted to assure him that she would not give in to the council and marry. She had thought he would have heard of what was planned. She thought he would care.

In truth, she had wanted to see him so badly that she had not let sense or reason stop her.

She walked to the table, pushing the damp prostitute's hood from her head. "The council meets tomorrow, to choose a husband for me."

"I know it."

She bent her head. Atop an open parchment, amid his

curious beakers and tools, lay the piece of black stone that he had purchased from the Egyptian—a lifetime ago, it seemed. Across the parchment were inked copies of the strange letters upon the rock. She traced the odd carvings with her fingers.

She looked sideways at him over the folds of the black-and-white hood. "What should I do?"

He gave a short laugh. "You pose it to me?"

She wet her lips, looking quickly down again. She had not meant to ask, but to tell him. But now—he was so cold. He seemed to feel nothing of the tumult she had inside herself, the pain and thrill in her blood, the sensation of merely standing in the same chamber with him again.

"You have told me that we are wed," she said to the stone and parchment.

"I lied," he said bluntly. "You are free. You have the Pope's own word on it, I hear."

She turned and leaned back with her hands gripping the edge of the table. "In my heart, I am not free."

He walked past her to the far side of the board. "You came to torture me, is that it? Monteverde bitch. I wonder that I have not killed all the women who ever bore the name."

She let go of the edge, watching him as he put his palms on the table and bent over an open book. The pearl-encrusted cuffs fell down over his hands.

"Do you think it does not torture me?" she asked.

With a slam he closed the book. He looked up at her. "Then why did you come?" he said fiercely.

"Why are you still here?" she asked. "I know that you could escape."

His hands opened wide across the leather binding, his fingers spread and white between the joints. "And go where? Do what? I would have fought Riata, and won, but I will not fight you."

"That is all?"

He gave her such a look that she nearly stepped backward, though the table was between them.

"You take pleasure in this, don't you?" he said softly.

She did take a step back then, when he came around the table toward her. He seemed to move with leisure, and yet he was before her suddenly, dauntingly, cornering her against the table.

"You take pleasure in binding me here, while you bid Franco to the citadel and play with your English knight." His black lashes were like smoke, lowered over his dark eyes in disdain. "I know you."

She shook her head. "Not in this!" she exclaimed. "I hate it."

"Do you want to know how much it torments me? Do you want to see for yourself that I have a poison ready at my hand, for when I can bear this no longer?"

"No!"

He stood back. "But that is a distraction only, to give me comfort. I will not die a suicide. Nay, I'm ten times worse a fool—I think I might claw my way into Heaven somehow, and be with you when our lives are ended, since there is no way now on the earth."

She sank down on the stool, holding her arms and palms pressed together, rocking forward with her face in her hands. "Oh, God, if you would only make peace with Riata," she said. "Then you could be free. You could come into the citadel."

"And see you wed to another, with that English dog prancing in and out of your bed as you please. What mortal bliss. Leave me here to contemplate my poison vial, grant mercy."

She lifted her face. "I will not wed. Never. I came to tell you so. I would take no one else to me."

Thunder rumbled. The candle flames swayed in a draft of air, but the blue lights burned steadily. The sound of an increasing downpour drifted from the far chamber with the cool scent of rain.

The grim set of his mouth softened a little. "You will not be able to hold to that. And you are mad to trust Franco.

You should not let him near you. I cannot give you any protection from him inside the citadel."

She let her hands slide apart. "What protection do you give me?"

"What I can. You have not made it easy."

She bowed her head. "Is there no way—no chance—that you could have faith in Franco's intentions?" she asked humbly.

"Aye, when the Apocalypse comes to annihilate us all," he said.

She gave a slight miserable laugh and put her fingers to her forehead.

He turned and walked to a shuttered window. He pulled it open. Outside the rain poured down, splashing and dripping, darkening the stone as he stared into the black night. "You would not take another to you?" he asked abruptly. "Not even your sainted Raymond?"

Elena stood up from the stool. "No. Or I would not have come here."

He shook his head slowly. The night air ruffled a lock of his hair that had come loose from the braid and fell over his face. "I am beyond a fool. Beyond it, to believe in this dream of Ligurio's. To listen to what you say."

"You believe in it?"

"I do. Sometimes." He sounded distant. "But there is no place in it for me, Elena. I was born for everything you want to bring to an end."

She squeezed her eyes closed. She wanted to deny it, and yet she could find no way. Already there had been loud murmurs in the council that Allegreto and Franco Pietro should be tried as traitors to Monteverde, and it was clear enough what outcome was intended.

She turned back to the table. The books and scrolls on it seemed to have little to do with natural science. A Bible lay open to the Ten Commandments. On another parchment was a list of saints' names with sums beside them, like the bankers' ledgers in Venice.

A brief memory flitted through her mind, of the abbot's

pleasure in accepting a score of Allegreto's unscrupulous orphans to his quiet house. She had thought at the time that he was an exceptionally kind and virtuous man, to receive them so happily and even refuse her offers to pay for their maintenance. She ran her finger down the list and saw the name of the patron saint of the abbey, with a startlingly large amount listed beside it.

"I am trying to buy my way in," Allegreto said as she touched the page of accounts. "If you know of any notably holy personages I might support, or a miracle I might sponsor, do inform me."

She smiled painfully. "I have only one miracle to desire of you."

"I am flesh and blood. I have no miracles within me, Elena. You know it well."

She turned her face away. "I seem to have none, either. Sometimes I think it has been a great mistake. That my grandfather was wrong. We are weak. We are still divided. I'm a maid—hardly yet nineteen. Milan is only waiting for me to fail. Or not that long." She drew a shuddering breath. "The stories I have heard of the Visconti . . . God save, they are beasts, not men. Sometimes I'm so afraid. And I wish you were there at my side."

The rain lightened to a steady mutter outside the window. She remained staring down at her finger on the parchment list.

"Now you torment me in truth," he said.

"And myself."

She felt him when he came to her. When he stood behind her silently.

"What do you want?" he asked softly.

She could hardly speak. "Oh—do not ask." It came out as a mere rush of breath, barely words. She knew why she had come here. Had known it all along.

She felt his hand touch the cloth wrapped about her head. It came free, drifting down to the floor as her hair fell around her shoulders. He moved near her, a heat and velvet touch all down her back and her hips. But no closer. He did not embrace her. Elena gazed at the woven mat on the wooden floor, feeling tears of anguish rising in her throat.

"I should go," she said in a broken voice, and did not move.

He pushed his hands into her hair and pressed his face to her throat. "Let me remember." He drew a hard breath beside her ear. "Let me remember first."

She let her head fall back. Oh, to remember . . .

She turned, lifting her face to him. He doubled her hair in his hands and pressed her cheeks between his fingers, kissing her, opening his mouth against hers. He leaned back on the table and pulled her to him fiercely.

The sound of the rain seemed to rise to a roar in her ears, merging with her heartbeat. She let herself rest on him, his body strong and alive and real against hers. So long it had been, she had near lost faith that he had ever been more than a dream, a vision she had seen once between sleep and waking. Her dark angel.

He pushed her abruptly away. Elena made a faint moan, gazing up at him. They did not speak. There was no need to say that she had set aside any truth or lie that they had wed, that to conceive a child now would be utter disaster. And yet she had come here to him, and she knew not how she could leave again.

A faint bitterness played at the corner of his mouth. "How you must enjoy to annihilate me."

She shook her head. "I cannot help myself. I cannot."

He cupped her face and kissed her again. "I can." His hands slid to her shoulders. "Though it slay me."

She whimpered, seeking his lips, pressing herself to his chest. Through her plain thin gown, through his silk, she could feel his phallus erect. With a lascivious move, she rolled herself against him, begging.

"Hell-cat," he muttered, tearing his mouth away. He pressed downward on her shoulders, pushing her to her knees before him. His fingers tangled in her hair, pulling her face against the hard shape of him under the silky cloth.

Elena slid her hands up his thighs. He wore no breech;

above his black hose and laces, her fingers touched bare skin. She drew her hands together over his naked shaft.

With a deep sound he arched toward her. She kissed him through the black veil of silk, skimming her nails over his hot skin. He let go of her suddenly and gripped the edge of the table as she explored him, his body growing taut. She could hear him breathing between his teeth.

She opened her mouth over his rod, sucking through the silk. Her own body wanted him inside; she drew on him with that desire, as if she could take him to her very heart. She closed her fingers hard at the base of his shaft and felt the pain she caused travel up through him as he thrust into her mouth in response.

She tightened her hold and pulled and worked, tasting the wet cloth and another essence that made damp heat between her legs. She served him like a wanton, with no thought but to the way he trembled and plunged himself deep in her mouth. The silk pulled taut over the head of his rod with each shove.

She drove her fingernails into him. Low in his throat he made a sound of agony. His shaft pulsed in her hands. He cried out, arching back, an echo of the rain and wind as his body seized and shuddered. Elena opened wide her lips to take him as he burst and spilled into the silken sheath.

The exotic, earthy savor was only a trace through the cloth. She would have tasted deeper, but he pulled her up against him, thrusting his tongue in her mouth, holding her hard to his chest. When he finally broke away, she was lost for air or thought. She clung in his arms, wanting him still, consumed with folly and desire.

"Beloved," he said fiercely. Suddenly he caught her up and carried her, ducking through the doorway. He laid her on the bed, half upon it, dragging up her gown. The edge of the high bed arched her body to him like an open offering; he leaned over her and kissed the mounded curls between her legs, thrusting his fingers up inside her.

Elena gasped and twisted, lifting herself to his mouth. Where his tongue touched her, her body convulsed. She closed her legs and strained, panting under the stroke and press of his fingers. Sweet hot sensation unfurled, rising to an explosion. She clutched at his hair, pleading for it. When it came in a fury of pleasure, she sobbed for breath, squeezing tears from beneath her eyelids as the peak rolled through her.

SHE HAD NO long hours to tangle in sleep beside him. Keys and the slide of a bolt awakened her from what seemed a moment's drowse at his side. Allegreto was already on his feet when a loud voice gave warning of the appointed time. Dario sounded gruff and irritable, but Elena heard the note of anxiety beneath. He would give her no longer than they had agreed. Less, she thought it seemed—or an hour had passed in the space of a moment.

She rose hastily. The fact of imprisonment struck her with force as guards came through the door without consent. Allegreto turned her into his arms, pulling the black-and-white prostitute's hood close around her face. He bent as if for a kiss, blocking her from the view of the guards. "Farewell," he said beneath his breath. "Farewell."

He let go of her without lingering. She could not look up at him again for fear of revealing herself.

"For the girl." Allegreto tossed a gold coin to the nearest guard as he turned away. Elena kept her face lowered under the hood.

"Ah." The guard gave a snort and waved her toward the door. "She must have been good."

ELENA BARELY HELD her head erect under her heavy crown as she dined at the high board between Raymond and the Milanese ambassador. Exhaustion pulled on her mind and heart. She would have been glad to lay her head down on the snowy white damask and lose all awareness amid the cups of silver for the wine.

The council meeting had been a monumental conflict of

wills between herself and some twenty men with no small opinion of their own judgment. She had clung to her refusal to wed, but the only thing that truly spared her was their inability to agree on a candidate. She feared that strong factions were forming, and none of them were behind her on this matter. It did not bode well for the unity of her rule. None had said so aloud yet, but some might think that if she would not marry at the council's hest, perchance her election should be overturned and a man put in her place. Or if she proved too stubborn for that, she might be removed by a more uncomplicated and fatal stratagem.

They had postponed a vote until the next meeting, at least. Elena broke bread and tried to master her weariness far enough for courtesy. Dario performed credence and kept a stony eye on the signor from Milan, but the plump representative of the Visconti seemed less inclined to poison Elena than to chide her incessantly in a gentle voice. In his face and manner he reminded her of no one so much as her sister Cara, reproving Elena for her reluctance to agree to his political proposals and insisting that Monteverde and Milan had always been friends and staunch allies. This was not what she had read in her grandfather's history. She had taken Philip's advice and paid handsomely from the treasury for an added protection if Milan should prove a true enemy.

She had not even dared speak to the council about it, for fear of spies, but hidden the sum in the expense of renovations to her chambers that had yet to be made. But the money went to another free company of soldiers, in the current pay of Venice, who ranged in the mountains to the north and held the passes open for commerce. It was a pure and simple blackmail—no doubt they would as happily close the way if no one paid them to do differently. But they were there, and Elena remembered Hannibal, and thought it worth her while to live with the same bed-hangings that had graced her chamber in Lady Melanthe's day.

She nodded to the Milanese diplomat with what courtesy she could muster. She raised her finger for the signor's wine to be filled, watching as his own taster took a ceremonial sip before the cup was passed.

The ambassador launched into a discourse on the ultimate futility of republican institutions, advising Elena to reconsider the wisdom of giving wide powers to an elected council. She was not overly pleased with the council herself at the moment, but his criticisms provoked her, as she knew they were meant to do. Before she could discover a suitably polite and clever way to undercut him, she was astonished to hear Raymond speak loudly in French.

"Nay, my lord, have you read Prince Ligurio's book on the subject?" he asked, leaning to look past her. "I have just finished it, and it is worthy of consideration by kings."

Elena looked at him, half-expecting him to grin and wink as if he made a jest. Raymond was no proponent of civil rule that she ever knew—he had served Lancaster as his liege and master without question, even to his marriage. But his face was serious as he took up a sharp defense of her grandfather's ideas, countering the ambassador's objections with quotes from the Latin and even Greek.

Elena stared at him in amazement. She had to be courteous herself, but Raymond grew quite heated on the subject, saying that he had spent the past fortnight in Monteverde in talking to people of all orders, and taking note of how they loved their elected princess. They were pleased with the new laws and just administration. A fisherman of unknown family could expect that he would receive treatment under the judges equal to that of any Riata lordling.

The ambassador mumbled about the disintegration of order, but Raymond said stridently that any bloodthirsty tyrant could keep order by spreading fear. Order in Monteverde came of respect and love for the princess herself, and the selfless way she governed. This was so near a direct insult to the merciless methods of the Visconti that Elena intervened before the ambassador's color rose too high. She turned the talk to the upcoming days of grape harvest and asked the Milanese diplomat if the weather had been favorable in Lombardy. They spoke of the country festivals that would honor the harvest once it was gathered in.

"Your Grace," Raymond said suddenly, turning to her with a smile. "Give me the honor of laying an idea before you. Let us have a celebration in Monteverde to mark the first year of your reign. It has been near a year now, has it not?"

She blinked at the notion. It hardly seemed a thing to celebrate—it had been a year of strain and misery and loneliness in her mind. But Raymond gave her a warm look, leaning near. He raised his eyebrow toward the ambassador and lowered his voice, changing to English.

"It would be a sign to doubters that all is going well," he murmured. "Arrange some processions and feasting. The people always love display." He offered her a sip of wine from his goblet. "Make liveries that they can keep. Distribute largesse, release some prisoners." He shrugged, giving her a sideways glance. "Invent some cheer, Your Grace. By hap if I am fortunate, it will make you smile again."

Twenty-six

⚬⚬⚬

ON A MORNING in late October they came for Allegreto.
The splotches of colored banners, the movement of a
troop—he had seen them marching on the fortress across
the lake where Franco Pietro lay, but he had thought it yet
another escort to take the Riata again into the citadel. Zafer
had heard no hint or suspicion of anything more, beyond
the plans to commemorate a year of Monteverde's new republic. Those preparations had seemed to grow apace each
time there was a new report. In addition to the procession
to the duomo and the special mass, there was to be a feast
and a hastilude in the tilt yard of the citadel, celebrations in
the market and streets of all the towns, everything from a
new ballad commissioned by the miners' guild to a bronze
statue of Prince Ligurio in a Roman senator's robes and
laurel crown, donated by Venice, to be raised in the piazza
while speeches were declaimed by every worthy who could
find an excuse to dally in the north of Italy.

The whole chaotic plan for celebration made Allegreto
uneasy. He did not approve of opening the citadel to
crowds, or the princess exposing herself at the head of a

procession that would begin at Val d'Avina and advance to the city. He had even sent messages to tell her so. But his cautions seemed to fall unheard. Word came that it was her favorite, the Englishman, who promoted the festivities, and whatever delight he suggested, the princess granted willingly.

She had said she would take no other to her. Allegreto did not believe it. Zafer said nothing of carnal connection; the rumors claimed that she never saw any man alone. But still Allegreto did not believe it.

So when the soldiers came without warning on the first day of the event, he understood instantly. Haps the Englishman had convinced her at last of the wisdom of it, or Philip, or the council in some secret gathering. Allegreto hardly cared. If she meant to have an execution as the centerpiece of her entertainment, ridding herself of Navona and Riata at one brilliant blow, he could only admire the drama of it. Such a thing would impress the people beyond measure. She had offered mercy and urged peace—Allegreto and Franco had refused it. So everything came to its preordained end, and this was the perfect time to make it count.

He had tried to prepare himself. He had some slight hopes, floating half-waterlogged in a sea of desolation. He had not yet received a reply from the Pope on his latest appeal and offering—perpetual masses endowed at Monteverde and Rome and Venice, all of the isle of Il Corvo dedicated to a monastery in the service of whatever saint His Holiness considered most deserving, and the three fragments of the Black Tablet that he had managed to collect at extraordinary expense, which contained portions of the Ten Commandments carved into stone that would take no scratch from a normal tool.

He did not go so far as to make any claims that the Black Tablet was a holy relic. He only offered what he had with as much meekness as ink could convey on a page. He had begged the Pope to forgive his inability to send an army; he had no army at his command, but to have his ban lifted, to have a slender chance at Heaven, he would abase himself before this absurd madman of a Holy Father in any other manner the lunatic desired.

But it was too late now for the Pope. There would be a priest there for Franco; if Allegreto was fortunate he also might be suffered to receive the sacrament in extremity. He could hope for it.

He stood without resistance as they dressed him in a green shirt and silver houppelande. The robes were beautifully made, with fitted hose and elegant deep sleeves that trailed to the dagged hem at his thighs. The braided circlet for his head held a single feather plume, a whisper of weight that curled down over his temple and fluttered white just at the corner of his vision.

It was great finery for a man condemned. In haps she meant it as a compliment. He would have been more thankful to be spared the manacles they clapped on his wrists, rendering him helpless for the ride down the mountainside. He kept his gaze level, staring straight ahead for pride, containing the frenzy against the bonds that rose inside him. Two soldiers led the horse. Zafer walked beside, one hand on the stirrup.

Bells began tolling as they reached the narrow strip of level ground beside the lake. The captain of the troops ordered haste. Allegreto prayed that if it was to be a bonfire, she would not have the courage to watch, for he was not sure he had the courage to endure it in silence. If he lost his thin hope and found himself howling in everlasting flames, at least there would only be the Devil and the rest of the doomed to hear.

The city gates stood open for them. Crowds lined the streets, staring as he passed, bizarrely silent under the deep toll of bells from every church in the city. It nearly broke his nerve—he thought he could have borne jeering and pelting with refuse better than the expectant waiting.

They passed his father's tower and the Navona enclave. It still bore marks of smoke and flame from the upper windows, but a new portico was under construction lining the street. He recognized faces—men loyal to his house stood atop the wooden scaffolding. He met their eyes, and they bowed their heads one by one as he passed.

There were other signs of destruction and renewal in the city—empty spaces where buildings should have stood, stacks of rubble and pallets of worked stone ready to be levered into place. But it seemed unchanged in its heart, in its fine tall towers that glared at one another across the piazzas and streets. Long banners hung below every window, a hundred colors and designs to mark each house and guild. The cloth drifted with lazy majesty over the streets, lifting and falling, a soft sound above the clatter of armor and hooves as the bells fell silent.

Allegreto felt a rise of his heart as the street turned. Down a narrow cleft of shadow between the towers, the colored walls and golden dome of the duomo stood framed in brilliant sunlight. The crowds parted. In a moment he expected to see what pyre or execution block would end his life, but the sight of the church was a glimpse of wonder through a dark tunnel.

He took courage from it as he rode into the open air of the piazza. From the other direction, in a stir of motion, a troop led Franco Pietro into the square. The mass of the duomo came wholly into view, dwarfing the horses and people, the great steps rising to a gigantic bronze door. The beautiful bands of green and white stone were like bannered stripes painted all the way around the walls, one atop the other. The sun struck full on the great mosaic of the Annunciation, a glitter of gold and turquoise and scarlet arched above the door. Allegreto knew every detail of it without turning his face, as he knew without looking directly at her that Elena stood beneath it at the top of the stairs.

The crowd began to rumble now. Next to the princess stood the bishop, and behind her a line of men. Allegreto knew only some of them; he recognized merchants and councilors, others who carried the badges of Venice and Milan and Ferrara. Near to her elbow stood a handsome peacock in parti-colored red-and-blue, his tunic adorned by white fleur-de-lis. Allegreto remembered the English insignia with clarity. He stared with cold venom at Raymond de Clare. It spared him looking at Elena, or knowing if she looked at him.

The Englishman paid him no heed. He seemed more interested in Franco Pietro, watching with a solemn look as the Riata was led to the foot of the steps. Allegreto dismounted under the rough command of soldiers. He saw no sign of preparations for an execution. He hoped then that she intended to pass sentence here before the church and withdraw to let her soldiers carry it out elsewhere. The noise of the people grew louder, anticipating.

Escorted by the guards, he climbed the steps with Franco. He would have thought to feel humiliation, but instead a sense of bitter victory filled him to see the Riata share his fate. She gave him that much at least, that there was some ultimate purpose and aim in the end. There was Ligurio's peace, this mad marvel of an idea she meant to make real, and a white blaze of hate for Franco Pietro that almost blinded Allegreto as he stood before the crowd. He closed his eyes. He did not need to see or hear; for once he needed no caution or defense. Vaguely he was aware that the noise of the assembly begin to rise to a roar. The tight grip on his arms loosened and left him.

He felt a cool touch lift his hands. The contact startled him. He opened his eyes in a sea of sound, the bellow of the crowd echoing and washing in thunderous waves from the walls of the duomo to the towers and back.

Elena stood before him. She was looking down at his hands, inserting a key into the manacles. He could hear nothing but the roar; see nothing but the heavy gold circle of her crown over the black braids coiled about her head. The chains fell away and struck the ground, the sound of it lost in the clamor. She turned to Franco Pietro beside him and did the same.

The noise of the crowd rose to a deafening pitch, a note of confusion and ferment and outrage. They had expected what Allegreto had expected. Not this. As he stood in disbelief, she raised her hand high, holding the keys.

Sudden silence rolled outward from where they stood, the crowd-sound falling away into the streets and the distance like something living that ran away.

"We are all Monteverde!" she called, her voice loud and strong. "*All* of us." She lifted her eyes to Franco, and then to Allegreto. She held his gaze for an instant, that open level look, the violet-blue depths of the lake. In the quiet she tossed the keys down onto the stairs, a faint clatter in the sudden immense stillness. "You are free. Do what you will."

He was aware of Franco looking toward him, half-turned to see from his good eye. Allegreto looked back, confounded. He saw Franco unbound—a thousand possibilities seemed to threaten on the instant. There were arms, men, riots; she was overwhelmed and taken down in a flood of combat; Franco declared himself in control; Riata took the streets and the citadel . . .

Neither of them moved. They both stood as if some sorcery held them in suspended motion while Elena and the crowd waited.

The silence stretched.

The guards had their weapon hands at ready. Allegreto saw that he could not kill Franco, not without ending in both of them slaughtered on the steps before her eyes. He thought it—saw Franco think it. Allegreto was willing to die, but he did not believe Franco was. Nay, the Riata had only to step back, avoid a blow, and watch Allegreto be cut down for trying.

He would not leave her that way, in the midst of an attempt at murder. He glared at Franco in defiance. It would be both of them or neither.

The Riata's lip twisted in disdain. He turned back to the princess as if Allegreto were some mongrel growling from the gutter. With a sudden intake of breath, Franco raised his fist and shouted, *"Monteverde!"* His voice echoed off the wall of the duomo as he went to his knee before Elena, bowing his head down in a clear act of submission.

The crowd broke into an uproar. Allegreto found Elena turned to him, looking at him steadily—expectantly. *Don't believe him.* He stared back at her, willing her to see through this mockery. *It's a ruse. It's a lie.*

But she gave him no choice. She made it impossible to reason. He could not refuse in public to give the same that Franco claimed to offer. He dropped to his knees and bowed his head amid the sheet of sound that broke over him. The hard stone pressed into his joints. He stared at her hem, the pointed toes of her green slippers peeking from under a heavy embroidery of gold and silver thread. He said nothing, shouted no declaration of loyalty to please the crowd. She had bound him long past.

After a moment she offered her hand. He took it and pressed it to his lips and forehead.

"Gardi li mo," he said against her skin, as if she could hear him. "You know I am yours."

She curled her hand into a fist and drew it away, touching his shoulder, bidding him rise.

It was like a dream as she leaned up to him and pressed her cheek to his. He would not look at her. He could not. He made her a stranger in his mind, the warmth of her skin a formal touch, the flash of gold and gems from her crown a barrier. He bore it as she let Franco kiss her hand and rise and press his scarred cheek to hers. Allegreto was ready to kill if the Riata made any deceptive move, any hint of a threat. But the soldiers, too, were ready, and the crowd roaring its approval was another safeguard. At their displeasure he and Franco would be torn apart.

She outwitted them all with this unexpected play. He felt a flash of admiration for the pure foolish boldness of it, and a profound desire to gut the smug Englishman who stood grinning behind her as if someone had just handed him the keys to the mint. When she turned away from Franco and gave Raymond de Clare a shy, conscious smile in return, Allegreto nearly lost his rule over himself.

Only for a moment did she glance at the English pig. But it was enough. Allegreto felt his mind and heart vanish down a black well, a darkness that finally swallowed him whole.

ELENA WENT THROUGH the processions and celebrations of the first day in a haze of dread. She had designed the list of events to keep Franco and Allegreto well-occupied and within sight of one another—and never beyond her view or Dario's. She made sure they had no time to make connection with any of their followers. She might have freed them, but she was not so rash as to give them easy opportunities.

Only Raymond had known of her plan. She feared that she was unjust to him, using his devotion to sustain her courage when both of them knew his love had no future. But he did not falter or turn away. He found reasons to linger in Monteverde. Philip and Dario were staunch friends, but their understanding was not wide. Philip was a soldier, and Dario a watchdog to his bones—they could not see beyond their concerns to the greater scope of affairs. They were horrified at what she had done by freeing her prisoners. But Raymond understood. He comprehended Prince Ligurio's words. Milan threatened, and they must— they *must*—all stand together.

But she thought of the look on Allegreto's face as he rose on the steps of the duomo, and her blood chilled. She had hoped that when they understood the danger, he and Franco would relinquish their enmity and work with her to form a defense. She had discussed it long with Raymond, and he had agreed that only a daring stroke could break the impasse. But now she was not sure.

A maid made a final adjustment to the net that held her hair and replaced the heavy crown. Elena was sick of it, of holding herself straight and unbending under the weight. She drew a breath and lifted her head, signaling the guard to open the doors. The chamberlain announced her grandly—the Magnificent, the Prima Elect, the Principessa Elena di Monteverde. She walked from her privy chamber to the presence-room, where Dario waited with Franco and Allegreto.

Franco bowed immediately, a smooth flourish, withholding nothing. Allegreto looked directly at Elena, his face calm. But she saw death in his eyes, cold and certain.

He made a mocking bow, not quite complete. In the failing light from the open windows, it seemed to Elena that they were all a set of gorgeously dressed puppets on a rich stage, surrounded by frescoed walls and tapestries, going through motions set by some unseen master. She gave them each a nod of recognition, equally courteous. But her heart was shrinking in her chest. She felt a girl-child among men, as if it were an effrontery even to stand in this room and claim authority over them.

"I will not delay us long before the banquet." She had to force herself to speak. "I called upon you to come so that I might explain what I've done. I can wait no longer for you to agree to peace between yourselves. There is word that Milan may make an attempt against us. I require the complete loyalty of your houses to Monteverde above all. Do I have it?"

"Certainly, Princess," Franco said. "Do you wish us to take an oath before God?"

Allegreto's mouth curled as he glanced at Franco Pietro. "I cannot take any oath before God, for the Pope says my face offends Him." He lifted his dark lashes and looked at Elena. "You know well enough where my loyalty lies."

For one moment she thought of the room in his father's tower, the brief days of love and pain. But she put it away from her; she could not bear it and find words to speak at the same time. "I do not require an oath." She lifted her eyes to Allegreto. "Someone once said to me that they are easily made and easily broken. But I do not think either of you wishes for us to fall before Milan, and as long as we are divided, we are in great danger. So I ask you to consider that, and restrain from creating discord and insecurity among the people."

"I understand, Princess," Franco said. His scarred face was reddened with some emotion, but she did not know him well enough to guess what he truly felt. This sermon on loyalty from the young maid who had overthrown him could hardly be sweet to his ears. But she hoped. She hoped. The meetings with Matteo had gone better.

She looked to Allegreto. "Will you hold your house in check?"

He did not reply, but watched Franco Pietro with a shadowed study, that steady, lethal contemplation like a wild creature hidden in the trees. Then, with a soft laugh, he glanced at Elena. "I have played this game with you so far, have I not? Princess."

The title hung in the room, a mockery. She knew she would get no clearer answer from him.

Franco gave him a glowering look from his one eye, his hand at his girdle, as if he wore a sword. Then he turned back to Elena. "What word do you have of this offense from Milan?"

"I mean for Philip to advise you both of all we have heard. The ambassador says it is not so, of course, but there is some possibility that they intend to use the lake for an attack from the south. It is well that we've repaired the castles there, but they have little yet to garrison them."

"The condottiere?"

She gave him a level glance. "I have felt I must keep the mercenaries close."

She did not say openly that it was because she feared an uprising or conflict within the city. But he made a grunt of acknowledgment.

"Hire more," he said. "Though the merchants will groan—if it is needed for defense, they will pay."

"We will all pay if I hire more," she said bluntly. "I will not tax the merchants alone for it."

Franco gave a shrug. "What you will, Princess."

"I have decided not to use outsiders for our further defense," she said. She held herself still, fighting a desire to step backward. "The main castles in the south belong to Navona." She looked at Allegreto. "I ask Navona to provide the garrisons."

"Him!" Abruptly Franco's acquiescence slipped. "Nay, you'll put weapons in his hands? No."

Allegreto made a cool nod, ignoring Franco's outburst. "I can do it."

"I'll not endure it!" Franco made a step, scowling. "That goes too far."

"Do you think it might inconvenience your plans?" Allegreto asked in a silken voice. "Why should you dislike the idea?"

Franco flung toward him, breathing hard. "Should I suffer a serpent at my back? Foul enough, that I've stood by and let you be raised again at my expense."

"At the expense of what you stole from Monteverde and Navona." Allegreto's hand moved over his belt where his dagger would have been. He opened his fingers wide, his body still. "If you have no intention to steal it again, why should it offend you if I garrison my own property?"

"You devil spawn! If she is fool enough to trust you, I am not," Franco declared. "You'd have a knife in my back as soon as—"

A sharp rap on the outer door interrupted him. Franco stopped and turned, striding to the window, taking a deep and furious breath of the soft evening air. He crossed his arms.

Elena was not sorry to suspend the talk. She glanced at the guard, bidding him to open. There was a commotion as the arched doors swung wide, voices . . . she heard Raymond speaking hoarsely and saw him half-standing, supported by some of Philip's men. He was bloodied, his doublet slashed and his face scarred with dirt. When he saw her, he stumbled forward.

"I came to tell you—" He dragged himself up, holding his arm around his ribs and staring toward Franco Pietro.

He clamped his jaw closed and leaned onto the arm of the man holding him.

"What has happened?" Elena hurried forward, reaching for Raymond to help steady him, but he pushed her away feebly.

"He was attacked on the way into the citadel, Your Grace," the man said. "Half-killed him, but he wouldn't have us do aught but carry him straight to you with the news."

"She must know," Raymond muttered, his face white as he gripped his doublet. Blood seeped through his fingers. His legs were failing under him. "Tell her."

Elena stood back in horror, a sudden coldness gripping her heart. "Tell me," she said.

"It looked to be Riata men, by their insignia," the guard said, averting his eyes from where Franco Pietro stood.

"Nay!" Franco exclaimed. He pushed himself from the window. "That's a lie!"

Raymond slid to his knees, panting. "Princess. I came. For you to know as soon as—" His voice trailed off. His eyes rolled and he lost his senses, going slack against the guard's leg.

Elena made a faint sound. She could not tell if he had been stabbed as well as beaten, but there was enough blood to terrify her. When his eyes flickered open again, she found her voice. "Bring the surgeon and a hurdle," she ordered, turning to Dario. "Now!"

Dario's face was brutal, his thick jaw set hard. He went to the door and issued commands, but made no move to leave the room.

"Riata had nothing to do with this," Franco snarled. "He's English! Why should we attack him?"

Elena glanced at Franco. She had already thought the same. Her lip quivered with a sudden dreadful weakness. She did not think she could look at Allegreto, she was so afraid of what she would see in his face. But she forced herself to turn to him.

He was observing Raymond without any emotion,

watching as they brought the hurdle and helped him onto it. But when he lifted his eyes and met hers, a subtle change came into his face, a defiance. He did not flinch from looking at her. He showed no sign of shame or triumph. He seemed to dare her to accuse him.

Franco did it for her. "Navona arranged for this, by God! To discredit me before you! We're not such fools as to kill some foreign envoy without reason, and wear our badge while we're at it!"

"And I am not such a fool as to let him live if I meant to kill him," Allegreto said.

"No doubt you intended for him to be left alive," Franco snapped, "so that he could prate of Riata insignia with his last breath."

"He is not breathing his last," Allegreto said with contempt. "More's the pity."

The surgeon came running into the chamber. He halted, as if it startled him to see Elena and the others there, and fell into a deep bow. "Your Grace! I beg your pardon! I was called here." He glanced at Raymond where he lay stretched on the hurdle, his face pale and strained. The surgeon bent to his knee, started to pull the torn doublet open, and then looked up. "Sirs! Take this man to the surgery. This is no fit place to examine him."

Elena stood back as the guards and Philip's men gathered around to lift the hurdle. To see Raymond lying still and bloody wrenched her with guilt. She should never have allowed him so near to her, never permitted friendship or intimacy, even as careful as she had been to make certain they were always in view of company. "Send me news instantly. No one is to speak abroad of this."

"As you command, Your Grace!" He bowed again, hurrying out with the others.

Elena stood looking after them until the double doors swung slowly closed under the hand of the guard outside. The wood made a hollow sound. She was left with Dario and Franco and Allegreto.

"No one is to speak of this outside," she said again, staring at the heavy door.

"I will swear on God's holy writ that I did not cause it," Franco said. "Whoever attacked him—it was no Riata."

She turned slowly. A vision was in her mind, of Allegreto's face leaning close to hers, his hands at her cheeks, pulling her hood close. *"Only me,"* he whispered in her memory. *"Unless you care to leave a trail of dead men in your wake."*

She felt him now without looking at him, felt his dark, still presence. She hugged her arms around herself. The daylight had almost faded, leaving the corners of the chamber in dimness. The candle flames swayed in evening air, making the faint shape of her shadow bend and rock on the wall.

Allegreto offered no oath of innocence. When she finally looked back at him, he gave a chilly laugh. He closed his eyes and shook his head. "Of course I must have done it," he said. "The Devil knows I wanted to." He opened his eyes with a look of disdain. "Arrest me, then, and let us complete this farce."

Beneath the scorn, there was something else—a barely contained wildness, a despair in him, as if he did not care what she did to him.

"Allegreto," she asked, "you did not cause it?"

"I did not." His voice seemed oddly helpless. "If I had aimed to kill him, he would be dead."

She knew that for a certain truth. Yet she had not seen Zafer since the morning; he had vanished among the crowds before the duomo. She hardly trusted herself or her own judgment. From outside the window came the sound of church bells tolling evensong. She bent her head, feeling the crown weight it forward.

It was beyond forgiveness, how she could love him when she knew what he was. She knew he could say false and make an angel believe it true. She had seen him hold a knife at Dario's throat. She had heard the crack of a man's neck in the darkness and felt the blood pool at her feet.

There was no one else who had reason to hurt Raymond;
the Riata knew nothing of what he had once meant to her.
It was a senseless attack on a chance victim—for anyone
but Allegreto.

In the deepening gloom he waited. He stood apart, her
beautiful killer, accused and tried and condemned by all
reason. She could hardly check herself from going to him
and pulling him hard into her embrace, holding him to her
heart.

He said he had not done it. With no reason but that she
was blind in love, she chose to believe him.

"It must have been a band of ruffians," she said slowly.
"I will see that Philip looks out for any further disturbance."

Franco made a growl of protest, uncrossing his arms.

Elena glanced toward him. "Consider well if you have
an objection, my lord," she said. "The only witnesses say it
was your men."

The Riata scowled at her, his eye-patch a black disfig-
urement across his face. But he said nothing. Allegreto
seemed to move and then stood uncertainly, his defiance
suddenly vanished, as if he was not sure what she had
meant.

"Let us proceed to the banquet," she said. "The surgeon
can attend me there with news."

Twenty-seven

———◆◆◆———

FRANCO HAD CHANGED nothing in his years of occupying the citadel. It was all as Allegreto remembered, still a mix of rough ancient stone and the improvements that Ligurio had begun to make, the intricate designs and colors of the brilliantly tiled floors, the windows cut into walls that had seen no light though them for centuries. But the thick old timbers of the ceilings remained untouched.

He knew the day that work on the plaster and frescoes had ceased. The stone masons had laid down their mallets. The painters had put away their brushes, leaving a painted drape of cloth that vanished halfway into the upper curve, never reaching the painted hook that awaited it.

He could see it from where he was seated at the high table, the long succession of frescoed damask drapes along the wall that ended on the day of Prince Ligurio's death. The great gilded chains and candle branches that the prince had installed still hung from the walls, adorned by dragon heads that hissed into space.

There were murmurs from the banqueters at the long tables below, as there had ever been. His presence, and

Franco's, was no doubt a topic of heated argument. As the
sweet fried bread and meat jellies were served between
courses, a trio of carolers presented a ballad that described
the triumphant entrance of the Princess Elena into Monteverde. The singers added some flourishes to the story—a
miracle dove of peace and a few battles won by valiant
miners against enemies unnamed. Riata and Navona came
away with more credit than Allegreto would have expected
in this paean to the new republic. He supposed that the
princess had made her wishes clear. She had been utterly
determined to drag him and Franco Pietro to seats at the
high table.

He sat before people who had hated him for years, next
to a young councilman whose father had been tortured once
by Gian for paying too openly amorous attention to
Princess Melanthe. They were courteous to one another,
having no weapons at hand. She used that much sense at
least: Dario's men had examined every guest at the gate for
any blade or means of mayhem.

Allegreto was yet benumbed by what she had done.
Even now, even here—especially here—he could not shake
himself of Ligurio's dream and how she stood for it.

He had no part in it, and yet he loved her and this fantasy of a place where it was not tyranny and fear that ruled.
He loved the fragile concord that she held together by sheer
will and faith and stubborn idiocy. If he had cast a hundred
horoscopes, he would never have foreseen it. His lady
queen, she had dared to make things true that no living man
had even hoped to dream.

He did not know if she truly believed him or not, that he
had not tried to kill her English lover. She had her reasons
to ignore such an incident in the midst of her celebrations,
to avoid any arrests or storm of accusations. But when she
accepted his word, only his word and no more, it had been
like one of Ligurio's windows punched through stone
walls, a shaft of sun into a place that had never been lit before. He sat with a hole inside of him, not sure if he was
bleeding or burning from the brightness.

Raymond de Clare would live. She'd had word of that before the boxes of spiced confetti were cleared from the table and the first courses began. Allegreto was separated from her by several councilors, her grandfather's old advisers who held first precedence in Monteverde, but he had seen the relief in her face when the steward had come to whisper in her ear. It cleaved him with jealousy, but he was still bewildered by the strange kernel of joy at her trust in him. It tempered malice, made it difficult to understand himself. Made it difficult to eat. Difficult even to breathe.

Dario and Matteo and one of Franco's men performed credence at the high table. It was another of the whispers that must be circulating wildly among the guests below— that Franco Pietro's son served Navona even yet. Matteo had grown. He had more assurance now, only tipping the wine a little too far the first time he came to Allegreto, spilling a few drops over his towel. The boy took his ritual sip, looking over the rim of the cup at Allegreto with a particular unblinking look.

It put Allegreto instantly on guard. He realized how he had been drifting on some thoughtless cloud. Long-ingrained habit made him attend always to what passed around him, but he had let his concentration slip too far in such an exposed place.

He realized that Dario, too, was noting Matteo's subtle move to place the clean silver trenchers and blunted knives. With an embellishment of courtesy, Allegreto bent his head deeply to the councilman beside him and offered to carve the meat.

He drew the platter toward him, lifting it just enough to feel the slip of paper beneath. In an excess of enthusiasm for his task, he pulled the trencher slightly too near, over the edge of the table, and gave his neighbor a wry smile for his clumsiness as the message slipped unseen into the folds of tablecloth over his lap. He pushed the roasted bird back and began to carve.

•   •   •

NIMUE LEAPED AND cavorted, a pale shape in the moonlit tournament grounds. Allegreto walked freely beside Matteo—hardly allowing himself to enjoy the sensation after the months of captivity. It had not been difficult to arrange this reunion. After the banquet and diversions finally ended, as the princess had retired to her antechamber with the wine-bemused guests from the high table, the boy simply said to Dario that he was going to take Nim for her last excursion of the day, and asked Allegreto if he would like to go along.

Dario had shrugged and said the princess would expect Matteo in bed before Compline, and given Allegreto a subtle signal of safety with his left hand.

Allegreto had acknowledged it and walked out. He had no doubt that there were watchers on him, but Matteo had chosen his ground well. As soon as they reached the lists, Nimue bounded immediately out onto the wide grassy yard, beyond the bedecked scaffolds standing ready for the hastilude in the morning. Allegreto and Matteo followed her. There were others strolling in the grounds and standing on the walls that overlooked the city, but no one in the center of the great open space. A half-moon gave light enough to see Nimue trot along the line of the wooden lists, investigating smells.

Allegreto stopped and leaned against the heavy railing. He had a moment's thought to say how tall Matteo had grown suddenly, and then recalled the disgust of his own childhood at the mention of such a thing. "What passes?" he asked instead.

"You don't have to be afraid of me," Matteo said, hiking himself onto the single rail. "If you are."

"I don't?" Allegreto looked aside at him solemnly. "Have you forgot all the means to kill me that I taught you?"

"No!" The boy jumped down, and then hiked himself back up again. "No. I meant—don't suppose I've turned to Riata."

"You are Riata," Allegreto said quietly. "I never meant you to forget that."

"No, I—*avoi,* I am. But—" He had an unhappy break in his voice.

Allegreto waited. He had not expected that Matteo alone would have some truly serious message for him, but he was not averse to causing Franco to writhe and fret over whether he meant to steal the boy again. And Elena had seen them leave together. She had not prevented it. She trusted him. The gap in his soul drank in the strange sensation.

"You must know that she wants me to be great friends with my father," Matteo said anxiously.

"I heard such."

"Do you mind?"

Allegreto shrugged. "He's your father. The Bible says to honor him."

"Were you friends with your father?"

Allegreto lifted his head and gave a short laugh. "No." He curled his hands around the railing. "But I was a bastard son."

"I suppose that is different."

"Very different."

Matteo dropped to the ground. He squatted on his knees and pulled at the grass. "Did you like your father?"

Allegreto began to wish he had not come. He watched Nimue gallop across the yard to some other scent. After a long moment he said, "I loved him."

Matteo ripped up a handful of grass. "I wish you were my father," he said in a muffled voice. "I love you."

Allegreto felt the gap inside himself tearing open. Like a vision through it, he could see wheels beyond wheels of hate and scheming, of never-ending fears. He could see how he had been Gian's tool, and had made Matteo his. All driven and pursued and drawn by love.

"Franco doesn't mind if I make mistakes," Matteo said, as if it were an affront. "He says he doesn't care, because I'm his son."

Allegreto was silent, gazing up into the dark. The stars were cold points of radiance hanging against the deep black arch of the air.

"I don't want to like him," Matteo hissed miserably. "I'm afraid that Englishman is going to kill him."

Allegreto turned his head. "Englishman?"

"Signor Raymond. When I was out with Nim one night, I heard him talking to someone. They were speaking low, but I heard my father's name. And they were trying to be secret."

Allegreto stood straight. "Who did he speak to? What language?"

"I couldn't see who it was. I climbed up to look, but they were above me on the ramparts. They spoke in the French tongue. I could tell it was the Englishman because of how he says the words."

"Did you hear else?"

"Only Franco's name, and talk of money. The other one spoke of gold."

"When?"

"Ten nights past."

"Did you tell Dario of this?"

"Nay. I don't care if they kill Franco. He's Riata." His young voice shook a little. "But I—" He stopped and then said, "I thought I would tell you."

Nimue suddenly ceased her investigations of a fluttering cloth that adorned the viewing stands. She turned and took a bound, standing stiff-legged, her plumed white tail curled up over her back. Her deep bark echoed in the yard.

From the top of the steep pavement that led down into the tourney yard, torches flared. Men came striding, their shadows a wild dance against the castle walls. Nimue ran forward, a rumbling growl in her throat. She stood between Allegreto and Matteo and the newcomers, barking a loud warning, until suddenly her ears lowered and her tail waved in welcome as she ran to make her greetings.

Franco Pietro ignored her, pacing forward aggressively, still showing a slight limp from the sword wound in his leg.

He had four of his men at his back. Allegreto held himself still, lounging against the railing, measuring the distance.

Franco halted, just far enough away. "Matteo," he said. "Leave him."

Allegreto put his hand on Matteo's shoulder and gave the boy a push. "Go."

Matteo resisted, leaning back against Allegreto's hand. Nimue turned from fawning and sniffing at Franco's knees and bounded happily to the boy.

"Go with him, Matteo," Allegreto said, giving him another light shove. "Honor thy father," he said mockingly. He did not care to linger in such an uncertain position, with no weapon on him. Matteo took a step forward. The boy grabbed Nimue's collar and stood sullenly.

Allegreto nodded once to Franco. "I bid you eve." He rested his hands on the rail and vaulted it, walking away into the dark.

ALLEGRETO COULD NOT breach the citadel from outside, but once he was within the gates, he knew how to move through every corner and stone of it. It was in Ligurio's old chambers that Franco had made his only mark—changed the paintings of ladies playing chess and plucking roses to scenes of hunts and tournaments. Allegreto covered his candle and walked softly through the dark rooms that occupied the upper floor of the great tower. The alchemical tools were long vanished, but Ligurio's library was still intact, the boards lined with books and unbound papers. Allegreto stood a moment, remembering the prince and a boy hungry for gentle words and wisdom, for things he had never known. They had spoken of science and history and politics. They had even argued sometimes, a thing Allegreto would never have dared with Gian.

Here amid Ligurio's books, his thoughts, Allegreto tried to reason what the prince would say. Allegreto did not understand Franco Pietro now. A year had passed. Franco should have made some move long since to reclaim Monteverde, to purge Navona in a final sweep.

This attack upon the Englishman—it was a clumsy attempt, pointless, far too inept for Franco. Matteo thought Raymond de Clare had accepted money to kill his father, but from what little the boy had heard, it might as easily have been the reverse, a pact for Raymond to perform some deed for the Riata. The Englishman was close to the princess; the word was he saw her daily. It could have been murder or information or only another meeting with his son that Franco desired.

And now someone in Riata livery gave the English whore a warning, but let him live. Or it was Franco's attempt to blame the thing on Allegreto and have him arrested again—a poor gamble with witnesses who had seen Riata badges on the Englishman's attackers.

Allegreto stared at a map of Monteverde that hung upon the wall. No thoughtful voice from the past spoke to him. No ready answers came. He only thought that Franco Pietro must be failing in his mind. They were both of them breaking somehow, splintering in directions that had no logic.

From the boards under his feet, he felt the faint vibration of doors closing in the chamber below. He blew out his candle and let his eyes adjust to darkness. After a few moments he moved quietly out of the library.

In the bathing room, faint moonlight from a narrow glass window fell on the naiad that still presided over the basin, spreading her marble arms and offering to pour water from her mouth. It was one of Ligurio's inventions, a piped system that would bring water down from a cask heated on the ramparts to Ligurio's bath and the ladies' quarters on the floor beneath. Allegreto walked to the statue and put his ear to the nymph's cool stone lips.

From this place, it was possible to hear all that passed in the ladies' chamber below, where Melanthe had resided.

Elena's voice came to him, her affectionate chiding voice that she used with unruly dogs and children. He closed his eyes, leaning his shoulder on the wall to listen.

She had a diversity of voices—the unyielding tone of the Prima di Monteverde, the brave cry that echoed over the crowds and claimed they were all one, the husky whisper that bid Allegreto take her deeply, rolling in his arms to arch and tremble beneath him. She spoke now to a maid and harried the dallying Matteo to his prayers, leading the boy in a recitation of names of the souls they asked God to bless and absolve. Allegreto heard Franco's name, and even his own.

Perchance it would have some sway with God, the prayers of a boy and a maid—no matter the maid was no pure virgin and the boy had already tried murder. To Allegreto it seemed there was an innocence, a sincerity about their voices that might have some effect. He did not suppose anyone else alive had ever raised a prayer in his behalf. He felt vaguely ashamed, and grateful to be included. He did not even begrudge Franco's name in the roll.

After prayers there was a small commotion as it seemed that Nimue tried to climb onto the bed with Matteo, and had to be cast out sternly and sent to her mat. Allegreto heard the familiar scrape of the bed-curtains drawn closed on their wooden rod as the maid bid her mistress and the boy good night. Then Matteo wanted to talk to Elena of the hastilude on the morrow, but she answered only with mumbles that Allegreto could not discern through the muffling curtains. The boy's voice finally faded away.

Allegreto waited a long time after he could hear nothing. Then he rose, his eyes well attuned to the darkness now, and went softly down the stairs from Ligurio's chamber. He knew the way by feel, knew the door at the foot of the stairs had no lock or bar; that it would open silently with the right steady pressure.

As he came into the bedchamber, Nimue lifted her head, a pale outline in the dark. She knew better than to bark at him—from the time she was a pup, she'd learned to give silent greetings to Allegreto or Zafer. Allegreto stood still as the dog rose and padded to him, sniffing and pressing against his legs. He rubbed her ears and scratched the place under her collar that she liked. Together they moved across the chamber to the window embrasure where Allegreto had always slept when Melanthe ordered him out of her bed.

He was taller now, and the stone had no pillows or cushion on it. He drew up one leg and let the other hang over the edge, resting his foot on Nimue's warm coat. From the bed came a faint, steady sound of sleep. He laid his head back against the window and kept his vigil, as he always had.

ELENA STARED THROUGH the crack in the bed-curtains. She lay tense, telling herself there was no one there. She did not rest well; any small sound could have woken her from the first light drowse of sleep. Matteo was breathing steadily, a child's soft comforting snores. Nimue drew a great breath and let go a sigh from somewhere by the window.

There was no one. The outer door was under guard all night. The dog would not have suffered any intruder. But she sat up, trying to see into darkness.

The attack on Raymond had unnerved her. She chose to believe Allegreto, but if he had not done it, then someone else had. Monteverde had its boisterous youths and a few street thieves, but they did not wear Riata's colors.

Nim sighed again, her toenails scraping wood as she turned on the floor and resettled herself. Elena tried to calm her thumping heart. She caught the edge of the curtain and drew it open as silently as she could.

She distinguished Nim's white shape beneath the window. And a shock of fear flashed through her to see the shape of a man against the glass.

"Do not fear, Elena," he said softly.

She made a faint sound, holding her hand over the pulse pounding her in throat. "Allegreto?" she whispered.

"Aye."

She let go a great breath of relief. For a moment she sat propped on her hand, trying to gather her wits. Then she carefully laid back the sheets and slipped from the bed.

She wore only a light shift. The night air outside the curtains was cool, the Turkey carpet soft against her feet. She did not know where the maid had laid her robe, but it was dark. Nim scrambled up as Elena drew near the window. She saw Allegreto rise, a black silhouette against the round panes of glass.

"What is it?" she asked, a bare whisper.

"Franco is at liberty," he said, so low she could hardly catch it. He shrugged. "So I am here. *Gardi li mo.*"

"You can't stay here." She could not judge the distance in the dark, and her leg touched him. She felt his hand on her arm.

He made a faint sound, like a slow moan in his throat, moving his hand up her shoulder. "I should not."

Her body took instant flame at his touch. He pulled her against him, enfolding her in his arms, crushing her to velvet and silk and his solid shape.

Elena allowed it, going pliant in response. Her head fell back as he kissed her, his hands sliding down her back, tangling in her loose hair; heat and desire like smoke rising through her brain.

He broke away, breathing deeply. "Elena," he whispered beside her ear. "You have driven me mad. I know not what I do anymore."

Matteo turned and shifted in his sleep, causing the bed to creak. Elena slid her fingers into Allegreto's hair. She held him close, tracing her lips over his jaw, barely touching. She could feel him restrain himself, his breath caught, his hands motionless, pressing into her skin.

Suddenly a shudder ran through him. He gripped her close, bending to her throat. "Come up the stairs." His whisper was hoarse against her skin.

She nodded, her spirits lifting with reckless joy. It was madness, after all. He twined his fingers with hers and led her. Her bare feet found cold stone at the step through the door. He closed the door behind them, leaving an inquisitive Nim in the bedchamber with Matteo.

Elena ran lightly up the chilly stairs. She felt enlivened, almost weightless without the crown and the furs and the heavy robes of office. It was a secret thing, a mystery between them. She turned at the top, shivering. He caught her in his arms and spun her, drew her unerring to the bed alcove in the dark.

She fell upon it with a sound of delight, stifling her hand over her mouth like a silly child in mischief. All fear and care and worry fell away from her as he came over her, pulling the shift over her head, kissing her throat and her breasts. He tore back the sheets and turned her with him into the depths of the bed.

She quivered, cold and heat and his touch pouring like light through every limb. She sought eagerly for his lips, drawing him close, naked beneath his weight.

There was more moonlight here. When he pulled back, leaning over her on his arms, she could see his face and the gleam of silver threads on the collar of his tunic. His beauty yet stunned her, even more now, when she had not seen him for months gone.

"How I love you," she whispered, touching his face.

He groaned and kissed her palm. Then he rolled away from her, casting a glance about the silent chamber. "It is folly. God shield us, this is folly."

She knew it was. She did not care. She caught the folds of his tunic and worked at the light belt that crossed his hips. He looked down at her as she did it, watching her as if he were bespelled.

The belt came free. Elena leaned and drew the velvet upward. He sat upright suddenly and tore it over his head, taking his shirt with it. She pulled him to her, kissing his chest, running her fingers along the fine shape of his collarbone and shoulder.

On a loop about his neck hung a ring, a soft flash of gold. She caught it in her fist and held it to her lips. Then she flung her arms about him and drew her teeth over his nipple.

He gripped her hair, his body going still. "Don't," he whispered hoarsely. "Have mercy."

She would not. She twined her leg with his, pressing up

against him, opening her body for him as she closed her teeth.

He gasped for air, holding her head against his chest. Elena slid her hands down and dragged at the ties on his hose. She slipped her fingers beneath into the hot gap, seeking the heavy shape of his manhood. She did not hurt him, but caressed the tip gently while his mouth pressed hard into her hair.

He made sounds of desperation, holding himself taut. He shivered as she ran her hand down the length of him. Then he wrenched away, pulling her upright. "Turn over," he hissed, rising. He made her roll away from him, quick and brutal, dragging her up by the waist and shoving his cock between her legs from behind.

Elena knelt, eager to be penetrated. But it was his hand that found her place, sliding over her, partly inside, sending waves of pleasure through her body. She arched against it, closing her legs on his shaft. He began to move hard against her, thrusting against her buttocks, sliding on the exquisite wetness between her thighs.

She pressed her face into a velvet pillow, panting, swallowing the whimpering cry that rose in her throat. She bent down before him, her hair falling around her, taking his thrusts, each pressure of his hand carrying her closer to ecstasy. When it came, it burst over her, a throbbing rupture that seized her limbs and made her cry out into the pillow. He held her hips and made a stifled groan, a sound deep in his chest as he arched, his body surging against her. Warmth flooded her belly, his seed spilling free as he gave a hoarse sob.

He wrapped his arms around her, holding her up against him. They knelt together in the bed, the last tremors of his climax still flowing through him. Elena leaned her forehead on the pillow, all her strength gone. She breathed deeply and pressed back up against him for the lingering pleasure of it.

For a long time he held her under him, his shaft growing soft. The wet sign of his completion slid and tickled between her thighs. He exhaled in a harsh breath, a warm flow over her back and her hair, and pushed himself upright.

Elena turned over on her side. The scent of him covered her. He pulled her back against him, lying close.

"Christ, we are fools," he whispered. "I will have to go away."

She caught his hands and gripped them against her. "No."

"I cannot endure it," he said, pushing up, pulling free of her hold. "I can't leave you to Franco. But I can't stay by you, or we'll . . ." He looked about at the disarrayed sheets like a man who had just woken from a nightmare. "This is too great hazard. Someone will discover it."

His seed had stained the bed; even in the dimness Elena could see it, and feel it spread slick on her belly and thighs. The musky perfume of coupling was strong. But she turned over and pulled him down again, holding him to her, drowning in the feel of his skin and the heavy heat of his body on hers.

He kissed her open-mouthed, resisting her pull even as his tongue searched deep. He wrenched free and rolled over, rising from the bed. As he grabbed his shirt and tunic, he murmured, "Wait here."

Elena watched him vanish through the dark mass of a doorway. She lay among the tousled sheets and breathed the scent of what they had done. She thought of the rest of her life without this, the rest of her life as the past year had been; a cold pretense of power, uneasy vigilance, never allowing what she felt to show. She squeezed her eyes shut and turned into the pillow.

She understood Cara's fears for her now. She knew why her sister had wept and turned away, as if Elena were already lost to life. And yet each day that she looked out of her grandfather's window over the city and the lake, she felt an ache in her, a love for the stern beauty of the stone towers, for the people crowding in the narrow streets below, the chaos of color and sound as the merchants shouted and donkeys brayed. The common people were like children, living each moment readily; quick to laugh and argue, to drop their work to gather and cheer whenever Elena showed herself in the city. The nobles and merchants of high family had more reserve, but they too lived with vigor, with a delight in paintings and gorgeous clothes and the eternal competition to build the most impressive tower. She had met men of education who spoke to her with respect, and talked to her of books as if she were a man able to have judgments of her own.

She did not hate Monteverde. She could not. It was hers. Her home and her own people, and the very thought of Milan ruling over them made her sick and angry.

She hugged the pillow to her breast, feeling the gold embroidery scratch her skin. When he said he would go away, she knew where he would go. Into exile again. Il Corvo and the black castle. Exile. As long as she had been able to look out the window, across the lake, and know that he was there, she could endure it. If he went beyond where she could see, she did not think she had the power to go on.

She could turn away from all of it. She thought of it sometimes in the dark, hearing the guard change outside her door. She thought of it now.

His silent silhouette passed from the door and moved across the chamber, returning. "Bathe with this," he said softly, passing her a dampened towel. "Then you must go. I'll do what I can to arrange the bedsheets."

Elena used the towel to wash herself. She sat up, cleansing away the traces as she could, and stood. "You will not go now," she said anxiously, holding his arms.

"Not yet." He brushed his lips to her forehead. "There is Franco. And—something else." He paused. He held her cheeks between his palms, frowning down at her. "For the love of God, be wary, Elena! Let me send Zafer to you."

She stood in his hold. "I have Dario."

"Dario is too trusting," he said. He gave a dry laugh under his breath. "He even trusts me. If Zafer were with you, I would never have been able to reach your bedchamber."

She swallowed. "Do not send Zafer, then."

He clasped her tightly to him, pressing his lips to her hair. Elena stood holding him hard, trying not to believe that she might never have this moment again.

"You must return," he said. "We've been too long here."

"Allegreto." She lifted her head. "Let us go back." She wrapped her fingers around his arms. "Back to the island. We can go together, and leave all of this."

His body grew still. He pushed her away, looking down at her face.

"We would be safe there," she said. "I could be with you."

He tilted his head a little, gazing down at her as if he looked at something far away and lost. "There is safety there no longer, Elena. There never was." He traced his finger down her cheek. "Wherever I am is hazard for you."

"I do not care," she said desperately. "Am I safe here without you? Nay—it is as you said—there is no place in the world without jeopardy."

He closed his eyes. His black lashes rested on his skin. "Elena, you tear my heart. And I do not have one."

"You do," she whispered. "You gave it to me to guard." She made a small sad sound, pressing her hand to the shape of the ring beneath his tunic. "I have done poor work of it."

He shook his head, lowering his forehead to hers. "My only queen." He took her chin and kissed her gently. "You are all that I will ever love, in this life and beyond."

She clutched the loose folds of his unbelted tunic in her fists, leaning to him, burying her face against him. "Do not desert me," she breathed.

"I will be here." He set her away, pushing her chin up with his thumbs. "Even if you cannot see me. Now you must go down, before Matteo discovers you gone."

Twenty-eight

※

ALLEGRETO SCORNED TOURNAMENTS and the ignorant blocks who galloped about on horses, knocking their heads together for the joy of it. Franco Pietro had accepted the princess's invitation to participate; he was striding around dressed in full armor, braying to his men like a heroic donkey. Allegreto did not know if it was the princess or Matteo that the Riata was so stirred to impress, or both, perchance, for he made great show of kneeling before the dais where they sat, his black armor gleaming dully under the blue shield painted with Riata's dragon badge.

He was good. It was an old thorn he had twisted often in Allegreto's side. Gian Navona had never allowed his bastard son to participate in the lists. Allegreto had not known if it was some concern for his safety or only because a bastard was not suffered to champion Navona in such a public entertainment. But Franco had taunted him with cowardice, urging Allegreto to ignore his father and at least join the boys in their practice for the events. Allegreto had never been such a fool as that. He would not give Franco a chance to knock him down with a blunted lance, or Gian a reason to doubt his obedience. So he had stood against the wall and watched, as he did now.

Knights from Ferrara and Tuscany and Milan fought. There were even some Germans, and a pair of Frenchmen sent to represent the condottieri. It was a hastilude, merely for pleasure, and so the weapons were dulled, but the Riata made an excellent showing by bashing several contenders off their mounts. The walls of the citadel were draped with banners and crowded with spectators who waved colorful flags, shouting wildly at each course. Above the low-pitched, eerie moan of the long mountain horns peculiar to Monteverde, the cheers rose to a passionate roar when Franco challenged the knight from Milan and rode off the field triumphant, leaving his opponent on the ground and leading away the warhorse as a prize.

Whatever bitterness they might have felt for Franco Pietro before, he was beloved of the crowd now. Even Matteo was standing, shouting with the rest as his father rode to the princess and presented the armored destrier with a bow. The boy said something eagerly to Elena, received a smiling nod, and sprang over the draped railing on the dais with a child's carelessness. Nimue came right after him, under the rail, nearly taking down a swag of cloth as she scrambled from the dais. Elena stood and clapped while Matteo took possession of the great warhorse and led it from the lists at his father's side.

Allegreto stood straight from the wall. He turned away.

With somewhat less than courtesy, he pushed his way through the swarm of onlookers. He found Zafer at the foot of the steep ramp that led down from the main fortress to the level of the tournament yard. He exchanged a glance with the infidel youth and walked on alone up the incline.

He avoided the imposing shadow of the great tower and circled instead through the smithy, where all work was suspended, even the bellows and tools carried down to the tournament grounds to provide repairs. In the nearly deserted precincts of the upper citadel, he passed through the empty guard barracks, ducking under the low beams, and entered a small courtyard. The walls resounded with distant sound, a faint rumble in the quiet. In the afternoon light, olive trees and herbs gave off a pleasant scent.

The tourney would be over soon. The princess was to journey part of the distance to d'Avina before nightfall, in preparation for the reenactment of her first glorious procession to the gates of Monteverde. Allegreto thought it a foolish scheme, a dangerous excursion from the city. But her favorite, Raymond, had put the idea in her head, and so country maids were harvesting sunflowers and mending their best clothes all along the road from the mining town, in readiness to laud the princess as she passed.

Allegreto paused in the court, looking at the small door that led to the guards' infirmary. It was a chamber cut into the side of the rock itself, bricked out by more stones to make a room. Broom weeds grew in the cliff beside the deep passage to the open door.

There was no sign of the surgeon. The single guard was snoring softly, propped insensible against the stone wall. Zafer had made sure of that. Allegreto moved silently into the doorway. Raymond de Clare lay on a pallet, sleeping. There was a bandage about his head, and another across his ribs.

Allegreto leaned on the crude frame of the door. The Englishman seemed to be resting easily for a man who had been almost beaten to death. Zafer had discovered from the surgeon that Clare had no bones broken, and only a few cuts across his chest. From the moment Raymond had stumbled into the presence-chamber, whining as if he were like to expire, Allegreto had been sure he was not gravely injured.

It would be easy to gravely injure him now. Easy enough to take one of the surgeon's knives from the box by the door and slip it into the Englishman's heart. The wound might even be overlooked—Allegreto could use the most slender pick and wipe the spot of blood on the bandages. The man died of some internal harm from the beating. And Raymond de Clare would no longer be a question, for Allegreto or anyone else.

For a few moments he amused himself with the possibility. The Englishman was a well-looking harlot. She had written of his first kiss as if he were Galahad.

It was tempting. But she would not like it if she found out. She believed Allegreto now. Took his word. He discovered that it would be a painful thing to lie to her.

Allegreto kicked a pebble across the floor. Raymond jerked on his pallet. The Englishman came upright quickly, reaching for his sword. Allegreto watched him realize that he wasn't armed, or alone. Raymond stared at Allegreto for an instant, started to scramble up, and remembered he was mortally wounded. He sagged back on the pallet.

"Are you in dire pain?" Allegreto asked, lifting his eyebrows.

Raymond shuddered and laid his head back. "Pain enough. Curse the Riata villains." Then he turned his head with a scowl. "You're Navona."

"I am." Allegreto gave a courteous nod. "And I will not dispute your opinion of Riata."

Raymond made a soft snort. He put his arm over his chest, as if it hurt him. "Villains, the lot of you! You've done nothing but cause her sorrow. Where is the guard?"

"Elsewhere," Allegreto said.

Raymond looked up at him. Allegreto leaned in the doorway, his ankles crossed.

"What do you want?" the Englishman said testily, tugging at the bandage across his chest. "Do you also wish to kill me?"

"I desire nothing so much," Allegreto murmured, "but it would cause the princess sorrow. Foolish as she may be for it."

Raymond plucked at the binding. His bare shoulders had begun to sweat. "I could say the same to you, Navona. I could find it in my heart to murder you for what you did to her."

"Get up and try it," Allegreto said.

The other man glared at him, then laid his head back on the wall, his face turned away.

"But you are injured," Allegreto said. "I beg your pardon. I do not wish to quarrel with you. Or to kill you. It was a small jest."

"I am hugely amused," Raymond said.

"Let us talk a little of money." Allegreto smiled. "By chance that will be more to your taste. Who paid you to feign this attack on you?"

Raymond closed his eyes. "Oh, is that what the two of you have invented to mislead her? I feigned it! Does she believe you?" He gave a laugh and caught at his ribs. "And what sinister mission do I have that makes me smash my own head and cut myself open?"

"That is what I wish to know."

The Englishman turned with a sneer. "I have no mission, Navona, but that I love her, though you'd comprehend nothing of that! I'll do what I can to protect her from you and Franco. I begged her—but she was so rash as to set the pair of you free to work your evil. She thinks you have some honor in you." He made a commendable groan as he turned his back, lying undefended on the pallet with his face to the wall.

"Honor I may not possess," Allegreto said softly, "but I have five thousand sovereigns for you, if you will work for me."

Raymond put his hand over his head. "You make me sick."

Allegreto observed him thoughtfully. "I wish your recovery well, then," he said to the Englishman's back. "If you think again, you can find me."

He walked quietly out of the chamber. Zafer waited in the shade of an overhanging oak. They moved together just inside the barracks.

"Do not lose sight of him," Allegreto said.

Zafer nodded. "You discovered anything, my lord?"

"Nay. Only that he does not believe I have five thousand in gold to line his purse. I set about it badly. I should have played his friend." He shrugged.

Zafer made no remark. He only said, "The guard will awaken soon, my lord. I will keep watch."

DARIO HAD SUMMONED them again to the presence-chamber, Franco with his hair still showing damp from a bath, and Allegreto wearing boots as if he meant to travel.

Elena too was dressed to ride. They were not alone now; the French knights and her retinue all stood gathered with Philip and Dario in readiness to escort her from the city. Philip's presence unsettled her while Allegreto was near. She had never had a father, but the old bandit seemed to read her heart with a father's insight. She felt herself grow heated as she caught Allegreto's dark glance. It was impossible not to think of the night before, of his kisses and his body thrust against hers. She had looked for him all day, and seen him sometimes, leaning insolently in the shadow of the walls, lounging like one of the young bloods of the city who bet their fortunes on the breaking of a lance.

She tried to avoid looking at him now. She complimented Franco Pietro, thanking him for his brave performance at the tournament. The Riata was in good humor, she thought, still proud of his victory. It was exactly what she had hoped for. The people had a new affection for him, and he had represented Monteverde against Milan, instead of Riata against another house. It had taken a toll on him; he was favoring his leg heavily as he walked. But he looked tired and pleased with himself.

"I will not ask you to mount a horse again, my lord," she said to him as he rose with difficulty from his knee. "I wish for you and Navona to remain in the city while I am absent. It is only for two nights—but all of the council will be with me. I will feel more at ease knowing that the citadel is in the hands of experienced commanders, even for a such a small duration."

There was a faint murmur in the room. They all gazed at her as if she had lost her reason.

She made a small shrug. "If you are going to fight one another, I cannot stop you," she said bluntly. "You could do it as well in my sight as here. But I pray that you will both be alive and at peace when I return, and greet me at the gates together with welcome. It would make the people happy."

Allegreto gave a soft snort. "More like they would be struck dumb with wonder, Princess."

She let her eyes meet his. The moments in the dark with him seemed to set them apart, as if everyone else in the room were a stranger to her. The scent of lovers curled about them, so vivid that she was afraid it was more than imagination and memory.

His lashes lowered. He bowed his head and made a dismissive gesture with his hand. "But I will remain. And I pledge that I will be alive when you return."

She tore her look away, fingering the cuff of her sleeve. It seemed the silence around them was too heavy, too curious. It was as well they would be apart for a day or two. "God grant you mercy for your service, my lord," she said formally, directing a nod to his left ear.

"Will my son stay in the city, Princess?" Franco asked abruptly.

"Matteo has asked to go with me." She forced herself to stop rolling the pearl on her cuff between her fingers. "He would like to see d'Avina again."

"What guard do you take?" he demanded.

"We have ten horse and a company of foot," Philip said. "Captain Guichard has also sent an escort." He nodded toward the French knights from the condottieri. "We will break the journey at their encampment, and continue tomorrow to d'Avina."

Franco cast a narrow glance at Allegreto. "I do not suppose it is wise to leave Navona at liberty alone here, Princess," he said. "I will remain."

THE SUNSET ON Monteverde's duomo was famous. The golden mosaics on the façade of the cathedral caught light and sent a glow like a halo onto the piazza and the towers and into the air itself. The domes and spires glittered white; stone-carved ice. Allegreto stood in the deepening shadow among a few pilgrims watching the sight wide-eyed, no doubt hoping for a miracle to appear in that golden mist of light.

He was watching for something else. Gerolamo had

brought word that Franco was attending vespers at the duomo—not such an odd thing, for Franco always kept his soul in good standing. He took communion often, sometimes even daily, and heard the evening offices with regularity. Allegreto supposed that it was an efficient habit—not only was Franco cleansed of his grievous sins shortly after he committed them, it also provided a suitable cover for meeting with his partisans and agents. The Riata made sure that he developed no certain habit; though he attended mass and other offices regularly, he heard them at churches all over the city, changing daily in some order that Allegreto had never been able to fathom.

The distant sound of the choir floated on the golden air, the last psalm fading into silence. Allegreto could have recited by heart the canticle of Mary that would follow as the priest mounted on the pulpit to read in a voice that echoed solemnly through the great aisles and columns. As the sun fell behind the mountains and the halo faded, the pilgrims rose and dusted off their knees. Allegreto keep his head lowered. He could just see Gerolamo and his other man, who stood in the lengthening shadows of the piazza and watched the duomo's side doors.

The service came to an end. After a pause for thanksgiving, the huge bronze doors swung open and a small straggle of the faithful came out, old women mostly, completely swathed in black veils. They moved as old women should move, with tiny steps and care on the stairs. Allegreto scrutinized them, but they were all too short and feeble to disguise any Riata, or Raymond de Clare.

It was Raymond who had brought him here. Allegreto would have let Gerolamo follow Franco to a normal service and report back. But Raymond had vanished from the infirmary and the citadel an hour since, like Lazarus from his tomb, and Allegreto had a suspicion as to where the Englishman had gone.

They had both entered before the service, Raymond and Franco, but neither departed with the congregation. Allegreto walked across the piazza and lightly up the steps. He slipped into the open door, kneeling and crossing himself, his head well down. Gerolamo had told him there was a scaffolding along the south aisle, tall enough to reach the upper windows. He turned his back on the sanctuary and pretended to dip his fingers in the holy water, though he did not touch it or the carved stone font.

It was unnerving to enter a hallowed place against his ban. It was the church where his father lay sealed in the crypt below, no easy memory. In the dimness the windows glowed with brilliant color against lacy black outlines. The huge space echoed with whispers that were not quite voices, sounds that carried and reverberated endlessly through the long double row of pillars that marched down the nave.

He moved near the scaffold, quietly dropping an offering in the plate and igniting a candle among the bank of lights against the wall. It would be as well to pacify Gian's tortured soul. Behind the cover of a massive column, he grabbed a rung of the scaffolding and hiked himself up. The wound in his shoulder gave him a twinge of reminder, even after a year, but he climbed quickly and silently up into the shadows near the roof.

From under the succession of arches that topped the pillars, he could see all the way down the length of the sanctuary. A small knot of men stood near the pulpit, highlighted in the fading radiance from the great rose window over the choir.

Allegreto scanned the empty nave below him. At the edge of one of the ponderous columns, he saw a movement. He stared at it through the gloom, distinguishing the shape of a man's hand fingering his sword hilt. As he looked along the line of pillars, he saw more—six men in all, concealed against the colossal pillars, waiting stone-still but for that single restless hand.

Allegreto held himself in heightened caution, chary of some trap laid for him, a deception meant to lure him here into ambush. But the men looked toward the choir and chancel. Allegreto moved softly along the single board, pausing before he crossed each window to be sure they were not glancing upward. He came to the end of the scaffolding, overlooking the transept where Franco Pietro stood with his men.

Allegreto had assumed that Franco came here to meet Raymond by some preordained plan. But there were men hidden, and Franco had a wariness about him; an edged impatience. His four men were disposed in a guarding position, two before him and two at his flank.

A single priest worked calmly in the chapel of Saint Barbara, the patron of miners and Monteverde. He trimmed candles at the altar, then knelt and crossed himself before he unlocked the spiked iron railing and departed the chapel. The filigreed gate closed with a clangor that rang loudly in the church. He exchanged a nod of courtesy with Franco, as if it were no uncommon thing to see the Riata lingering after the holy offices were complete, and walked across the nave, under Allegreto's feet, to the side door.

The door closed. As the boom faded away in the sanctuary, Franco said loudly, "Show yourself."

His voice echoed. Allegreto knelt on one knee, watching.

After a moment Raymond de Clare stepped from under the spiraling stair that led up to the high pulpit. "I asked you to come alone."

"I take no orders from spies," Franco said coldly. "If you have news of what Navona plans, then tell me. Or you will find yourself assailed by Riata in truth."

"Not I," Raymond said. With a sudden move he lifted his arm and shouted, *"For Navona!"*

His yell echoed down the nave. Men swarmed from concealment, a sudden drumming of boots on stone. Franco cursed and unsheathed his sword, swinging around to defend himself. He lunged just in time to parry a thrust, pulling back as his closest guard drove a point deep into the attacker's chest.

Allegreto rose to his feet, staring down. The Riata made an instant ring of defense, their blades flashing in the circle around Franco, catching colored light from the windows. Raymond drew his sword, backing away.

They were a dozen to Riata's five, pushing forward, trying to reach Franco. Allegreto stood incredulous. It was a church. He heard the flat clanking sound of a crossbow, a hiss—and one of Franco's men pitched backward with a bolt lodged in his chest. Another assailant lunged into the gap left by the fallen man, his sword tip aimed at Franco's unprotected side. The Riata turned and kicked the assassin's exposed knee, stopping the charge. Raymond's man stumbled and took Franco's blade through his throat.

Blood began to spread, polluting the marble floor of the sanctuary. Allegreto pressed his hand against the arch beside him, breathing harshly. He had never thought he would be sorry to see Franco cut down like a dog. He had spent a lifetime hoping for it. But this . . . in a church, in Allegreto's name . . . if Franco died like this, it would be Navona to blame. And it would be war again.

Raymond could mean nothing but war. Nothing but to break the fragile peace of the houses and the republic. Nothing but to make the princess fail.

Rage gripped Allegreto. He watched the Englishman stand aside while Franco fought for his life. The Englishman who claimed he loved her, who had fawned on her and kissed her and inspired poems of ardor and devotion.

Franco could take two against one of these hired killers—they fought like cattle, with no skill—but he was favoring his leg, his footwork clumsy, his arm a fraction slow. The tourney had taken its toll.

His men had dispatched four of the assailants. But he had lost two of his own already. He was going down. In the sounds of blade on blade and the harsh grunts of men in combat in a place of God, Allegreto saw Elena's dream falling to destruction before his eyes.

He looked down between the boards of the scaffold, toward where the bolt had been fired. A man crouched near one of the pillars, hastily reloading a crossbow. Allegreto slid over the edge and jumped down the shaky arrangement of supports. As his boots hit the floor, he was already turning toward the hidden archer. He went in low and at an angle, moving fast.

The man was sighting carefully down the length of the bow, doubtless trying not to shoot any of his companions. A noble thought, for his last. Allegreto slipped behind him, gripped a handful of curly hair, grabbed the man's jaw and twisted his head violently to the left. Cartilage popped and snapped as the archer's neck broke. Allegreto caught the crossbow as it fell, preventing it from clattering to the stone. He left it on the dead man's body, already in motion toward the Riata. Franco had no guards remaining, but his men had made a ferocious defense. In the light from a tall candelabra, the sanctuary was like a battleground, a chaos of fallen bodies and blood. Franco still fought fiercely against his last two assailants, moving sideways as if in some bizarre dance to keep one of the assassins between himself and the other. If he had been fresh, he would have cut them in pieces, but he stumbled and slipped on the fouled floor, going down on his knee. With a shout, his attacker lifted his sword for a final blow.

Allegreto stepped from behind a pillar, grasped the tall iron candleholder and hurled it with both hands. The heavy piece of iron caught the man in his belly. He went sprawling, his sword spinning across the floor. He screeched and rolled as burning wax splattered his flesh. Allegreto drew his sword, lunging over Franco just in time to meet the blade of the last man. He struck it aside on his arm bracer and impaled the assailant through his heart.

He yanked his blade free as the body fell, consumed by blood rage. The burned man still rolled on the floor. Allegreto kicked him in the face and killed him before he could rise.

A sudden silence descended, the last echo of the combat dying away to sounds like grieving sighs. Allegreto stood still, looking down at the dark pools and smears of blood defiling the sanctuary floor. He felt covered with it, drowned in it. He could taste it on his tongue. If he had not been so full of rage he would have wept.

The Englishman had never joined the fight. Allegreto glanced up at a motion along the aisle. He saw Raymond slip out the side door—and into Gerolamo's waiting grip.

Franco had made his feet. He was sweating, his chest heaving with exertion. He looked at Allegreto as if he were some baffling vision that had stepped out of a streamer of light.

"It was not me, Riata," Allegreto said. "Not me." He dropped his sword. "It is betrayal of us all."

THE THREE TOWERS of Navona brooded over an open square with a fine stone well at the center. A woman drawing water in the last of light looked up, stared for an instant, and hurried down the steps from the well. She ran away across the square, splashing water from her urn down the front of her skirts.

The great arched doors faced the piazza, walls of wood strapped by iron and marked now by old blackened tongues of smoke. Allegreto kicked the half-burned wicket door, holding Raymond by one arm while Franco gripped the other. What was left of the bolt gave with a crash. Gerolamo shoved the entry full open and they passed under the arch of stone.

"Discover a light," Allegreto said. He shoved Raymond up against the wall, holding his hand to the Englishman's throat. Raymond made rattling sounds as he tried to breathe.

The small flicker of a candle rose in the darkness, illuminating a chaos of burned timbers standing askew where they had fallen from the floors above. A crushed chest lay in splinters, with scorched leather horse trappings spilling from it across the floor. Allegreto cast a glance at Franco, but he had no fury to spare for the Riata at the moment.

"We'll take him to the cellars," he said, giving Raymond a hard thumb against his windpipe for the pleasure of it.

The Englishman gasped and struggled. As Allegreto released him, Franco yanked him away from the wall. Between their daggers, as Gerolamo held the candle high, they took him in a pool of flickering light down the stairs.

Everything of value had been looted long ago from the towers. But the fire had not reached here; the stone vaults had held up the floor. There were still manacles in the cells where Gian's enemies had been questioned. And the rack and cudgels; the pulleys and ropes of the strappado.

Raymond was drenched in sweat. He set his heels when he saw the strappado—and so Allegreto instantly reached for the cord. "Who pays you?"

"The Visconti!" Raymond exclaimed, with an upward break in his voice. "You don't have to put me to question— I'll tell you all!"

Franco pulled the Englishman's hands across his back. Allegreto looped the rope and made it fast.

"I'll tell you!" Raymond cried in panic as Gerolamo began to turn the wheel at the wall and work the pulleys. Raymond's hands rose backward above him until he was standing on tiptoe. He swung and wailed, foolishly fighting, trying to lift himself on his arms.

Allegreto signaled his man to stop.

"They said they'd pay me to murder Franco," Raymond gasped. "But I did not agree. They said they'd kill me if I didn't!"

Franco made a sound like a snarl. "Raise him."

The wheel creaked. Raymond whimpered as he was lifted from the floor, his head and shoulders hanging forward on his arms. Allegreto had a vision of Elena's face, a sudden glimpse of her steady gaze leveled at him. He blinked, shivering.

"You finish it," he said to Franco. "I'll kill him. I can't kill him."

"Don't kill me!" Raymond squealed.

Franco laughed. "Has your stomach grown so delicate, Navona?"

Allegreto walked to the stairs and stood staring up into the darkness as Franco ordered Raymond to be dropped. The Englishman fell with a shriek. He sobbed and groaned. "I was to slay Franco . . . to make way for Milan," he mumbled.

"It was no men from Milan with you," Franco said. "Who was it?"

"The French! The condottieri!" Raymond screamed, gasping as the wheel began to crank, lifting him again. "Love of Christ, don't!"

"What do the French care for killing me?" Franco demanded.

"French captain . . . they'll murder him—tonight. His second takes command!" Raymond wheezed. "Milan . . ."

Allegreto swung around. Comprehension washed over him, a huge dark wave, as Franco met his eyes. "The condottieri," Allegreto said. "They've turned. God save, she's gone out there."

"Matteo!" Franco breathed. He took a step toward Raymond's dangling figure.

"Drop him!" Allegreto shouted, striding forward. The rope went slack, and then caught hard, jerking Raymond's arms from his frame as the Englishman shrieked. "You worm, you knew it! You knew it all along." Allegreto drew his knife. He stood where Raymond hung moaning and put the blade to his throat. "You said you loved her, you puling maggot, and you sent her out there to them."

"Don't!" Raymond gasped, rolling his eyes at the dagger. "I'll tell you! My signal . . ."

"What signal?" Franco demanded.

"Two lanterns . . . please, please God don't . . . in the tower—the prince's chamber."

"What of the princess?" Franco asked, while Allegreto's hand trembled, drawing blood from the tip of his knife.

"She'll be safe! They promised me . . . rule here. Marry her. But I didn't want to!" he screeched as Allegreto moved.

Fury held Allegreto mindless; he was just sane enough to know it. He looked at Franco, finding some reason there— the Riata put a hand on his shoulder, staying the blade.

"When do they expect the signal?" Franco asked.

"This night," Raymond croaked. "It was to say . . . Riata is dead. Then the French captain—they'll murder him. Rally—" His head fell slack as he lost his senses.

Franco signaled to Gerolamo to lift him again. He came awake at the pull of the rope on his ruined arms, making gibbering sounds of pain.

Franco looked up at him. The Riata's scarred face was like stone. "And then they attack?"

"Send a message. Open gates or . . . slay councilors— one by one."

"What of Navona," Franco said coldly. "You were to kill him, too?"

"Riata . . . first." Raymond barely spoke through his pants. "For disorder. To seem Navona . . ." He passed out again for a moment, swinging like meat on a hook. Then his eyes fluttered open. He tried to lift his head and only flailed weakly, whimpering.

"And my son?"

Spittle dripped from Raymond's mouth. He made no answer. At Franco's nod, the wheel began to crank him higher.

Raymond squeaked. "The boy . . . not me! Not me! I would not kill your boy! The soldiers!"

Franco's scarred lip curled. "You meant to murder us, and then take Monteverde with the condottieri force," he said in a deathly composed voice. "Milan paid you to do it. They said you would wed the princess and rule here. Tell me if this is true, and I will let you down."

"It is true!" Raymond quivered. "I swear on the holy writ, it is true! Let me down!"

"Drop him," Franco said cordially.

His body fell halfway and caught, bouncing. He screamed and wept and snuffled, hanging limp.

"Is that enough?" Allegreto asked Franco, with a strange sense of helplessness. "Do we need more of him?"

"It is enough," Franco said. "We must act."

Allegreto grabbed Raymond's hair and lifted his sagging head. He put his blade to the Englishman's bared neck and cut his throat.

Twenty-nine

⸺⊶⊷⸺

ELENA DISMOUNTED BESIDE a line of gaily striped tents, glad to reach the encampment just at dusk. Fires were already lit, sending smoke into a soft sky above the light-silvered plunge of the mountainside. Captain Guichard of the condottieri welcomed her with flattering words in French, making her free of his camp and his provisions. She thought wryly that he could afford to be generous; she had paid him a years' worth of Monteverde bullion that had drained near half the revenues from the mines and the taxes. But it calmed the people to have the troops near. She had hopes of creating a civil militia around a core of professional soldiers, according to the plan in her grandfather's book, but for now, with the strongest Monteverde houses still at dagger-point, they depended for all of their defense on the French mercenaries.

Philip stood talking to Captain Guichard amid a bustle of activity as baggage was stowed and the councilors escorted courteously to their tents by his second-in-command. The old bandit worked well with the French captain; they seemed to speak a common language of martial understanding. But Elena knew that Philip was careful to maintain a distance, and some secrets. He had warned her himself of the dangers. The French were mercenaries, after all. They would sell themselves to the highest bidder.

For the moment, while they grew fat on Monteverde's silver, they seemed content to lie on the road to Venice and await her directives. But Philip thought they should be better occupied, and was in negotiation with the captain for some raids into the mountains in search of bandits. It did not seem to bother him that he'd been a bandit himself only a year ago. Elena had learned from Philip that soldiers needed to fight, and idle men were trouble.

It was one of the reasons she had finally decided to set Franco and Allegreto free, and try to bring them into voluntary service to Monteverde. There was danger if they were at liberty, but danger, too, if they were at leisure to make mischief that she could not see.

She glanced at Zafer, who stood quietly beside her tent after he had dismounted and made his infidel prayers. He had joined them outside the city gates, waiting on his donkey beside the road and silently falling in alongside the ranks of councilors behind her.

She saw some scowls now from the Riata men sent to guard Matteo, but Elena acknowledged his presence with a nod. She knew who had sent him, and it gave her a warm sense of shelter.

"Give you good eve, Zafer," she said. "Is Margaret well?"

"Your Grace, she is well," he said with a precise bow. "God is great."

"And her babe?"

"He grows apace, my lady."

Elena pressed her lips together against a weakness in her throat. She had missed them all, Zafer and Margaret and the children. She looked about at the darkening sky and hugged herself. "Send her to me when we return," she said suddenly. "I would have her in my service."

His solemn face softened a little as he nodded. "Your Grace, it would give her great joy."

"And we must find a bed for you," she said with a half-smile. "I will not have you sleeping on the ground like a watchdog at my feet."

"It is no matter what I sleep upon, Your Grace," he said softly. "I will stay by your tent, if you permit."

She looked about with significance. "I think you will find several Riata men beside you," she said. "I will suffer no conflict over it."

Zafer bowed. "As you command, my lady."

She called Philip and ordered more bedding brought. The older man gave Zafer a brusque assessment and went to do her bidding. When an invitation came to join the supper that the captain had readied for his guests, Elena pleaded weariness, eating her meal in private with Matteo.

She could not make light conversation with the French captain and the councilors this night. While lamplight glowed on the red silk lining of the elegant pavilion and Dario served her, she sipped at a broth of ravioli and worried. She was in dread that Franco and Allegreto would come to blows while she was gone. And she was uneasy about Raymond. He had been too badly injured to accompany the procession to d'Avina. She had visited him in the spare quarters of the infirmary, but could not convince him to remove to his old chamber in the castle while she was gone. He was wary of Franco, convinced that the Riata had tried to kill him, and Elena could not in truth deny the possibility. She thought of how Allegreto had entered her chamber without even passing the guard, and agreed that the infirmary was more secure. There was but one door, and she had set a sentinel on it day and night.

After prayers, she lay down in her shift amid the furs and silk sheets that had been prepared for her. Here in the camp, with so little privacy, she left her hair modestly wrapped and covered. Matteo and her maid had their own pallets. Nim settled happily beside the boy. The ground was hard even under the padded mattress and furs, but Elena was exhausted.

She did not sleep, though. She lay drowsing in a foolish dream that Allegreto came to her here, too, even through all of the guards that Philip and Dario had set. Through the thin air, somehow, to take her down with him in hot darkness and secret delight.

"HOW MUCH NERVE do you have, Riata?" Allegreto squatted beside the stone well, washing blood from his hands. His sleeves and chest were soaked in it, but he had no time or use for other clothing. He walked in a dream of violence, every step inevitable, the final sum of all that he was.

"Navona's and twice again," Franco said, watching the shadows cross the piazza.

Men were already gathering, the clandestine call to both Navona and Riata bringing figures hastening from the dark, men who were mortal enemies, who paused in arrested disbelief to discover Allegreto at the well with Franco.

Allegreto had received no thanks for saving Franco's life, nor wanted any. "Can you bear fire on your skin, if it does not burn?" he asked, flinging drops of water from his hands as he stood.

"Demon! What scheme do you have?"

"Your hand-picked men and mine. Into the camp, under a diversion that will quail the soldiers' hearts. We bring out the hostages in one body before they know we are there."

"There are three thousand men in that company," Franco said.

"Are you frightened of three thousand men, Riata?"

He heard Franco spit, though it was too dark to see. "Nay, but I'm no fool either. If we fail once, all is lost."

"You wish to negotiate for Matteo's life? Sell the city to buy him back, and all you will have is his body for your treason. If you live long enough to see it."

Franco was silent. It was self-evident. They had no defense, no grounds to bargain. If the French took the city for Milan, Allegreto and Franco would be the first to die, after the council and the princess.

Around them, the still shadows of men waited.

"Tell me your scheme then, you false-hearted bastard," Franco said scornfully. "If anyone can work a fiend's ruse, it would be you."

SHOUTS WOKE HER as Philip's rough hand came down on her shoulder. The blaze of a half-shuttered lantern hurt her eyes.

"Hurry!" Philip hissed. "They've murdered Guichard."

"What?" Elena scrambled upright. She lunged out of the furs, but he did not even give her time to find her robes. He was hauling her toward the door as her maid rose with a horrified look.

"They're coming to secure you. Dario has a cross-bolt in his back." His gloved hand gripped her. Before she could do more than cast a wild look to see that Matteo and Nim were with them, he had her outside in the starlight. Zafer came running with a pair of horses out of the chilly dark. There were torches rising to life, and she saw men in Monteverde's livery fighting at the far edge of the tents.

She threw herself onto the horse in her bare shift. Zafer thrust Matteo up behind her. Philip mounted and hauled his horse around, headed in the direction of the city, back through the camp where they had come. She urged her mount after his, dashing past men who were stumbling from their tents and bedrolls.

The road to Venice cut through the encampment, giving them a sudden opening. Elena let the horse gallop, pounding alongside Philip, asking no questions. The dark masses of tents flew past.

Matteo grabbed hard at her. "Hold!" he cried in a high-pitched voice. "Princess! Hold!"

Elena saw it. She dragged the horse to jolting halt, staring at the torches and mounted knights ahead, a dozen of

them, twenty—she could not tell in the dark, but they held
the road with lances ready. Philip halted beside her.

One of the knights raised his torch and shouted. "We
wish you no harm, lady! Surrender, and you will be made
safe."

Elena looked at the blocked road, at the soldiers running
toward them from the sides. "Philip!" she said low. "You
must go north!"

"Your Grace—" His horse backed against hers. "I can't
leave you."

"I command it! Now—while you can!"

Philip threw her a wild glance. She turned from him and
made her horse walk forward, lifting her hand.

"I am in your protection!" she called. "I surrender myself."

The knights began to move forward in a line, a dark soft
roll of hooves under the glare of torches.

"Now!" she hissed to Philip. "Go!"

He turned his horse. He spurred it, driving back along
the road as renewed shouts broke out. The line of knights
parted, galloping toward her, some of them hurling past
after Philip while others reined their horses beside hers.
Matteo hugged her hard around the waist. In the flashing
shadows mailed hands gripped her bridle. She looked into
the armored faces of her captors and prayed to God that
Philip had not paused too long.

SHE UNDERSTOOD ALLEGRETO'S dread of chains
now. To be manacled was more frightening than she had
ever imagined. She felt utterly helpless, left alone with
Matteo in the same silk-lined tent, knowing nothing of what
passed outside. Dario lay grievously wounded from the bolt
that had pieced him through; they had torn it from him and
carried him into her tent in the night, as if to show her their
intentions.

She had done what she could for him, though she could
barely work with the way her wrists were chained and fas-

tened to the heavy pole in the center of the tent. She bound
his wounds as best she might with the length of cloth that
had covered her braided hair. He nodded and blinked up at
her in the lantern light, drifting in and out of his senses. She
had not thought he would survive the night, but in the dawn
he was alive. Every breath was a labor for him. Matteo gave
him water and stared at him, reciting silent prayers.

The camp outside was restless, with men on horses passing up and down the road, distant shouts and arguments.
But there was no open fighting that she could tell. She
thought once she heard the voices of her councilors, raised
in fury, but then they were silent and she heard them no
more.

The day passed in such terrible waiting, with only Matteo's wide eyes and Dario's hoarse breath and the dread that
Philip had not made it out of the camp. Her maid and Zafer
were gone. Elena stared at the bread and wine they brought
her and could not eat it.

In the late afternoon a guard yanked back the covering
on her tent. She recognized the officer who strode inside—
Guichard's second captain, the tall and lanky officer who
had so courteously led his guests to their places.

He looked down at her where she sat on one of her
chests. Elena lifted her chin by instinct, refusing to lower
her eyes.

"Your Grace, I am Pierre de Trie," he said with a deep
bow, baring his head, as polite as he had been in the evening
before. "I am in command of this company now, under the
order of Bernabó Visconti of Milan."

Elena gazed at him, saying nothing.

"It grieves me to report that our good Captain Guichard
has returned to his maker, may God forgive his soul. And
we have sorrowful news from your city—Franco Pietro of
the Riata is also dead, God assoil him."

Matteo made a small sound. He grabbed Nim and
hugged the great dog to him.

"Your Grace," Trie said, "it seems some disorder has

broken out in Monteverde. We ask your permission to enter
the gates and quell it."

She stood up. "What happened to Franco? What death
caught him?"

"We were told it was his enemy, the Navona."

Dario ceased his harsh breathing and made a sound, a
word lost in a groan. She stared at Trie. The condottiere
looked back at her, a little bent under the tent-cloth, his thin
eyebrows and trimmed beard like ink drawings on his face.

"Why am I confined?" she asked.

"For your protection, my lady," he said. "We were sorry
you were so imprudent as to try to flee last night."

She knew what they would do if she allowed them into
the city. They would loot and pillage at their will, burn what
they would, and worse. Far worse. She had heard of what
the Free Companies would do if they ever breached a city's
walls.

"If I do not permit you to enter?" she asked coldly.
"What then?"

"Then I will take one of your councilors before the gate,
and ask for entry. If I am not permitted, he will be hung
there for the city to see. Each time I ask, and am refused, I
will hang another." He glanced at Matteo. "I will begin with
the boy."

She gazed at him, speechless. He smiled a little.

"You have the night to consider it, Your Grace. My men
wish to celebrate their new command this eve, and I will
allow them the indulgence. In the morning I will return to
hear your decision."

ELENA KNELT BEFORE the little altar in her tent, her
hands gripped together as if in prayer. But she was not praying. She was thinking, trying to set aside the horror that
wanted to rise up in her throat and choke her.

She had no surety that Philip had escaped. If he had,
there was some hope, some faint hope, but only after a
delay that would be too long to save many lives. If she or-

dered the gates open tomorrow, she might spare Matteo and the councilors—if the condottieri did not kill them all anyway after they took the city—but at a cost of destruction that she could not even bear to contemplate. Three thousand armed men among the undefended people of her city—she pressed her fists against her teeth until her knuckles bled.

Even if everything had gone as she hoped, even if Allegreto and Franco had kept peace, they could not have shielded the city against this. She saw no way to protect it. She could agree to the demand, go before the gates and order no one in the city to fight. Let them loot. Let them burn. But she did not trust the condottieri to restrain themselves even if they met no resistance. She had read of France and Burgundy, where women were raped and children cut to pieces before their father's eyes for trying to hide a few coins from the brigands.

It was a cruel jest now, the silver she had spent on the French company. She had no doubt that Trie had taken his share, and stolen Guichard's, too. She would have denied them entry, stood before the gates and cried out to her people to fight, told them there was hope of rescue if they could hold out—and let the soldiers hang her for it if they pleased. But she could not live and let them take Matteo first.

He was very quiet, sitting beside Dario and looking down at his chains with a scowl. Nim lay sprawled beside him, resting her head on his knee. The dog had wandered out on her own in the evening, as the sounds of men drinking and laughing grew louder, and then come back, flopping down beside Matteo as if she had no cares.

Elena prepared her words for Trie—she would try to convince him that with Franco dead, no one in the city would care much for Matteo's life. Trie should threaten to kill her instead before the gates if he wanted them opened to him. But she feared that it would not avail—Trie knew he had her and Matteo and all of the council for his victims, and enough force to besiege and conquer the gates if the city still held beyond that.

She bent her head into her hands in despair. She thought

of Allegreto, who had warned her and warned again not to leave the citadel. He might finally have killed Franco, but she had done far worse a crime.

"Princess," Matteo whispered, without looking up at her. He gazed down, holding the back of one hand in the depths of Nim's thick white fur.

He kept his head lowered, turning his arm a little. She saw him fold his hand, twist it, and slowly withdraw it from the shackles. He opened his fingers, gave Nim a long quick stroke, and slipped his hand back into the iron cuff. He lifted his face then and gave Elena an impish smile.

Her heart lifted with a bound. If Matteo could get himself free . . .

Before she could even think of more, he suddenly bent over Nim. He turned her collar, sliding his hand under it, his face intent. He glanced toward the opening of the tent and then back at Elena. With a quick move, he reached out and pressed a rolled slip of parchment into her hand.

Elena's pulse began to thud. She held the slip down close in the folds of her skirts and unrolled it.

Midnight, it said. *Be ready.*

Thirty

———⟡———

AT MIDNIGHT ELENA was lying rigid, listening for anything over the sound of Dario's feverish breathing. Matteo
had already made two stealthy trips to the councilors' tents,
slipping out in the dark through a slit made with a cloak-
pin. She died a hundred times while he was gone, and urged
him under her breath to make an escape instead of returning, but he came back. In the pitch-black darkness inside
the tent, she felt him lie beside her and work gently at her
manacles with some tool she could not see.

His days with Allegreto were rewarded. The iron fell
away. Elena watched the thin line of brighter darkness that
was the opening of the tent. Dario coughed, a deathly
sound. But he was sitting up as well as he could. She had
leaned over him and whispered when she gave him water,
and he nodded and opened his eyes. He seemed aware
enough to understand her, though his forehead blazed with
heat. That he had lived so long gave her some hope, but she
did not know if he could rise.

Distant bells marked midnight from some village

church. Outside, there were still a few voices, a snatch of song from a drunken soldier. Elena clenched her fists.

When it began, she knew instantly.

A noise started, almost below hearing. It was like a trumpet, but playing a note that belonged in hell, an eerie timbre that rose from somewhere far away. She could not tell what direction it was; it seemed to come from everywhere at once, low at first, a wisp of imagination that became real, gathering strength as it echoed through the camp.

She sat up. Matteo leaned beside her. Nimue stood with a growl low in her throat. She barked savagely. And then she sat down and began to howl.

Dogs all over the camp joined her, their mournful voices rising in long uncanny notes, linking with the rising note of the hellish horn.

The guard outside their tent spoke sharply to his comrade. "What is—"

His voice ceased. The other guard cursed and then blessed himself. Elena slipped to the opening and dared to look outside.

Her tent was in a circle that faced the commander's pavilion. At the entrance to Trie's tent, she saw a flicker of blue light in the darkness. It became a thing that glowed— a thing, a man—a figure seething with blue radiance. It threw back its head and raised its arms and gave a ghastly roar, a sound like a soul in agony. Vaporous flames shivered up and down its arms. It turned, scanning the tents. With a shock of horror Elena saw the eye-patch that burned in ghostly sapphire across its face.

At the instant that she recognized Franco Pietro, he turned to Trie's tent. Men were running from out of the dark, but they all came to a dead halt at the sight of him. *"Treason!"* he howled, a voice that reverberated under the sound of the horn. The dogs moaned in concert. A man's head appeared at the door of the tent, shouting angry orders.

Franco Pietro's ghost pointed. *"Murder!"* it wailed.

With a boom and a hollow whoosh of air, the tent exploded in flame.

Elena scrambled to her feet. Screams and shouts rose from the burning tent. One man plunged out, his clothes aflame, another fell and rolled in the burning silk. She stumbled over a body at her feet; realized it was the guard who had cursed only a moment before.

Franco turned, pointing again, and another tent burst into fire. Soldiers began to run, not toward the ghost, but away.

And Allegreto was there, out of the darkness and chaos, with Zafer and men she could barely see. She grabbed his hand without a word, running behind him as he ducked among the tents. They split off from the others, but she had seen Zafer take Matteo, seen Dario on his feet and a glimpse of the councilors running in a cluster from their tents.

All around them, explosions lit the camp. Men were shrieking, sounds of pain and fear and dread. Loose horses bolted, dragging their stakes. Allegreto pulled her behind a tent, holding back for an instant just as a pavilion went up in flames, so close that the heat licked her skin like a white-hot tongue. She caught a glimpse of his face in the burst of reddened light, his features frozen in diabolic beauty.

He gripped her hand and ran, one way and another, avoiding the men who stumbled with sacks and buckets to the fires. At the edge of the camp, he plunged into a black hole, bending low and dragging her with him. Leaves and branches brushed her face, and something soft and weighty bumped against her hair. She realized it was a vineyard, with grapes hanging heavily from the trellis. She could hear others moving around them, crashing through the vines. At the end of the row, she grabbed her skirt and climbed behind Allegreto up onto a bank.

She smelled horses and stale blood. A tiny light shone from a shuttered lantern, just enough to illuminate the door of a stone house.

By threes and fours the others came, a crowd of shadows

gathering. From behind, the camp flared with fires, smoke rising in pale gray spires against a black sky.

"Count them, make sure we leave none behind," Allegreto muttered by her ear. "There are horses and mules with the men in the yard. They'll take you to the city."

Someone opened the door, a sudden square of light spilling onto the ground. In the brief flare, Elena saw that Allegreto's doublet was soaked in a dark stain, completely covered in it. "You are hurt?" she whispered, reaching for him.

"Nay," he said sharply. He caught her hand, putting it away from him. The door had closed again, the light vanished, but she felt him looking down at her. "Elena—" His voice was strained. He pushed her toward the house. "Go. Make certain they are all there. Hurry."

She obeyed, hastening into the farmhouse. Only a fire was lit in the open hearth, but the illumination seemed to glare in her eyes. Councilmen caught at her hands as she entered, clasping and kissing them. She tore away, pushing through the milling of her councilors and men she had never seen, hushing those who spoke. With a flair of pure relief, she saw Matteo holding Nim's collar in the corner. She hiked her skirt and stood on a chest, overlooking the crowded room and pulsing shadows in the firelight.

In a low voice she called each of their names. They responded with soft ayes to the roll that she had read at each meeting until she had it memorized. All were there—a miracle. She gave a prayer of thanks and jumped from the chest.

"Signor!" She put her hand on the eldest councilman's arm. "We have escorts in the yard. Go out the back. See that all have a mount. I will return in a moment."

A path opened for her to the door. She slipped out. Allegreto stepped forward, a silhouette against the flaring skyline of the camp. "They are here," she murmured. "All of them, praise God." She swallowed an uneasiness in her throat, looking up at him. "Allegreto—I saw a thing that looked like—as if Franco had come alive."

"He is alive."

She closed her eyes and let go of a harsh breath.

"Did you think I had killed him?" he asked. In the darkness his voice was tense and clipped. "I did not."

"What passed?" She touched his bloodstained doublet.

The faint light glowed along his cheekbones, made his face a sketch of light and shadow. He wet his lips, backing a step from her. "Ask Franco," he said, with a crack in his voice, an anguish that she had never heard before. "Go, Elena. You must leave quickly." He turned from her toward the camp.

She caught his sleeve. "You are not going back?"

"Dario," he said. "He fell behind." Before she could speak, he had vanished into the black night.

ALL THE BELLS of Monteverde had rung without stopping for two days, calling the people of the countryside to shelter within the city gates. The chaos among the condottieri had broken them into groups and factions, leaderless soldiers, angry and frightened by the uncanny assault, by tales of demons and ghosts and blue flame. Some of them had bolted into the mountains, but most of them remained, seething with agitated confusion.

Elena's head seemed to ring, too, even though the bells had finally stopped. She had not slept since they had escaped to the city. She sat at Dario's bedside while he fought off fever, receiving messengers and reports, giving directions for the refugees to be fed and housed, watching to make sure the surgeon treated the terrible wound with useful herbs and elixirs and did no more harm.

"The night patrol has just come in, Princess," Franco Pietro said, entering without formal greeting. They had no time or heart for courtesies. In the dim early morning light his hair and eyelashes still glowed in patches from Allegreto's strange powder.

"What word?" she asked quickly.

The Riata were yet missing five men, Navona three.

Zafer had found Dario at the edge of the vineyard at dawn, just beyond a smoldering tent where four men had burned past recognition. Dario's clothing was singed. He lay insensible and alone.

"We discovered two more bodies, Princess," Franco said.

Elena glanced up in fear.

Franco shook his head. "Not Navona's, Your Grace. My men."

She pressed her hands together. "God assoil them. I am sorry." She turned back to watch Dario's beard-shadowed face. His bones seemed to stand from his skin, making him look years older than the sturdy youth she had met on the island.

"Your Grace, it strains our resource to continue searching," Franco said. "I need what knights and men we can field to patrol the encampment. We cannot let them disperse and raid. While they quarrel among themselves, we have been fortunate, but if they begin to band in large numbers, or find a leader—"

"I know," she said sharply. "Philip is coming. His messenger said he was two day's march."

"Pray God it is so, Your Grace. This circumstance cannot continue long, and grows more dangerous. I ask your leave to abandon the hunting. I need all men that I have to watch the camp."

She rose suddenly. "Because it is Allegreto!" she exclaimed. "You do not want to find him!" She turned her back. She walked to the basin beside Dario's bed and began to wring a cloth.

"Your Grace," Franco said in a harsh voice, "if I thought there was a chance that I could find and aid Navona, I would do it."

She twisted the cloth hard in her fists. "There is a chance. He is out there. He is hurt somewhere, or captured."

"We have searched. He never returned to the meeting point. The infidel has been through the camp and every tent in it these two nights past. There are corpses that cannot be recognized." He nodded toward Dario. His voice softened. "This man's clothes were burned. The compounds that Navona carried—you saw what they could do, princess."

Elena stood, staring down into the basin.

"My lady," Franco said, "do not think I would abandon a search for him lightly. We have been mortal enemies, but he stood with me when the Englishman would have cut me down. I remember that."

"Raymond," she said bitterly. "I cannot comprehend it."

"A fool will do much for gold and dreams. The Visconti know how to twist a man's heart with promises."

"I never saw it," she whispered. "I trusted him. He was my friend."

Franco grunted. "Sometime it is those who seem most anxious to give compliment and esteem who must be suspected."

She turned. "He was killed in the church? When you fought?"

"Nay, Princess, we were not so kind to him. We took him to Navona's tower and showed him some of Gian's mercy."

"Gian's mercy?" Elena echoed faintly.

The Riata shrugged. He rubbed at his nose beneath the eye-patch and glanced at the faint glow of powder that came away on his fingers. "We needed to know the whole of his scheme. He would have lied. But he did not lie when his arms were torn from their sockets, I promise you, my lady."

Elena put her hands to her cheeks. "Raymond," she whispered.

"Spare no grief for that one," Franco said. "He was a dog, and died as a dog. I might have made him regret his treachery a little longer, but we had no time to spare. Navona slit his throat."

She pressed her hand over her mouth and looked down, thinking of the massive bloodstain on Allegreto's clothes. Raymond's blood. Gay, handsome Raymond, with his charming smile. Raymond who had called her a sparkling diamond, an extraordinary woman. She began to shake and could not stop herself.

"I am sorry if I cause you pain, my lady," Franco said brutally, "but it was better so. If Navona had not done it, the task would have been yours."

Elena made a faint sound, nodding. When finally she had swallowed down the nausea and found the ability to look up again, he was standing awkwardly, a slight scowl on his face beneath the patch.

"Va bene," he said gruffly. "I will appoint a pair of men to continue to look for Navona, if you wish it."

"Grant mercy, my lord!" she said. "I fear he is hurt or trapped somehow."

He hesitated, as if he might differ, then compressed his lips and gave a bow. "I beg your leave, Princess. I will make the rounds of the gates now."

She nodded, dismissing him. He walked heavily from the chamber. The guard closed the door behind him.

There was a sound from the bed. Elena turned as Dario struggled to sit up. He winced and held himself on his elbow, panting. "Grace," he said. "Navona—" He lifted his head a little. "He is hurt?"

"He did not return," she said, kneeling beside the bed. "Do you want water?"

Dario nodded. He took a deep sip from the cup she held to his lips. "He was—with me. In the dark."

"Where?" she asked.

He closed his eyes. He made a grimace and shook his head. "In the dark."

"Outside the camp?"

"Aye," he said hoarsely. "Carried me." He coughed and winced. "There was—fire."

"Fire?" Elena repeated anxiously, but he was fading back into the fever. He sank onto the pillow, his lashes fluttering. With a rasping breath, he turned his head away.

•   •   •

BY THE NIGHT Philip was in the pass to the north, and word had come to Monteverde. The condottieri had heard it, too—there was renewed turmoil in the camp as they found themselves trapped between the lake and the mountains and another force the equal of their own.

Suddenly they sent emissaries and claimed a desire to parley. Elena returned a message with a single word. *Go.*

But there was nowhere for them to go easily. Philip had divided his company and sent part of it around the mountains, to block the pass to Venice.

The messages became more frantic. They begged the Prima to forgive any trespass. They offered the store of Monteverde's silver back. They pleaded to join her personal guard. Through the night Franco's men cut down the soldiers who bolted from the camp, and stories of ghostly visions and angels grew at a rampant pace.

In the dawn Philip's army was visible from the citadel, like Hannibal marching from the north. Elena sent word to him to halt a league from the city and prepare for battle.

From the ramparts of the great tower she could see the condottiere camp swarm like an anthill kicked open, motion without purpose. She received two of the officers, who claimed to speak for the rest.

They apologized copiously for any crime their dead leaders had committed. They were only simple men, soldiers, who acted under orders. They could see that it had been an ill-advised, impudent plan to meddle in Monteverde's affairs. They would go, immediately, but for the obstacles in their path.

Elena listened to them. She took them to the western rampart and pointed toward the mountain crags that were already covered in snow. "Every man must swear upon the Lord's word that he will never raise arms against Monteverde again," she said. "And then you may depart. That way."

To the west. The high, bleak, pathless mountains, where men would have to struggle to even walk, far less gather and fight or destroy what few outposts lay there. And be-

yond them, for those who made the journey before winter
froze the trails . . . Milan.

Let Milan take back the dregs of what they had wrought,
and if the condottieri turned bandit before they reached Visconti lands, then perchance it was God's judgment on them.

Elena held out her hand and accepted the grateful kisses
of the soldiers on their knees. And for nigh a week she
stood with Philip in the western reaches of Monteverde's
lands, at a castle—hardly more than a gatehouse—that
guarded the remote trails into the mountains. As the condottiere passed one by one through Philip's ranks, they took
their oath to shun any war with Monteverde, relinquished
all plunder and weapons but a knife, and received a bag of
flour and a flask of olive oil. They were given a cloak and
a tinderbox if they did not have one. While Elena watched,
one of her bodyguards interviewed each soldier for any
news of Allegreto.

There was none. They had seen specters and glowing
angels and barking fiends that looked like dogs, but no one
had news of a living man with black hair and a comely face,
dressed in green-and-silver dyed with blood.

The guard brought a ring to her, discovered in a soldier's
pouch, because it was engraved with Navona's motto. It
had been found on the ground, amid some blackened
grasses inside a burned-out tent.

Elena took it from the guard's hand. The metal was cold
in her fingers. In the harsh light of an October frost, she
could see that there were letters on the inner curve. Her
eyes were not quite clear, they were blurred in the icy air,
but she did not need to read it.

She held the ring in her fist until it warmed. Then she
thrust it on her left hand, her fingers trembling, forcing it
over her knuckle though it was too small to fit.

He would come back. She could not believe he was
gone. She would not. She dreamed nightmares of men
rolling on the ground in flames.

•   •   •

"YOUR GRACE!" AT least five councilors were on their feet in objection, but the eldest took advantage of his precedence. "You must not depart on such a scheme! We cannot allow it!"

Christmas and Easter had come and gone, and letters that had wandered astray for months had arrived, informing the bishop of Monteverde that in light of the solemn repentance and offerings made by his worshipful child in God, Allegreto della Navona, the censure of excommunication laid on him would be lifted after he made his penitential offerings and traveled to the Pope for absolution.

"Allow it?" Elena said. Her hands were cold in spite of the white fur that draped over her wrists. "Do you think I am a prisoner here?"

"Nay, Your Grace, certainly not, but—"

"Then I will go."

"Your Grace, we comprehend and share your grief, and understand that you desire the proper observances to be made, but to go to Rome! It is not necessary. Let us send an envoy to carry our respects and reverences, and beg what you will of the Holy Father."

"I will go myself."

The old councilor gave her a reproachful look. "Your Grace has pressing duties here."

"To listen to further debate over who I am to wed? I will not wed. I will go to Rome. I wish for this letter from the Pope to be made public in every corner of Monteverde, so that Allegreto della Navona may hear it and know."

They only looked at her, their familiar sober faces lined down the long table. Since the night of the escape, they had been more gentle, less contentious among themselves. It had united them as brothers, and their devotion to her had grown to stifling proportions.

She saw what they thought. She braced herself, but she was failing, losing her conviction in the days and weeks and months that passed.

"Your Grace," the old man said, with a kindness that cut

her to the heart, "it would be wiser to have a mass said for his soul in every church."

She shook her head, refusing.

He looked up and down the table. "Signori, I propose that we gather a sum and cause an epitaph of intercession to be made on behalf of Allegreto Navona, to be placed in some honored spot in the city, so that all who see it will be reminded to say a prayer for his soul. And in tribute to his valiant action in the recovery of the Prima and all of the council, that we request a special mass to be said for him throughout the realm."

"No," Elena said. Her voice rose a little; she heard the high-pitched note in it herself. "I will not have you speak as if he were dead."

The elderly councilor pursed his lips. He lowered his eyes and sat down without calling for a vote.

She sat still and upright in the huge throne-like chair. "I will go to Rome and make certain that his offerings are carried out properly, and that no faults can be found in them, so that his anathema may be absolved."

No one said aloud that it was too late for absolution. They averted their eyes. The great dark chamber echoed with shuffles and aimless shifting.

"It is not your responsibility, Your Grace," a councilor mumbled far down the table.

"It is. It is the least—" Her voice caught. She paused. "It is the least we can do. He saved all of our lives, and Monteverde."

"Franco Pietro did as much, Your Grace."

"Franco did well. But he could not have executed the plan that freed us. He has said so himself. And I will leave him in command of the citadel while I am gone, with Philip under him."

Before the rebellion of the condottieri, they would have gasped in outrage. Now they only murmured, less concerned by the Riata than by fear of her departure. Like parents with a sickly boy child, they dreaded to have her out of their sight. They put forth all of their arguments—she had duties, she would alarm the people, she was acting without thought or prudence. She rubbed her fingers over the ring. They averted their eyes, pretending not to see it, pressing her on and on. Finally she put her face in her hands and ceased to reason with them.

"I must do this!" she cried, her voice echoing from the walls and timbers of the roof. "If it slay me, I must do it!" She lifted her face. "Elect another in my place, if you will, for I cannot give you more."

Twenty shocked faces stared at her.

The elder councilor rose again, pushing himself up with a slow move. "Your Grace, you force me to speak with perfect frankness. It is apparent that you allow your sentiment to outweigh your wisdom. For you to leave the realm on such a foolish and worthless undertaking is unpardonable. If you refuse to put the welfare of Monteverde first, Your Grace—perchance an election should be considered," he said heavily. "Though it rends my heart to speak of it."

"Then do so." She took up the weighty scepter and let it fall on the table before them with a thud. "Haps you will find someone wiser than I to lead you."

Thirty-one

———✦———

ELENA LIT CANDLES. She prayed, but it was without humility or gratitude. It was with anger and desolation, with rebellion, and so she knew none of her prayers were heard. But she could not find humility in her heart, or acceptance.

She had made Dario and Zafer and Margaret wait with Gerolamo by the lakeside. They were all she had taken for escort, leaving the pomp and safeguards of Monteverde's walls behind. Dario was still weak, but he would not be abandoned, moving awkwardly and stubbornly beside Zafer, both of them falling easily back into their old ways of keeping mutual watch.

In the small church that overlooked the abandoned piazza, she prayed. She did not wear a widow's weeds this time, or veil her face. If the old Navona recognized her, or had any notion who she was, he did not speak of it. He only asked her if she wished for confession and absolution, and when she refused, gave her the same unhappy look that he had before. She thought he might have remembered her then, for he gazed down for a troubled moment before he murmured a blessing and turned away.

She knelt at the plain railing before the altar, her head bent. She felt as if there were a hole in her chest, a place where even air could not enter. She pleaded with God, an incoherent prayer that held no sweet expressions of adoration or petition; her prayer was a drum that beat in her heart, *Please do not let him be in Hell, please do not let him be in Hell, please do not let him be in Hell.*

She had paused at every church and prayed it. But here, where he had entreated her to be shriven when he could not, it was not even words. It was a dagger cutting over and over in her mind, please and please and please have mercy.

She heard no answer. The church was still and cold, the priest gone away to some other duty. Her journey to the Pope seemed futile, a hopeless task, too late and too little. Six months she had insisted that they search for Allegreto, that they not give up, but there was no sign. Only the two known Riata dead and a score of corpses that had been buried in a common grave, burned beyond telling what they had worn or who they had ever been in life.

The door opened behind her, sending light down the length of the little church. She crossed herself and rose, gripping the rail as she stood. Her knees hurt. She did not know how long she had been there, but her fingers would hardly unclench in the cold.

She walked back with her head lowered, watching the well-worn stone floor beneath her feet. When she came to the open door, she was aware of someone standing in it, waiting. She thought it was the priest, and lifted her head to speak to him as she left.

She stopped. Haloed against the strong light from outside, Allegreto seemed a vision for an instant, an unbearable hope. Then he moved one step inside the church. His outline took on shape and form, simple substance. In the moment of perceiving him, every detail seemed clear and perfect, the dust motes falling slowly about him, his unadorned tunic of blue; his wine-colored sleeves, the low-slung, plain belt and dagger at his hip. His face; his smooth hard jaw and the long eyelashes that brushed downward over his skin; his flawless mouth unsmiling. He only looked at her.

She closed her eyes and opened them, and he was still there. Her knees gave way beneath her. The jumbled noises that came from her throat had no meaning; they were his name, and dry gasps for breath, and peeps and sobs of frenzy as she pressed her face to his soft boots. She clung to him, unable to speak, unable to weep, unable even to breathe—able only to touch him and feel that he was alive.

"Elena—" He knelt with her, catching her arms, pulling her up to face him.

She pressed her forehead to his chest. "I thought you were gone. I thought you were gone." Her voice was hoarse and deep. "Allegreto."

He cupped her face. She looked up at him, and the tears came then in a furious burst; she grabbed his tunic and pressed her face to his shoulder, weeping so hard she could barely draw breath, kneading at him with her hands as if she could make certain he was not a phantasm of her desperate mind. Then she sat up, hiccoughing, running her palms over his face and shoulders and arms. The fabric was rough and crisp beneath her fingers. The shape of him did not vanish. She could feel him. He was real.

He caught her hands in his, looking down at them.

"They found your ring." Her voice shattered into husky squeaks. "Everything was burned around it." She made a little moan. "Oh, God save—you are alive!" She brought his hands to her cheek and pressed them hard to her skin.

"Elena," he said in a muted voice.

"Where have you been? Why didn't you come? Everyone thought—you made me think—"

Her words trailed off as he drew his hands forcibly from hers. He lifted his lashes.

"It was better so." His mouth curled into a bitter smile. "But I could not stay myself, could I? When I saw you." He shook his head and gave a laugh. "God help me, I shall have to go to the ends of the earth."

He sat back on his knees and rose. He pushed open the

ancient wooden door and shoved it behind him, leaving Elena to scramble to her feet and catch it before it slammed in her face. The bright spring sunlight washed the broad steps of the church and reflected off the lake. The mountains still held snow at their peaks, but the air was warm and fragrant as Allegreto strode across the pavement, crushing wildflowers and new weeds beneath his feet. As she watched him walk away, a wild wave of anger rose on the heels of relief.

She ran after and caught his arm. "You do not think to leave!" she demanded. "What cruelty is this?"

He swung around, his face dappled by the shadows of a huge olive tree. "It is not cruelty, but mercy. Take pity on me, Princess, for I love you as my life."

She dropped her hand. "And you will go away from me?"

He closed his eyes and drew a shuddering breath. "I should stay, aye. I should stay and guard you. But I have no armor left. Christ, I have no skin left! I am no use to you." He turned away again and ducked under the porch of a half-ruined house. He disappeared through the doorway, leaving Elena standing in the empty piazza.

In a cold dread that he would vanish again, she hastened after. But he was there; he stood in the remains of what had once been a handsome chamber, though only broken pieces of the tile floor and a ceiling painted in red diamonds remained. But the room had been swept clean. A pallet lay spread in the corner, with a chipped mug and basin beside it. She had sent men to search here, and in the castle on the lake, and even to the island of Il Corvo, but they had found nothing.

He had not wished to be found.

"It was not your usefulness that I wept for," she said. Her voice broke. "Allegreto. It was that I thought I would never see you again in this life."

He propped himself against the wall, crossing his arms. "Or the next?" he asked dryly.

She remembered her journey, and the purpose of it.

"Look!" She reached for the purse that hung at her girdle, where she carried the precious letters always with her. "The Pope has written! He wishes you to be absolved."

"I know."

She dropped the drawstrings, looking up. "Then let us go to Rome. I will go with you."

"The holy vicar of God is in Genoa, not Rome. I have been to him there."

"Your ban has been lifted?" she exclaimed.

"He said the words. So I suppose that it is." Allegreto's tone was ice cold. "He did not have much time to spare me. He had just had his cardinal priests murdered, and their bodies thrown in the bay."

Elena blinked at him. Her lips parted. "You jest."

Slowly he shook his head.

"Depardeu." She swallowed and crossed herself. "May God forgive him."

"He is out of his reason." Allegreto closed his eyes. A sudden anguish came into his face. "Elena, I don't know if it is God or the Devil who has him. I don't know if it is true, what he said." He gave an aching laugh. "I have been afraid to go into a church."

She thought of him there, standing in the open door. One step inside, but he had turned and gone out again.

"I went into the duomo," he said. "I went into the sanctuary, and then they attacked Franco, and there was blood all over the floor." He took a shuddering breath. "I should not have gone in. I'm under anathema, and blood was shed, and now it is not a true church anymore." He gave her a look of such sorrow, like a lost child, a bewildered angel that had fallen down and picked itself up and found it was a demon.

She walked to him and caught his hands. "Franco told me what happened there. You saved his life. And many more, too, before it was done. The duomo will be consecrated anew—the bishop says by Ascension Day it will be sanctified again and the doors unlocked."

His hands closed hard on hers. He looked down at them,

his jaw taut. Outside, birds sang and chattered in the trees, but his face was set in winter cold. "Did they tell you that I killed the Englishman?"

"Yes," she said steadily.

For a long moment he stared down at their hands. "You loved him," he whispered.

She pushed her fingers between his, locking them with hers. "Love?" She felt tears slide down and fall onto her wrists. "I did not know what it was until I lost you."

"I am no loss to you, Princess." He broke away. In the corner of the room he stopped and turned, bracing against the wall. "There has been peace since I left Monteverde, has there not? You have even tamed Franco." He squatted down on his heels, taking up some lengths of rope coiled on the floor. "All the way to Genoa there is talk that any man who raises his hand against you will be cursed, and perish of some dreadful death of fire. The Visconti can field no soldiers now who will dare it."

"If it is so, Monteverde has you to thank."

"Aye," he said, rolling the pallet and blanket together. "I have a talent for striking terror in the hearts of decent men."

She watched him as he knelt. "Haps there is peace in Monteverde." She stood still, refusing to recognize what he was doing. "But it is not whole."

"What is missing?" he asked ironically. "Is there not enough evil left for your liking?"

"What is missing," she said slowly, "is a man who has given any price—even his soul—for those he loved. And received nothing in return."

He paused. He looked up at the painted ceiling. Then he turned his face down and slid a length of rope under the roll of bedding.

"If you depart," she said, "I will go with you."

He shook his head. "Do not speak like a fool. You are the Prima."

"I told them to elect another."

He stopped his work. He looked at the hem of her dress, not lifting his eyes beyond.

"I prefer to play morra," she said with a shrug. "I prefer to be with you. In grievous sin, if there is no other way."

He dropped the ties and rose slowly. "Hell-cat," he said incredulously. "You told them to elect another?"

"They made a resolution that the Prima di Monteverde could not wed into Navona or Riata. So they can now find another to hold that office, for I mean to wed you."

He closed his eyes. "You witless babe."

"Even if I must seize you and force you to my will. Do not think you can justly complain, for you did the same to me. So I will serve you the like, if I must go out and command Dario and Zafer to bind you hand and foot to do it." She felt heat in her face and neck. Her heart was beating strongly. She stood between him and the doorway, in full resolve to stop him if he tried to leave.

He gave her such a lethal look that she quailed inside. But she held still, breathing fiercely, daring him. She threw away Monteverde, but she had learned how to stand her ground. Before Franco and the council and ambassadors, before the threat of treachery and poison; in the face of everyone who said she could not do what she resolved, because she was weak and a woman and full of absurd ideas.

But to hold sway over crowds and courtiers seemed an effortless task, compared to facing Allegreto. In the simple chamber the leopard looked back at her, dark-eyed and beautiful, creature of inhuman haunts. She dug her fingernails into her hands until they hurt.

He moved. He walked to her and put his hand behind her neck. His breath warmed her lips. "Oh, you have learned to live perilously, hell-cat. For one who wanted so well to be safe."

"There is no safety," she whispered. "You told me so."

His lips parted a little, showing his teeth. "Not with me," he said.

"Then peril is what I choose."

His fingers tightened. "You would give it all up? Monteverde and your place?" he asked. "When you know what I am?"

She took a deep breath, swallowing tears. "Will you never understand? Allegreto—it is you I will not give up, no matter what you are."

His hold on her slackened. "No, I do not understand," he said helplessly. "I cannot."

"Then take it as gift. Without understanding." She looked up into his dark eyes. "Like grace."

He stood still. But she felt the tremor in him, deep and silent. He blinked. Then the tension in his body seemed to fail him. With infinite slowness, like a wounded animal sinking to rest, he bent his head into her shoulder. "Elena," he said in a harsh whisper. "I am afraid."

She lifted her arms around him, pulling him close. His fingers dug deep in her skin, holding her tight as he breathed against her throat. She could feel his heart beating fast and hard.

"Afraid!" she said, pressing her cheek to his. She turned and kissed his ear. She leaned on him, consuming the scent of him, the essence of him, with every breath. "You know not how fortune smiles on you. Emperors and dukes stand begging at the gates for my hand."

"Fools," he said into her skin. "You would cut their hearts to ribbons."

"Well for me, then," she whispered, "that you do not have one."

He made a groan, catching her closer to him. He rocked her without lifting his face. "You want to wed me?"

"At any cost," she said.

He held her away. He shook his head, closing his eyes. His fingers opened wide on her arms, as if to set her from him—his beautiful manslayer's hands, clean and perfect, with no trace of blood on them now. Outside the door a raven croaked, its great shadow passing across the chamber wall and vanishing.

Elena gripped the loose fabric of his sleeves, in dread that he would pull away and turn from her again. She looked up at him, drawing him toward her with a steady pressure. He set himself against it.

"Warrior," she murmured, lowering her lashes. "Will you make me command you?"

He gave a harsh laugh. "My queen." He jerked her close. He slid his hands up to her throat. "You want me?" His voice had a break in it, almost wistful.

She reached up and tangled her hands in his hair, tugging at it. "I will drag you before the priest," she said fiercely.

He stared down at her. His hands barely touched her skin, resting lightly over her pulse "Nay, I cannot." He stepped back, breaking from her. "Go back. They are not so half-witted as to elect another. They'll fall into turmoil if they try, and Franco will step in."

"Then let them fall!" She sucked in her breath. "They can read Ligurio's words as well as I. If they cannot live by what he taught, without me to remind them every moment, then let them fall to Franco!"

"No. You will not let that happen now."

"I have done it," she hissed.

"You must go back!" He turned. "I should never have shown myself. It is dead, Elena. I am dead to you. Go back."

"No!" she cried. "Why are you doing this?"

He stared down at the clay mug and bowl beside his pallet. He kicked out with a savage suddenness, sending them both smashing into shards and splinters against the wall as the bundle of blanket and pallet unrolled across the floor. "Because I cannot be near you and not have you!" he shouted. "I am a man, not some block of stone, though God knows I have tried to be."

His voice died away in the empty room. A goat bleated in the piazza. Its bell tinkled, soft above the sound of his uneven breathing.

"I told you that I have renounced the office," she said quietly. "There is nothing the council can do to keep us apart now."

"The council be damned," he said. "It is not them."

"What then?" she demanded.

"I thought that I would be absolved," he said tightly.

"You said—"

"I don't know how that creature could forgive any sins," Allegreto sneered. "He screamed at the clerk—I thought he would have killed the man for speaking my name. And then he looked around at me and turned red in his face and shook like a demon had his throat. He made some sounds and went out, and the clerk told me it was done."

She wet her lips and shook her head, knowing nothing to say.

He leaned his shoulder heavily against the wall. "Elena, it was like an audience with the Devil," he said between his teeth. "I think it was the Devil." He stared at the floor as if he saw into the Abyss. "I don't think God will come to me, not even in the Holy Father."

"No," she said faintly. "It cannot be so."

"I want you to go back," he said. "There is one thing true in my life, and it is what you have done in Monteverde. Do not let it fail."

"And leave you here as if it made no matter? As if you were some rag that I have cast off and forgotten?"

"Yes. Forget me."

"Oh, God." She closed her eyes and gave a laugh. "As well command me to forget to breathe," she whispered.

He made a wordless curse, turning toward her. He spread his hands like a man who did not know what to do with them.

Elena walked forward to him. She took the loose cloth of his tunic in her fists and buried her face in his chest. "I will live with you in iniquity if you will not let us wed."

"No," he said. "I will not drag you down to Hell with me." But his arms came up around her, searching into the coil of her braids, denying what he said.

She lifted her face for his kiss, knowing it would come. She opened her mouth and arched her body into his, greedy for the feel of him, for the hard way he dragged her against him, for his taste and his heat, for everything they did together in shameless sin.

"It is too late." She her lips drift over his. "Take me down."

"I cannot bear it." He released an agonized breath, turning his head a little away. But still his body denied his words. She could feel him hard for her; in the empty chamber, his hands pulled at her skirts, taking them upward to the curve of her back. He let them fall and ran his palms up her sides and under her breasts. He set her back, but only to look at her, his gaze hot.

She lowered her lashes, Jezebel and Delilah, and traced her fingers along the skin below his ear. He gave a harsh breath, leaning into her hand. His mouth held a derisive curl. Then he closed his eyes and bared his teeth like a man wounded, gripping his arm around her and pulling her down with him, one step away from the wall and to the floor.

She spread her legs as they went down to the pallet, rose on her knees over him in a tangle of skirts and blanket. He leaned back on his hands, thrusting his tongue in her mouth. She held his face between her palms and raked his searching tongue with her teeth. His heavy groan vibrated under her, against her breasts. He arched his head back as she drew her teeth down his throat, tasting him, kissing the pulse beneath his skin.

He held against her, resisting as she pressed forward, shoving at his shoulders. She slid her hands down his arms, feeling the shape of his dagger and the arm-guards beneath the cloth. He lifted himself to turn her beneath him, but Elena locked her hands in his and kissed him, leaning her weight on him until he gave way and let her push him down.

For a moment she hung over him, holding his arms spread, her hands braced on his wrists.

He looked up at her, his chest rising and falling, darkness and male heat at her command. His shaft pressed against her naked thigh under her skirts, with only the thin veil of his tunic between them.

She leaned forward over him. She felt the tunic fall away. The tip of his cock touched her bare skin. He shuddered under her. In full clothing the contact was intimate and secret, hidden between them.

"Elena—" His arms tightened where she held him. "The others are outside."

She smiled. "They cannot see," she whispered wickedly.

"Hell-cat." He swallowed, panting.

She spread her legs and pushed down on him. "Come into me."

He strained, his body arching upward for release, but she did not let him go; she held him pinned as she rolled her hips to take him deep inside. She licked her tongue across his lips and held herself just above him, feeling the muscles across his chest work as he shoved himself up into her.

She sat back then, bringing his hands to her breasts, closing her eyes and reveling in the thick intrusion, in the sharp sensation in her belly from holding him at such a slant. Through her gown and shift he brushed his thumbs across her nipples, the nails raking; even through the fabric it sent a surge of lust to the place they were joined. She looked down through her lashes. "Serve me," she murmured.

He plunged his hands under her skirts, running his palms up her bare thighs to her hips. He held her down as he thrust upward, moving in her in a way that brought her instantly to gasping. She licked her lips and whimpered, riding herself down on him, feeling his legs come up behind her to force him deeper, so deep that it exploded at once with a cry of ecstasy from her throat.

He rolled with her, pulling her under him down on the pallet. He came over her and thrust inside again, ramming up hard in her body. He braced above her, his throat exposed, the muscles taut as he took her without any mercy, as she had never given him, a quick and violent assault against the hard pallet. She arched up and felt a throbbing climax come on her again as he groaned and held himself forced deep, a sound of agony and pleasure. He jerked and shuddered, his teeth bared, and then dropped his head to her shoulder.

Elena clasped her arms about him. Her ability to reason slowly returned—she saw the room again; the painted ceiling above, the web of shadows on the wall from the branches outside. She held him in her, as if she could keep him that way, and feared when he pushed up on his elbow.

His hair had fallen loose. It brushed her cheek, and she turned her face into it, breathing deeply.

He bent down and brushed his lips gently at her forehead. "You see," he said softly. "I cannot be near you."

Elena squeezed her eyes shut. Then she opened them and stared up at him. "I see only that you lie when you say you love me. That you will use me and then abandon me like a lover with a whore."

"No," he said.

"How not?" She pushed at him, struggling to sit up. "I am in sin like the lowest prostitute, to lie with you as we have done."

He let her go, sitting with his back to the wall. "Then go and repent of it," he said.

She pushed down her skirts and cast him a fierce glance. "Not without you," she said. "I have waited for you."

"Oh, you have not been such a fool." He scowled. "Do not tell me—all this time—you have kept to that thoughtless promise?"

"All this time." She pushed herself to her feet, shaking her hem. "Yes, I am such a fool."

He sprang up. "You have not confessed since we were here before? It is nigh two years!"

"I am steeped in mortal sin," she said violently. "I hope that I am! Haps then I *will* see you in another life, since you must go away from me in this one. And it will not be in Heaven."

He put his hands on her shoulders. "Do not jest of such a thing. Go into the church and do it now!"

She tore away. "Willingly! If you will go before me."

He stepped back against the wall.

"The priest here is a good man," she said despairingly. "If you spoke to him—"

He closed his eyes, resting his head back with a slight uneasy laugh.

"Allegreto—you asked me this once—if I would spare my own soul at the cost of what I love." She lifted her chin as he opened his eyes. "I did not know my answer then. But I know it now."

He stared at her, a lock of his dark hair falling down over his temple. His breath grew shallow and uneven, like an animal in distress.

"I will risk eternity for you. What will you do for me?" she asked softly.

He looked down at her beneath his lashes, standing frozen, his body pressed back against the wall. Then he squeezed his eyes shut and opened them, as if he tried to see what was before him, and could not make it clear. "Must I go in the church?" he asked ruefully. "I'll be struck down by lightening bolts."

All the air seemed to slide out of her. She had not known that she feared to breathe. "Then let them strike me, too," she whispered.

"Elena." His voice cracked. "Help me."

HE STRODE TOWARD the church as if into battle.

Elena had gone before him, to find the priest and make sure he would hear a confession at once. Mad and murderous the Holy Father might have been, but none could doubt the sanctity of the sweet and patient old man who clasped her hands in his blue-veined fingers and smiled with honest joy to have the privilege. She thought he knew Allegreto well; there was a perceptiveness in his face when he looked at her, though he asked no questions.

The priest stood watching for them from the porch. Allegreto went up with light steps, but his determination seemed to desert him at the door. He paused uncertainly. The old man stepped forward and took him by the elbows. He pulled Allegreto close with a strength that belied his age and pressed a kiss of welcome on either side of his rigid jaw.

Elena stood back. Allegreto looked around for her with
an expression that was suddenly distraught, as if he had just
realized where he was, but the priest held his arm and
guided him slowly under the portal and into the nave as if
he could not find his way alone. In truth, she did not think
he could have.

The priest knelt. Allegreto went to his knee, his head
bent, and hastily crossed himself. There were no bolts of
thunder or explosions of wrath. There was only the twitter
of common birds from outside, and the cool silence of the
church, and the harsh sound of his breath, halfway to weeping with fear.

After a moment the old pastor rose, pressing his hand
under Allegreto's elbow. As if he guided a blind man or an
untutored child, he took him down the church toward a corner near the altar.

It was too poor a place to have a screen for privacy. Elena
made her own obeisance and waited by the font, far enough
away that she could hear only indistinct murmurs. She saw
the priest touch Allegreto's shoulder. He dropped suddenly
to his knees, his hands gripped together. He bowed his forehead onto his fists. His shoulders were shaking.

In Elena's life she had gone through the ritual many
times, heard the exhortations and suffered the examination
of all her venial sins, even resented the persistence with
which the priest at Savernake had insisted on prying into
her every thought. But she had never been afraid. She had
never thought that Hell awaited her.

She watched Allegreto, too far to catch what he said with
her ears, but hearing with her body what his body spoke—
courage and despair and shame—his mumbled words tumbling over one another as he began: *Forgive-me-father-
for-I-have-sinned.* . . . He bent down nearly to the floor, his
face in his hands.

She tried to say a prayer to aid him, but she found no
prayer. She only watched, her fingers clasped hard, as the
priest looked over his head and listened. The old man did
not flinch all through it. He asked no questions. He seemed

like a gnarled tree robed in dark vestments, standing still and crooked against the background of the simple altar and the cross above.

What mortal sins and murders that he heard, what of vengeance and wrath and hatred, it caused no horror or despair on his face. The confession fell in uneven torrents, like a storm beating against an enduring wall, words and hesitations and outbursts. Elena felt love and grief rise up in her until it spilled over into tears and she could not see either of them clearly anymore. Only light and shadow.

She did not know how long it lasted. Finally the broken sound of Allegreto's voice drifted to a whisper, and then to silence.

The priest said nothing for a long time. Elena blinked and cleared her eyes. Allegreto sat on his knees, leaning his mouth on his locked hands, rocking himself a little.

Then, with amazement, Elena watched the old man do something that she had never seen any priest do before. He knelt down onto the floor and took Allegreto's face between his hands, speaking earnestly close to his ear.

Allegreto listened. He nodded, and then nodded again as the cleric murmured to him. When the priest let him go, he caught the old man's knotty fingers and kissed them reverently.

With an effort, holding to the rail, the pastor rose to his feet. "In the name of the Father, the Son, and the Holy Ghost," he intoned in Latin, making the sign of the cross over Allegreto's bowed head. "I forgive you."

Elena murmured amen along with them. Allegreto rose and turned toward the door. He looked as if he did not know himself. He came down the nave, walking with his graceful stride, dangerous and tear-stained.

He stopped beside Elena. She gave him a tentative smile.

He caught her arm hard, pulling her near. "You'd best have yourself shriven quickly now," he said hoarsely. "I'm not going to Heaven without you, hell-cat."

Thirty-two

— ⊗ —

ONE TINY MIRACLE took place at Elena's wedding.

She wore a garland of flowers for her headpiece, and the fine gown of blue damask that she had brought for her audience with the Pope. A brisk spring breeze lifted her loose hair from her shoulders and her long train dragged over weeds and uneven pavement as she walked with Margaret toward the church. The day could not determine if it wished to storm or shine; blue-black clouds rolled over the mountaintops, but the lake gleamed under brilliant shafts of sun. Far out on the silvered surface, the oars of a bright-painted galliot flashed, conveying some rich merchant to the south.

Every Holy Day for three weeks, the Navona priest had given his sermon to a few shepherds and a fisherman's wife, and then in his quavering old voice intoned the names of Allegreto della Navona and Elena Rosafina di Monteverde and asked if there were any impediments to the marriage.

No one in the tiny congregation had any objection. Elena did not think they had any notion of who she might be—a humbling discovery, when her every word and breath had been the subject of such intense import in the city. But she wanted the banns read and their names recorded. She did not intend to keep her marriage a secret, or allow anything that might put it into question.

She and Allegreto had not spoken of where they would go when they were wed, but it could not be anywhere in Monteverde. She had rejected her office, but married to the head of Navona she would still seem a dire threat to any new authority.

They could not remain here. It was her only sorrow. She had not ever thought she would love the land that her sister feared and despised. But like a swan compelled by her blood to this lake, these drifting clouds and blue mountain cliffs, to the towered city and bright-colored banners, she understood now what had driven Allegreto any length to return to Monteverde. It would be exile, in truth, but she did not know where.

Already the citadel seemed far away. Like a peasant maid, Elena came with Margaret as her only attendant, with no white palfreys or canopies of golden cloth in her array.

Zafer waited a little distance from the church, dressed in oriental finery, a coat of scarlet and heavy gold such as Elena had never seen him wear before. He held Margaret's boy by one grubby little hand, preventing the child from sitting down in the dirt while wearing his best Sunday smock. Elena glanced at Margaret. But the English girl had her gaze on Zafer, a look of shy and smiling wonder.

Elena thought Margaret showed a little rounder in her cheeks and waist than she had used to. She caught the maid's hand and pressed it.

Margaret gave her a conscious look, heat rising in her freckled face.

"Zafer is most handsome today," Elena said. "And he is kind to take charge of your son."

"Oh, my lady!" Margaret stopped. "I should—" She bit her lip, and burst out suddenly, "We have done a dreadful thing! I can't—I couldn't—" She bowed her head. "I couldn't bring myself to tell you."

Elena stopped, turning. "Perchance I can guess."

"We are handfasted," Margaret barely whispered, her head lowered in shame.

"He loves you greatly, I think," Elena said.

"But he will not convert," she said miserably. "I have begged him and begged him."

Elena looked down at the maid's bowed head. There would be no wedding blessed by the church for Margaret, or any charity for her true heart and Zafer's. "You can stay with us," she said. It was all that she could offer. "Both of you. Allegreto will allow no one to part you."

"Grant mercy, Your Grace." Margaret lifted her face. "Thank you. I am weak. I cannot find the strength to go away from him."

"It is not weakness," Elena said softly. "It is love. I cannot think that God condemns it, even if the world does."

Margaret's lip quivered. "Do you think so, my lady?" She looked over at Zafer. Her son was laughing, dangling from his hold, grabbing at the horn of a grazing goat. "I cannot leave him," she whispered. "Not even for the sake of my mortal soul."

"I know," Elena said.

Margaret nodded. She returned the pressure on Elena's hands. "God grant you and my lord mercy, my lady." She smiled a little and lifted her head. "We must go to the church. They await you."

Together they walked across the piazza, passing beneath the huge olive tree, among cloud-shadows racing across the weed-grown pavement. Elena kept her eyes lowered. She did not lift them until she saw the steps of the church before her.

Allegreto and Dario stood with the priest at the door. Dario wore the green-and-silver of Monteverde, but Allegreto wore silver only, the glittering tunic of the first time she had ever seen him, when she had wondered if he were a demon or an angel or a man. His hair was uncovered, tied back, a black fall over the silvery cloth. He hardly looked like a man cleansed of all sin—he looked as if he were sin itself, pagan, everything of earthly life and beauty come together in pure temptation.

After his confession, though, he had become as fastidious as a nun. For the weeks while their banns were published, they had camped like a band of tinkers in the empty great hall of the Navona castle on the lake. Its roof had been repaired and the walls rebuilt, but there were no tenants beyond a few lingering workmen and Gerolamo's sister to cook. Allegreto had insisted that cloth be draped from the workmen's scaffolding, and the men and women sleep each on their own side. He had not touched Elena, or hardly spared a look at her as he and Zafer prowled in and out on whatever business they found to do.

Margaret lifted Elena's train as she mounted the steps. The priest smiled at her. It was no beatific beam; to her consternation it was a mischievous, knowing smile, like an old gnome grinning over his newfound hoard. She could hardly help from smirking back at him, as if they were childish conspirators who had succeeded in some clever game.

It all passed quickly then. The priest asked them for their free consent, and assisted them to say the proper vows. Elena had the words ready, but Allegreto seemed to forget them and had to be led through line-by-line. He looked at her, a dark look from beneath his lashes, and then glanced away, frowning out toward the lake and back again.

It was as the priest took Elena's hand and drew it to her bridegroom that her small miracle occurred.

The day before, she had forced the Navona ring from her finger, with great pain and effort, and given it to the priest. Now the old man blessed it and handed it again to Allegreto, jostling him a little to attract his attention away from the lake.

Twice before, she had put on the same ring, and each time it had been a struggle to make it fit. She held her hand stiff, expecting a difficult moment. Allegreto closed his hand over hers. "With this ring I wed thee," he said hastily. The ring slipped onto her finger without effort, as smoothly as if it had been made for her. "With my body I worship thee."

Elena looked up in amazement. Allegreto seemed not to notice, still glancing in distraction toward the water. The old priest nodded benignly. He smiled at her.

Suddenly Zafer made a low shout from his position a little distance from the church—and it was not celebration.

Elena finally turned to see what it was on the lake of such palpable interest. She gripped Allegreto's hand.

A painted galliot came rushing into shore, the oars backing water and the scarlet canopy rippling as it swung around for landing. Another was behind it, holding off. She could see a crowd of passengers under the shade. The delicate arched prow rode down the reeds and the oars pitched upward smartly as the first vessel came to rest against the abandoned quay.

"Do not offer violence," the priest said quietly.

She realized that Allegreto and Dario and Zafer all had their hands ready to draw weapons.

It was Matteo who first bounded off the galley, even before the plank was laid. Nimue hesitated, her paws and white head hanging over the side, and then came in a great leap after him, racing across the piazza.

Elena turned as the eager dog bounded up the steps and pressed against her skirts. She looked toward the priest. "Is it done?" she exclaimed anxiously. "We are wed?"

He made a calm nod. "In the eyes of God and the holy church, your union is established and sanctified."

She could see the eldest councilor of Monteverde being helped ashore. There were others standing, preparing to disembark; she could not make out their faces in the shadow under the canopy, but she thought Franco Pietro was there. The law against her marriage to Riata or Navona rang in her head. Thoughts flew into arguments she might use: It was a edict meant only for the Prima, and she had resigned that office. It was a civil motion, and could not be held above the rule of the church. It was complete, and there was no way they could prevent it now. There were witnesses, Margaret and Dario and the priest, who would vouch for the certain truth of it.

The penalty was death or exile—not for her, but for the man she married.

Allegreto strode down the steps without a word. He and Dario and Zafer made a line, a waiting defense, though they did not bare their blades.

The old councilman seemed to be in no hurry to come nearer. He straightened his robes and looked back as the other passengers were helped down the plank by servants.

"It is Lady Melanthe!" Elena gasped.

She gathered her skirt and train and ran down the steps to Allegreto, with Nim cavorting at her heels.

"It is Lady Melanthe!" she squealed, grabbing his hands. She dropped them and rushed to the landing. She came to where her godmother was just setting foot on the stone and fell into a deep curtsey. "Oh, madam!" she exclaimed. "Oh, praise God!"

"Ellie!" Her godmother leaned down and raised her. "You wayward child!"

Elena found herself cloaked in a hard embrace. She pressed her face into her godmother's perfumed shoulder with a sob of joy.

Lady Melanthe patted her back and set her away. "Pray do not weep all over my wedding clothes. I'm not the only one who comes to see what mischief you've made here."

Elena stood back, blinking. Just a few feet from the plank, with cheeks already reddened and wet with tears, her sister waited uncertainly, as if she were not quite sure what country she was in.

"Cara," Elena whispered in wonder. "Oh, Cara!"

Timidly Cara held out her plump hands. "I wished to see you again."

Elena took two steps and caught her sister's hands. And then she was locked in a deep embrace, both of them weeping like foolish maids. She could hardly see for crying when Cara finally stood back. "We should not make a spectacle," she murmured, with a little hiccough. She dabbed at her face with the swag of her sleeve. "It is not decorous."

Elena gave a laughing sob. "No." She reached out and squeezed her sister one more time, feeling the familiar, soft comfort of her shoulder. "But you came. Cara! You came *here.*"

She turned back, finding she was surrounded by a crowd of councilmen and attendants, all dressed in their richest robes. A little distance from her, with a space about him, Allegreto watched. He had a wary look, flanked by Dario and Zafer, the three of them standing apart.

Elena walked to him and took his arm, looking back at the others with defiance. They seemed to be dressed for celebration, but she did not know why the council and Franco Pietro would have come to rejoice at her wedding.

"Allegreto," Lady Melanthe said composedly. "Well met."

"My lady," he said, with a slight inclination of his head.

"As comely as ever. The years do you favor."

His lip curled. He made a bow. "And you, my lady."

She gave a soft laugh and a riffle of her bejeweled fingers. "Grant mercy for your chivalry. But has this priest done his business? Have you wed my little Ellie in truth this time? I hardly know what to think from one report to the next."

"In truth," he said shortly, "we are wed."

Elena closed her fingers on his arm. "I am grieved if it displease you or the council, my lady, but—"

Lady Melanthe smiled. "But what? You will put him aside if you are bid?"

"Nay, I will not." She glanced at the elder councilor with determination. "Nor let him be arrested! I am not the Prima, and I will not be bound by their decree in this."

Lady Melanthe shook her head. "Are you certain you wish for such a meek bride, Allegreto? Depardeu, if only she would learn to speak up for herself!"

"I have no choice, my lady." He lifted his arm slightly, with Elena's hand still on it. "She has abducted me."

Lady Melanthe raised her eyebrows and shook her head. "Elena. You are well-matched with this wicked rogue. As I thought you might be. But the good signor has a declaration to make, and then a feast awaits us on the other vessel."

Elena hardly knew what to expect as the elder councilor stepped forward. He unrolled a scroll, and she hoped it might be a formal dismissal of her from the office of the Prima. But she was wrong. It was not addressed to her at all, but to Allegreto. With all of the pompous words and compliments that could be crammed into every sentence, the wise and magnanimous council of Monteverde invited and urged and begged Allegreto della Navona to return with honor to his native city. On consideration of his service to Monteverde and the Prima, the resolution prohibiting her marriage to one of his distinguished house was rescinded. The council sent their effusive wishes for a long and fruitful marriage, and appointed him to the newly created office of Guardian of the Prima's Life and Person.

By the time the sonorous voice fell silent, Elena felt a wild urge to smile at the absurdity of this groveling declaration. Guardian of the Prima's Life and Person! And not even a mention of her resignation—how like the council, to simply ignore what they did not care to acknowledge.

But she looked up at Allegreto, and her smile faded. He had the same lost expression, the same bewildered gaze as after his confession, as if he were not sure where he should look. He seemed like a man who thought it might be some elaborate jest, and waited for the final line that would make everyone burst out in laughter at him.

She pressed his arm, to remind him to reply.

He glanced up, scowling. "You mock me," he said. "Or it is a trick." He looked toward Franco Pietro. "You never agreed to this."

The Riata narrowed his good eye. "No trick. I saw but disadvantage in the barring of our houses from marriage into the highest office of the Republic. It was a foolish act. As to the other—that you return covered in honors—" He shrugged, as if it were a trifle he disdained. "My son has asked it of me, as a boon."

In the space between them, Matteo stood beside Nim, not looking up, stroking his hand hard through the dog's thick fur.

She felt Allegreto's arm tighten and work beneath her fingers. She saw what he thought. It was a strange proclamation. A ruse, to bring him into the city where he could be arrested and even killed. This sham of celebration and feasting—they might do it; the marriage was completed, and it would be the only way to free her now for some alliance more useful to the council. It was the old way, the Monteverde that Cara had feared, that had made Allegreto what he was, that Prince Ligurio had fought and failed to overcome. Lies and treachery and murder behind the smile—as Raymond had smiled at her.

Allegreto stepped forward suddenly. The Riata touched the hilt of his sword; a ripple of motion and reaction that went through the men around.

In the taut silence wind blew a strand of Allegreto's black hair across his face. He held out his hand. "Peace forever between our houses, Riata. I want it. Let the priest bring a Bible, and we will have it done this instant."

Elena blinked. She stared at Allegreto.

He did not look anywhere but at Franco Pietro. He waited, with his hand held out across a lifetime of hatred, an abyss of suspicion.

The Riata made a sneer with his twisted lip. He reached out and gripped Allegreto. Their fists locked together. "Let it be done."

Elena did not dare speak or even move, for fear of somehow altering their minds with the wrong word. But when the Bible was brought, and the priest stood between Allegreto and Franco, she found Lady Melanthe at her side. They stood and watched while Riata and Navona swore on God's word that they were no longer enemies.

There was a silence after they spoke. The galliots bumped with hollow wooden thuds against the quay, moved by a rising wind. A few raindrops spattered over the ground. The clouds rumbled with thunder.

"I believe that is Prince Ligurio, looking down in wonder," Lady Melanthe said, casting an amused glance at the sky. "I hope he will not shed tears of joy all over our feast."

Matteo suddenly made a cheer. *"Bravo!"* he cried in his boy's voice. *"Monteverde!"*

Elena turned and knelt down and hugged him while he leaped and danced in her arms, hardly aware of Nim's black nose at her cheek and the voices raised in jubilation around her.

ALLEGRETO KEPT HIS gaze on Elena, avoiding any other encounter, still half-lost and uncertain of his place in this new circumstance. He watched uneasily as she received congratulations and honors and even embraces. When Prince Ligurio's oldest councilor turned to him, reaching out to catch his shoulders, it was an effort to hold himself still and not reach for his dagger while the old man kissed both of his cheeks. But when the others seemed inclined to follow their senior's example, Allegreto stepped back, unable even for courtesy to tolerate such close quarters.

Lady Melanthe beckoned him, offering reprieve and excuse with a knowing smile. He returned a nod, relieved to attend her. Melanthe understood him well.

She extended her hand as he went to his knee before her. He touched his lips to her fingers, the gesture and the scent of her so familiar that he could almost imagine his father standing by them, feel again the terror of discovery if Gian should guess how they had cheated him of all his aims.

Long ago now, that moment when both of their futures had dangled on a sheer thread of lies and fear. But Melanthe had never faltered in her nerve. Not once. Allegreto rose, meeting her eyes. She seemed smaller, even with her proud bearing and tall headpiece. He had to look down at her, something he never recalled before.

"My lady," he said coolly, exposing nothing of the un-expected emotion that rose in him. "Your husband is well?"

"Lord Ruadrik is well, God be praised. And my son and daughter." Abruptly she held his hand so hard that her rings cut into his fingers. "I wish the same blessings for you, Al-legreto."

"Blessings." He gave a slight laugh as he looked away from her, out toward the lake. "That is a strange thought."

"It will soon feel more familiar," she said. "I pray so. For my Ellie's sake."

He looked back at her and tilted his head. "Do you care so much? I've wondered at the incompetence of those knights you chose for her protection."

"The Hospitallars? Ah. Yes, hopeless fools, indeed." She watched Elena laugh as Matteo and Nim cavorted before the crowd, then added softly, "Are all accounts in balance between us now?"

"Damn you, my lady," he murmured. "What a risk it was."

She gave a small shrug. "A chance. When there was no other. Elena was equal to it."

"Aye, she is worse than you in her daring, God defend me."

Lady Melanthe smiled, still watching Elena. "And are we even now, Allegreto?"

"We are, my lady," he said.

"Take care of her," the countess said fiercely. Her rings glittered as she pushed a silken veil back from her shoulder. "There is no other I would trust as you to do it." She turned away, leaving him standing alone amid the gay assembly.

IN GIAN'S TOWER Elena held open the shutters and looked out at the sunset over the lake. The chamber was cleaned and refurbished, draped in white Damascene silk with red roses woven through it. Nothing was the same—all of Gian's furnishing were gone. Even the bed had been replaced, and the floor covered over in soft rush mat. But the clear rain-washed air and the mountains looming far across the water were still bathed in pink and gold like a vision of eternity.

She wore a loose robe. She had not allowed Margaret or even Cara to attend her in the tower. She felt fortunate that the whole of the council had not decided to lend their dignified presences to the bedding. But they seemed content to confine themselves to rowdy song and the clatter of metal pots and spoons in the courtyard below. Even in the tower, she could hear Nim's barking and Matteo's excited voice among the others. It was the first wedding he had attended, and he found the gay feast and noisy *mattinata* much to his liking.

Allegreto did not. By the time he came into the chamber, still dressed in his wedding clothes, breathing deeply from the steep flight of stairs, he leaned back on the door and glared at her balefully. "God spare us," he muttered. "When did you sister learn to become amorous in her cups?"

"Oh, was she?" Elena asked airily. "I did not notice."

"Only because I would not allow her to sit in my lap." He pushed off from the door, looking at Elena as if she were to blame.

"I think she was a little—nervous."

"No doubt she thought I would poison her wine. Although that did not prevent her from drinking a vat of it."

Elena clasped her hands. "So you did not find your love for her revived?"

"Hell-cat," he said darkly, "I *will* poison her wine, if she does not comport herself with better modesty."

Elena pressed a smile from her lips. "I know you prefer modest females."

He stalked to the big traveling chest that held her clothing and sat down on the game boards painted on the top. He pulled off his soft ankle boots. Then he sat up, keeping his gaze averted from her. He seemed to find the black-and-white dagger points on the playing table to be of great interest.

She kept her hands clasped together. "I thank you for the vow you made. With Franco."

"It was my penance from the priest." He lifted his head, his look traveling from her toes up to her face. "It was that or walk barefoot to Jerusalem, so . . ." He shrugged.

Silence prevailed between them. Elena stood by the window, her hair all down about her like a virgin maid's, her chin lowered a little. From under her lashes, she looked at his feet clad in the silvery-white hose.

"You are not trying to appear modest, are you?" he asked suspiciously.

Elena blinked, her eyes wide.

He rose with an easy move. She lowered her face even more as he walked across the chamber to her, until she could only see his belt and daggers hung low on his hips, and his feet set apart as he stood before her. She kept her fingers clasped and her eyes down as he lifted her chin on his thumb.

"Mary!" he growled. "Have me thrown in some dungeon, before I suppose I've wed the wrong bride."

She ran her tongue over her upper lip. "You would like that?"

"Oh, yes." He lowered his mouth to hers, barely touching. "If you will come and torment me there."

"Allegreto," she whispered, looking up into his dark eyes. "I love you."

"My heart is in chains, hell-cat," he said. He pulled her close, his hands in a merciless tangle in her hair. "If I had one."

Acknowledgments

Many of you know that for a time, it was quite a struggle for me to finish *Shadowheart*. I owe thanks to a number of people for helping me make it through when my fickle muse went on strike. The patience and support I received from my agent, Richard Curtis, and Leslie Gelbman, president and publisher of Berkley Books, were invaluable and went far beyond anything I deserved. To all the online chat "regulars" at Holly Lisle's Forward Motion Writers' Community, my deepest appreciation for word wars and brainstorms and helping me realize that writing was fun again. In particular, June Drexler Robertson, Andi Ward, and Sheila Kelly were my enthusiastic partners in plotting twists and encouraging me to keep at it when I faltered. Charles R. Rutledge, my "fight man," generously offered his expertise in choreographing all that good violence and assassin stuff. My thanks also to Holly for creating such a wonderful resource and support system for writers on the Internet, and to my volunteer "checkers" who helped me catch errors in the manuscript.

And as always . . . I owe the most to David, who said it didn't matter either way, writing or no writing, we'd be okay.

Thank you.

Laura Kinsale

www.laurakinsale.com

Carnival Elation

7 Day Exotic Western Caribbean Itinerary

DAY	PORT	ARRIVE	DEPART
Sun	Galveston		4:00 P.M.
Mon	"Fun Day" at Sea		
Tue	Progreso/Merida	8:00 A.M.	4:00 P.M.
Wed	Cozumel	9:00 A.M.	5:00 P.M.
Thu	Belize	8:00 A.M.	6:00 P.M.
Fri	"Fun Day" at Sea		
Sat	"Fun Day" at Sea		
Sun	Galveston	8:00 A.M.	

TERMS AND CONDITIONS

PAYMENT SCHEDULE:
50% due upon booking
Full and final payment due by July 26, 2004

Acceptable forms of payment are Visa, MasterCard, American Express, Discover and checks. The cardholder must be one of the passengers traveling. A fee of $25 will apply for all returned checks. Check payments must be made payable to **Advantage International, LLC and sent to: Advantage International, LLC, 195 North Harbor Drive, Suite 4206, Chicago, IL 60601**

CHANGE/CANCELLATION:
Notice of change/cancellation must be made in writing to Advantage International, LLC.

Change:
Changes in cabin category may be requested and can result in increased rate and penalties. A name change is permitted 60 days or more prior to departure and will incur a penalty of $50 per name change. Deviation from the group schedule and package is a cancellation.

Cancellation:

181 days or more prior to departure	$250 per person
121 - 180 days or more prior to departure	50% of the package price
120 - 61 days prior to departure	75% of the package price
60 days or less prior to departure	100% of the package price (nonrefundable)

US and Canadian citizens are required to present a valid passport or the original birth certificate and state issued photo ID (drivers license). All other nationalities must contact the consulate of the various ports that are visited for verification of documentation.

We strongly recommend trip cancellation insurance!

For further details call 1-877-ADV-NTGE or visit www.GetCaughtReadingatSea.com

---

For booking form and complete information
go to **www.getcaughtreadingatsea.com** or call **1-877-ADV-NTGE**

Complete coupon and booking form and mail both to:
**Advantage International, LLC,
195 North Harbor Drive, Suite 4206, Chicago, IL 60601**

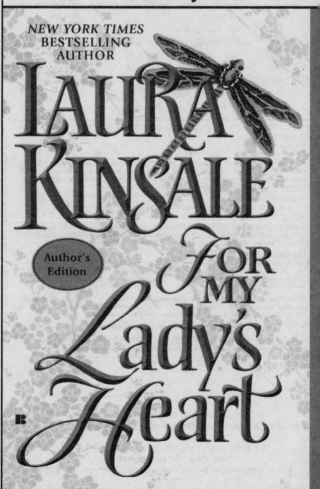

NEW YORK TIMES
BESTSELLING
AUTHOR

LAURA KINSALE

Author's
Edition

FOR MY Lady's Heart

0-425-14004-0